MAR 02 2020
P9-DWF-846

THE TRIGGER MECHANISM

ALSO BY SCOTT McEWEN AND HOF WILLIAMS

Camp Valor

THE TRIGGER MECHANISM

SCOTT McEWEN

and

HOF WILLIAMS

St. Martin's Griffin
New York

First published in the United States by St. Martin's Griffin, an imprint of St. Martin's Publishing Group

www.stmartins.com

Designed by Omar Chapa

Library of Congress Cataloging-in-Publication Data

Names: McEwen, Scott, author. | Williams, Tod Harrison, author.
Title: The trigger mechanism / Scott McEwen and Hof Williams.
Description: First edition. | New York : St. Martin's Griffin, 2020. | Series: Camp Valor series ; 2
Identifiers: LCCN 2019045669 | ISBN 9781250088253 (hardcover) | ISBN 9781250088260 (ebook)
Subjects: CYAC: Hackers—Fiction. | Cyberterrorism—Fiction. | Spies—Fiction. | Adventure and adventurers—Fiction.
Classification: LCC PZ7.1.M43455 Tr 2020 | DDC [Fic]—dc23
LC record available at https://lccn.loc.gov/2019045669

First Edition: February 2020

10 9 8 7 6 5 4 3 2 1

This book is dedicated to the next generation of patriots. May you always have your own Camp Valor to prepare yourselves.

PART ONE

CHAPTER 1

Jalen fired up the gaming console, grabbed the controller off the dresser, adjusted his VR headset, and stared at the giant flat-screen. The reflection of a thin, somewhat serious African American teen looked back. Jalen felt disconnected from the image reflecting back at him, as if his own eyes were saying, "That's all you got?" He looked away.

From the console, Jalen launched Twitch, a free software tool that allowed him to stream his gameplay live. Checking the sound to make sure the tiny webcam mounted on the TV was recording him, he now saw a different Jalen sitting on the bed—tall, confident, and athletic, despite his apathy for sports.

"Damn waste of my good genes," his dad had said more than once. Jalen's father, Ronnie Rose, had been the one to buy Jalen's first gaming console. And sometimes when Jalen visited his father and the awkward silence was just too much, he played games on the living room floor, his dad sprawled out on the couch behind him, talking like Jalen wasn't there.

"I bred a boy who could play in the NFL or NBA," his dad said, "but all he does is stare at those screens." Jalen wanted to point out that his dad was a hypocrite. Not only did he devote his life to a game—football—Ronnie was also a huge videogamer, and until he moved out, he would hog the TV with endless rounds of *Halo, Madden,* and *NBA Live*. He even got addicted to *Candy Crush*. Jalen wanted to tell his father to focus on himself and stop shaming him, but that would only set him off. "Waste of time, money, and DNA!"

"You think you're responsible for those good genes?" Jalen's mom laughed. Tyra Rose immigrated to Florida from Brazil as a child, and with a little help from her dedicated father, she became one of the best women tennis players in the world, at one time holding a number-one rank. She'd won seven majors—Wimbledon twice—before having Jalen and his sisters. "Tell me, Ronnie, how many championships did you have with the Lions?"

"Don't you give me that," Ronnie groaned. He'd been a five-time, all-pro wide receiver for Detroit. "You know the team sucked. Can't expect me to carry the world on these shoulders." Ronnie grinned down his right and left side. "Broad as they are."

"Okayyyy, blame it on the team." Tyra turned to her son. "Baby, I want you to take note: your father's attitude is the reason he hasn't worked a day since he left the league thirteen years ago."

"Goddamn." Ronnie stood up. "This is exactly why I got outta this house. Jalen, you take a note. Pick a woman who pulls you up, not pushes you down."

Tyra followed Ronnie to the door. "There's a difference between pushing someone down and challenging them to be their best. I challenged you. You gave up!"

"How 'bout you challenge our son to get off his damn ass." Ronnie slammed the door.

Sanjeet Rao, the CEO of GoTech, the leading developer of autonomous vehicles in the United States, strode confidently toward the modified Peterbilt semitrailer truck with *CBS Nightly News* anchor Chris Moriarty, and his cameraman, in tow.

"The strategy behind GoTech's business model," Sanjeet said to the illustrious reporter, "is to provide the autonomous operating system—the brains of the car—to vehicles." Sanjeet motioned to the GoTech technology mounted over the truck's cab. "We don't want to make cars or trucks, we want to make the technology that *drives the future*." Sanjeet smiled, letting the line—the bit of branding he'd paid hundreds of thousands of dollars for—sink in. "Think of it like an open operating system in a cell phone. Samsung, Google Pixel, and LG all have different housings, different features, but the thing that makes the phones work—the brains, if you will—is the Android operating system running on the phone, the open system any phone can use. We are like the Android operating system for vehicles. We're the brains and you can put us in any brand, any body type, pretty much anything with four wheels. We just want to make the driving experience more efficient, more productive, more enjoyable, and much, much safer. Doesn't matter if it's a car, truck, or even a golf cart."

Chris nodded and his cameraman panned the cab of the truck. "I can tell you that everyone at my dad's country club would be a lot safer if he had a self-driving golf cart."

"Good." Sanjeet laughed a little too hard. "We're up for the job. But in all seriousness," he said, clearing his throat. "We exist so you can do the things you want to do in your vehicle and let us do the driving. Our GoTech Model One is outfitted with LiDAR VR voice recognition software. We have thirteen mounted cameras, 750 sensors in the exterior and interior of the vehicle, including the most advanced telematics reporting system available. But the secret sauce, if you will, is our local computing power within the vehicle, supported by a cloud-based computing power and the Qualcomm Snapdragon chipset within the GoTech module, which leverages 5G and 4G plus LTE connectivity with the cloud."

"Quite a mouthful." Chris Moriarty flashed a smile, his veneers fitting for a nightly news anchor.

"Yes," Sanjeet chuckled. "Simply put, there's no faster, safer, or more tested solution in the market, whether driving a sedan or an eighteen-wheeler like this one."

"Yes, I know," Moriarty said. "I've seen your tech riding on top of cars and cabs in my neighborhood in New York and when I travel to Silicon Valley. Very distinctive."

"We have a lot of cars out there learning how to be better, and we've logged billions of miles with AI technology in virtual simulations." Sanjeet strode around to the driver's side of the vehicle. "For today's demonstration, we're going to sit here." He opened the back door with a grin. "Your cameraman can take the jump seat behind the driver's seat." He stepped inside the cab of the truck, which had been outfitted ahead of time by Moriarty's film crew with mounted mics and cameras. The CEO took a seat behind the wheel of the big rig and motioned for the other two to follow, saying in a pandering Southern drawl, "Hop on up in here, y'all."

With the cameraman sitting behind them, toggling between the two men, the GoTech-outfitted semi pulled away from the curb and into the streets of Austin, Texas.

"And safety?" Moriarty asked as the unmanned steering wheel gently oscillated right and left.

"I'm sure I don't have to tell you that there are some bad drivers out on the road. Our vehicles, however, are not among them. It's estimated that it takes three billion miles for AI technologies to become as proficient as a very good human driver." He gave a snake-oil grin. "We've clocked 150 billion miles on roads and simulators."

"Wow," Moriarty said.

"Yeah, that's a lot of time behind the wheel. Our AI driver—the technology that's guiding this vehicle right now—is a far safer driver than any human. Layer on top of that the sensor and computer-viewing technologies, and this car has the ability to see and sense vastly farther ahead than any human eye could. You, and the people around us—the cars we are passing—are all exponentially safer with GoTech autonomously driving this vehicle."

"Okay," said Chris. "That makes sense. And what about cybersecurity?"

Sanjeet laughed. "Everyone worries about cybersecurity when they think about autonomous, because it's the most obvious breach. But the fact of the matter is, the first moment companies like GoTech conceived of autonomous vehicles, we began to execute on that vision. We anticipated that problem and have designed security precautions to make a breach absolutely impossible."

"Absolutely impossible?" Moriarty raised a skeptical eyebrow.

"As impossible as possible," the CEO corrected. "The universe is infinitely complex and there are conceivably eventualities we haven't considered, but I can tell you that there is no safer device, no safer visual environment, than the vehicle you're in right now. For someone to compromise this technology would require more effort than developing a nuclear weapon. Trust me, this technology is unbelievably safe."

Jalen put his laptop and homework assignments in the center of the dresser in his bedroom. He stared at the sixty-inch flatscreen and game console underneath. Of course he had work to do, but the compulsion to sneak in one more game before studying Mandarin was just too compelling. Plus, he'd recently been playing his favorite—a throwback, pixelated, world-building game called Kill Bloxx. He'd been playing online with a guy named Pro_F_er, who was incredibly fun to game with.

With the camera working, Jalen launched Kill Bloxx and stepped from his broken, boring life into a digital wonderland where he was known to gamers on the platform and in videos online as the all-masterful gamer Javelin.

The game Jalen had chosen that day was *Jaylbreak,* in which an avatar escapes from prison. As with any massively multiplayer video game, Jalen knew there could be tens of thousands of people playing at the same time, in the same world. He was familiar with many of them, and some he even considered friends, though he only knew them as their digital avatars. This was the case with Pro_F_er, who'd first chatted with Jalen while livestreaming through Twitch. The text came on the screen in red letters, Pro_F_er using Jalen's Kill Bloxx handle.

Pro_F_er: *Yo, Javelin. I've been developing a new world. Wanna meet me?*

On the Kill Bloxx's platform, participants and developers could create their own games using software made available by the original developers. Jalen wanted to develop those skills himself one day, but for now, he was content to explore the worlds created by other people.

Javelin: *Sure man. How do I get there?*
Pro_F_er: *Turn around.*

Jalen turned and saw Pro_F_er's avatar.

Pro_F_er: *All right. Follow me.*

The two avatars ran down the long hallway of the jail, the digital alarm blaring as it would in real life. Jalen followed Pro_F_er to a set of stairs and then stopped.

Pro_F_er: *I put a door here.*

Somewhere, in some room across cyberspace, Pro_F_er entered a code that caused a door to appear onscreen. He opened the door and went through, and Jalen's avatar followed, entering a world that was similar to most Kill Bloxx games, except they'd crossed from night to day, and instead of being inside a jail, they were on a sun-kissed city street.

Pro_F_er: *The object of this game is to steal a car . . . hit as many pedestrians as possible. It's a point system. One point for men, two for women, three for teenagers and kids, and half a point for anyone with a walker.*

Javelin: *Dude this is sick. Where do I find a car?*

Pro_F_er: *Gotta go hunting.*

Jalen followed Pro_F_er down a series of suburban streets. In the world he had designed, there were wide lawns and split-level houses. It did not take them long to find the first car to steal—a futuristic semitruck.

Pro_F_er: *You drive. Wanna see what you think about this game.*

Pro_F_er opened the passenger door of the digital vehicle.

Javelin: *On it.*

Javelin's avatar opened the driver's side door and climbed in.

Javelin: *Where do we find people?*

Pro_F_er: *Just gotta start driving, my brother, and let the bodies pile up.*

Jalen peeled out.

CHAPTER 2

"So where do we want to go?" Sanjeet asked Moriarty.

"Since we're in Austin . . ." The journalist patted his belly. "How 'bout barbecue?"

"Okay." Sanjeet addressed the vehicle. "GoTech, can you recommend a barbecue restaurant?"

"Sure," the soothing female voice of the intelligent driver sounded through the car. "I can help you with that. Today, I can see there is a special pop-up at the Midway Food Truck Court for Franklin Barbecue, Austin's top-rated barbecue restaurant. Shall we try that?"

"Sounds good," Sanjeet said, smiling at Moriarty as the semi made a left and headed toward South Congress.

It was a beautiful day in Austin, still early enough that it wasn't scorching hot, though temperatures were supposed to reach into the midnineties by afternoon. It was Saturday, and the University of Texas was in the midst of Graduation Weekend, so parking was a challenge. But for the GoTech, this would not be a problem.

"As ride-sharing and vehicle renting is the ultimate goal of our system, we've made it unnecessary for GoTech to park—

except for service—so the asset is always engaged. For commercial vehicles, the cost of training and managing drivers is a major expense, so this is a game changer." Sanjeet again addressed the computer. "GoTech, if it's crowded, will you let us out and find an appropriate spot to wait for us?"

"Yes, Sanjeet, I will do that for you," GoTech said, and the semi continued past the food trucks lining a green park that was thronged with people, buzzing around the Franklin Barbecue truck.

"Maybe we should go somewhere else," Moriarty said, looking out the window. "We weren't the only ones who thought this was a good idea."

"Sure," Sanjeet said. "GoTech, would you make another recommendation?"

"Yes, I am happy to do that—"

"Actually, how about we just head out to Hill Country? We can go to the Salt Lick. That place is always good," Sanjeet said.

"Yes," GoTech responded. "Changing course for Salt Lick."

The tablet mounted on the dash showed the course rerouting.

"Great. Thank you, GoTech."

"Turning right," the voice chimed.

But the truck did not turn.

"Uhhh, looks like you missed the turn, GoTech," said Sanjeet, chuckling.

But the truck did not respond. Sanjeet's thin body swayed as the electrical motor revved, and the red line on the speedometer tipped to seventy miles per hour.

"Is this supposed to happen?" Moriarty looked at Sanjeet, who braced against the seat.

"GoTech, slow down and proceed to Salt Lick," Sanjeet said with feigned calm. The semi did not comply, hurtling toward the park packed with food trucks and people.

Sanjeet repeated the instructions again and again, each time his voice a little less calm. "Go to Salt Lick. Salt Lick. Turn around. GoTech, stop the car. GoTech, pull over now! Stop!"

"Okay, Sanjeet. Stopping now." The British computer voice echoed in the cab of the speeding truck. But the Peterbilt only sped up.

The hood of the vehicle struck the first pedestrian at approximately 11:37 a.m. on Saturday, May 19, 2018. It was a man on a bicycle. The truck thundered on, passing a row of picnic tables and plowing into a group gathered for a birthday party.

"Look out!" the cameraman screamed from the back. "Oh my god. You killed them!"

"The motherlode," Jalen said into his mic as he saw the crowd of digital bodies milling around a series of food trucks. Jalen had changed to "hover view" and could now see a hundred feet in the air above the digital car. The first person he hit was an avatar on a bicycle. He watched the figure of a man bounce off the hood and fly over the roof. He then angled the digital vehicle toward a group of eight to ten people who looked to be gathered around a birthday cake. "Aw, man, jackpot."

The points calculator on the side of the screen clicked to seven. "Looks like I just hit four men and a kid."

Pro_F_er: *Dude . . . police.*

Sirens blared.

Pro_F_er: *Do some damage and get out.*

Jalen mashed the controller, speeding between food trucks. The points calculator clicked again as he crushed digital forms that darted left and right in surprisingly realistic fashion.

He reversed the semi and backed over a lady in a business suit. "Wait, can't miss this one."

Jalen was good at this game, but as he drove the truck around the oval park, smashing through trash cans and wooden barriers, he felt a pang of something slightly gruesome. The world he was in was a game, without real-life consequences, but even so, he felt slightly nauseous as he ran over people, guilty almost, a touch remorseful. The crunch, their screams—it was a little too realistic.

This pang of uneasiness, however, was quickly buried, so deep he couldn't quite put his finger on it, nor did he want to. And as the police cars came swarming up, he figured if he was going to be bad, he'd take it to the next level. Toggling quickly, he pointed the digital eighteen-wheeler at the lead cop car and pressed down as hard as he could on the speed button, tearing up a boulevard and slamming head-on into the police sedan. The first vehicle pancaked on the front of the semi and rammed another police car before the truck slowed to a stop.

"Oh my god. That was insane." Jalen laughed and addressed the camera across from him. "Hope someone out there was watching that. If not, I've recorded this session, and I'll add it to my YouTube channel. Please leave comments down below. Thank you, Pro_F_er, for introducing me to this sick and twisted world. Javelin out."

Jalen took off his headset and was about to go downstairs when he heard his laptop ding from the desk across the room.

Commenters already, he thought.

He opened his email and saw the sender was someone he didn't recognize—Encyte. He wondered if it was spam, and he read the subject line out loud: *REALITY IS BROKEN.*

The words intrigued and chilled him. He paused, then opened the email. The message only contained three words: *You did it.* At the bottom was a YouTube link. Jalen clicked and was suddenly viewing his own livestream. "What in the world . . ."

On one side of the screen was the typical Twitch video—the game format and the view of the gamer in his room. Jalen saw a boy sitting on a bed, wearing a VR headset playing a video game on Twitch. Because of the VR headset, it took Jalen a half second to realize the boy in the video was him. On the other side of the screen, there was actual footage of the actual food truck court. The hairs on the back of Jalen's neck stood up and his stomach soured as he realized it was the same as the game he'd just played, except this food truck court was real, and the people were real, enjoying a beautiful day in some town, in the United States. They were getting lunch, hanging out, having fun, and then, just as the Twitch video showed Jalen driving the stolen eighteen-wheeler into the food truck, a real eighteen-wheeler with high-tech gizmos on the roof sped onto the screen. The truck plowed into bodies—humans. Jalen could hear himself laughing in the video over the screams of people being slaughtered on what should have been an ordinary Saturday.

Jalen's hands shook. He ran to the bathroom, fell to his knees, and vomited.

CHAPTER 3

Wyatt's head was not in the game. Sure, he wore a helmet and cleats and held a long titanium stick. His eyes followed the gameplay from the sidelines where he waited to be sent back in, but his mind was elsewhere, lost in a moment nine months before when she was taken from him, from her family, from this world, and no one aside from a small band of misfits and outlaws knew it. Not even his teammates—many of whom considered him a great friend—had any idea who Wyatt was and what he had lost. Wyatt kicked at the dirt, wanting to shake the thoughts in his head, but he couldn't. He wanted to be present for his team, especially now, but Dolly kept creeping back in.

His team, the Bulldogs, was playing in the Virginia State Championship semifinal for high school men's lacrosse, and even though he'd started the season with the other freshmen on the bench, his aggression and speed had earned him a spot as a long-stick midfielder with a reputation as a go-to in clutch situations, an enforcer who could make things happen. Wyatt, with his slight, scrappy build, should not have excelled in this sport he'd only played for a few months, but the truth of the matter was this: he was 165 pounds of pure, raging teen. The shaggy hair, the jaded eyes, the jutted-out chin—from across the field it was easy to see that an anger had set in him so deep it went to the bone, and he took it out on anyone who dared to stand in front of him.

It was how he coped. Pushing his body to the brink. Letting physical pain distract from what was inside him. If his thoughts settled for even a moment, he knew what would surface—Dolly: gagged and bound, the life gone from her wide, dark eyes. And then he would see Mr. Yellow, the pit rings around his button-up when he told Wyatt the news: "We found a body in South America. Washed up in the river. Dental records are a match."

Wyatt had not saved her. And worse, he was the reason she was used as bait.

"Get in there and take somebody out!" Wyatt's coach screamed at him from the sidelines, shaking him from his trance. The Bulldogs were down one point with two minutes left and as always, Coach used Wyatt when he needed to shake things up.

"Yes, sir!" Wyatt called out and ran onto the field. Because his captain had fouled out, Wyatt's team was a man down, and the player cradling the ball in front of him was the opposing team's best attackman. The ref blew the whistle, and the attackman ran at Wyatt, then rolled. Wyatt tripped. The attackman got a step ahead and ran toward the goal and hitched his stick back to shoot, but Wyatt, teeth bared, caught up to him and with his six-foot titanium shaft, snapped hard on the boy's ascended stick. The white rubber lacrosse ball popped out, and with a practiced flip of the wrist, Wyatt swung the head of his stick and secured it, running in a slight arc toward the other team's goal. Wyatt ran with his own stick out in front of him, so the players chasing and lashing him with their sticks weren't able to jar the ball loose.

Wyatt ran down the field and crossed over into the other team's defensive zone, creating a four on three. Normally the defense would "slide" toward Wyatt, opening up an attackman who Wyatt could pass to, but this wasn't happening. The other team was making the bet that Wyatt—with his long stick and less than perfect stick skills—would not attempt a play on the goal. But he did. Moving the stick from his right hand to his left and cutting hard toward the center of the field, he sped toward the crease in front of the goal. Angling straight for the goal, still switching his hands back from left to right, Wyatt's eyes shifted to the lower left corner of the net. The center defenseman, a 240-pound senior who'd already committed to play at an Ivy League school, slid off his attackmen and ran full speed at Wyatt, his stick pointed like a spear at Wyatt's chest. Wyatt took the shot, expecting to get hit, wanting to get hit. But he saw the defenseman slow and turn his head, tracking the ball with his eyes. Wyatt figured the guy was going to hit him a second before. Why deprive him of the chance? He lowered his head and rammed the six-foot-three defenseman, planting his shoulder in the giant player's chest, knocking him to the ground and then stepping over him, like a boxer after a knockout blow.

The defenseman writhed on the ground, cradling his forearm. Within seconds, a couple of medics rushed the field and began checking, but Wyatt just stood there, watching him squirm. He could hear the crowd screaming. He finally looked over to see if he'd scored. The ball had stopped rolling somewhere behind the goal, far out of bounds. He'd missed. Game over. But he'd tagged his man.

"Hey."

Wyatt heard a voice behind him and knew immediately who it was. He turned to see his father, Eldon Waanders, standing outside the locker room. As usual, his father's sunglasses sat a little crooked, his left ear missing from his previous summer as a hostage of the psychotic killer the Glowworm.

"Good game," Eldon said somewhat cheerily as they walked

across the gravel parking lot. "Except for your crappy attitude." His tone turned stern. "I don't care that you lost, but you took a cheap shot and you almost hurt that guy."

"Whatever," Wyatt said, slinging his bag over his shoulder and crunching gravel. "That dude was twice my size. His fault if he can't take it."

"Look," Eldon said, following his son. "I know it hasn't been easy since we've been back, but you're gonna have to get control of yourself."

Wyatt slung his gear into the back of the car and slammed the trunk.

"If anyone has a reason to be angry, it's me." Eldon pressed the finger of his mutilated hand into his son's chest and held his gaze. "And if anyone has a reason to want revenge . . . it's me."

"Come on, Dad, you still have Mom. The woman you love didn't get stabbed to death because of you. Don't you get it?"

"No, but she's lived alone for the better part of twenty years. Thinking I just ran off on her. She was hurt too—"

"Hurt, but alive—" Wyatt said and then added, "Why didn't she come to the game?"

"I don't know." Eldon hesitated. "Maybe—I think she still has a tough time being out with me in social situations."

"That's great," Wyatt said and kicked a patch of gravel across the lot.

"I'm sorry, buddy," Eldon was saying when he caught a glimpse of a familiar car out of the corner of his eye. They'd been so engrossed, they hadn't realized they were being watched. Two faces peered through the windshield of the sedan parked a few rows over: Mr. Yellow, the fixer for Camp Valor, and Avi Amit, the former Mossad agent and Valor's less-than-cuddly security expert.

"Are they here for you?" Wyatt asked his dad.

"Something tells me they want you." Eldon waved as Avi got out and pulled down his sunglasses.

"Eldon!" Avi called out with a nod. "We need Wyatt."

"Nice to see you too!" Eldon joked. "Have at him."

Avi started toward Wyatt, speaking as he got close. "Wyatt, there's a kid we need you to talk to. About the attack in Texas that a criminal or criminal network, Encyte, took credit for. He's in Detroit and we need you there tonight."

Wyatt looked at his father, waiting for an answer.

"Sure." Eldon shrugged.

"Really?" Wyatt said. "I'm not punished?"

"You're not a kid anymore, Wyatt," Eldon said. "Go do something useful with yourself."

"We'll have him back by midnight." Avi opened the car door for Wyatt. "We'll keep you in the loop."

Mr. Yellow aimed the sedan out of the lot onto the highway, heading for Charlottesville's Albemarle Airport. The damp, late spring air swirled through the car, smelling sweet, like young leaves and distant barbecue smoke.

In the back seat, Wyatt had changed from his wet undershirt to a dry T-shirt with a soft hoodie and a clean pair of mesh lacrosse shorts. He was still sweating slightly but the breeze cooled his skin.

"You need a shower." Avi scrunched his nose and rolled down the window farther.

"You were the one in the big hurry," Wyatt said, slipping on his headphones.

Mr. Yellow drove them to a private terminal and parked outside a nondescript hangar. They cut through a small lobby, reminiscent of a car dealership—wafting gasoline and a burning pot of coffee. They passed onto the tarmac, where a Citation jet waited for them, gassed and ready. The pilot welcomed them aboard, and a few minutes later, they were airborne, en route to Detroit, to an airport that catered to military and private aviation.

Mr. Yellow found Wyatt staring out the window seat facing the rear of the plane. "Could you take those off?" He motioned to the Bose headphones.

Wyatt obliged, the punk rock bleeding from the headphones.

"So the official death toll from the Austin attack is fifty-three." Mr. Yellow slid into the seat beside Wyatt and began his brief on the developing situation. "Dozens more injured, some gravely—paraplegics, one quadriplegic, amputations. Victims include Sanjeet Rao, the CEO of GoTech Industries, and Chris Moriarty, a CBS news anchor, and a cameraman, all killed after the truck rammed into the first police car."

Mr. Yellow passed a folder to Wyatt, who paused before opening it. In it, the faces of the dead. He looked over them—elderly, children—his eyes glazed over.

"Law enforcement on the scene opened fire into the cab of the truck," Mr. Yellow said. "It's unclear if all three inside were killed by gunfire. The cameraman wasn't wearing a seat belt and may have died from head trauma before being shot."

"A couple dozen students from UT were also killed," Avi joined in as Wyatt looked through the images. "Three professors. A high school civics teacher, four middle schoolers, a nun, a family with young children, and a grandmother."

"The digital operator of the semi, Jalen Rose, is a teenager," Mr. Yellow added. "Bright kid, no record or any major trouble. Attends St. Mary's Prep School. Mom and dad are athletes, but the boy is pretty big into gaming."

Wyatt looked at Jalen's face. "I saw the YouTube video on the news."

"That video," Avi added, "has made him the most hated human in America, the scapegoat. The unedited version was viewed eleven million times before it was pulled. Thankfully, he was wearing the VR, or he'd probably be another victim. Everyone is trying to figure out the boy's identity. He's been getting death threats, so authorities put him in protective custody outside Detroit."

"He is a victim," Wyatt said somberly. "Even if he pulled the trigger."

Avi nodded.

"But how could these even happen? I mean, technically speaking?" Wyatt asked.

"An interesting and complicated question," Avi said. "You want the simple version or the real answer, the one cloud technology PhDs are trying to figure out?"

Wyatt gave Avi a look. "When I need to bore myself to sleep, I'll ask for the extended version, for now let's shoot for simple."

"Okay, so the servers that allow the video game to work and the GoTech-outfitted truck to drive both reside in the cloud—meaning, on remote computers accessed through an internet connection, where they have massive amounts of computing power, so the cloud can tell the car where to drive and so players can interact in a virtual game environment. These servers reside in separate data centers, and in the case of GoTech, in *highly secure* data centers that supposedly cannot be accessed by anything or anyone but the remote GoTech devices. You follow?"

Wyatt nodded.

"Somehow Encyte was able to hack into the GoTech data center, find the server for that truck, and replace the part of the cloud computer that tells the truck where to drive with part of the gaming computer that received instructions from the gamer's controller. At the same time, Encyte took all of the live video, LiDAR, and live data the GoTech computer was using to see the street and converted it to the data the gaming computer's virtual reality engine was using to produce the graphics environment the gamer was experiencing while playing. This combination let the gamer control the truck while seeing everything the truck's computer saw in real time, but in his video-game world."

Wyatt paused. "So that was the simple version?"

"As simple as I could make it."

"So basically, Encyte hacked into the GoTech computer and put the videogamer in control with a video-game view of the truck."

Avi shrugged. "Sure. That's one very simple—almost absurdly stupid—version of what happened."

"Thanks." Wyatt smiled. "I assume the FBI's Cyber Division is investigating. Any leads?"

"They're going through Jalen's home internet, computer, and console, as well as GoTech's servers now, looking for evidence of the hack. It's going to take a long time—the servers are massive. So there's nothing yet. We do have the email Encyte sent Jalen. It contained the subject line: *REALITY IS BROKEN*. That mean anything to you?"

"Actually, yes. I first heard it doing research into Glowworm Gaming. It's a phrase used by gamers," said Wyatt. "And a book. *Reality Is Broken: Why Games Make Us Better and Can Change the World.*"

"What's that supposed to mean?" Avi asked.

"It's a worldview," Wyatt explained. "Gamers think the worlds they experience in a video game are superior to reality. Reality, in their view, is flawed and doesn't follow the perfectly ordered logic of a well-designed game. Games are logical and designed from the ground up to match our needs perfectly. Games provide the things we need in reality, like a sense of accomplishment, total engagement with the world around us—what we don't get from life. Anyway, that's the gist."

"Now you have me confused. Gaming is not reality, so it has no consequences?" said Avi.

"Games do have consequences. You can make money, or lose it—a lot. The gaming economy is massive."

"And just look at Austin," Mr. Yellow said. "Those are very real consequences."

"I think what he's trying to say is that the world we live in is broken," Wyatt said. "Games can make us better, games can improve life. And now he's playing a game with us. Trying to change the world through his games." He stared out the jet window at a vast sunset the color of a drying bloodstain. "Or that's my thought at this time."

"Avi, let's get this book Wyatt is talking about," said Mr. Yellow.

"Already on that," said Avi.

Wyatt looked back at them. "Is this Encyte's first attack? Or do we have a preexisting criminal profile?"

"Interesting you ask," Avi said. "Do you remember the Sneaker Riot this past year?"

Wyatt shook his head.

"Weezo, the sneaker company owned by rapper Young Tarique, makes collectible shoes and decided to do a drop. You know what a drop is, right?"

"Yeah. To hype a product. You announce a drop in an area with a limited supply."

"In this case, Weezo—or someone claiming to be Weezo—released an app to locate the pop-up, but when fans got to the drop—a church basement in SoHo, in New York—there were thousands of people and just a few pairs of shoes."

"The reaction was completely out of hand," Mr. Yellow said. "A riot ensued, inside the closed area."

Wyatt looked incredulous. "But a riot? Over shoes?"

Mr. Yellow held up a can of Sprite and shook it. "But everyone was trapped, like the gas in this can, excited, bouncing off each other. The room was ready to explode. And then it did."

Wyatt eyed the can. "You got one of those unshaken?"

"Yes." Mr. Yellow cracked a different Sprite and poured it into a plastic cup. "It was like a Black Friday brawl on steroids. Got very violent. The press blamed it on the hip-hop element. Weezo denied any knowledge of the drop. And it faded away in the news cycle. But what the public didn't know was that the shoe company that supposedly organized the drop was entirely blameless. The app—our intel informs us—was created by Encyte and used to corral thousands of people, many of them impressionable teenagers, in a church basement that been suffused with a lethal cocktail of norepinephrine and adrenaline."

"Hormones," Avi said, "were released into the air so the people, who were already stressed and excited by the sneakers, experienced a chemical shift in their brains—and bingo."

Wyatt nodded. "All it took was someone to throw the first punch."

"Some of the most gruesome details were kept from the press," Mr. Yellow said. "People gouged each other's eyes out. Some were trampled. It was the stuff of gladiators, the basest form of human behavior possible, and we believe the real Encyte engineered it."

"How do you know it was him?"

"Encyte didn't claim credit directly," Avi said. "But from the development of the app, to the knowledge of these psychiatric drugs, to the kill mechanism—the weapon of choice is a human pawn. That's what we are learning is the method of operation used by Encyte."

"It's a little thin, but a workable theory." Wyatt peered at the bubbles in his cup, swirling it. "So we have two attacks—one with video games and one with an app and a fake sneaker drop. Why involve me? What am I supposed to do?"

"Talk to Jalen." Avi leaned in. "Check him out. He seems pretty distraught, but it could be an act. One theory is that Encyte is a hacker/developer from Glowworm Gaming. If there are ties, you might be able to find a strand of the truth for us to pull on. Maybe help us both."

"I'll talk to him, but I can't promise anything. The only thing I want to focus on this summer is finding Hallsy and making him pay for what he did to Dolly, to us . . . to Valor."

Mr. Yellow leaned forward, locking his eyes on Wyatt's. "We are working on Hallsy day and night, Wyatt. We have a team of people trying to track him down. The best, the Golden One

Hundred. You have to trust in the team and in the process. You know this."

Wyatt shrugged. "That's what you tell me. All I know is that murderous traitor is out there getting away with it."

Both Avi and Mr. Yellow nodded.

Wyatt leaned back in his seat. "Reality is broken." He repeated the line as he watched the clouds whir over the jet's wing. "What is Encyte going to break next?"

CHAPTER 4

The safe house for Jalen Rose and his family was located in the village of Clarkston, a quaint commuter town about forty-five minutes north of Motor City. The house sat at the end of a cul-de-sac on a street dotted with a mix of ranch-style homes all set on large parcels of land. Its long driveway was lined with black SUVs and police vehicles tucked out of view from the street.

Mr. Yellow edged the loner FBI sedan past the string of cars and onto the muddy grass, trenching the yard in the process. He threw the car in park and turned to Wyatt.

"You have an hour."

"Roger." Wyatt pulled up the hood of his sweatshirt.

"And I'm sure I don't need to remind you," Mr. Yellow said as they followed Avi to the house through the garage. "You were never here."

Wyatt nodded and they entered the room, raising the heads of the police and FBI agents who'd been interrogating Jalen under the guise of protection. Seeing the three men approach, the agents scattered, and Avi continued down a dim hallway before crossing through a kitchen littered with disposable coffee cups and pizza boxes. A soggy Greek salad sat untouched in a plastic clamshell, reminding Wyatt of a terrarium. Outside the window, the law enforcement officers huddled, peering inside, trying to figure out who the mysterious visitors were.

Avi led them into a spacious dining room with wood-lined walls and a large table in the center. The blinds were angled shut and a chandelier glowed warmly above them. Jalen's mother, Tyra, sat on one side of him, and a man in a nice suit—Richard Lee, Jalen's attorney—sat on the other. Jalen's father, Ronnie, paced in the back like he was in the locker room, ready to ball. Jalen slumped in his chair, arms crossed, chin down, staring at an uneaten garlic knot on a paper plate in front of him.

A thick-necked, sweaty interrogator sat across from Jalen, shoulders hunched. "I know you know more than you are telling me," he said, the patience in his tone belied by a sinister smile. "You have the blood of dozens of people on your hands. If you tell me what I need to know, I'll help you wash it off. Otherwise, it's on you. On you, Jalen!" He pointed a fat finger at the boy like an umpire during a strikeout.

"I told you everything." Jalen's voice just barely audible.

"Stop lying!" The man slapped the table, but Jalen didn't even flinch.

One look at Jalen's posture and Wyatt knew the kid had shut himself off. "These guys are trained to deal with serial killers, not kids," Wyatt whispered to Mr. Yellow. "How many hours has this been going on?"

Mr. Yellow shook his head. "Don't know."

"Now what?" Ronnie broke the silence, pointing at the new faces in the room. "Who the hell are these people?"

The interrogator swiveled around, his face cardiac red. "I said I didn't want anybody in here but me. This is my interview!"

Mr. Yellow flashed a Department of Defense badge. "We're here under orders. Sorry to interrupt, but we need a few minutes with Jalen."

"I don't care. I work for the attorney general's office, and if you have a problem with that, you can talk to him."

"Department of Defense," Ronnie said incredulously. "What the hell do they want with my son? I'm about done with this, Dick . . ." Ronnie turned to the lawyer.

"We can end this right now," Richard Lee said calmly. "Jalen's under no obligation to answer any questions and has the constitutional right to remain silent. He's trying to do the right thing—which I, personally, think is misplaced, as he did nothing to harm anyone intentionally. You gentlemen should be interrogating the makers of these violent video games, not my client!" Richard Lee shouted as if he were speaking to the press, which, in fact, was something he was itching to do.

"These clowns," said the interrogator, "need to back off."

Wyatt stepped past Mr. Yellow and pulled the hood off his head. "Jalen," he said, "want to step outside with me?"

"What's this?" Ronnie grunted. "Bring your kid to work day?"

"The opposite," Mr. Yellow said. "He brought us to work."

"Sure he did." Ronnie laughed.

The interrogator now rose to his feet. He was huge: 250 pounds, six foot five, with a thinning flattop. "Kid, get your punk ass out of this house right now and take this old man with you." He reached out and pushed Wyatt's chest.

The man's fingers had just touched Wyatt's shirt, when Wyatt's right hand came up in a blur, pinning the man's hand to his chest. He leaned forward on the man's thick wrist, nearly breaking it, and the man howled. Wyatt kicked his legs out and slammed the interrogator to the ground, rattling the entire house and knocking the wind from the man's massive chest.

The man lay moaning and sputtering. Wyatt looked up at Avi and Mr. Yellow, who each took an arm and dragged the investigator out of the room.

"Damn," said Ronnie.

Wyatt turned his eyes on Jalen and nodded outside at the basketball hoop glowing above the garage. "Just a quick game of H-O-R-S-E?"

Tyra patted her son's leg. "Honey," she whispered, "if you want to stop now, it's okay."

"Hoops?" huffed Ronnie. "Good luck. Been trying to get him to play—"

"All right." Jalen rose to his feet.

"Wait—" The lawyer caught the boy's arm. "If there are any questions, I need to be present."

"We're just hanging out, Richard," Wyatt said. "Off the record. Where's a basketball?"

Tyra raised a long, hot-pink fingernail. "First, tell me who you are before you go anywhere with my son."

"My name is Wyatt. And all I'll say is that I've been in his shoes before. I think I can help."

"Help my ass," Ronnie said.

"Twenty minutes." Wyatt smiled at Tyra, trying his best to be charming.

"Ten." Tyra cocked her head at Wyatt. "I saw a ball in the garage . . . but I'm watching you from here."

The sun had set, and the air was considerably cooler in Michigan than Virginia, though still comfortable and fresh. Wyatt could see the security detail on the property, dim figures moving among the trees and shrubs in the distance. Jalen was a good shot—a leftie who put the ball up in clean, tight arcs. They played in relative silence for a few minutes, just shooting and passing, before Jalen cleared his throat. "Thanks for getting me out of there."

"Sure." Wyatt nodded.

"So you said you've been in my shoes before," Jalen continued. "Hard for me to imagine *anybody* else in these shoes." He looked down at his new Jordans as he dribbled.

"I just meant I've been sitting under the noses of a bunch of cops, sniffing around, trying to get something outta me that I didn't understand."

"Yeah, but I've killed people. That's different." Jalen took a shot, drained it. "So you don't know. You can't know . . . I didn't mean to do it, but I did and they're dead."

Wyatt scooped the ball under the net and passed it to Jalen, giving him his change.

"Of course I know what that's like," Wyatt said. "You think you're the only person in the world who's been tricked into something horrible, something you regret every day of your life?"

"What do you mean?" Jalen held the ball up for a shot. "You've killed someone?"

"Yeah," Wyatt said flatly.

"More than once?" Jalen asked.

"Pass the ball if you're not going to shoot."

Jalen fired it at the hoop, and it bounced off the rim. "But how? You're a kid."

"How?" Wyatt said. "*You're* asking me how?"

"I didn't know what I was doing. It was a game."

"Maybe it was the same for me. And in that moment, reality was broken for me." Wyatt squared up for a jump shot.

"You know that's a book, right?" Jalen's eyes perked up.

"By Dr. Jane McGonigal," Wyatt said as the ball hissed through the net, hitting the blacktop and bouncing back to him.

"And you know in the book, this doctor says playing games is good?"

"It *is* good," Wyatt said.

"Not for me. Not that day." Jalen's eyes fogged slightly. "I was just playing a game and all this happened. And now I'm broken." Tears clouded his eyes and he blinked them back. "I wish I could turn it back. I wish I'd been the one to die. I don't even want to live anymore. I've been thinking about how I can just end it for me, too."

"I wouldn't want to live either." Wyatt tucked the ball under his arm. "And I wouldn't blame you if you tried to do something about it."

"Huh?" Jalen looked up. "Aren't you like supposed to tell me not to say stuff like that?"

"No, man. It's your choice. You can wallow . . ." Wyatt dribbled the ball around Jalen and went for a layup. "Or you can keep moving. And right now, you have a chance to do something good."

"Like what?"

"Like helping us find Encyte."

"Who is us?" Jalen shot back. "You dropped that FBI agent like he was a kindergartner. The old man with you said something about the DoD—who's asking me to help?"

"Someone who can do something about what Encyte did to you and those people in Austin."

Wyatt let that hang in the air for a few moments. "Going back to your original question, I think what Encyte means by reality is broken is that there's a new reality, a digital world that links us all in a giant game, both real and virtual—that's the reality, and he's telling us he's breaking it."

"Certainly broke it with me." Jalen took a shot, missed badly.

Wyatt tossed it back to him. "You're bent, not broken."

Jalen thought for a moment. Then fired up a three-pointer that swished through the net.

"When'd you first start interacting with Encyte?" Wyatt asked.

"To be honest, I don't even know, 'cause he may have approached me with multiple avatars. I've been streaming my gameplay for a little while, trying to get a fan base on Twitch or become a YouTuber, but it's like, not that easy. So when someone follows you and wants to play Kill Bloxx with you, it's cool, it's like an honor, and I guess the only person out there, who I know is associated with Encyte, went by Pro_F_er. He just started chatting with me one day. I think over Twitch, but then we were communicating over Kill Bloxx, too. He knew the game really well, and he designed some games of his own, with Kill Bloxx studio. You know that tool, right?"

Wyatt shrugged. "Loosely."

"Well, within the Kill Bloxx platform, those in the community are encouraged to create their own games and let other people play them. He'd done that, and it was fun, but then . . ." Jalen's voice trailed off. "The last game he brought me into was different. It looked like Kill Bloxx, but it was a simulation." Jalen dribbled, lost in thought.

"Did Pro_F_er—or any avatar you communicated with—ever mention the name Glowworm? Or Glowworm Gaming?"

"Nah." Jalen shook his head. "I've heard about their games, but they're banned now . . . totally off the internet. But I think you can still find versions on the dark web."

Wyatt looked back at the house, then at Jalen. "Ever been on the darknet?"

"I've logged into the Tor browser, but only just to do it. I haven't played the games."

"Well, don't. I don't know who's still developing them or how they are functional, but those games are also a trick . . . a way to lure people in."

"Aren't all games?" Jalen laughed and passed Wyatt the ball. "How do you know so much about Glowworm Gaming?"

"Like I said, I was in your shoes before, not playing the game per se, but part of the collateral damage."

"One thing I heard—a rumor among gamers—is that Glowworm was secretly some kind of terrorist. He was captured and black-sited by the U.S. government. Some people think he's in Guantanamo right now."

Of course Wyatt knew this wasn't true. He'd been the one to kill Glowworm. He'd watched him die, the bullet from his own gun firing into Glowworm's brain. The one life he didn't regret taking.

"Jalen!" Tyra called down. "Your daddy's leaving. Come say bye."

Jalen hesitated. "If you want," he said to Wyatt, "I can come back."

"Nah, it's cool. But just one more question."

"Okay."

"What didn't you tell the FBI?"

"Man." Jalen shook his head. "Thought you were going to be cool."

Wyatt smiled. "Come on, dude. You're too good of a gamer to have told them everything. Gotta be something you held back. At least, I know I would have."

Jalen glanced around the property, letting out his breath.

"Hurry up!" Tyra called again from the house.

"Okay. But it's not about me." Jalen's eyes narrowed. "There's someone in the games . . . I just didn't want her to get tangled up in all of this."

"A girl?"

"Yes. But if I tell you what I know, can you promise me you'll keep it a secret?"

"I can promise you I won't tell the FBI."

CHAPTER 5

Wyatt thought about what Jalen had told him, and he even considered keeping it from Avi and Mr. Yellow. He had the boy's trust. And he didn't want to betray that trust, but he knew all too well that innocent people are an inevitable casualty of psychopaths.

They'd been midair, en route back to Virginia for a good twenty-five minutes before Wyatt spoke up. "So . . . I think there's someone else we should look at."

Avi and Mr. Yellow glanced up from their devices.

"Go on," said Mr. Yellow.

"I don't know if this is gonna go anywhere, but Jalen told me something. One time he entered one of the games Pro_F_er created. And he briefly played alongside another avatar named Hi Kyto."

Avi's face scrunched up. "Should that mean something to me?"

"I don't know if they're the same. Coulda been a copycat avatar, but Hi Kyto is the name used by Julie Chen, one of the most popular gamers on *Fortnite*."

Avi's head immediately dropped back down to his tablet as he Googled Julie Chen.

"Wait a minute," Avi said. "She's not just a gamer, she's a prodigy." He began reading aloud, *"The gamer, known as Hi Kyto, was born in Shenyang to Chinese national parents, and moved with her parents to the United States at the age of four, where her father taught diplomacy at the Freeman Spogli Institute at Stanford University, and her mother was a professor of computer science. Chen showed an early propensity for linguistics, reportedly fluent in seven languages by age nine. She's a polymath who has developed her own codebase. A highly regarded game developer in her own right, she has developed Kill Bloxx games and was an early adopter of* Fortnite. *She's one of the few female players to have risen to prominence within the platform. A highly controversial figure, she remains both a fascination of but still aloof from the gaming community. In 2017, she was the first youth to be awarded—"* Avi paused, then read on slowly, *"She was the first youth to be awarded the distinguished Darsie Fellowship, selected by John Darsie himself."*

"Wait a minute," Mr. Yellow said. "John Darsie . . . that the one I'm thinking of?"

Avi tapped his iPad and pulled up another Wikipedia page and held it out for Mr. Yellow.

"Well, this changes things." Mr. Yellow leaned back, satisfied.

"What are you guys talking about?" Wyatt said. "Who's John Darsie?"

"Valor alum and . . ." Mr. Yellow said, distracted by his thoughts.

"And what else?"

"Have you ever heard of Red Trident?" Mr. Yellow asked.

Wyatt shook his head.

"Red Trident is a business Darsie founded. It's probably the largest private-sector, big-data intelligence supplier to the U.S. government."

"What does that mean?" asked Wyatt.

Avi chimed in. "It's a spy agency with web-crawling spiders

instead of actual spies. Basically, Darsie created a technology that can watch a lot of what we do online—say over the phone—and he sells that information to the government."

"Shouldn't our government have that technology and not some privateer?"

"A lot of people feel that way, but John Darsie has beaten all his critics and made billions. He's one of the most powerful people in the U.S. and the world . . ."

"And so this billionaire private-sector spy who's a Valor alum is associated with Julie Chen, who's possibly associated with Encyte?" Wyatt asked. "Sounds like something we need to be all over."

"Yes," Mr. Yellow said. "Of course, with Darsie's connections in the government we will need to tread lightly. But we will investigate." Yellow looked at Avi, who nodded. "But tell me, why would Jalen keep this from the cops? This could really help his case."

"He's a young, impressionable kid." Wyatt shrugged. "And in the gaming world, this girl—Hi Kyto—is royalty. He didn't want to rat out his star crush."

"Crush?" Avi said. "Idiot."

"Avi, you know Darsie, right?" Mr. Yellow asked.

"I do."

"We may need you to reach out to him," Mr. Yellow said.

Avi nodded and looked again at Wyatt. "Was there any connection to Glowworm Gaming?"

"Jalen didn't seem to think so. It's possible Encyte might've been a developer there, but I haven't seen anything to indicate it."

"What about Hallsy? Did Jalen mention him?" Avi jotted some notes on a cocktail napkin.

Wyatt shook his head, then glared at Mr. Yellow. "He's the one who's supposed to be looking for Hallsy. Maybe you should ask him."

"I told you earlier. We're still pursuing leads, putting out feelers," Mr. Yellow said, addressing the question he'd hoped to avoid. "Gotta be something on this damn plane other than Sprite." He pushed up from his seat and bumped his way to the front of the cabin.

Wyatt turned to Avi. "Come on, man. You've got some skin in this game, too. You want Hallsy, so shoot me straight."

Avi turned from the window and looked at him. "Of course I want him. I think about my brother every day . . . what Hallsy did to him. And one day, I will avenge him."

Avi blamed Hallsy for his brother's death, and rightfully so. Avi's brother was part of the security team when Eldon was kidnapped. He was the driver, trying to get Eldon out of Israel. But the escape was a setup. Hallsy had learned of a fifteen-million-dollar bounty placed on Eldon by the Glowworm, and that was enough for him to betray his lifelong friend.

Wyatt checked behind him, making sure Mr. Yellow was out of earshot. "Enough sitting on the sidelines. We need to be part of the hunt, Avi. You and me. Let's get in the game."

Avi flexed his jaw and returned his gaze to the window. "Mr. Yellow seems to think Hallsy's made it to South America."

"South America?" Wyatt sighed. "Well, that really narrows things down."

Outside, more clouds and the craggy browns of West Virginia somewhere below them.

"Do I have any reason to believe they'll find him?" Wyatt said.

"Well . . ." Avi let out a breath, calculating. "Given the time he's been gone . . . I'd say you've got a three percent chance."

It was just before midnight when Wyatt approached his house and saw a light still glowing in the kitchen window and a TV flickering inside. The full moon hung in a clear sky. Haloed in the far distance was Monticello: an architectural masterpiece, the plantation home Thomas Jefferson designed and had built for himself. As a student in Charlottesville, Wyatt had taken several field trips to the home and learned many things about Jefferson. Not only was he a Founding Father and a chief author of the Declaration of Independence and the Constitution, Jefferson was also a scientist and inventor, a collector and a tinkerer. Monticello itself contained many items that, at the time, were considered almost futuristic. Like the dumbwaiter for his wine, and the Great Clock that could be heard from nearly three miles away.

Wyatt stared at the glowing dome and wondered if, in his wildest imaginings, Jefferson could have conceived of the world today—computers in everyone's pocket, nuclear weapons, automobiles, self-driving ones at that. Cars that could be hacked and used to kill. Jefferson was a diplomat. He had an interest in spy craft and cryptography. What would he have thought of Camp Valor? Of the small army of child soldiers using the latest technology to protect the ideas that he and the Founding Fathers had etched into parchment with a quill and iron gall ink? Wyatt thought Jefferson would've thoroughly approved.

Wyatt pushed open the door and found his father at the kitchen table with a decaf coffee. The TV played quietly and Eldon's head was craned toward the screen. It was the same loop that had been playing for the last three days of the news cycle. A talking head was interviewing the new secretary of defense.

"Madam Secretary," the interviewer said. "It goes without saying, this administration has seen some . . . turbulence. Under the current president, officials have been leaving office right and left. The terrorist known as Encyte has carried out one of the most horrific attacks in U.S. history. As secretary of defense, what are you going to do about it?"

"Well, I can tell you one thing, I'm not going anywhere." The SecDef was a small woman, but she had a commanding voice and a villain's polished smile. "And the answer to your question is a multifaceted one. Of course, we're going to work to protect our freedoms and make Americans feel safe again. But we're also going to clean house and initiate reforms. My job is to get our military back on track. No one loves the bureaucratic process, but I think we all saw—with the previous administration—the chaos that occurs when leashes get too long and we have too much freedom."

"Too much freedom . . . ridiculous," Eldon groaned. "This damn administration." He snapped off the TV and turned his attention to his son. "I was trying to work, but I got distracted. Easy to do lately. How are you?"

"Good." Wyatt locked the dead bolt behind him. "Hungry."

"Mom wanted to make sure you ate that." Eldon motioned to the meat loaf, mashed potatoes, sautéed string beans wrapped in cellophane.

"She still making you sleep downstairs?" Wyatt popped the plate in the microwave.

"You're too young to know about that stuff."

"Come on, Dad. Mom's pissed."

"She'll be fine. She just needs some time to adjust."

As Wyatt smelled the food warming, he realized it had been almost twelve hours since he'd had a bite to eat. He sat down next to his father and began tucking into his dinner.

"How was Detroit?"

"Avi didn't brief you?" Wyatt raised his eyebrows at his dad. "I know he helps you keep tabs."

Eldon shrugged. "He said you might've found a link that'll help the Encyte case."

"Yeah, so that gamer kid, Jalen . . ." Wyatt stalled, considering his words. "Think we could find a place for him at Valor?"

"I don't know." Eldon sighed. "Camp is a few days away. Candidates have been selected, and from what Avi told me, this kid's legal battle hasn't even started yet."

"I'm talking about him redeeming himself. Right now, the kid probably wishes he could go to jail."

Eldon slugged the last of his coffee. "I'll think about it."

"He's a good kid."

"You think that now, but—"

"No. I know it. He's scared to death. He isn't Encyte. He was a total pawn. He's smart, and if someone doesn't intervene, he'll be lost. And you know what gamers can be like if they're lost."

Eldon didn't look up but Wyatt could see he'd struck a nerve. At one time, Eldon's best friend had been the infamous Glowworm. They were teenagers together in the '80s, and their love of the early games was part of what made them best friends.

"I'll bother Avi about it in the morning."

"Thank you." Wyatt set his fork on his empty plate and pushed back from the table. "Look, Dad, I've done what I can to help with Encyte, but truthfully, it's not my problem. I'm going back to camp, but I'm going on my terms . . . I wanna find Hallsy."

"Wyatt, there will be a time and a place—"

"I'm done waiting. I'm going after him."

"The most elite operators in the world have turned up nothing in nine months, and you think you can just waltz in and find him?"

"They don't care like I do." Wyatt's eyes narrowed.

"We'll get a team together, but right now, you need to finish training. You need to be there for the next round of campers—"

"Cody is gonna be fine."

"I'm not just talking about your brother. We follow a code. You're a part of the Valor community. You don't get to choose your orders."

"But Mr. Yellow—"

"Let me tell you something about Mr. Yellow. Sure, he's our ally, but he's not your friend. And things can get pretty dangerous for you pretty quickly if you take the assets the government has invested in you and you go rogue. People do that and they disappear. And I can't help you."

Wyatt nodded.

"Do you understand?"

"Ten-four, Dad," Wyatt said as he went toward the stairs. "I'll go and I'll do what I'm told. But you should know, I'm not sure I believe in this place anymore."

Wyatt walked down the creaky stairs toward his bedroom. For the first time that day, he felt the stiffening from his lacrosse game that afternoon. He cranked on the shower and stepped under the hot spigot. Water coursing down his back, he thought about the day—Jalen Rose, the massacre, Hallsy—all of it tumbled around in his head.

He toweled off, dressed, went back to his room, and knelt beside his bed. Wyatt waited for his father's steps to retreat down the hallway before grabbing the headboard and pulling the bed from the wall. He reached down to the molding, feeling around behind the base of the headboard until he found the spot. He pressed into the wall, lifting it up and out, and then retrieved an encrypted cell phone from a cavity inside the wall. He pressed the power button and the phone glowed to life.

Wyatt scrolled down his list of contacts until he found Avi's name. He texted: *I wanna move on Hallsy. We can't wait. Find someone who can help us get him.*

Wyatt returned the phone to the hiding spot and pulled out the photo of Dolly, bound and gagged. He studied her as he did every night, using the fear in her dark eyes as fuel for revenge. He would find Hallsy and bring him to justice, even if it meant dragging him back by his broken neck.

In his dreams, that night, once again the scene was the same—the gray lake, the echo of birds in the wet, green treetops, the girl: tall and athletic, she had something slung on her back. It looked like a weapon—a rocket launcher—that jangled as she ran. Wyatt ran behind her, down a path in a thick wood, and then it was dark. The girl was wading into water. He followed her, the cool water rising above his waist. She waited for him, and he swam out to her and pulled her close to him, her body warm against his.

"Never let go of me," she whispered into his ear.

"I won't." He pulled her in tighter, but his arms collapsed against his own chest. He opened his eyes. He saw her—her face pale, almost greenish. Her eyes, terrified. She reached out to him, but something grabbed her, pulling her away. Wyatt swam, but the harder he kicked, the faster she was dragged into a watery abyss. Wyatt felt his lungs burning—deeper, deeper, until he could bear it no more and he turned and swam for the surface.

CHAPTER 6

The secretary of defense, Rear Admiral Elaine Becker, sat down for a rare quiet dinner at the Boatyard Bar and Grill not far from the United States Naval Academy, her alma mater. It was early for dinner, blue-plate-special hour, and her security detail had effectively shut down the restaurant to all other visitors, save for her predecessor, Admiral Henry McCray, also a Naval Academy graduate. McCray lived in Annapolis, where he was taking a year to write a tell-all memoir about his time at the White House and his work as a contributor to Fox News.

Though he'd been the one to ask for the meeting, he'd arrived late enough for his successor to have a glass of wine and get annoyed. When he finally arrived, he was wearing khaki pants and a T-shirt and entered the restaurant carrying a glass of rosé. After greeting his former bodyguards, he gave the current secretary a kiss on the cheek and slid into the chair across from her. "Elaine, good to see you."

"Likewise."

"Sorry I'm late. I was just wrapping up a fly-fishing class."

"Fly-fishing?"

"Yep. Never had time for a hobby," he said, fanning the

white dinner napkin across his lap. "Figured I'd pick one that was time consuming and photogenic."

"You like it?"

"Mehhh." The former two-star admiral shrugged. "I spend a lot of time swearing and getting my flies out of hairy messes. Kinda like being the secretary of defense." He winked.

"Well, I have a few messes. That's for sure," she said.

"From what I've read, it sounds like you've been cutting the messes out. Heard you shut down some black sites."

"Cleaning up what you left behind has taken me several months, but that's the easy part. That's not what's keeping me up at night. Our homegrown terrorist is doing that."

McCray looked into her eyes. "This Encyte—does anyone in any of the agencies have any leads?"

"Classified," the SecDef said with a flat smile. "If I knew, I couldn't tell you, but the truth is—no. No one has any clue. I need some suggestions, Henry. I gotta find this guy."

McCray tapped his fingernail on the table. "Wish I could help you there," he finally said. "My only advice—be careful what programs you cut. The job of today's military is like fishing. And you're not going to catch anything without three things: time on the water, numbers, and luck."

"Thanks for the tip," Elaine said dryly. "Nice catching up, but why did you want to meet?"

"Nothing like getting to it," he said. "So you've heard the story of Khrushchev? The two letters he was given by his predecessor which he then gave to his successor?"

"Yes, Khrushchev wrote two letters to his successor that he should open when things got really bad. The first one read, 'Blame it on me,' the second one said, 'Sit down and write a letter.'" Elaine rolled her eyes. "You here to give me that advice?"

"No." McCray leaned in. "But I'm going to tell you something my predecessor told me, and it's far more valuable than the Khrushchev trick."

"What's that?" Elaine raised her thin eyebrows.

McCray looked over his shoulder, then whispered, "Are you recording this or being recorded?"

Elaine could smell his breath—summer sausage and wine. I never want to retire, she thought. His breath smelled like wasted time.

"No," she said. "I'm going to need to get going."

"There's an elite training program the United States has been secretly developing and covertly funding since 1941. Its existence is only known to the president—though some presidents are not informed—to the secretary of defense, to those who've attended the camp, and to a handful of people in the espionage business. But it must be kept secret. If its existence were public, it would be incredibly damaging to the program and to the administration."

"Is it legal?" Even after a second glass of wine, she'd suddenly straightened up in her chair.

McCray tossed another look over his shoulder. "Not by a long shot."

"So why are you telling me about it?"

"Because it's an incredibly powerful tool for you to deploy or destroy. But know that it can also destroy you." McCray swigged his rosé. "Remember the rumor last year that the Glowworm Gaming Network, which had been blackmailing politicians, was broken up by a group of covert operators?"

"Yes, I remember being debriefed on that."

"The threat was real and it was dismantled by these warriors I'm talking about."

"Sounds great," Elaine said. "So what's the problem?"

"They're kids. Teenagers. Some younger." He leaned back and shot her a squinty-eyed smile.

"Children?" she said, her voice loaded with indignation. "And you supported this effort?"

"Absolutely. They're not just kids. They're bad kids. Juvenile delinquents given a second chance. And they deliver."

"I'm not sure I want to be hearing this." She started to rise.

He reached out and touched her wrist. "Wait. Sit down."

She wanted to slug him, but she sat. "What?"

"I'm old school," he said, tossing back his wine. "So I don't get rattled like some of the new blood does when a couple rules are broken. Members of this organization have assassinated world leaders on behalf of the U.S., they've collected intelligence, prevented horrendous crimes and catastrophes."

She scoffed. "As the United States of America, we can't have children doing that on our behalf. I can't let our president be exposed to something like this. I can't condone—"

"Shhh." McCray held his finger to his lips.

Elaine glared.

"It's your right to shut it down. But before you do, I strongly suggest you take a look. Eighty years of your predecessors have supported this program."

"And ninety years of U.S. presidents chose not to abolish slavery!"

"Listen, Elaine," McCray said, rising to his feet, which she noticed were in flip-flops. "One thing you're going to learn if you haven't already is that this country is not made secure by laws—because we're playing everything safe and fair—it's because a select few chose to defend our freedoms. This group deserves medals, not your disdain."

"You must be drunk."

McCray belly laughed and rose to his feet. "You betcha."

"What's the group called and how do I find it?"

McCray swiveled his head at an unassuming man standing in the back of the restaurant. Even across the room, she could see the pit rings on his button-up shirt. "He'll take you when you're ready."

McCray walked out, and the man came over to the secretary's table and handed her a card, all black with a golden CV embossed on the front and only a phone number on the back.

CHAPTER 7

Great time, effort, and resources had been put into keeping both the existence and location of Camp Valor confidential. The list of those who knew about it was short: graduates of Group-A and B, qualified staff (mostly graduates themselves), junior campers, and those who had, at a minimum, qualified for Group-C. Valorians aside, there were a few select persons in the U.S. government who were also privy to it, but Eldon Brewer did everything in his power to ensure his nosy sister-in-law was not one of them.

"I love y'all, but I ain't getting up to say goodbye when you leave for camp in the morning," Aunt Narcy warned. "Now that I'm in business for myself, I can decide when I do and don't get up, and I don't get up unless I'm getting *paid* to get up."

Prior to moving to Charlottesville, Wyatt's aunt Narcy, formally Narcissa, had performed various odd jobs. She'd been a limo driver in the days before Uber, which, according to Narcy, was the reason she couldn't get off disability. "My back is completely destroyed."

She'd worked in toll booths, sold time-shares. In her late twenties, she'd even been a card dealer at a low-end casino. "That was when I still had my figure," she told anyone who'd listen.

"You shoulda seen how the men would tip me when I wore a tight bustier."

And after she relocated to Virginia with Wyatt and the rest of his family, Narcy had gone into business for herself, working as a realtor. To help launch Narcissa in this career, Wyatt's dad had invested in several new pantsuits for her, because, as Narcy put it, "A strong woman needs to look strong." He also was convinced to buy what Narcissa called her *attaché*: an old briefcase that contained nothing but a pen, lipstick, a Twix bar, and a thin file of work-related documents. To date, Narcissa had sold a grand total of zero homes, but she got to make her own schedule. "And Sunday," she told the Brewer family, "is my day of rest."

Despite her threats, at 5:15 in the morning, Sunday, June 3rd, Narcissa was in the kitchen, hugging up a storm. Although Narcy had never quite warmed to Wyatt, she had become a surrogate mother to Cody. This was especially true during the bleak months the previous summer, when Narcy believed Wyatt was in juvie. In fact, he was at Valor. And when Wyatt's father had been missing, Wyatt's mother had been grieving, minimally competent, and clinically depressed. So Narcy stepped into the mothering role for Cody, while her sister, Katherine, checked out. Cody happened to be one of those nearly perfect kids who needed little guidance, which was fortunate because for all of Narcy's bossiness, she was a loving, yet completely inept parental figure.

"Take care." Narcy smothered Cody in a tearful hug. "Remember to eat. You're so thin. Don't want you coming back any thinner, you hear?"

"I will, Aunt Narcy." Cody obliged her with a smile. "Don't worry."

"Wyatt," Eldon called up the stairs. "Time to roll out."

As was typical, Wyatt had waited until the last minute to pack. He pulled out his old canvas backpack, the beige military rucksack he'd found in Narcy's garage a couple of years before. "What the heck am I gonna do with that?" Narcy had said when

Wyatt had asked to have it. "It's your dad's anyway." Though he'd been angry at his father at the time, when Wyatt slipped the heavy straps over his shoulders, he'd felt the weight of something important. So he made the bag his own. It had a pocket for everything—water bottle, favorite jacket, comic books, ChapStick, candy, cell phone, and a few protein bars. Wyatt had even gotten his mom to add loops to hold his lacrosse sticks and a mesh bag attachment for his ball. The center of the bag contained a waterproof liner that he filled with neatly rolled shirts, pants, and socks, and then cinched closed.

Wyatt stepped out of his room and was making his way to the athletic closet, where he'd pick out an old lax stick to bring to Valor, something he could use to toss around a ball if he wanted, but not his long stick. The closet was beside the garage entrance. As Wyatt stepped up to the door, he could hear his parents talking in his father's study, which was down the hall a short distance. The door was ajar. He could see his mother pacing, frantically cleaning the room—anything to avoid eye contact—as his dad sat on the edge of his desk, arms crossed, trying to persuade her to join them at camp.

"James," his mother was saying, "or whatever the hell your name is. I know this is something you have to do, but"—her voice softened—"I'm dealing with twenty years of lies."

"I was protecting you," his father interrupted, putting a hand on her shoulder. She shrugged it off and stepped away.

"Protecting me? I'm going insane. First you're a truck driver, then I think you've abandoned us, then I think you're dead. And you come back with . . ." Wyatt could see her looking down at Eldon's mutilated hand and he knew where this discussion would go—nowhere. This argument, about the lies his father had told his mother about his work for the U.S. government and the sacrifices he had made for their family not only had dominated the relationship between the two but had become the entire family dynamic since his father had come back from the dead.

His mother was no longer in a relationship with his father, but in a perpetual reckoning of what she had thought their life was and what the reality had been.

"I'm sorry. But I can't," his mom now said. "I don't know who you are yet, I don't know who my son is even, and most of all I don't know who I am. I just can't go to some mysterious camp and be somebody else."

Katherine Brewer was not, by anyone's standards, a traveler. Born and raised in the dusty, middle-American town of Millersville, she was a classic homebody. With the exception of the patently chaotic way in which the family was relocated to Charlottesville, she had rarely wandered more than a few hours from where she was born.

"Kathy," Eldon said softly, trying to reach out to her again. "You know this is not what I want. I want you with me. But if you can't come, I will call you every day. I'll make the boys speak to you. You will know everything about what we are doing—no lies—anything that does not cause a security breach to share I will share—"

"No. No!" Kathy pushed Eldon away. Wyatt could hear her voice get gritty. "I can understand and accept that you and Wyatt and now Cody have some responsibility to our country. That this responsibility takes you and our sons away from me. But I cannot and will not be on pins and needles. I can't take that. I spent countless months wondering what had happened, waiting for the call. I don't want this, I can't." She was crying now. "You can go play war and I'll be here when you get back. But I can't and won't be waiting every day to know if you're alive, in danger—"

"We'll mostly be training," Eldon said. "Low to no danger this summer."

"Mostly. I don't want to suffer through *mostly*. Just do me one favor . . . You just take care of my sons." Her voice began to shake. "Because if anything happens to them, so help me God—"

"Wyatt! What're you doin' over there," Narcy came barreling around the corner.

"Just getting a lacrosse stick," Wyatt said.

His dad and mom came out of the study, his mother wiping tears from her face.

"Kathy, you okay?" Narcy asked.

"Yeah." She smiled. "Just a lot going on today."

"Okay . . . Now, Eldon, what about a physical address? I mean, I could have an emergency . . ."

"You don't need one." Eldon walked through the cramped hallway carrying his own rucksack into the garage. "Cody! Time to go." Everyone followed. "You have the email and the PO Box in Washington, D.C."

"Washington. That's good. Glad you'll be close," Narcy said, fishing for an address.

"No, Narcissa. If you need us, email, okay?"

"Oh, I'll be so worried." She dramatically pawed her forehead.

"Don't worry," Wyatt's dad said, loading his bag into the back of their Suburban. "We'll be great, Narcy . . . and Kathy, I love you." He gave his wife a long look.

"I love you too," she said quietly, then turned to her sons. "If you don't want to go, you can stay with me. You can choose any life you want to lead."

Cody looked up at Wyatt, who spoke first. "Mom, we love you. And our choice is to go to Camp Valor for the summer."

She pulled them close. "Be careful. I won't stop worrying until you are back here safe—both of you."

"You mean all three of us?" Cody looked at his father.

Katherine nodded. "All three."

"Put this on." Eldon handed his youngest son a blindfold.

"For real, Dad?" Cody asked. "Wyatt isn't wearing one. And I get carsick as it is."

"Sorry, but it's protocol for new candidates. As much for your safety as anything else."

Cody tied the blindfold around his head and leaned back against the pillow as Eldon backed out of the garage into the still-dark morning.

By the time they got to Andrews Air Force Base, Cody was sound asleep, blindfold snug over his eyes as Eldon drove out onto the tarmac and into the belly of a C-130. Wyatt, who'd been snoozing in the front passenger seat, was startled awake when the car bumped up the ramp. He glanced around to get his bearings, then dozed back again. The plane took off without the rest of the Brewer family even stirring.

An hour into the flight, they awoke, surprised to find themselves in their car, tightly secured to the floor of a military aircraft thirty thousand feet in the air.

"You all right?" Wyatt said, looking back at Cody. A couple summers ago, he'd had to retrieve his little brother from the high-dive at the city swimming pool. Cody had been up there for forty-five minutes, paralyzed by his fear of heights.

"Yeah, first flight," Cody said. "I'm actually glad this plane doesn't have windows. Don't have to worry about my stomach dropping."

"We'll be touching down soon."

"This how you got to Valor last summer?" Cody asked. "'Cause it's pretty freaking cool."

"I was coming from jail." Wyatt shrugged. "Your commute is nicer."

Two hours later, the plane began to make its descent, and again the blindfold was pulled down.

While Camp Valor itself had a landing strip, it was five hundred feet shy of the runway requirement for a C-130, so the plane came down smoothly some twenty miles from Valor, on a remote airstrip used mainly for getting supplies into the rough, mountainous country.

Eldon hitched a trailer with a load of supplies to the back of the Suburban and after a short, bumpy drive, Wyatt turned to Cody. "Okay, you can take it off now."

Cody lifted his blindfold, eyes widening at the entirely different world than the one he'd left. The flora and fauna looked much like the Pacific Northwest—tall pines, lush green vegetation, thick fog in the morning air. Not to mention the scale and size of the place. Everything, from the mountains and the trees, to the boulders in the distance, was simply awesome, especially if you'd grown up in Millersville.

"We're here?" Cody stared out at a weather-beaten concrete slab stretching into a gray lake, forming a sort of industrial pier.

"Almost." Eldon nodded at the mist, and Wyatt saw the familiar prow of the *Sea Goat,* the stout work boat and ferry Valor used to shuttle supplies and campers to and from the island. At her helm was her captain, Mackenzie Grant, a heavyset Native American man with long black hair and a ready smile.

Mackenzie secured the boat to the dock. "Hail to the new chief," he said and stuck out his hand for Eldon to pull him up onto the dock. An older woman was behind him. She could've just as easily been in her sixties as in her eighties, her blue eyes and youthful spirit seeming to defy age. She hugged Eldon, her white-gray hair billowing on the breezy dock.

She turned to the Brewer boys. "Would've thought you were Wyatt one summer ago," she said to Cody. "I'm Mum. Your dad has told me about you for the longest time."

Mackenzie high-fived Wyatt. "Good to see you, buddy. Looking swolt."

Wyatt smiled. "I'm still half your size."

"I see you brought your mini-me," Mackenzie said.

Cody held out his hand. "I'm Cody." Like his brother, Cody's cool, unassuming demeanor was most evident in new situations.

"Need to get this boy into my kitchen," Mum said. "He's skinnier than you were your first day, Wyatt."

"Ready to get back to that kitchen." Wyatt patted his stomach.

"Are we the first ones back?" Eldon asked.

"Nope." Mackenzie began unhooking the thick ropes from the cleats. "Picked up Cass yesterday."

At the mention of Dolly's older sister, Wyatt tensed and looked out over the gray-blue water. "How is she?"

"She looks great, considering . . ." Mackenzie said. "Don't think she's been out of the hospital much more than a month, but she's already back in the Caldera, training." He motioned to the fast-moving clouds overhead. "Enough pleasantries. Better get going before the weather turns."

The wind blew a slight surf across Lake Tecmaga, but it was still calm enough to transport the family and the supplies they had pulled by trailer off the C-130 to the dock and loaded onto the *Sea Goat*. Mackenzie eased the old ferry away from the pier and pointed her toward Camp Valor's entry facility, nestled in the archipelago in the distance. Wyatt watched Cody looking out from the small pilothouse, the wonder in his face reminding Wyatt what it was like to come to Valor for the first time. The sights, smells, even the taste of the moist air in his mouth brought back memories, but even the good ones caught him like a stitch in his side.

The camp was situated on the tallest of the numerous rocky islands all blanketed with emerald-green pines. Drawing up to the beach, one would think there was nothing particularly special about it—a narrow strip of sand in a horseshoe cove bisected by an L-shaped concrete dock. At the end of the dock was a post with a simple wooden sign that read, CAMP VALOR.

The beach, which was normally lined with canoes, paddleboards, all manner of watercraft, was vacant. Even the clotheslines above the crabgrass hung empty, awaiting the coming campers.

A path from the beach wound up to a red-and-white clapboard lodge with a broad porch, and just off it, a pole with an American flag fluttering in the light wind. To the right of the lodge and back from the water were crude white cabins. "Is that where we are staying?" asked Cody.

"Yeah—you and me. Campers are in the cabins. Dad, as director, has a different residence."

The cabins were divided male and female and organized by groups, starting with the most junior program—the Mounties—for those under twelve. Then there were the Junior Rovers, ages twelve to thirteen, then the fourteen- to fifteen-year-olds in Group-C, the fifteen-to sixteen-year-olds in Group-B, and finally Group-A, composed of the most senior and elite campers. The ages of campers only served as general guidelines; the more important divisions were individual ability and readiness.

Beyond the cabins and the lodge, a nondescript path led into a tall old-growth forest. As Mackenzie edged the *Sea Goat* up to the dock, Cody pointed to the ridgeline in the distance. "Is that it?"

"Yeah." Wyatt nodded. "The Caldera."

Though Wyatt and his father had spoken of Valor only in whispers, Cody had heard about the Caldera, an ancient volcanic crater several miles wide that housed the secret training facility where the real Camp Valor was located.

"Cool." Cody squinted, his long blond hair falling into eyes filled with curiosity and wonder.

Eldon, who couldn't wait for Mackenzie to finish tying off, leapt from the bow. "Come on!" he called over his shoulder. "Got a lot of work to do. Let's get moving."

CHAPTER 8

While he had not yet been convicted—or even formally charged—with a crime, thirteen-year-old Jalen Rose found himself under what amounted to house arrest. This was done for two reasons, the first being that local police and multiple three-letter agencies wanted unimpeded access to interviewing Jalen. The other reason for the isolation was for his own safety. Everyone in the U.S., from the press, to private citizens, to nutcases, was trying to figure out the identity of the kid in the video wearing a VR headset gleefully running over actual human beings.

He was an accidental mass murderer. After a couple of weeks, his confinement had become reality and the safe house in the podunk town of Clarkston his new home. It was as if he were a castaway, trapped on an island that was not only physical, but emotional as well. Once his picture started circulating on the national news—even with the VR headset obscuring his identity—Jalen felt exposed. If someone knew it was him, he'd be America's most hated human and a target. He deactivated all his social media accounts. He turned off his iPhone and left it in a bowl on the kitchen counter. The only account he left active was Twitch, but when he finally went online to delete that one as well, he found the government had already done it for him: *User not found*.

And if the overbearing, unwelcome eye of the U.S. government's security detail was not enough, Ronnie had hired a guy of his own, Willie Green. Willie had been Ronnie's teammate with the Lions, and he supplemented his retirement working private security detail.

"I tell you what," Ronnie said to Tyra. "I'm not gonna trust no FBI to keep my family safe. No, sir. We take care of our own."

Since Ronnie had already disclosed the Rose family's whereabouts to Willie Green, it was decided that it was safer to go ahead and let him stay. So Jalen spent most afternoons with a three-hundred-pound ex-linebacker eating hot wings and working on crossword puzzles.

Which was just as well to Jalen. He had given up TV after the first morning he saw the news footage of the park in Austin. It seemed they would never stop talking about it. Night after night of candlelight vigils. The loved ones crying for the fifty-three people killed. The first time he saw the small towers of flowers piling up in front of the picnic tables, he flicked the TV off and hurled the remote at the screen.

While most kids would be happy to have their divorced parents reunited under one roof, Jalen knew it just meant he'd be in the middle of the verbal equivalent of a UFC fight. When the yelling got to be too much, Jalen would sneak out at night, lifting his bedroom window and dropping down silently into the grass. He never wanted to go anywhere in particular; he just needed to get out of the safe house. So he could think. He figured if he spent the rest of his life trying, he could do enough good to offset all of the harm he had caused. On one of those nights, he was walking, thinking about how he could fix things, when he realized he'd reached the filling station a mile from his house. He saw a bum slumped against the wall outside the gas station, an empty Styrofoam cup in his limp hand.

Jalen pulled a couple of dollars out of his pocket and bent down. "Here you go," he said to the man.

"Two dollars?" the man yelled. "Come on, man. Can't even buy a Big Mac for two dollars!" The bum's eyes were wild, and the whites of his eyes yellow. He crumpled the money and threw it back.

Later, alone in his bed, Jalen pulled the thick tartan comforter over his shoulders and went to sleep, praying, as he did every night, that tomorrow would be different. That like in his video games, he might somehow die and begin again.

Before Wyatt even opened his eyes, he heard the sound of birds. Their early-morning warbling cut through the woods outside his window, growing louder with the coming dawn. Wyatt stirred in his cot, under the wool blanket, unwilling to open his eyes, forgetting for a minute he was back.

He dressed quickly and stepped out onto the porch. He knew he could not do anything until he talked to someone, but it was not a conversation he was eager to have. He went to the lodge, poured a mug of the hot chocolate Mum made every morning. He took a sip, sweet and hot. Maybe too sweet. He tried something he'd seen older campers do. He poured out some of the hot chocolate and added half a cup of coffee to his mug. He tried it. Not bad. Bitter and sweet. He drained the cup and walked out under the evergreens, heavy and wet with the morning, and made his way down to the Caldera.

From a distance, the Caldera looked ominous, but within the rocky bowl was another world altogether—green and thick with plant life. Pools of clear water dotted the basin, and woven into the interior was the heart of Valor: an obstacle course and shooting range, swimming pool and soccer field, a climbing wall and helicopter landing pad, all manner of military vehicles, camp offices, storage areas, indoor training facilities, and of course, Avi's secret security lair. All housed in a series of cave-like bunkers dug into the rock cliffs that ringed the inside of the Caldera.

Wyatt hadn't seen her yet, but he had a good idea where to find her. He punched the buttons on the keypad and entered the bunker that served as the armory. A cold, sterile locker filled with every weapon imaginable. Wyatt had only taken a few steps across the concrete floor before he heard a familiar *click* and felt the cold metal at the nape of his neck.

"What are you doing in here?" The woman's voice was raspy and calm.

"Looking for you." Wyatt turned slowly. He held his hands up, staring beyond the barrel of a Desert Eagle into a face that was half drop-dead gorgeous and half laced in burn scars coming together to make a terrifying yet beautiful face. "Hey, Cass."

"Heard you were back." She drew the gun back and put it in the holster on her hip.

Wyatt forced a smile, but he could not keep eye contact. His stomach swirled with butterflies. Her dark eyes. Her tan, perfectly sculpted shoulders. She was so much like her younger sister it caught his breath, except for the fine scars that she wore like a veil on the right side of her face.

"Why won't you look at me?" Cass said, stepping closer.

"I am." Wyatt lifted his chin and gazed at her through his shaggy bangs. Still, he could say nothing.

Cass's long dark hair had been shaved months ago when the doctors removed the 9mm that had been lodged in her skull in the firefight with the Glowworm, but it was now growing back.

"I know what you think." She stepped even closer. So close he could see the slight deviation of her fake right eye. "And it's not your fault."

A huge knot swelled in Wyatt's throat. "It is."

"No, what happened to my sister—"

"Was because of me. I was supposed to keep her safe and I got her killed."

"Don't you dare cry."

"I'm not." Wyatt gritted his teeth and pushed the knot back.

"It was her time. She knew the risks. Dolly was a soldier. And soldiers go when it's their time. You can't control that. Nobody controls that. It's what we sign up for."

"But Hallsy and I were close . . . I should've known."

"*You* should have? Hallsy and I were together at one time. If anyone was close enough to know, it was me. We can't undo what's been done . . ." Cass drew a Sig Sauer P229 Compact from the back of her belt and laid it in Wyatt's palm. "But we can go after him."

Wyatt curled his fingers around the cold grip and looked her square in the face. "That's the only reason I came back."

"If you're going to be sneaking into my lair without permission . . ." a voice said behind them.

They turned to see Avi, drone goggles propped on his head. "Then you better let me help."

CHAPTER 9

The next few days at Valor were designated to prepping for the arrival of campers and candidates, most of whom would be sprung from juvenile facilities across the U.S.

In many ways, the preparation for their arrival looked like it would for a traditional summer camp—dragging out canoes, sweeping acorns and mouse droppings from musty cabins, mowing grass around the baseball diamond. Then there were other activities, ones more specific to Valor—fueling the military vehicles and motorcycles on base, inspecting the weaponry (RPGs, M4s, and flamethrowers, pistols, carbines), testing the drones, and so on.

To Cody, the division of labor between these two types of tasks seemed a little unfair, as he and Mum, along with Fabian Grant (Mackenzie's brother, who helped in the kitchen), took care of the more mundane tasks. Meanwhile, in the bowels of the Caldera, his father, brother, and Avi prepped the weaponry. Supplies for the summer were flown in by military plane or helicopter and brought in by boat, loaded onto the *Sea Goat*. At the end of each prep day, as a reward for hard work, Eldon would take his sons to the shooting range and let them practice their marksmanship with handguns, M4s, and Uzis.

Cody might not have been the strongest one physically, but one thing was clear: the kid could shoot. "This is just awesome," he said, expending a magazine and watching the bullet rip through the target.

"Believe it or not," said his father, "a couple weeks from now, the only thing you're going to want to do at the end of the day is crawl into your bunk. Or take a swim in the lake after it warms up a bit."

"No," said Cody, hefting his Glock. "I'm gonna be right here . . . practicing."

Crackling embers and glowing ash rose from the great bonfire, reaching into the vast northern sky in a column of air, only to flame out and drift back down to earth. Wyatt stared into the fire, remembering the previous year's End of Summer ceremony, which concluded with the somber orange glow of three funeral pyres. Of the three, only one contained a body—Old Man, who fought valiantly but died in a shoot-out. The other two heaps were empty, devoid of human remains, but the effect was the same. Three Valorians—two campers and one staff—had given their lives. Of course, they could not have known that Sergeant Eric Hallsy, who'd led the funeral ceremony, had been conspiring against Valor during that sacred moment.

And once again they had gathered—Eldon, Avi, Mackenzie, Wyatt, and Mum. The purpose, this time, was to tie loose ends that hung like nooses around the camp's neck. There was one new face around the circle: Viktoria Kuokalas, an eastern European immigrant who had spent a year at Valor before becoming a naval aviator and F/A-18 pilot. And former instructor at Top Gun. Together, the leaders sat in the firelight, each with a stack of dossiers on their lap.

"The purpose of this meeting," Eldon began, "is to arrange

the groups and teams that operate within them while we await orders from the DoD."

Everyone nodded, knowing without Eldon having to say it that there was a more pressing agenda—quickly assembling the team that would hunt down Hallsy.

"This year," Eldon continued, "we only have three members of Group-B from the class of Group-C that graduated last summer: Wyatt and two others who will be coming soon—Rory and Samy. Three operators, no matter how good, are not enough to support a group or a team. So, as I see it, there are two options. We can select two Group-A members from the dossiers in front of you and pull them down to Group-B. Or, we can pull the three Group-B members up into A for the summer, creating a team at the highest level. As my son is part of this discussion, I'm going to recuse myself from this decision."

Viktoria was the first to assert herself. "Here's the question: Is it fair to effectively demote qualified Group-As? Or promote Group-Bs that haven't progressed through that level?"

"Well," Mackenzie said, "if we're strictly following protocol, then Group-As should be pulled down."

"Agreed," Viktoria said, "making an exception for these three would set a precedent."

"That precedent has already been set." Cass stepped out of the woods and took her place in the circle by Avi. "We've pulled members of Group-B into Group-A before."

"But never an entire group," Viktoria said, not missing a beat.

Cass took the stack of papers from Avi and set them in her lap, the gunpowder on her palms smudging black all over them.

"You're late," Avi said under his breath. "Bomb-making again?"

"Defusing." She smiled.

Viktoria continued, "Sergeant Hallsy is former Golden One Hundred. To say he is a highly trained operator is a huge understatement, and to send young operators after him before they've completed their third summer of training is simply reckless. I motion to let this issue rest and pull two members back."

"Not so fast." Mum sat on the other side of the fire, stoking it with a long stick. "As you know, I'm here on an honorary basis. This program was my husband's baby, his dream. He considered it his greatest achievement—building each one of you into the operators you are today," she said, the firelight catching her watery eyes. "I never personally operated in a mission, never shot a gun in combat, but I've supported all of you. Forty years of campers—I've fed them, clothed them, buried more than a few. And I've never seen a group of campers who've been through more real experience, who've shown more promise and aptitude, than Rory, Samy, and Wyatt."

Mum paused, looking over at Wyatt. "And because of that, I think it's within the bounds of Valor to promote the three to Group-A for the summer. I vote that this point be settled."

"All right," said Eldon. "All in favor say aye."

A series of ayes rang up around the fire.

"Okay, then," Eldon said. "Wyatt, looks like you're in Group-A."

Wyatt nodded, fighting hard not to smile.

"As you were Top Camper last summer and team leader," Eldon went on, "it's your responsibility to request team selection."

Wyatt adjusted his headlamp and looked at the pages in his hand. The dossier for each camper included their police report, a short biography, and their performance record at Valor.

"The first thing I'd like to request," he said, "is that Rory and Samy remain on my team."

"Any opposed?" Eldon asked the circle.

Again, Viktoria spoke: "I don't oppose it, per se, but we all know that the teams benefit from operating with different groups, providing varied experience and teaching the members to not rely on familiarity. This was a key lesson I learned flying for the navy. We always rotated pilots with WSOs."

"Yes, Lieutenant Kuokalas, I agree with you," Wyatt said, "and under normal circumstances, I'd like to work with the other members of Group-A, but we have a critical mission: finding Agent Hallsy. Learning the idiosyncrasies of each other's operating styles is a luxury we don't have. So for the sake of time, I'd like to retain the team I know best."

"Okay," Viktoria conceded. "Who else would you like?"

"Well"—Wyatt cleared his throat—"our primary challenge is the absence of a trail. Hallsy has reduced his digital footprint to nil, so I think we need someone with old-school tracking ability. Mackenzie Grant's nephew, Pierce Grant. He's sixteen—young for Group-A—but he's already a world-class tracker."

"True." Mackenzie chuckled. "Growing up in Alaska with Fabian will give you some of those old-school hunting skills."

"We need someone with experience in covert ops." Wyatt shifted through some papers. "I noticed an interesting camper here . . . Mary Alice Stephenson. She's participated in Group-A two years in a row and been operational the past two summers, so Hallsy would have interacted with her very little, if at all. She's been on intelligence-gathering assignments in Europe, Russia, and the Middle East, posing variably as the daughter of diplomats, a Live-Aid intern, and a beauty contestant. Mary Alice can help by planning a traditional espionage-intelligence gathering role so that Hallsy doesn't see us coming."

Viktoria piped up. "I understand your rationale, but I'd planned on Mary Alice leading the entire Group-A this year. If she's part of your team, the entire program will not have her experience and leadership here. Also—as the director said"—she looked to Eldon—"the DoD is going to instruct us where to apply our resources. I think aligning our teams to track down one traitor when the leading threat to the United States is the terrorist known as Encyte is putting the cart before the horse."

"With all due respect," Cass interrupted. "I think there are plenty left behind to fill the leadership gap."

"Yes, but we're all forgetting that there's an internet terrorist on the loose—one who killed over fifty people. Do you really want to send our best kids on a revenge mission and spread ourselves thin when at any moment we could be called upon to help with Encyte?"

"Lieutenant Kuokalas, when were you last at Valor?" Cass asked calmly.

"I graduated fifteen years ago. Attended the U.S. Naval Academy, flew combat missions in Iraq and Afghanistan, and since then, I've been leading programs with the CIA. I'm here for the summer, at Eldon's direct request."

"And I deeply appreciate your service. But I don't think you've ever met my sister."

"No, not in person, but I've read her file." Viktoria lowered her eyes.

"Well, she was a Blue, an elected leader of her group as a Rover, and the best member of Group-C last year. She did not go down easily. Her body was found beaten, likely tortured, and the person who did this to her is the same person who killed Avi's brother. He did it to cash in on a multimillion-dollar bounty on Eldon, his former mentor!" Cass cut her eyes at Avi, who stared blankly. "This man has waged a full-scale assault on the Valor family for a payout. He has no scruples. Not only does he know our secrets, he knows some of the most classified information at the highest levels of U.S. intelligence. So we need to set our other goals aside, do our duty, and bring this bastard back."

CHAPTER 10

The weather, which had been crisp and sunny, turned hot. A front shifted in from the north and mingled with the warm air hovering above Camp Valor and brewed into a violent, almost tropical storm. With pouring rain, high winds, and lightning, preparations ceased and all the staff ran to the lodge to wait it out.

Given the enormous expenditure of energy—the average camper burning in excess of seven thousand calories a day—one of the rules of Valor was that everyone ate well and as much as they could shove down their throats. So Eldon stoked the fire in the huge stone fireplace, and Wyatt and Mum boiled water for coffee and busily whipped up a late-night snack.

When the storm started, Wyatt ran to his empty cabin, but the drafty old structure seemed to quiver with every clatter and thunderbolt, so he donned his rain gear and hustled across the exercise field along a path that was a variable river of mud. He climbed the steps and, sopping wet, entered the lodge, where Cody sat by the fire with a snack.

Once Wyatt had shed his wet layers, he took a seat next to his brother. "What you got?"

Cody raised his mug. "Hot chocolate . . . and Mum made scones."

"Ah." Wyatt nodded. "Good day today?"

"Sure." Cody blew across the surface of the cocoa. "Dad's been busy. I'm kinda ready for the other campers to get here. Ready to do some shit."

"Watch your mouth."

"Sorry . . . so I got a question."

"What's that?"

"Why are you up there?" Cody pointed to the line of photographs hanging just inside the entrance of the lodge. Each portrait had no name, but there was an inscription.

Wyatt turned and saw his own image high on the wall—tousled hair, chin up, the look of someone who thought he could never be burned. It was a bittersweet victory, knowing what he knew now and what he had lost. "Camper Wall," he said softly.

"*Top* Camper Wall," Mum corrected as she whisked through the lodge behind them. "For each year, there's a portrait of a Top Camper, going all the way back to 1941. Your brother was last year's," she said, pushing through the kitchen doors.

"That's pretty awesome." Cody beamed, unable to hide his own naïve desire to prove himself.

"Yeah, well," Wyatt said. "Doesn't mean much."

"That's not true." Cody began reading the inscription under Wyatt's name, "*The truest form of bravery is selfless—*"

"Stop," Wyatt said firmly.

"What? Why?"

"Just don't. I don't want to hear it."

"Fine . . . Oh my god." Cody turned his attention to another photo from years earlier. "That's gotta be Dad. Look at his hair. He was so young." Cody laughed and began reading the inscription from three and a half decades ago: "*Some men are built strong, some men imbued with courage, daring, and grit. Some men are simply built for glory* . . . Cool."

"Yeah," Wyatt said. "Dad was a hero. Still is."

"I think I know another one," Mum said, putting her hand on Wyatt's shoulder.

Wyatt's face instantly scowled. "Don't waste a word like that."

Wyatt hated being on the Top Camper wall and he wanted to get away from the faces, from Mum and her insinuation that he was a hero. He looked at the scone and no longer had an appetite. He started putting his rain gear back on.

"Well, I hope there's room up there for me," Cody said.

Mum studied Cody's freckled baby face—blue eyes innocent and hopeful. "Sure there is." She pointed at the hot cocoa. "Need a refill?"

Wyatt had his head down and nearly barreled into Avi, who burst into the lodge, water from his rain gear pooling on the floor.

"Wyatt!" Avi called out. "We need some help. There's a shipment of supplies on the dock on the mainland. It couldn't get transferred in the weather, and it's gonna spoil if we don't get it."

"In this?" Wyatt looked out the windows blurred with rain.

"Just a little drizzle." Avi pulled his hood back up. "This camp has gone soft."

"Let me check with the boss." Wyatt nodded at his father, who sat by the fire, a letter in his hand, eyes staring out. Wyatt caught the embossed seal of the Department of Defense—an eagle with wings spread—before his father slipped the letter back in a manila envelope and tossed it into the fire.

"Hey, son." Eldon looked up over his reading glasses. "What's up?"

"Uhh," Wyatt said, watching the documents burn. "Avi needs my help on the *Sea Goat* for a few hours, but if you need me, I could stay . . ."

"No, that's fine."

"Sure?"

"Yeah. Go on."

"Okay. Don't think we'll be late." Wyatt turned, then he stopped. "Dad, what was that letter?"

"Just a little junk mail."

"From the DoD?"

"Well," Eldon sighed. "From the man you call Mr. Yellow, about the secretary of defense."

"Not McCray. You mean the new SecDef?" Wyatt asked. "Elaine Becker?"

"Yes," Eldon said, keeping his eyes on the fire. "She wants to come . . . *evaluate* us."

"When does she get here?"

"It didn't say. My guess is they'd like to surprise us. Could be any day."

"So what do we do?"

"Go about our business, and in the meantime"—Eldon rubbed his creased forehead—"I need to make some friends. Valor has survived nearly eighty years because the Old Man had powerful allies. And political instincts. I have neither."

"What about Mr. Yellow?"

"He's helpful and connected, but the Old Man always had a direct line to the White House. I know Admiral McCray, but he's out and this new SecDef is clearing out all the old guards. Not sure who will silently take our back."

"Who else knows about this?"

"Mr. Yellow, obviously. Avi . . . and now you." Eldon's damp eyes twinkled with firelight. "Avi's waiting. We'll talk about this later."

Wyatt secured the waterproof wide-brimmed hat over his ears, checked the buttons on his raincoat, and stepped out onto the porch, where Avi was impatiently waiting.

"Took long enough?" Avi said, charging off into the storm, and Wyatt fell in step behind him.

Down by the beach, the *Sea Goat* bucked in the water off the end of the dock. Waves sprayed over its bow as its engines whined.

"Really want to do this now?" Wyatt yelled.

"Yes," Avi replied in his matter-of-fact Israeli accent. "This cannot wait."

They hustled down to the end of the dock. Mackenzie eased the boat up, and Wyatt and Avi jumped onto its slippery deck.

"Hell of a night for a grocery run, eh?" Mackenzie said as they eased out into the thickening storm.

"No kidding. You guys are just crazy."

"Gotta make sure our Wheaties don't get wet." Mackenzie winked at Avi.

The ferry, sturdy as she was, pitched in the black surf, which was lit only by the occasional flash of white lightning. The lights from the camp receded in the distance and then disappeared as they wound their way through the archipelago toward the mainland dock and depot. About halfway to the depot, Mackenzie glanced out into the darkness through the foggy pilothouse windshield. On one side of the glass, a small heater, on the other, a wall of solid rain. Mackenzie squinted, studying the black water, and then suddenly, he idled the motor.

"There it is," Mackenzie said. Through the transmogrifying lens, an apparition appeared. A human form seemingly riding a wave.

Wyatt leaned in and saw the outline of a black Jet Ski, its rider easing to the side of the *Sea Goat*. Mackenzie leaned over and grabbed her bow, steadying her as she came along the port side.

"What's going on?" Wyatt asked.

"All right, Wyatt," Avi said. "Remember when I told you about the gamer Hi Kyto, the Darsie Fellow?"

"This is related to Encyte?" Wyatt said slowly.

"Yes. Well, I reached out to Mr. Darsie. Of course, I didn't speak to him directly. I didn't hear anything until this afternoon when I received instructions for you."

"Me?" Wyatt asked incredulously. "How does he know who I am? Isn't my identity secret outside of Valor?"

"Supposed to be. But he's a former Valorian and has access to people who give him information. And," Avi sighed, "he's a billionaire many times over and his businesses are enmeshed in U.S. security."

"So what does he want?"

"You, Wyatt, are to be at the following coordinates." Avi pressed a phone into Wyatt's hand. "They're loaded into the GPS. You need to be there in exactly one hour and forty-five minutes."

"I don't understand the mission. What am I supposed to do?"

"Move quickly," Avi said, then gestured to the helmeted Jet Ski rider. "Mary Alice is going to pretend to be you for the next three hours while we make this run."

Wyatt turned to a young woman wearing the same exact rain gear. "A girl? Pretending to be me?"

"With the rain and her attire, it won't matter. To anyone watching, it'll just be a body on the boat. They'll assume it's you," Avi said.

"My only worry is I might actually make you look tough," Mary Alice said. "You got a problem with that?"

"Nope." Wyatt steadied the Jet Ski in the pitching surf.

"Take the Jet Ski to Logan's Point," Avi continued. "In the brush, just up the hill, you'll find a motorcycle. If you move quickly, you should be able to make it to the coordinates in time."

"So wait, I'm going to meet John Darsie or—"

"I don't know who's going to be there," Avi cut him off. "All I have is a location . . . for you—and only you."

"What if it's a setup? Could even be Encyte."

"Could be," Avi conceded. "Which is why I brought this." He handed Wyatt a 45.

Wyatt waved it away. "Cass already gave me this." He showed Avi his Sig Sauer P229 Compact and waterproof, clippable holster.

"Well, take this too." Mackenzie held out a switchblade. Wyatt secured the gun to his belt under his rain gear, and feeling around his midsection, tucked the switchblade in place.

"Can I trust Darsie?"

"No," Avi said with an exasperated shake of his head. "You can't trust anyone. But you should go for one reason."

"What's that?"

"You told me to find someone to help us move on Hallsy. Well, I did. If you do a favor for Darsie, he's the kind of guy who will pay it back tenfold. Plus he's the only person outside the U.S. government who could find him. In fact, he owns the company the U.S. would contract to track him digitally."

Wyatt thought, the sideways rain pelting him.

"Are you going or not?" Avi called out.

Wyatt snatched the phone with the GPS coordinates.

"You are set to arrive at 11:38 p.m.," Avi added. "You have exactly a two-minute window. If you are even a few seconds outside that timeframe, you will miss it entirely."

"Got it." Wyatt pocketed the phone and hustled out onto the deck. "I can take this from here." He nodded to Mary Alice, who dismounted the Jet Ski. Wyatt grabbed the handles and climbed on.

"Good luck," Mary Alice said.

"Roger." Wyatt squeezed the accelerator, and the Jet Ski rocketed away from the *Sea Goat* into the night.

CHAPTER 11

Jalen Rose, like every other potential candidate, began his summer at Valor with a piece of paper. It was a crisp white document; the letters "CV" were painted in gold in the center, and the inscription read: *United States of America * Department of Defense.*

"Here you go." Mr. Yellow slid the paper over to the boy.

"Seems pretty . . ." Jalen scanned the document, searching for the word. "Intense."

"Think of it like a Wonka ticket," Mr. Yellow said dryly. "Without it, you're not getting in."

> I, <u>Jalen Alexander Rose</u>, being of sound mind and body, have agreed to commit myself to three months internment at Camp Valor. I swear to keep the existence of the camp and all activities therein confidential. Any mention of the camp and its programs will result in imprisonment. I understand my sole compensation will be the experience itself and the liberty to return to society after a ninety-day period of service. I hereby waive any right to hold the U.S. Government, Camp Valor, and its staff and any participants accountable for any injury, physical

or mental trauma, death or dismemberment during my internment.

Jalen glanced at his parents, sitting sullenly on the other side of the dining room in the safe house, electric animosity between them. He took a breath, then scrawled his name at the bottom of the page.

"Stupidest thing," Ronnie said under his breath. "Doing shit and takin' risks you ain't need to."

"It's his decision," Tyra said, but then looked at her ex with more softness than she could typically muster. "But I can't say I disagree with you."

"That should do it." Mr. Yellow scooped up the paper and tucked it in a manila envelope. "You have twenty minutes to pack."

Jalen ran through his room, gathering essentials—underwear, a few T-shirts and shorts, a sweatshirt, two pairs of boots, gym shoes, and an old pair of Gucci sunglasses from his dad. Packing complete, he was led from his home in handcuffs, his next-door neighbor watching from the window as he ducked into the back of a police cruiser.

It was midday, and the sun shone brightly en route to the Birmingham Police Station. The squad car pulled in front of the building, and from there, a few bystanders looked on as Jalen was transferred from the cruiser to a windowless van.

"Put this on," the pale-skinned driver said as she handed him a hoodlike blindfold. She was wearing a midwestern cop outfit and spoke with a thin, eastern European accent.

"Who are you?"

"Viktoria. Your staff from Valor," she said. "Lie down on the floorboard."

As the van pulled away, Jalen contemplated his decision in the darkness. It seemed like an hour, but twenty minutes later, the grumpy fake cop again opened the sliding doors.

"Where are we?" Jalen asked from inside the hood, putting his hands out dramatically.

"FBO outside of Pontiac," Viktoria said dryly. "The plane won't have windows, so you can lose the blindfold for a bit."

Jalen did as he was told and followed Viktoria, climbing the rollaway stairs onto a small plane where six other handcuffed camper-candidates sat, waiting to begin the journey.

"This the last of them?" the copilot called from the front.

"Good to go." Viktoria climbed up into the pilot seat as the heavy door slammed closed.

A few moments later, the plane glided from the runway, the same way the candidates had been seamlessly lifted from their lives.

Several hundred miles away, Wyatt's Jet Ski tore through the dark water. He had no compass, but thanks to his relentless water training, especially during Hell Week the year prior, he knew the waters around Camp Valor like his own childhood neighborhood, and so he didn't need a map—or daylight—to locate Logan's Point. He simply drove, guided by familiar contours lit intermittently by lightning flash.

Logan's Point was on the mainland, and it only took him twenty or so minutes to find it. Wyatt gunned the Jet Ski up onto a small beach on the leeward side of the point, got off, and dragged it all the way up to the foliage, hiding it under the low-hanging branches of a cedar tree.

"Now what?" he said under his breath, but it only took a little searching before he discovered it: a dirt bike, lying on its side under some freshly cut pine bows. The bike, he recognized, was a KTM Freeride E-XC 2018 NG. He pulled the handlebars, lifting it into a rideable position—it felt light, maybe just over a hundred kilograms. The bike was electric and had knobby tires and no headlamp—a strictly off-road vehicle.

"How the hell am I going to ride this?" He peered into the

night, picturing himself flying down dirt trails through the dark forest.

And then he noticed something tucked under the pines—a camouflage bag. He unzipped it and inside, a tactical helmet, fitted with night vision goggles. He checked the coordinates one more time, and zooming into the map, he loosely plotted a course to the meeting spot twenty-seven miles away. He studied the device, puzzled. The red dot on the map was literally in the middle of a forest—ten miles from the nearest road, in the center of a remote, protected woodland area.

Who the hell was going to meet him in the middle of the woods, in a two-minute window? A billionaire? It felt like a setup. He suddenly thought about what his father had said. About unsanctioned missions. But there was no time. He had to ride, trusting in Avi's judgment and the Sig Sauer clipped to his belt.

He started the bike, slipped his phone under his rain gear, pulled on the tactical helmet, and the dark night was suddenly outlined in green. He tugged the chinstrap and gunned the bike out of the small ravine and onto a narrow path so indefinite that Wyatt assumed it had been worn down not by humans but by animals seeking access to water.

He pinned the throttle and felt the tremendous torque—at least 40 NM, he guessed—from the electric motor. It was oddly quiet, the bike silent except for its tires grinding on the muddy path and the cold wet wind whistling past. It was slow going, somewhere around fifteen to thirty miles per hour. He worried he might not make it to the rally point. It was stop and go, Wyatt constantly getting off the bike to move around fallen trees and black rushing rivers. He wiped out four times, each time getting up, thankful he was only bruised and battered. He didn't know what he would have done if he'd broken a bone alone on the dense forest floor.

Wyatt reached the rally point with less than three minutes

to spare. He rode down the hiking path, jumped off the bike, and ran toward the location—a damp, mossy gully thirty yards away. There he waited, panting, and at exactly 11:38, he heard the click of a metal spring, similar to the sound of an IED. He froze, and this time he thought of his mother. She was right. He had made the wrong choice. Death. But then, something above him drifted through the air. It looked like a floating jellyfish, but as it came into view, he realized it was a parachute with a note attached. He unfolded it and studied the hand-drawn map. The paper was so fine, it literally began to dissolve as soon as it was unfolded. The map revealed another five-mile leg of travel and on the bottom of it were the words *seven minutes*.

Wyatt ran back through the wet foliage, righted the bike, and gunned it toward the new checkpoint. The map, which had completely dissolved in his clenched fist, was seared in his mind as he followed the trail up a very steep cliff then leveled off to a plateau with a wide open plain. The rain had let up, and the moonlight shone through the thinning clouds as Wyatt rocketed across the flat ground, his destination visible, just on the other side of the thick copses of trees. He arrived at the destination and saw a raised railbed that glistened in green night vision. He put his hand on the rail, feeling the vibration before he heard the train roaring down the track.

"Holy crap!" Wyatt backed up ten feet just as the train screeched up the tracks. The locomotive before him looked like no other he'd seen in his life. It was matte black, newly built, elegant, but as he strained to look closer, he saw it was covered in thin armored plating. The train cars were windowless, so clean and dark that the surface ate all available light and hardly registered in his NVGs. A phantom train cutting through the night.

Wyatt pushed his rain gear down and eased the Sig Sauer out, keeping it clipped to his belt but still accessible over the gear. The engine pulled ten cars, all armored and custom built. Once the last car lurched to a stop, a garage-like door clattered opened and a ramp eased out and anchored into the rocky railbed.

In the light of the boxcar, a figure appeared—a man—tall, thin, wearing khaki pants and a cardigan. Wyatt recognized him immediately from the Wikipedia page back on the plane: the elusive, eccentric billionaire John Darsie.

"Coming aboard?" he asked.

Wyatt said nothing, staring into the bright compartment.

"This train is leaving in thirty seconds."

Wyatt took a breath. He flipped the throttle, and the motorcycle raced up into the boxcar just as the train hissed into motion. Wyatt dismounted and pulled off his helmet, and instantly two military-looking men approached.

"The boys will secure your bike." Darsie motioned to the men hovering around in tactical gear. "And your weapon. Don't worry. You're safe. Leave your rain gear and come with me."

Wyatt slipped off his jacket, and did as he was asked. A security guard motioned for the gun, which Wyatt unclipped and handed it over, leaving his knife still hidden against his torso.

Not the best security, Wyatt thought.

The man passed Wyatt a towel and grunted something about dripping on the carpets. Toweling off his head and neck, Wyatt followed Darsie through a series of train cars. Where the train's facade was dark, foreboding, militaristic, the interiors were the opposite—sleek and minimalist, like a luxury high-rise in Manhattan, the kind that overlooked Central Park, timeless in any epoch. Fastidiously clean, organized, expensive looking.

"I apologize if you had any inconveniences in meeting me. I've always found a few extra hoops to jump through . . . can save your life, even if it inconveniences others." He smiled. "And it separates the nimble from those who stumble."

"It was no problem," Wyatt lied.

"Well, there are two factors I consider critical above all else.

The first, of course, is security." Darsie looked out where the windows should have been, but in their place, a wall of 4K screens displayed the dark night as it blurred past. Wyatt assumed the screens were linked to cameras outside the train's armor, but the picture was unnaturally detailed, like a nature film. Through Darsie's lens, the world Wyatt now saw was somehow cleaner.

A security guard came forward for Wyatt's damp towel. Wyatt put it in his hand, and Darsie began to pace.

"And the second is secrecy. If we are to do anything substantial in this life, we are to do it with *utter* secrecy." He looked at Wyatt intently. "Are you able to keep a secret, Wyatt?"

"Depends on whether it's worth the effort to keep it . . . or if it's a secret at all."

"How's that?"

"I'll give you an example," Wyatt explained. "The Americans spent years and billions of dollars during the Cold War trying to keep their spying on the Russians secret. But all along, thanks to superior Russian spies and double agents, the Russians knew everything we ever did. And while we were worried about the Space Race and sending cosmonauts and dogs into orbit, we missed the big signs—the breadlines and phony grocery stores. The Soviet government was failing, communism itself had failed."

"Of course," Darsie said. "It's also worth noting Americans in the Cold War were relatively new to the spying game. It was like sending a middle-school soccer team to the World Cup. Europeans have been spying on each other since they could grunt. Hopefully, as Americans, we've gotten a tad better at it in the past few decades."

Wyatt looked around the office, thinking of the many ways he was likely being spied on at that moment. The office reminded Wyatt of works he'd seen by the architect Frank Lloyd Wright. It was modern, but the furniture and decor felt timeless, like the room could exist in the 1960s as well as today. The only pieces of ordinary tech are a slim laptop, closed on his modernist wooden desk, and an iPad. Wyatt stared at it.

"Like the desk?" Darsie smiled. "It was made by a hero of mine, Donald Judd. He was quite a fancy artist, actually. This piece alone is worth hundreds of thousands, if not millions."

"Nice," Wyatt said, less concerned with furnishings than where recording devices might be hidden.

"Would you like something to warm up? Tea?"

"I'm okay," Wyatt lied again, his teeth nearly chattering as he spoke.

Darsie nodded, and again a man in black appeared. In his hands, a gleaming silver teapot, complete with service.

"Thank you," Darsie said as the man poured tea for both of them. "Wyatt, please. Have some." He extended a fancy saucer. "Perhaps I should give you my own personal history."

Wyatt nodded.

"I was born John Thomas Darsie, to British parents in Hong Kong," Darsie began. "And like yourself, I was a troubled youth. Also like you, I displayed an intense precociousness early on, and at the age of nine, I became an international chess champion. This opened doors to other pursuits, and by fourteen, I was studying at the college level."

"Can't say my precociousness was that productive," Wyatt offered. "Mine just got me in juvie."

"Well, it wasn't all impressive. I had a pathological propensity for theft—I won't bore you with details, but it resulted in my own admission to Camp Valor."

"A klepto," Wyatt said knowingly.

"Mischief often levels the playing field, so there I was, just like all the other delinquents, a scared candidate of Group-C. But I held on. I progressed through three summers, from B to A, but midway through my A summer, we were on operation in Switzerland, and I'd had enough. I blew the horn. I tapped out."

"What?" Wyatt interrupted. "But you were an A. I didn't even know it was possible."

"Of course. Like the Old Man always said—you can quit at any time. I was done with the program, so I left. Naturally, no one appreciated this decision, especially not your father and not the Old Man."

"You were in Dad's group," Wyatt said, suddenly understanding.

"Yes. And so I packed a go-bag, but instead of returning to Valor, I stole some Swiss francs, boarded a train in Zurich, and rode it all the way to Amsterdam. From that moment on, I've loved trains. I have a plane or two, but I despise flying. So I appreciate you meeting me in this little office of mine."

"Why'd you leave Valor?" Wyatt heard himself asking.

"Good question. My experience at Valor was complicated to say the least. One thing I learned was that to be successful, you must be independent . . . and after I realized I could think and operate on my own, I knew I could no longer stay. A lot of people at the camp resent me for it, but I'd become the thing they designed me to be. I left because I was ready."

"Let's get back to why I'm here," Wyatt redirected.

"Right. Hi Kyto," Darsie said, motioning an attendee to bring Wyatt something to drink and eat. "Now, what do you know about Encyte?"

Wyatt accepted the delicate cup and took a couple of cookies from the tray. "Only what I've been told in debriefs or read online—"

"Only what you've been told or read?" Darsie asked flatly. "You didn't fly to Pontiac, Michigan, and spend two hours with Jalen?"

"If you're referring to confidential information, I can neither confirm nor deny," Wyatt said.

Darsie rolled his eyes. "You know Mr. Yellow, correct?"

"I know someone who is called that, yes."

"Does he know you're here?"

"You'd probably know better than me."

"Don't try to guess at what I know or don't know. Just answer the question." Darsie grinned and tapped his foot, waiting.

"Not that I'm aware of. The only people who know I'm here are Avi, Mackenzie Grant, who drives the *Sea Goat*—"

"Ahh . . . Mackenzie Grant. Always liked him."

"And a new addition to Group-A."

Darsie considered something for a moment. "Small enough group—if you're being honest—so perhaps secrecy is attainable. Never know where you might have a leak. Take Hallsy, for example. A Valor poster boy defecting right in front of the Old Man's nose."

"Well, there's *your* honesty to consider"—Wyatt motioned around—"and the secrecy of these men to consider. But what does it matter? I don't even know why I'm here."

"Then why did you come?" Darsie asked.

"Because Avi said that if I helped you, you might be able to help us . . . find someone."

"Now that I like." Darsie laughed. "A clean commercial exchange, a favor for a favor." Darsie took a sip of tea and studied Wyatt. "Suppose you'd like me to go first."

Wyatt bit another cookie and chewed slowly, saying nothing.

"My interest in all this," Darsie said, "is significant. Jalen told you about the gamer Hi Kyto, correct?"

Wyatt nodded.

"Awful mess Jalen's in," Darsie said as he walked over to a chessboard. "Poor kid was lured into something far above his understanding."

Wyatt wondered if Darsie knew that Jalen was currently en route to Valor at his request. Maybe he was fishing again.

"Well, the girl, Hi Kyto," Darsie went on, "is a genius polymath wonderkid. She lives in California, and tries to be a normal fourteen-year-old named Julie Chen. Her parents—both former members of the Communist Party—became friends of mine. How is unimportant, but the point is, my real interest was not in the

Chens, but in their daughter. I arranged for her parents to have positions as professors at Stanford; I gave her a fellowship."

Darsie sipped tea, and Wyatt also took his first sip, figuring that Darsie had been drinking from the same pot and enough time had passed that he did not have to worry about it being laced with any kind of sedative.

"Julie's mind is a powerful asset," Darsie continued, "one that belongs to the United States. And simply, it was a good business investment to acquire that kind of talent. So in exchange for her ideas, I allowed Julie to work directly under me at Red Trident. As a fellow, she has access to everything we're doing."

"Isn't some of that classified?"

"Yes, like I said, it's a new program . . . somewhat experimental. In general, we follow every security protocol, except when it comes to Darsie Fellows. I suppose you understand the value of making exceptions to the rules?"

Wyatt shrugged. "Who doesn't? But breaking the rules can come back to bite you."

"Or to benefit you. Usually benefit. Hi Kyto—Julie—was by all measures a huge success. She blossomed—the raw talent, the propensity for discipline, the hunger . . ." Darsie trailed off, looking into the train's 4K windows. "She was supposed to be my protégé, my confidant, my friend." His face softened and his tone grew wistful. "She may be the closest thing I'll ever have to a daughter."

Then, silence. The whirring of the rain on the screen was the only sound.

"And what makes you think she's gone rogue?" Wyatt asked.

"Well, it didn't dawn on me until I was contacted by Avi. But lately, she's been acting strange . . . withdrawn. She was always a private person, but she's become secretive in new ways."

"Such as?"

"A few months ago, she started to routinely lie about her whereabouts. And she's spending an exorbitant amount of time playing violent video games."

"So does, like, seventy-five percent of the teenage population."

"Yes, but of that seventy-five percent, only one works for me and has access to the tools and platforms we've developed at Red Trident. And there's the connection you discovered to Pro_F_er, who we now know is Encyte. And to Jalen."

"Jalen told me he'd only encountered her once," Wyatt said.

"That proves my point. It looks like a mistake. A slip . . . You see, at Red Trident our core business is creating spiders that crawl the internet and darknet looking for suspicious content."

"Spiders?"

"Yes, bots. Google does the same to improve the algorithm. We did it to . . . learn."

"You mean spy."

Darsie shrugged. "And to save lives. We had conversations—a web chat—from one of Osama bin Laden's drivers, that tipped us off that the driver might be working for OBL. Information can be like dead bodies on a hiking trail or like a spring of a trap. It can provide both evidence of a crime and tip you off to one that's about to happen."

"So what does that have to do with Encyte or the Austin attack?"

"As I said, we started in the spider business, gathering intelligence, but eventually, all customers ask the same question: Now that I know what's happened or what's going to happen, what can I do about it? How can you, Red Trident, help me, the U.S. government, to act on information?"

"And by *act,* you mean take an action? As in, how can you take an action once you're armed with information?"

"Exactly."

"So you were asked to develop a weapon?"

"Here's the more specific question we get: *Can you weaponize the internet?*"

CHAPTER 12

Adam Drake bought his first drone when he was in China in 2008. He was walking through the Beijing airport when he heard buzzing and saw a clerk flying what looked like a tiny helicopter with multiple rotors around the narrow store. Though in his late twenties, Adam was a kid at heart, and at the time was a copywriter for an advertising agency, specializing in packaged goods, specifically candy. Adam was the kind of guy who made the fun commercials that would crack you up—a caveman who does his own taxes, a waterskiing squirrel who loves chocolate—that kind of thing. So a flying toy that reminded him of his favorite remote control car from childhood was a no-brainer. He bought one of the devices, took it home, set it up, and promptly crashed it.

His girlfriend at the time could only shake her head. "That was three thousand Chinese yuan you just flew into our wall."

"Test flight," Adam said, picking up the pieces. "I'll figure it out eventually."

And he did, and the drone technology got better. More sensitive gimbals created steadier flight patterns; innovations and battery technology allowed for faster, longer flights, and artificial intelligence programmed into the drones themselves allowed many of the high-end commercially available drones to fly themselves, navigating through spaces with the kind of precision that even a hummingbird does not possess.

Along with his growing passion for drone technology, Adam developed an equally strong interest in photography. Photography and drones made for a happy union, which was good for Adam, who now had a wife and daughter, as he could enjoy both hobbies at the same time. And so it wasn't long before he bought his first drone equipped with a high-quality camera. "But honey," he told his wife when she saw the credit card bill, "now we can take a family photo from the air, in front of our house."

But that wasn't all Drake captured. There were sunsets and boats skimming along the East River and Long Island Sound, nature areas, rocky hides, sweeping majestic marshes with birds in flight—all of these screen savers his wife saw playing over and over on their TV, the sheer magnitude of them only made bearable by images of their baby girl.

The hobby had even become a family affair. Adam flew his drone at the park, his daughter cooing in a carrier strapped to his chest. So he spent many happy mornings, walking with a baby and a flying photo studio. He'd left the big agency, quite thankful to no longer be at someone else's beck and call. He ran his own small agency, and though there was more freedom, it did not eliminate the presence of overbearing clients, but at least Adam himself was allowed to decide when to react.

And so when Monday mornings rolled around, before he dropped his daughter off at daycare or his wife slipped out of their Brooklyn apartment to catch the train to Manhattan, Adam could sit on the roof of their brownstone in the predawn darkness in an ever-present attempt to capture the perfect sunrise.

On one particular morning, at two thousand feet in the air, a good thousand feet from max range and a solid two miles from any flight path, the drone he'd affectionately named Kitty was hovering, snapping photographs that Adam could see on his cell phone, which served as the viewfinder. The city, just starting to step into the electric morning all in stunning 4K HD. From the baby monitor in his pocket, Adam could hear his daughter, now three, singing in her crib. He squinted into the sky, hoping to see Kitty, but he knew the drone was too far away to be visible. After years of training his ear to the pitch, he could just barely hear the buzz in the distance and worked the toggles on the transmitter, bringing the drone home like an electric dog. He didn't need to see it, he knew how to guide it in, but something was wrong. He knew the direction Kitty should be flying in, but he could see from the camera that she was going in the opposite way—flying northeast instead of southwest. And then, something even more worrisome occurred: the drone began to sharply descend, speeding toward the ground.

Beep, beep, beep. The device blared a warning signal. He hit the auto "return to home" button, but nothing happened. He'd always felt perfectly safe with Kitty in the air, but now, he was panged with uncertainty, imagining the two-pound hunk of plastic falling from a couple thousand feet and hitting someone on the sidewalk below. A proverbial penny dropping off the Empire State Building. His mind reeled, trying to recall facts from an old physics class—*wasn't terminal velocity 53 m/s?*

But then Kitty leveled off and continued in a northeast direction. Adam shook the controller. "What the hell's happening?" Again he worked the toggles, but the drone still would not respond. The camera went black somewhere between the Queens Zoo and LaGuardia.

"Babe, what's going on?" Adam turned to see his wife standing behind him.

"I'm not sure . . . I think I lost it." He looked out at the skyline, the intense oranges of sunrise now dissipated into the haze of a regular day. He held up the transmitter. The screen was off. "It was flying that way . . ." Adam pointed off into the distance, vaguely aware of an airport he flew in and out of all the time, some ten miles away as the crow flies. Then Adam had another, perhaps more disturbing thought: before the camera cut out, he saw what looked like geese, flying in the V formation like tiny dots somewhere in the airspace below Kitty, but he wasn't positive that's what they were. He couldn't put his finger on it, but he had photographed enough wild birds to know that these weren't quite right, that there was something almost mechanical about their wing movement.

CHAPTER 13

"You're going to have to explain the internet as a weapon thing," Wyatt said.

"Are you familiar with the term 'IoT'?" Darsie asked. "The Internet of Things? Let me show you." Darsie moved the chessboard to the table between them and scattered pieces around it. "In the early days of the internet, you had computers and people who created a network that would intercommunicate." Darsie pointed from pawn to pawn. "Creating a network for the open flow of information. With this model, the computers did the thinking and the network served to transfer the information. Today, the model has shifted." Darsie pulled out a bottle of Fiji and put it next to the chessboard. "The thinking occurs in the cloud, where the processing and storage power is far greater than on any one local device. In this model, the cloud, or those who control it, become master and the device is slave."

"Okay, I get it. I can tell my computer to do something from the cloud." Wyatt pointed to an iPad. "But how can you weaponize that tablet? It's not like it can come over there and attack me."

"Well, it could blow up and harm you. Or if you were a pilot using that iPad to navigate, it could harm you or others. But the iPad is just one device. Today we put computers or processors inside everything, from light bulbs, to door locks, to robots on a factory floor. We call these devices 'smart.' They're controlled, quite often, through the cloud. Should anyone have access to that thing called the internet, they could, in theory, tap into the cloud and make these devices do their bidding. This, in my opinion, is the most dangerous weapon created by man. And I'm not alone in thinking this."

Wyatt squinted, trying to follow. "The weapon is the cloud?"

"The cloud is the system, Wyatt. And the warheads are the 'smart' devices on the network."

"I'm still struggling to see the horror movie you're describing," Wyatt said. "So what—a light bulb? You're acting like there are little Terminators running around chasing us."

"Not yet . . . but that, of course, will come. If we make it that long. A light bulb can be infinitely dangerous. Just depends where it is. If it's in an oil refinery, it could create a spark that's lethal. Look at the Austin attack: a smart truck, programmed to be magnitudes safer than the typical truck, kills fifty-three people when its smarts become psychotic, when the device is taken over. There are currently nine billion smart devices in the world. They're in everything—our TVs, headphones, power plants. We've put these weapons in our homes without even knowing it."

"My head is hurting," Wyatt said. "Bring this back to Julie Chen."

Darsie maneuvered the pieces on his chessboard. "At Red Trident, we have a project to weaponize the internet called Infinite Warhead. To make Infinite Warhead work, we built a platform that can hack into almost any system and hijack the smart devices on it."

Wyatt knew the answer to the next question, but he wanted to hear Darsie say it. "And Hi Kyto works on it?"

"Hi Kyto *is* it. I made her the chief designer in building the model."

"She's fourteen," Wyatt said. "Should she have that responsibility?"

"She's a genius. And coming from you—a proud Valorian—I'm surprised that age is an issue." Darsie smiled.

"I'm not sure I'm a proud anything," Wyatt said, feeling his anger build. Men like Darsie also played games with the world. They were not too dissimilar from the Encytes who wreaked havoc on it. He tried to refocus. "So could Hi Kyto have stolen the software?"

"No, thank god. No information can get in or out of our lab without us knowing." Darsie reconsidered, obviously thinking about how he would do it. "It's nearly impossible, though in her case . . . she wouldn't need to steal it. She's smart enough to copy it and build her own version."

"Jesus Christ," said Wyatt. "You taught her how to weaponize all the devices in the world if she wanted to."

"I didn't teach her. I just gave her the tools and asked the right questions. She taught herself. But in practice, you're right." Darsie nodded. "She could. And now you see why I need to know. If she's Encyte, it's not just my exposure—the very world is in danger if that girl wants to do it harm. And I'll be damned if that is going to happen on Red Trident's watch."

Wyatt wanted to reach out and choke this man, whose ego and ambition had put the world at risk. Like Victor Frankenstein, he had created a monster, a fourteen-year-old child prodigy, who slipped out from his lab and sowed the wind.

"I know what you're thinking." He looked over at Wyatt. "I played god and now we are in danger."

"Yes."

"What you will learn, if you stay in this business long enough, is that we're always playing god. It's how society advances. Messes are made. Genies get out of the bottle. It's up to people like you to put them back in. To clean up the spills."

CHAPTER 14

Darsie looked at the black digital window, millions of bits and bytes flow-ing past, and studied his own face in the smudgeless glass. "If Hi Kyto is Encyte, I need to be the first to know, and I need you to help me."

"I'll talk to my father. This sounds like the perfect mission for Valor."

"No!" Darsie snapped. "You can't ask your father."

"Why?"

"For starters, Valor will be inoperable this summer."

"What do you mean?"

"Trouble is coming and Valor's going to find its hands are tied."

"So what do you want me to do? I'm on the island. I'll be there all summer."

"Blow the horn. You need to leave the program."

"What? Hell no. I'm not a quitter. And if I do that, I'll never be able to come back," he said, rising to his feet. "We have other missions besides Encyte—"

"Look, I know it's not an easy decision, but you need to think about this. If Hi Kyto is the killer, I'll dissolve Red Trident immediately. I'll go to jail—I don't care. That's not the issue. I need to solve this my particular way, and that brings me to the offer I have for you . . ."

Wyatt looked over, arms crossed but listening.

"Mr. Yellow and the Golden One Hundred are in the middle of a search, but I don't think I need to tell you that they're stuck."

"Then you know about Hallsy?"

"Of course I do. And the girl he killed."

Wyatt's jaw again stiffened and his face flushed. "How do you—"

"Dolly Allen was her name, if I remember right . . ."

Wyatt glared.

"I'm sorry," Darsie added flatly. "You loved her, huh? Look, there's very little I don't know."

"Then you know where he is?"

"Right now, no. But that's only because Sergeant Eric Hallsy is not a priority."

Wyatt took a step toward Darsie, fists balled, still feeling the switchblade tucked in his belt.

Instantly, the security was on him, guns drawn. Reflected in the glass screen of the phony windows, Wyatt saw the dots of laser sights on his forehead, neck, and chest.

"Ease down, all of you," Darsie said. "Wyatt, I understand you don't want to leave Valor, but the world needs you."

"It does—at Valor."

"Sounds like something Eldon would say. You're better than that."

"I've only completed Group-C. I need more training to truly be of value."

"Not so," Darsie said. "Why do you think I made it so difficult for you to find me? Security, of course, but it was also a test. Now, if you will help me, either clear or close Hi Kyto as Encyte, I promise I'll help you find Hallsy."

Wyatt sat back in the chair.

"I don't expect you to tell me now. You can't just go up to Hi Kyto. She's too closed off. I need to find the perfect intersection for you two to meet. It must be organic."

"But if I blow the horn, they'll wipe my memory. I won't even remember this meeting. I mean, how will I even remember you or our plans?"

"Good question," Darsie said. "First, this is Year Two for you. With time, it's harder for the camp to erase it all. Besides, I know the chemical formula they use to erase memory."

"Then you know how to counter it . . ."

"Exactly. There's a chemical compound I can give you. It'll lessen the effect of the memory-erasing agent. I'll need something to jog your memory to reverse the loss completely."

Wyatt thought a minute. "There's a photograph stitched in my backpack. But," he quickly corrected himself, "I didn't say I was helping you."

"If you leave, I'll meet you and apply the antidote, and your memory will return. Most of it, anyway. There's a reason *I* remember Valor," Darsie said. "When I blew the horn, I did the same thing to myself."

"Feels a lot like you just want to cover your ass." Wyatt watched the 4K screen, contemplating. Darsie was right. All efforts to find Hallsy had fallen flat. He had no faith in Mr. Yellow, or even the Golden One Hundred. If he wanted to avenge Dolly's death, the torture his father had been through, and the attack on Valor, he would need Darsie's help. "How will I give you my answer?"

"You won't. Words mean nothing to me. Either you do it, or you don't. I'll see if you leave. Either way, there's one last caveat. You cannot tell anyone about this mission. And if you do, I will know, and I won't give you the memory-reversing agent. I'll let you drop out, and it will be like this meeting—and Valor itself, for that matter—never existed. You'll just go back to being a regular old teenager, frustrated by the nagging sense that you could have done and been more. But you'll never be able to put your finger on why. Do you understand this?"

Wyatt nodded.

"Good boy." Darsie glanced at one of his assistants, and the train began to slow.

CHAPTER 15

Wyatt looked at his compass and then at the sky. The train had effectively taken Wyatt back in the direction of Valor. The ride home would be shorter. He would race along the railbed to a dirt road, which, at midnight, would be empty. The train was gone now, disappearing into the forest, and he did not know where it would end up.

The night was wet and cold and thick with fog. No longer negotiating a narrow hiking path, Wyatt's mind could wander slightly, but the mist was no easier to navigate than his own mind—the quandary of morality and ethics, duty and responsibility. Would he ring out? When would he do it—and how? And Jalen? Had he recruited the kid only to abandon him before the summer started? At least Cody would have his dad if Wyatt left him behind.

The main issue, he supposed, was the finality of it. If he sounded the horn, one thing was certain: he could never, ever return. Camp had been his crucible. In its fires, he'd gone from a delinquent, angry teenager to something that looked a lot like a man.

Wyatt slowed, tabling his thoughts, and he turned toward Logan's Point. He ditched the bike and pushed the Jet Ski back into the icy Lake Tecmaga. He waded to his ankles and pulled out his phone: a text from Avi. He followed the instructions, speeding across the black water until he found the *Sea Goat*.

"Did you see him?" Avi asked before Wyatt had even stepped aboard.

"No," Wyatt blurted out. "I missed the rendezvous."

The boat floated in dark waters, the rain now having stopped. Mary Alice drifted away from the boat's side, fired up the Jet Ski, and disappeared across the water.

Mary Alice now gone, Avi pressed, "You were away for several hours . . . and missed the rendezvous?"

"Yeah. With the weather . . . there were too many obstacles. Wild-goose chase. I'm sorry."

Avi stared at Wyatt in the pilothouse, then shifted his eyes to Mackenzie, who was also staring at Wyatt. Both of them clearly not believing the story.

"Suppose we'll never know what he wanted," Avi said, holding his hand out. "Your gun, please. I'll see that Cass gets it back."

Wyatt unclipped the Sig Sauer and slapped it into Avi's waiting palm, then handed the switchblade over to Mackenzie.

"Let's go," Mackenzie said and he bumped the throttle into gear.

The first campers began arriving on the fourth day. They came in waves, and it was evident from their looks which group they fell into. Group-A and Group-B were clearly the elite. Polished, confident, they moved with a crisp definitiveness of those in the know. At the opposite end of the spectrum were the Mounties and Rovers. Generally wide-eyed and innocent, these were the youngest and freshest on campus.

Most potential campers were selected for the camp based on a blend of potential, skills, and a penchant for mischief. Although the straitlaced were by far the minority, there were other kids, like Cody, whose parents were Valor graduates or fallen warriors. Not surprisingly, this category of camper actually had the highest rate of completion. But by and large, Camp Valor recruited delinquents and incorrigibles. Children whom society had deemed "bad seeds." In some ways, Valor was an Island of Misfit Toys.

Still, the younger campers, for the most part, had less of a criminal bent. Maybe they'd broken into a neighbor's house, maybe they'd stolen a car and gone joyriding, maybe they'd hacked into a teacher's computer to get answers for a test. These displays of poor behavior from eleven- and twelve-year-olds could be simply misguided potential. However, the older campers, those trying out for Group-C, generally were a more evolved class of criminal youth. Many of their crimes were violent (breaking into a neighbor's house to steal a gun), or dangerous (crashing a car in a police chase—which was true for Wyatt), or pathological (hacking into multiple systems—schools, banks, and government records). While there were no set rules for recruitment, the deeds or misdeeds that attracted the attention of Valor recruiters generally involved noticeable creativity or courage, out-of-the-box thinking. Intelligence, propensity for risk-taking, aggressiveness—these qualities were silver that could be mined from the dross of troubled youth. But perhaps most important of all was the motivation. Camp Valor was a chance to get out of jail free, to start again, and failure meant going back to the foster care system, juvie, or worse.

But having potential was just the beginning. In order to truly become a part of Valor, campers had to complete a rigorous series of trials and trainings. And as is true for most elite military units, there's always the opportunity (and sometimes the incentive) to drop out—and most do: over eighty percent leave. The rest press on to complete the summer and are given the opportunity to return and serve their country when a need arises.

Wyatt had known the new campers were arriving and made sure to be waiting when the plane touched down.

"Dude, what's been up with you?" Cody walked behind, nearly clipping Wyatt's heels. His energetic demeanor was downright obnoxious.

"What do you mean?" Wyatt yawned.

"You've been out of it all day."

"Just a lot going on. New campers coming in." Wyatt nodded at the wide-eyed kids stepping off the jet and onto the roll-away ramp.

"Blindfolds off. Come out and line up!" Viktoria called.

Jalen was the first off, stepping out into the green, glistening world.

Wyatt waved at Jalen, then turned to Cody. "You're right," Wyatt said. "Just had a long night. Now, go join your group."

"Those are the Rovers?" Cody asked as the group filed out. He suddenly looked like what he was—a little kid. A scared boy on the first day of school.

"Just get over there." Wyatt put his arm around Cody's shoulder and walked him toward the group. "Hey guys, I'm Wyatt. That's my brother, Cody. He'll be joining you for Indoc."

A sullen delinquent, Rayo Hernandez, who was thirteen but whose 'stache made him look more like fifteen, took one look at Cody and laughed. "Who's this soft-ass punk?"

"You just heard," said Jalen, "his name's Cody."

"And who do you think you are? The Equalizer? I'll set both of y'all straight."

"I'm just saying." Jalen stepped back.

"How about you don't speak?" Rayo said. "That work?"

Cody and Jalen edged away and Rayo laughed.

"Yeah, that's it," Rayo called after them.

It was clear that neither Cody nor Jalen had had much experience dealing with kids like Rayo. Wyatt thought about interceding, but decided to let his brother and Jalen fight their own fights. They'd need that in order to survive and thrive at Valor. At least they had each other.

"Okay, everyone," Avi called the group together. "In order for you new campers to be processed, we're going to need some biometric data."

Out of nowhere, a drone hummed into view.

"First order of business," Avi continued. "Eye scan." The drone buzzed up to one of the candidates—a goth-looking girl—and stopped. "A simple picture of your iris is all that's required." Avi turned to the girl. "Okay, Dragon Tattoo, let's start with you. Your eyes look strangely green. Are you wearing contact lenses?" he asked.

The girl nodded.

"Well, take them out."

She obeyed and tucked them into a case in her purse.

"Okay, hold still."

"Scanning now," the drone bleeped out. "Five seconds . . . four seconds . . . scan complete."

The drone continued through the other half dozen kids who laughed nervously as the robotic bird weaved between them.

"All right, now the fun part," Avi said blandly. "A blood and tissue sample." He pulled out an EpiPen-like device and motioned for goth girl to remove her hoodie.

"Right shoulder, please." Avi prepared the needle.

"Why am I the guinea pig?" the girl said.

"'Cause you just a pig," Rayo cracked. "No one jabbin' me with a needle unless it's for a tattoo."

Wyatt was about to teach Rayo a lesson when Cody stepped forward. "I'll go first."

Wyatt felt a surge of pride.

"Fine," Avi said and stabbed Cody's upper arm.

"Ouch." Cody drew back, but Avi was already taking another needle from its sanitary wrapper.

"Next!"

Samples collected, the drone whizzed back from whence it came, and Avi gave his final instructions. "I will use this data to get you all processed in. Meanwhile, Wyatt will escort you to the main lodge, where you will join the rest of the staff for your first meeting."

There was some grumbling and confusion among the newbies, but they all gathered their belongings—a single backpack each—and followed Wyatt down the steep hill toward the lodge. The hike was only a mile and a half, but the terrain was unforgiving, and the new campers moved slowly, sweating and complaining.

"Man, I'm hungry," Rayo said. "Hey, Camp Boy, when do we eat?"

Wyatt stopped and turned quickly, taking a step toward Rayo.

"Whoa. What's up?" Rayo raised his hands like he was going to punch. But Wyatt was too fast. In one move, Wyatt had Rayo on his knees, his finger twisted in a painful grip.

"You can put dirt in your mouth. Or food. I'll let you choose. But if you speak one more impolite word to your staff or your fellow campers, I'll make the choice for you."

"Okay, okay . . . I swear I'll be nice."

"Wyatt, dude, let it go," Cody said to his brother.

"Don't talk to a senior camper like that," Wyatt barked.

Cody shook his head, almost laughing in disbelief.

"You think I'm joking, Brewer?" Wyatt said. "Get down and do fifty push-ups."

Cody just looked at him, confused, a little horrified.

"Now!"

Cody dropped and began pushing out.

"All of you, hit the deck and start pushing out," Wyatt fumed. He let go and the boy collapsed at his feet. "You, Rayo, do a hundred or you're getting right back on the plane."

Rayo slid to his chest and followed instructions, his arms shaking before he even got to ten.

"I'll take it from here," a voice interrupted. They looked up and saw Eldon standing above them. "Wyatt, they need you at the beach for a swim test."

CHAPTER 16

As Wyatt headed toward the water, he couldn't help but remember his own first day, when he'd seen a fellow Group-C member, Hudson Decker, deftly handle an unruly camper. He'd been shocked by Hud's effective use of violence, but he learned a valuable lesson. Bullying, in any form, can't be tolerated. It must be dealt with swiftly and sometimes savagely. Still, he wondered if he'd been too hard on Cody and taken it too far.

Wyatt had just finished the last swim test for the new Group-Cs as a boatload of campers eased toward the dock. As the *Sea Goat* neared, Wyatt thought he saw a familiar face. He craned his neck, and there, squinting in the midday sun, was Mackenzie and four other passengers. One was a tall, Arab-looking kid wearing a white velvet jumpsuit and white Air Jordans. He leaned cockily against the pilothouse, his gold chain glinting in the sunlight.

"Swim buddy!" the dude shouted to Wyatt as the boat drifted in.

"Samy!" Wyatt grinned.

On board with him was a young girl with short, tousled hair, standing just over five feet. She might have been described by some as mousy, but anyone who spent ten minutes with her could see she was a lion on the inside.

"Rory," Wyatt said, extending his hand to help her off, but she jumped to the dock and gave him a high five.

"Been pretty lonely, being the only member of my own team." Wyatt smiled. There was a vast void in their team and all of them felt it: Dolly. The bittersweetness of their reunion must have been evident. And just as he felt a wave of excitement at seeing his old friends and comrades he felt a wave of guilt for having considered blowing the horn so he could work with Darsie on finding Encyte and avenging Dolly's death.

"Don't worry, dude." Samy pulled Wyatt into a bro hug. "We can't bring her back, but we can make Hallsy pay."

"Damn straight," Rory added.

"Yeah," Wyatt said, fighting emotion. "Now please tell me," he said, stepping back to take in Samy's velour getup, "what the hell are you wearing?"

"Don't pretend you ain't jealous," said Samy. "This is high fashion, man. Haute couture. Cost me three hundred fifty dollars."

"It's a onesie, bro. But you wear it well."

"So, Wyatt," Rory asked as they hoofed back to the lodge. "Now that your dad's the new director, you wanna tell us what's going to happen with Group-B, with it being only the three of us?"

"Don't quote me yet, but I think they're gonna move us up into A and create two teams, so we can train with them this summer."

Rory and Sam looked at each other, then looked at Wyatt, huge smiles on their faces.

"Seriously, they're pulling us up?" Samy asked.

"It's not official till it's official, but that's the plan."

"Upgraded." Rory pumped her fist. "Much better than getting held back. Who's joining us?"

"They escorted you over." Wyatt nodded to the two other passengers on the boat.

"Those guys?" Samy asked. "I thought they were staff."

"See the tan guy?" Wyatt said. "That's Pierce. Mackenzie's nephew."

"Ahhh," Rory said, staring at the good-looking Native American boy as he finished tying off the boat. "That makes sense. Mackenzie let him drive, and he never lets anyone drive."

"And that's our other teammate, Mary Alice." Wyatt nodded at the towering blonde wearing an immaculate summer dress and a haughty grin. She looked nothing like she did on the Jet Ski that night.

"Is she wearing . . . heels?" Rory asked, her nose crinkled as much in confusion as disgust. "We'll see how long she keeps that pretty dress clean."

"Wait to judge till you see her operate," said Wyatt, winking. He considered vouching for her effectiveness based on the mission he'd completed with her, but that information was need-to-know. For all Rory and Samy knew, Mary Alice was arriving at Camp Valor with them that day to start the summer.

"Dude." Samy leaned in, gesturing to the pair in the boat. "We're back in the big leagues."

"Yup." Wyatt turned and started up the hill. "Come on. Cass is waiting in the Caldera. Training starts now."

CHAPTER 17

It was a typical Monday morning at LaGuardia. Flights from Philadelphia, Chicago, Boston, West Palm—packed with tourists and morning commuters—maneuvered around one another in a coordinated airspace ballet. Next up for landing, the Embraer ERJ-190 returning from Toronto Pearson International. The captain was hand-flying the aircraft toward LGA's runway some twelve hundred feet below when he saw something in the distance.

"Oh my god . . . birds," he said, pulling the yoke to rise above what looked like a perfect V of geese.

"What's going on?" the copilot asked, but then saw what the captain was talking about—the birds, also course-correcting, at least a dozen of them buzzing closer and closer to the jet's twin engines.

"They're not birds," the captain responded with cool horror. "They're drones."

And in that instant, the hunks of carbon fiber began thudding into the fuselage.

"They're targeting the engines," the copilot said as the machines whirred themselves into the massive turbofans. The first engine going, followed by the next as it coughed and backfired.

"Mayday, Mayday, Mayday," the copilot radioed in. "Air Canada 717 hit."

"Gotta keep her out of a stall," the captain said, still trying in vain to restart. "Dual-engine failure checklist."

The copilot rattled off the protocol. "Uh . . . airspeed two hundred sixty-five knots minimum, Ram Air Turbine manual deploy lever-pull . . ." he said, voice cracking. He began reading from an electronic checklist display.

"We got more of them." The captain looked out as a second mechanical V barreled into the smoking engines, the plane slowing and slowing. "We are in a nonrecoverable stall," the copilot said, his last words into the radio as the nose of the jet began torpedoing toward the river.

CHAPTER 18

After a hearty meal prepared by Mum and Fabian, the campers, candi-dates, and staff trickled from the Mess Hall into the lodge's Great Room, where bearskin rugs dotted the floors.

Eldon stood in front of the fire that roared in the tall hearth and began his first formal address as director. "Welcome . . . well, to some of you I say welcome . . ." His eyes shifted from the fresh faces of new candidates to the cluster of Group-A and Bs. "And to others, I say welcome back. My name is Eldon Waanders, and I'm the new director. I can tell you, the shoes I'm expected to fill . . . it's an impossible task. Many of you knew the Old Man. He was our fearless leader and champion. But not only was he the gold standard of Valorians, he was my mentor, my predecessor, and my friend. It's my greatest hope to do his memory honor by living up to the example he set."

Eldon paced in front of the group. "For those of you who are new, the next three months will be more challenging than you can possibly conceive. The staff and senior campers surrounding you are here to help. You'll learn quickly what to do, when to do it, and how to make it through, but if there's one rule you need to remember, it's simply this—don't quit." Eldon walked over to a nearby table and lifted up a prop. "This, candidates, is the horn. Something you'll get to know very well. Dorothy may have had her slippers, but here at Valor, there's no clicking your way out . . . there is only the horn." He held the horn out and gave it the gentlest sound.

Everyone jumped. Eyes wide, they listened as he continued. "On any day, during any activity, you have the freedom to take it. But you should know, the moment you sound this horn, you will be removed from the program and sent home. En route, you'll be given medicine that will wipe your memory of this place and you'll go back to where we found you, with Valor as nothing more than a vague dream you can't seem to recall after a deep sleep.

"For those who don't quit . . . glory and a new life await you." Eldon gazed over at his son. Wyatt shifted, wondering if the others would notice that it seemed like his father was talking just to him. Was it possible that Eldon knew Wyatt had been approached by Darsie and that he was considering sounding the horn? For a brief moment, Wyatt despised himself for ever considering quitting.

"Eldon, I'm sorry to interrupt," Avi said, coming in from the porch holding his iPad. He showed Eldon the screen and the two conferred for a minute.

"Something's happened." Eldon looked up, eyes grave. "I think everyone should see this."

Avi held out the iPad as dozens of campers crowded around the tablet like kids would gather around a radio to hear a ballgame or to listen to news of WWII.

The video loaded slowly, and Wyatt pressed play. "We have breaking news," the pale-faced reporter said. "At approximately 9:15 this morning there were a series of simultaneous drone attacks on major airports across the U.S. Some twenty-five airports have reported planes downed on landing and takeoff."

Behind the reporter, a pop-up screen showed shots of dozens

of crash sites, holes burning in the ground. "We do not have final estimates, but so far, we anticipate the death toll to exceed three thousand fatalities, which would make this attack the deadliest since 9/11. Based on a video posted to YouTube at 9:30 a.m., the terrorist known as Encyte has claimed credit. If confirmed, this will be his second attack. The video appears to contain images obtained by the drone during the crash. I warn you—this is difficult to watch."

First was clouds then blue sky as the drone soared majestically through the air, almost floating. The camera tilted up, recording the plane as it flew straight toward it. The plane tried to veer, but the drone cut back, moving closer and closer to the whirring engine before it went black. Then, another shot from a second drone, targeting the same engine, which spewed fire and smoke. Text over the image read: *Book of Encyte, Chapter G. 1:26.*

The feed cut back to the reporter. "While we at CNN are not aware of a *Book of Encyte,* it seems the reference mocks the Book of Genesis: 'And God said, Let us make man in our image, according to our likeness; and let them have dominion over the fish of the sea and over the birds of heaven and over the cattle and over all the earth and over every creeping thing that creeps upon the earth.'"

The reporter stared into the camera. "Encyte, why are you doing this? Are you punishing us for having dominion? What is your intent? You have the world's attention. We are listening."

Avi paused the video.

Mum came in from the kitchen, tears streaming. She held a list and began to read from it. "Mark Lemont and LeQuan James, please come see me."

Two young campers, one from Rovers and one from the Mounties, stood up.

"Is everything okay?" LeQuan asked. "My dad flies almost every week for his job."

"My mom is a stewardess," Mark joined in, his lips trembling.

"I don't . . ." Mum swallowed. "You both need to go home. Please go into the kitchen and wait for me there."

The campers stared as two of their own filed out. A buzz of concern went through the lodge.

Can I call home?

My parents fly every day for work.

My cousin's a pilot.

Mum held her hands out, addressing all the questions at once. "I know we're all worried. I want to assure everyone here that we are working with our government partners to check on the safety of your loved ones. For now, the two boys I have spoken to are the only ones who need to go home."

As the group processed this collective tragedy, Eldon cleared his throat. "For many, this is the first time we stand as citizens, united in grief, for people we do not know. And for those we do know, we are but a few degrees separated from the gravest tragedy. Some of us lost more than others, but today we have all lost. Let's take a moment to pray." Eldon lowered his head. The children, teenagers, and staff followed. "God, take care of our souls, our nation, and soothe the wounds inflicted today. Amen."

Tears flowed. Wyatt felt Cody's arm wrap around him. Wyatt hugged him, and then a voice cut through the sound of mourning.

"Let's go find this bastard and get him!" Samy slammed the table.

"Hell yeah!" Pierce said, rising to his feet. Rayo behind him.

Eldon stood, arms crossed, his hand holding his chin. "This right here." He pointed at the screen, the replay of the plane in its speeding, helpless dive toward the dingy water. "This is why we exist. To protect our own against evil. To defend the defenseless. But . . . we wait until called."

The campers began to sit.

"Our time will come." Eldon clapped Pierce on the back. "For now, we train . . . so we'll be ready. Avi, Cass, meet me in the Cave Complex. The rest of you, stay here with Viktoria."

The campers solemnly nodded, unable to break away from the carnage as Eldon and Avi slipped out the door, likely going to call Mr. Yellow.

"This is your 9/11," Viktoria said to the young faces. She shook her head. "You will remember where you were at this moment for the rest of your life."

CHAPTER 19

Activities were canceled for the afternoon and the campers slipped off to their cabins, their minds still replaying the footage of fire and smoke. Contact with home was strictly forbidden at Valor, but in the wake of this crash a few exceptions were made; parents could call kids or vice versa. Still, those at Valor strictly adhered to the fiction that they were at a summer work program, or in some cases, that they were still in juvenile facilities hundreds of miles away. The cage around Valor's collective consciousness had been rattled, and Wyatt knew who would be affected by this more than anyone else: Jalen. So before going down to the Cave Complex, he cut across campus toward the Rovers.

He found Cody sitting on the porch stairs, shoulders slumped. In his hands, a rifle that he polished with an oily cloth.

"Dad know you took that off the range?" Wyatt asked as he climbed the steps. "Rovers aren't supposed to have weapons yet."

"No," Cody said. "Isn't loaded." He dismantled the weapon in a smooth series of clicks. "Seeing how fast I can take it apart, then put it back together . . . I can even do it with my eyes closed."

"Well, you should let Dad know you have that."

"You gonna tattle?"

Wyatt sighed. "You okay? I mean, about the plane crash and all?"

"I'm fine. It's scary." He looked out toward the beach. "I'm just ready to do something."

"Me too. Where's Jalen?"

"Inside lying on his bunk."

"Okay, need to talk to him a minute."

"I'll come with you."

"Probably better if I go alone." Wyatt motioned his brother to stay seated.

Cody rolled his eyes.

Wyatt found Jalen alone in the cabin lying in a heap, hugging a pillow like a doll. "Hey, dude." Wyatt tried to be normal, taking a seat on the opposite bunk. "Just checking in. Wanted to make sure you're good."

Jalen said nothing, his eyes locked forward, tears gathering in the corners of them.

"So you're good?" Wyatt asked again, hesitantly.

"Good?" Jalen sat up. "No, man. I'm not *good*." Wyatt watched as the tears Jalen had been pushing back rolled out.

"I mean, I was . . . I was getting better," Jalen said. "I like it here. I learned how to forage yesterday, Day One of survival training. I ate ramps and blueberries. It's been ten days since I've played a video game—maybe the longest I've ever gone in my life—and I don't even miss it. It's like this was my escape, no one knew me here. No one knew what I'd done except you and the staff, I guess. But now this nightmare has followed me."

"Has anyone said anything to you or asked about your connection to Austin?"

"No. And I can only imagine what would happen if Rayo found out. How he'd use that against me."

"You gotta look past the Rayos of this world. If he doesn't

change, he'll wash out of this program and out of your life. This is a new start for you. Eventually, no one will know what you were before Valor."

"I know," Jalen said, "and I'll never forget. Today just reminded me of that."

"Listen, I've been there. I'm there now, just in a different way . . . I don't even want to talk about it. Just trust me," Wyatt said. "Sometimes it's one step forward, two steps back. But you can help. You *will* help. Valor is going to get a call and you will help bring in Encyte by . . ." Wyatt thought of saying *her* but decided against it. "By the proverbial throat."

"I don't want to wait for the call! I want to do something to make this right. I *have to make this right*." Jalen was yelling now.

"Okay," Wyatt said, lowering his voice. "I promise you can help with Encyte. I just can't tell you what I am thinking." Wyatt's plan, which was coming together, was to marshal a team and leverage the resources at Valor to find Dolly's killer. Perhaps he would not need to sound out after all. "Just know, I need your help on a mission, a personal mission I am running—"

The door creaked behind them, and Wyatt looked over to see his brother standing at the threshold. "Cody, I told you! We need a second."

"What's going on?" Cody stood there with the door open.

"Give me one second. We'll be right out."

Cody didn't move.

"Please," Wyatt said, patience fading. "Get out!"

Cody's face fell and he turned, gun slung over his shoulder.

"I'm sorry, dude," Wyatt said. "I'll find you in a minute, okay? Go take that rifle back before Dad finds out."

"Whatever," Cody said and shut the door.

Jalen wiped his face. "So what's the mission?"

"Can't say just yet. Let me ask you a question. Your mom is from Brazil, right?"

"Yeah . . ." Jalen said. "Why are you asking about my mom?"

"You know any Portuguese?"

Jalen scoffed, "You're kidding, right? I had to study it as a kid. Was the only way I could talk to my grandma. She's dead now, so I haven't used it in a while, but yeah, I'm fluent. Why?"

"I'll tell you when the time is right. For now, I might just pull you into some Group-A training exercises. You cool with that?"

Wyatt held out his hand, and Jalen slapped it. "I'm cool to try."

CHAPTER 20

It took a few days for everyone to come out of the haze, the bits of plane and human debris seared in everyone's mind like the charred holes in the ground. Even with the threat of Encyte looming, the newly formed Group-A could do nothing until authorized, so each day they waited for the call. And while they waited, Wyatt kept his group busy by preparing to find Hallsy.

From the outside, Wyatt's handpicked team didn't look like the warrior core one would expect to go after a Rambo turned serial killer. Wyatt himself, though physically hard and wiry, still had the brooding, shifty-eyed look of a juvenile delinquent or a professional dirt biker.

Then there was Samy, a huge figure with gangly limbs, who dressed like a cross between a genie and a rapper. He might have been mistaken for a Palestinian card shark, except for his constant joking.

And Rory—thin, diminutive, quiet. With her pale skin and innocent puppy-dog eyes, she was far more punk-rock pixie than predator.

The new members, for their part, didn't make the group appear any tougher. Pierce Grant, the dark-skinned pretty boy, might've been able to trek from Juneau to Nome, Alaska, living off the land, but in his flip-flops and polo, he looked like the kind of kid who summered on golf courses, letting his caddy carry his bag. If anyone in the group had the potential to be physically commanding, it was Mary Alice—tall, blond, gracefully assertive, she'd shine in any organization; however, based on appearances, you'd sooner think Junior League than military. And yet, the five of them were highly experienced operators and stone-cold killers. In one firefight alone, Wyatt and Samy had dozens of kills apiece. Rory had also been a critical player, providing cover and intelligence via unmanned drones. And Pierce, though he'd never felled a human, had killed all manner of big game, from bear to elk to deer, using rifle, crossbow, arrows, and even a knife he'd made from flint.

Mary Alice, too, had taken lives, though in a more indirect manner. Before her fifteenth birthday, she'd poisoned two men: a Russian spy and a Saudi royal who'd been funding terrorism. Her third kill was a female Chechen rebel, responsible for dozens of bomb-related deaths. Mary Alice dispatched her while on a ski trip in the Dolomites when she used a small, carefully placed explosive to create an avalanche that buried the legendary bomb-maker alive.

Finally, there was Jalen. Though not officially part of Group-A, he was pulled out of the Rovers to do one-on-one language immersion with a CIA language instructor they had flown into Valor. Immediately, Jalen's training with the Rovers was modified to provide more time with Group-A, and Cody's scowl deepened, as Wyatt stole more and more of Jalen's time away from the Rovers.

The team, which Wyatt dubbed "the War Dogs," began training immediately. After nine months away, the skills acquired over the previous summer, or summers, once razor sharp, had now dulled.

"What we do," Wyatt told his team as they lined up at the

shooting range, "is art and skill. But it's also sport. So we gotta be on point in the field."

"I *am* on point," said Samy.

"Your gut is on point and poking out," cracked Rory.

"Who cares about my Buddha." Samy rubbed his belly. He'd put on a good twenty-five pounds since last year. "I can shoot just as good with a paunch. Gun don't care. We all rarely miss a beat."

"Rarely isn't good enough. Not for Hallsy. We're like the gifted pianist who plays perfectly at a recital. But then he takes a few months off and plays again. Sure, a layman won't be able to tell he's off, but another virtuoso could," Rory said.

"Huh?" Samy said.

"I'm saying, Hallsy is an expert. Hallsy trained most of us."

"Can we stop talking and start shooting?" Mary Alice was wearing tennis whites and holding an M16.

Wyatt motioned her forward. "After you."

Along with sharpening skills, there was, of course, the physical training. (Samy discovered quickly that his "Buddha belly" didn't seem so benign on his first ten-mile jog.) Finally, there was the most challenging task: integrating two new members into a core of three and having all five operate like an organism with one mind.

To meet these challenges, Wyatt and Eldon, with input from the rest of the senior staff, designed a program of training that focused on tactical skills like shooting, driving, hand-to-hand combat, and bomb disposal. There was also a strict PT regime with running, swimming, and obstacle course work, as well as situational group training such as group reconnaissance and close-quarters combat, or CQC.

The tactical training, PT, and group reconnaissance were relatively easy to implement. Valor had the facilities for shooting, the planes for jumping, and some pretty fast cars. The driving was actually a blast. These kids, who were much too young to ever stand in line at an American DMV, were driving modified versions of some of the newest, fastest cars coming out of Germany and Italy. And instead of using a racetrack, the camp halted planes flying in and out of the airstrip and used the runway to practice driving in reverse at 70 miles per hour and forward at 140, all the while developing both evasive and chasing skills. If they were lucky enough to find Hallsy, a car chase of some variety would be likely, and given their experience last summer, Wyatt, Rory, and Samy knew firsthand that driving skills can save your life.

Close-quarters combat created more unique challenges for the team as they progressed as a unit. Under a staff's supervision, they performed CQC drills in Valor's custom-built "kill house," by training in three phases.

Phase One involved using electronic SIM, or simulation, rounds. Here, the team used laser beams and gears in the kill house in what looked like an elaborate game of laser tag. Both groups wore bodysuits that recorded hits on target (lethal areas) and "flyers" (when a round hit a buddy).

In one particular hostage-recovery scenario, Samy, carrying a SAW (a heavy machine gun with SIM rounds), rounded a corner and opened fire on Mary Alice, pumping her full of thirty rounds of harmless laser beams.

"Samy," Mary Alice screamed. "If these were real bullets, you woulda cut me in half!"

"I'm sorry," said Samy, unusually cowed.

"You better be! Sharpen it up! I don't want to get killed one day—or lit up with plastic pellets moving hundreds of feet per second—because you think you *rarely* miss a beat."

"I'll do better next time."

The nonlethal pellets Mary Alice referred to were used in Phase Two of SIM training, in which the team ditched the laser beams for something more realistic—guns that shot actual rounds of ammunition, albeit nonlethal rounds. Though the hard plastic pellets didn't kill, they hurt like hell, even with armor. The addition of the actual fire, the sound of gunfire, and smoke increased the reality of the exercise, introducing pain, heightened confusion, and blurred senses to the kill house.

For the final phase, live rounds were fired at targets in the kill house. In Phase Three, a flyer would not be tracked on your buddy's bodysuit or helmet but would blow her face off. Safety, precision, and teamwork were life-and-death requirements. Fortunately, three weeks in, the ragtag War Dog team had risen to the occasion, operating flawlessly in their first live-round CQC.

Jalen was also pulled into tactical training as often as Wyatt could work it in. The rest of the Rovers might not have thought much about it, but when Jalen came back covered in dirt, sweat, and something that smelled like cordite, it was obvious to Cody that something was up.

He cornered his brother one day at lunch in the lodge. "Wyatt, what are you doing with Jalen?"

"Language school."

"My ass. He's getting kinetic with you guys. Tell me what's going on," Cody said, trying to keep his voice down.

"Dude," Wyatt said. "It's need-to-know, and you don't need to know."

"The hell I don't. I'm the Blue for the Rovers. I'm the leader, and I'm your brother."

"I need him," Wyatt said. "You got that, brother?"

Cody shook his head. "Who are you, Wyatt? That *need-to-know* as well?"

Wyatt laughed. "Yeah. Now let me eat in peace."

CHAPTER 21

Looking out the dirty windshield of the car he'd been living in, Daniel Acoda knew there was something karmically just, even poetic, about his addiction to Zovis. Daniel's father, Maurice R. Acoda, was the chief exec of International Pharma Corporation, the maker of the painkiller and various other synthetic pheromones, and that year alone had made a fifteen-million-dollar bonus, thanks to record-breaking sales of the wildly addictive drug.

As is most often the case, Daniel's dependency was born of necessity. He broke his leg on the first day of a family ski vacation, and after the five-hour surgery—the screws and rods to ensure that he could walk again—his father came into the hotel room with a cup of soup and a warning.

"Danny, I know the doctor prescribed this shit . . ." Maurice took the orange bottle from the nightstand and gave it a shake. "But you shouldn't touch this stuff . . . Tough it out," he said and shut the door.

But after the vacation, Maurice was never around to see that his advice was taken. And so one day, without much guilt or forethought, Danny pulled the bottle from his hoodie and popped two pills down his throat. The buzz was nearly instant. A vibration, a hum, a warm light stretching to the darkest, achiest places inside him. Simply put: the pain was gone.

It wasn't long before the bottle was empty, but with the aid of his doting mother, Danny secured another thirty. The problem was when the drugs wore off, Danny now had two sources of pain: the one in his leg, and one much deeper than nerve and bone. An unreachable pain that started in his skull and radiated to every nerve and fiber of his body, from the top of his head to his fingertips and toes and the core of his person.

The bottle sat on the second shelf of his medicine cabinet, behind the mirror, and each time he approached it, the image reflected a slightly different face. Before that bottle was gone, Daniel had figured out ways to ensure it would be filled again. But by his junior year, his classmate sources were already inadequate or had been kicked out of school altogether. Danny himself, despite extremely generous donations to the school by his family, had been placed on academic leave, and had spent twelve weeks in a rehab in Malibu.

After his seventeenth birthday, Daniel's parents tried a tough-love tactic and kicked him out. They did let him keep his car—the Mercedes E-Class he'd been given for his sixteenth birthday—and he packed it with clothes, his laptop, and phone and charger and drove away.

One method Daniel used to protect himself against arrests was trading online. He would swap his ever-dwindling array of fancy watches and clothes for small stashes, and it was this bartering system on the darkweb that led Daniel to a supplier, a guy who went by the handle Star_Man.

Star_Man was different: instead of trading physical objects, he wanted Daniel to perform tasks—the delivery of a package, that kind of thing. Of course Daniel knew he'd become a mule, but Star_Man had promised him that he'd never be given much, nothing that would amount to more than a slap on the wrist if he got caught. And perhaps it was desperation that caused Danny to believe what was so clearly a lie. So there he was, carting parcels around the greater Los Angeles area under the hot summer sun. At the end of each task, he was given a location where he would find an envelope stuffed with enough Zovis to tide him over until the next task.

I have an insurance scheme, Star_Man's Wickr message said one afternoon. *I want you to start a fire that will burn across a piece of property I own.*

He sent Daniel a copy of a deed and an insurance policy with a rider for fire in excess of three million dollars for an old wooden barn. For this bit of pyromania blended with insurance fraud, Star_Man offered Daniel a month's supply, a nicely sized carrot.

All you gotta do is light a fire in the ring and walk away, Star_Man's message said. *The wind will do the rest.*

It was unseasonably warm, the Santa Anas whipping through the Valley at over forty miles per hour, the night Daniel drove his Mercedes to the property with a gas can, a cigarette lighter, and a copy of the *LA Times*. He'd grown comfortable with felony, as long as it didn't do direct harm to anyone, not even an animal, so the first thing he did was make sure the barns were empty. Confident this would be a victimless crime, he walked around the field until he found the crude firepit—a brush pile ringed by cinder blocks. He dragged branches from around the ranch, erected a nice, tall pile of brush, lit the wad of paper, and stuffed it into the middle. He blew furiously and stepped back to watch the flames lick up through the dry branches. The heat was so intense he turned his face from it, and he heard horses in a barn in the distance, neighing frantically.

Just as the Santa Anas began scattering ash across the sagebrush, Daniel wondered what he had done. But it was already out of control, fire jumping through the acreage and consuming the barn in a matter of minutes. Daniel looked around the wide field in futile panic. He fled to his car, and sped toward the pickup spot for the envelope, hoping, praying, for rain.

The devastation was something Daniel could never have fathomed. By 10 a.m. the following morning, forty thousand acres in rural and suburban Los Angeles had been consumed. The parcel of land where the barn had been positioned was much like the wadded-up paper in the pyramid Daniel had built—the center of the tinderbox in the Valley north of Los Angeles, and with the direction of the winds, the fire had all it needed to accelerate.

It raged on for five more days. On Day Seven, when the fires were officially out, reports estimated 3.5 billion dollars in damage, eighty-five lives lost, and 459,000 acres burned. And on that same day, Maurice sat at his desk in his high-rise office, the wall of windows behind him framing a city still shrouded in the aftermath of smoke. His phone buzzed with a text from an encrypted number. A link. Normally he would never have clicked on it, but the caption caught his attention: *There is no greater wildfire than Avarice.* A YouTube video began playing, showing his son Daniel popping a handful of pills before lighting the great bonfire that would turn Southern California into a crematorium.

CHAPTER 22

"I've got a new test," Avi said one afternoon, a rare smile on his usually blank face. "And I don't think Jalen can join us."

"What are you thinking?" Wyatt asked.

"A local police force has agreed to let us help with a raid on a synthetic heroin processing facility."

"Could that possibly be legal?" Samy asked, drenched in sweat after a day's drills in the kill house.

"They'll deputize you before going in," Avi said flatly.

"Like I said," repeated Samy. "Can that be legal?"

"I'm not a lawyer," Avi replied, "but if I'm guessing . . . no—not legal at all. Let's go."

"Okay, give me forty-five minutes," Wyatt said, running back toward the Caldera.

"Where are you going?"

"To pull Jalen out of language class."

"I said he shouldn't go on this one. This could get dicey."

"Exactly why he should come," Wyatt called back. "If it makes you feel better, he can stay in one of the cruisers."

And so, the team plus Jalen suited up and flew to a nearby town and the six members were deputized (even though only

Mary Alice was over eighteen) and then driven in an armored vehicle to raid an illicit drug lab. While this situation was loaded with the possibility for disaster, they caught the drug cookers with their guard down, literally playing video games and smoking pot. They scooped up the entire operation without firing a weapon.

"The only thing I was worried about," Mary Alice admitted to her teammates afterward, "was one of the local cops accidentally shooting at us."

"Agreed," was the consensus.

While Wyatt was happy with the War Dog performance, the drill had not really tested them. It was an easy win. Meanwhile, Hallsy was still out there, Encyte too, and he couldn't help feeling they were hamstrung by protocol: sitting around and wasting time. But Avi, in a good mood from the successful operation, pulled the van over and stopped at a local butcher at Pierce's request.

"All right, guys," Pierce said, licking his chops. "Anyone ever had a tomahawk steak?"

The same YouTube clip that showed a junkie striking a match in a California field was sent to every major news outlet in the United States. Word of Encyte's latest attack traveled faster than the wildfire—a matter of milliseconds—to places even as far away as Valor.

"He going to be okay?" Mary Alice asked, nodding to Jalen, who, having heard of the latest attack, had withdrawn into himself. He sat silently to the side of the group, a pained look on his face.

"He'll be okay if we actually do something this summer," Wyatt said.

"Maybe he should eat. But it's hard to have any appetite at all." Her face soured. "Especially for something cooked in fire."

"For once, I agree with you," Samy said.

"You can't think like that. The fire was blameless." Pierce piled the hardwood high around the campfire, leaving space for the air to blow through and stoke the flame. "Another one of Encyte's tools. Just because your tools might be dangerous and crude"—Pierce dragged two flat stones the size of shoeboxes up to the firepit—"doesn't mean dinner has to be."

Once the bonfire reached just the right temperature, the wood literally shrieking, Pierce speared the logs and crumbled them into a pile of thick, ropey cinders. He fetched two large cast-iron skillets from the kitchen and placed one on each of the rocks. "Feel this," he said, holding a thick tomahawk rib eye by the long angled bone. "Feel how soft that is."

"Like you could put your finger through it," said Mary Alice, probing the meat.

"We're going to want this to feel like the flesh just above your thumb—it's how you can tell the perfect doneness for a steak without a thermometer. Should only take a few minutes." Pierce cut a little piece of fat from each rib eye and used it to grease the pans. He then sprinkled salt and pepper on the steaks and laid them down in the skillets to sizzle and pop. Five minutes on each side, and the three-inch steaks were cooked medium-rare and the potatoes and onions, which had been wrapped in tinfoil, were retrieved from the ash. Hot and fluffy, the potatoes were stuffed with sour cream and butter.

"This would be my last meal. Like, for real," Samy said. He'd been annoyed with what he called Pierce's "champagne taste," but now, the whole team was more than grateful. Dinner was served with cold spring water and cherry pie that Mum had baked earlier that day.

Avi, who'd taken over as the group's staff leader, debriefed the team on the recent operation, going point by point through the raid on the drug mill. The operation had been smooth, and the debrief was short and perfunctory. Chitchat ensued, and as soon as the food was served, the Buck knives came out and cut deep into the thick, crusty seared steaks, reaching the soft pink interior.

"Hey, Rory," Wyatt said, making his way over. "Let me borrow your knife?"

"You forgot yours?" Samy asked, but as soon as the words were out of his mouth, he realized his mistake. Wyatt's knife had last been seen the previous summer. Hallsy had taken it and killed someone with it to send Wyatt a message.

Rory looked down, awkwardly. "Sorry, brother," Samy said to Wyatt, "You can use mine." Samy handed him the grease-smeared pearl handle of his own razor-sharp Buck knife. Wyatt cut a few slices, split open his potato, and loaded it with sour cream and cheese. He found a log positioned just where the warmth of the fire and the cool of the night met.

"Bring a steak for me?" Wyatt heard his father's voice call out as he approached the campfire.

"Here you go, sir," Rory said, cutting off half her steak. "It's like five times more than I can eat anyway."

"Thank you." Eldon fixed a plate and sat down next to Wyatt. Avi, seeing the two, came over and squatted down on a rock across from them.

"So," Eldon said. "Avi tells me the mission in training is going well."

"It is."

"What about repeating the training cycle?"

"Honestly?" Wyatt asked.

Eldon nodded.

"We don't need more training." Wyatt looked at Avi, who said nothing, but imperceptibly gave his consent.

"You always need more training, son."

"Okay, let me rephrase: we're ready enough and we're running out of time."

"Ready for what?" Eldon asked. "We don't have orders."

"To get a team together and find Hallsy. It's time to do something. We're sitting in the woods, cooking steaks around the campfire while there's a terrorist burning California. Let's not wait to get called into the game but force our way in."

"All right. So what would that entail?" Eldon looked across the fire, the other members of the team laughing and chowing, for a few moments just being kids. "I presume you have a plan?"

Wyatt shot Avi another look. "Yes, sir," he said.

Avi came closer. "Well, with the help of Cass, we've developed one."

"Lemme hear it."

"Well, the last sighting of Hallsy was in a fishing village in Panama. The assumption," Wyatt said, "is that Hallsy chartered a boat, made landfall in Colombia, and entered South America that way. But there are rumors of a girl traveling with him. He's saying she's his daughter."

"The boat was recovered a thousand miles out into the Pacific with no one on board, its steering wheel secured and throttle powered at just above idle," Avi added. "Like a ghost ship."

"That was the last sighting?"

"Yes. But Dolly's body was found washed up in the Amazon on the far eastern edge of the Colombian border," Avi said solemnly. "So we think it's safe to assume he's penetrated the jungle."

"Hallsy's a skilled survivalist," Eldon said, nodding. "If he made it into the jungle, he's disappeared, just like he was checking into a damn JW Marriott. So what do you propose? Send a team to South America to comb the jungle?"

"In short, yes." Wyatt drew a sketch in the dirt that resembled the top of an ice cream cone with three lumpy scoops. "This is northern South America. The borders between these countries—Colombia, Venezuela, Brazil—are some of the most lawless parts of the world. Exactly the kind of place Hallsy would gravitate to. Our intention is to deploy there, under the cover of Mormon missionaries. With the aid of locals and unmanned drones flown by Rory, we'll move village by village, scouring the region, looking for Hallsy."

"Hasn't the Golden One Hundred already done this, Avi?" Eldon asked. "If the last contact three months ago was, as you say, in a fishing village . . . I would assume they've been all over northern South America."

"Yeah," said Avi. "They've been in the region. But there's a difference."

"What's that?"

"Meat eaters can smell other meat eaters."

"What's that's supposed to mean?"

"As Wyatt told you. This is an outlaw region, with three borders. You get a bunch of American pipe-hitters prowling through the jungle. Anyone—from narco to ex-military to your average criminal evading justice—can sense the guys are operators and they keep away. Given that will let us fly better under the radar, attracting less suspicion. Classic Valor."

"What about assets? That will take months to establish if you're going to the South American version of the Wild West. Does anyone even speak Portuguese? You think you can trust any old translator on the street?"

"Actually . . ." Wyatt hesitated. "We were going to ask you about this last, but Jalen's mother is from Brazil." Eldon looked over at Jalen, who seemed to come back to life and nodded.

Jalen said flatly, "Sim eu falo portuguese."

"You're shitting me," Eldon said. "You want to take a Rover to Brazil to hunt Hallsy?"

"I know he's young, but he'll keep his head down. And stick close. His accent is flawless. And he's been training with us as much as possible to prepare."

"Yeah, I know that," Eldon said. "Your brother and others at Valor have been complaining that you've hijacked his summer."

"We need him. He will pose as a street urchin turned guide."

"Aren't LDS missionaries a little older than Rory?"

"Most of us can pass for nineteen. Cass will go too, as our mother," Wyatt said. "If we're supposedly student missionaries on summer break, we've six weeks left and a lot of ground to cover. We need to deploy now."

Eldon sighed. "You're literally walking into his perfect environment for setting up a defense, laying traps, and going on the offensive."

"Yes," Wyatt said. "But there's a difference. The woman he's traveling with might be gravely ill."

"How do you know that?"

"In the village where he was spotted, a pharmacy had been robbed. Many drugs had been taken, mostly recreational—Oxy, Demerol—but two doses of malaria pills were taken as well. What we think," said Wyatt, "is that Hallsy raided the pharmacy for the malaria medicine and used the narcotics theft as a cover."

"Hallsy could also be sick. That's also a possibility."

"If he's sick that could mean he'd act even more dangerously. Dad, it makes sense to act. At least one of them is sick. We can find them, if we move now."

"Okay," said Eldon, pushing up from the log and rising to his feet, the joints in his knees popping as he stretched. "I'll call Mr. Yellow about manufacturing the documentation to get you in. Likely will be Colombia, but that'll be his call."

"Oh my god. Thank you!" Wyatt, for a moment forgetting the chain of command, jumped to his feet and hugged his dad, the first hug he could remember giving him in almost a year. He also felt a wave of relief. Now that he had been given the green light on this mission, there was no chance in hell Wyatt was giving in to the offer from Darsie and sounding out of Valor.

"I'll go tell Cass," Avi said, excusing himself.

"Yeah, well, you two better figure out what I tell anyone if we're called in for Encyte while you're gone," Eldon said, somewhat joking but also serious. "We have the secretary of defense doing a surprise visit at some point this summer. If she shows and we're tapped to go after the world's most dangerous terrorist, and you guys are on a revenge mission, it will kill Valor. We will be shut down."

"You will *not* regret this, Dad." Wyatt suddenly noticed that the rest of Group-A had ceased their fireside antics and were listening in on the conversation. "We'll do good by the camp. We'll bring Hallsy back with honor and glory."

"If you want a chance of getting out of here tomorrow, you'd better get some shut-eye."

The entire team let out a cheer.

CHAPTER 23

Wyatt sat up in his bunk at 0600 hours, his chest heaving and hairline dripping with sweat. Though it was unusual the night before a mission, he had slept, and in his dreams, the black ghost train sped through Grand Central Terminal, killing everyone in its wake. *You chose this, Wyatt,* the Darsie in his dream told him. The blood splatter crusted against the armored plates.

"Hey!" Avi was kneeling down on the floor beside Wyatt's bunk, rechecking the backpacks they'd prepped for the mission. Hundreds of pamphlets with images of Jesus riding a cloud and a dozen copies of the Book of Mormon, each packed with contraband—C-4, magazines.

"Where's the plane?" Wyatt whispered.

"Heavy fog," Avi replied without looking up. "No flights in or out of the Caldera until it lifts. Go back to sleep."

But Wyatt knew that at this point, sleep was impossible. Finally, a mission was at hand, and though he didn't let himself think about it, he just hoped he had chosen the right one. He had said nothing to Darsie. Sure, Encyte's terror was raging on, but Wyatt was still convinced that this wasn't his battle. He would not blow the horn and be cast out of Valor just to appease the curiosity of one man, no matter how rich. Soon, he would board a plane, taking the first real step to revenge. So he rose, got dressed in his Mormon polyester finest, and combed over maps of the Amazon while he waited for the weather to clear.

A few hours later, the fog still hung in the air, but it was dissipating, and the members of Group-A, Team Z could actually see their own footfalls as they double-timed up the path toward the Caldera. They summited the ridge and headed down into the old crater, which looked to Wyatt like a giant bowl of soup, its center brimming with water vapor.

The team made their way down to the flight operation area, left the gear on the edge of the tarmac, and stood beside the runway. The flight operator, a former pilot named CJ, was on the radio, speaking quickly. A staticky voice, some ten thousand feet above them in the fog, responded. Then all was silent.

"Is that our plane?" Wyatt asked.

"Nope." CJ shook her head. "Someone is waiting to fly in."

"We were due for a visitor." Avi's face was tilted toward the sky, his tone foreboding.

"Yeah, supposedly it's somebody important," CJ added with a smile.

Wyatt felt his heart beginning to jackhammer. "Ask them if the secretary of defense is on board."

"Yep, that's the one," CJ called over.

"Avi, we have a problem." Wyatt looked over, but Avi was already taking the phone from CJ's desk.

"I need this." Avi dialed a number while CJ looked on, confused. "Eldon," he said. "It's happening. Get down to the Caldera. Now."

Thin and standing no taller than Rory, Secretary of Defense Elaine Becker was the kind of person who seemed to swim in her clothes, even those that had been tailored to her. Still, arriving in a dark pantsuit and thousand-dollar Christian Louboutins, she presented an extremely aggressive posture from the moment her private jet—not military transport—touched down in the Caldera.

Stepping out behind her, her entourage: Ken Carl, her gangly chief of staff in ridiculous reflective sunglasses, and a shifty-looking overweight Samoan who looked like a street cop.

Eldon strode toward the plane, passed Jalen in the rags of a street kid and the confused and disappointed members of Group-A, Team Z lined up along the tarmac. He attempted to salute the SecDef as she deboarded, but the little woman had something else on her mind.

"Sir, these kids," she said, motioning to the Group-As, "should not be within fifty yards of an airstrip during landing." She looked around. "If we crashed, we could've killed them all."

"Yes, ma'am," Eldon explained, "but these *kids* are awaiting the next transport outta here." Eldon nodded to the camouflage C-160 taxiing on the far end of the runway.

"Oh, really?" The SecDef swiveled her pointy nose from the plane to Wyatt and his team standing by their gear, dressed like missionaries. "And may I ask where they are going?" She arched an eyebrow.

Eldon hesitated. "Colombia," Eldon said softly.

"Ahh . . . Colombia. And I guess you don't mean South Carolina?"

"No ma'am . . . South America."

"Of course. May I ask the reason?"

"This ought to be good," Avi said to Wyatt under his breath.

"Well, Madam Secretary . . ." Eldon paused. "Their mission is to seek out and locate Sergeant Eric Hallsy, a rogue operator hiding out in the jungle. This operator is a former camp staff member and former Navy SEAL. He has betrayed his comrades and even murdered some of them in cold blood. We believe he is a wealth of confidential information and a great danger to our country if not found and recovered."

"Annnnnd we're done here," Avi again whispered to Wyatt.

The SecDef blinked a few times, processing what she'd just heard. "Rogue operator . . . camp staff member . . . cold blood . . ."

"I'm assuming," Eldon added, "that former secretary Admiral McCray apprised you of the Hallsy situation. McCray and I discussed the search effort at length, and he approved it. But of course," Eldon added, "we would not engage militarily without consulting you."

"Of course," she said. "And no, Admiral McCray did not apprise me of any such situation." She grinned uneasily. "I'm starting to think the former SecDef may have a drinking problem or has for years suffered from a prolonged mental and moral lapse."

At that, her chief of staff, Ken, swallowed a laugh.

"Let's hold off on the field trip to South America for the moment," she said.

"Yes, ma'am," Eldon said.

The Group-As and Jalen grumbled, and Eldon cut their mutterings with an icy stare. He turned back to her. "Welcome to Camp Valor. How can we help you?"

"I suppose you could start by giving me a tour of the facilities."

"Wonderful. We can start with a walking tour of the Caldera, then—"

"Let's not waste time with walking," Elaine snapped.

"I'll grab a Gator," Cass called from behind Eldon.

The SecDef's gaze shifted from the director to the woman who stood in his shadow. "Nice costume," Elaine said, taking in Cass's beautiful, scarred face and Mormon dress. "Looks like Halloween came early."

"Yeah," Cass said, eyes ablaze. "Trick or treat." She jerked up the hem of her frumpy skirt and fumbled down the hill toward the Caldera.

CHAPTER 24

"Ken, thank god you're here," the SecDef mumbled to Ken as he drove her down the dirt path in Avi's personal Gator—a fifteen-thousand-dollar golf cart—slinging mud the whole way. "This place has been getting rubber-stamped, and it's time for some accountability."

"Yes." Ken nodded. "Eye opening, to say the least." From a physical standpoint, Ken was the polar opposite of his boss—male, thick build, blazing red mustache. But his voice had the thin, weaselly pitch of the brown-nosing sycophants all too common on Capitol Hill.

"But I've just got too much on my plate," she said. "Encyte is running a tour de force of terror, half of my home state is in flames. I don't have time to deal with this. I may need you to stay behind."

"You got it, boss," Ken said as the cart bumped down the path behind Eldon's.

"Hope I'm not staying to babysit," the Samoan cop chimed in. Weighing down the back of the Gator was Tui, Elaine's general henchman and occasional bodyguard. Born and raised in Memphis, the only thing exotic about Tui was his name. A repo man turned cop, Tui saw possibilities of upward mobility in government, so he left his Southern barbecue behind and headed for D.C.

"No, Tui. You're coming back with me. I have a feeling there won't be much to see here once we leave."

After a quick inspection of the firing range and munitions depot and a tour of the weapons storage facility in the Caldera led by a disgruntled Cass, the SecDef leaned back in the Gator, clicking her teeth, thinking. "Commander Waanders," she said with eerie calm. "An hour at your camp, and I feel like I'm visiting the DEVGRU compound in Oceana."

"Well, that's no accident," Eldon said, happy for any comparison to SEAL Team Six. "That's the goal. Our facility, training, and safety protocols at Valor are modeled after the Virginia Beach compound."

"With one major exception," she said with an acidic grin. "No children."

Eldon bit his tongue. "Who's getting hungry?"

After a full spread of hamburgers, baked beans, and home fries (which Ken Carl declined because there wasn't a vegetarian option), it was time for a kitchen inspection.

"Well, we try to grow whatever food here we can," Mum said, nervously. "These kids eat a lot, so it helps to source what we can."

"Peanut oil," Ken Carl said lifting up the jug.

"For the potatoes," Mum said with pride. "Makes it so the oil flavor isn't so overbearing." She smiled.

"Well, that's an allergy hazard. Kids these days, everyone is allergic."

"There's an EpiPen in the first aid kit," Mum pointed out, wringing her hands on her apron.

"And you are sure to use it," Ken chided, "with the slack food safety and all the peanut products you are using."

"Look, I've been running this kitchen for forty years. I've yet to have a camper die from dry goods," Mum tried to joke.

"You're right," the SecDef snapped. "I think we should be more worried about the C-4 in the Caldera."

Mum geared up for a retort, but Eldon stepped in. "Point taken, Madam Secretary. We'll address that. Thank you for pointing it out."

After lunch, the SecDef asked to observe a training exercise. "Sure," Eldon said, scrambling to change the daily schedule, "let's head to the beach."

"Wait," Ken said, pointing across the lodge to the chalkboard on the wall. "The day's flight plan says 'HALO jumping, Group-As & Rovers, Caldera.' Why don't we stick with that?"

"Thought you guys might want to see some canoeing. Maybe a swim test?" Eldon offered.

"No, Ken's right." Elaine pivoted on her red heels. "We're here as silent observers. I insist you go about the day as planned."

So the Gators sped to the airstrip, where Viktoria was impatiently waiting to demonstrate parachute jumping to middle schoolers. Eldon, having no time to forewarn his senior staff of the importance of the observers, hoped that by some miracle Viktoria would deviate from her typical Ukrainian bluntness and decide to sugarcoat.

But as soon as he saw her in her Costas and full flight suit, Eldon knew there wasn't a chance.

"Today, campers, we're going to be performing what's known as the HALO jump," Viktoria said. "This exercise used to be reserved for older campers, but since we've found the skill set crucial to so many missions, we've decided to include it in junior camper training so they'll have years to perfect it. As Group-As will attest, there's safety in numbers, so we'll be jumping tandem. Now, anyone know what 'HALO' stands for?"

Mary Alice's hand shot up. "High altitude—low opening."

"Right. And any idiot on spring break can jump from an airplane, but this technique is different. In a typical HALO exercise, the parachutist free-falls until terminal velocity, at which time the chute flies open, sometimes at altitudes as low as twenty-five hundred feet AGL, depending on the mission."

Samy scratched his head. "AGL?"

"Above ground level, dum dum," Mary Alice said under her breath.

"All right, know-it-all little bi—" Samy joked.

"If you're gonna be an A, start doing your homework."

"Enough." Viktoria eyed the SecDef as she stood arms crossed on the hill just beyond them. "The purpose of this kind of jump is twofold. As you know, we are often sent to hard-to-reach places. Many times you'll be jumping with cargo, or into the ocean with your Zodiac. High downward speed, minimal forward airspeed, and carrying only small amounts of metal will deter radar detection, allowing for a stealthy insertion. Likewise, the low release minimizes the risk of midair targeting."

"So it's less time for us to hang up there like sitting ducks?" Rayo chimed in.

"Yes. And while this activity might seem easy enough from a physical standpoint, it's not. At thirty-five thousand feet—six thousand feet above the peak of Mt. Everest—the air is a balmy negative-fifty degrees. At those temps, it's not uncommon for goggles to shatter . . . I've even heard of jumpers whose eyes have frozen shut."

At this, Wyatt looked over at Cody, who stared catatonically into the sky, the excitement drained from his face.

"Are you listening, Brewer?" Viktoria said to Cody.

"Yes, ma'am." Cody shook from his stupor.

"In flight, you'll breathe several minutes of one hundred percent oxygen. This will prep you for the jump and help you avoid the bends. Hypoxia is a risk and blackouts are possible, so a device called a CYPRES"—Viktoria held out a small sensor with two black cords attached—"will ensure the chute opens even if you, and your partner, black out."

"Okay." She clapped her hands together. "I'll be going over the mechanics again once we're in flight, but remember, this requires extreme focus and execution. Do it wrong," she said, still smiling, "and you'll be flatter than a crepe."

"Man, I'd love some crepes right now." Samy rubbed his belly.

"Pair up, and we'll begin suiting up."

"Lieutenant Kuokalas," Wyatt said. "Don't you think it makes more sense to pair older campers with younger ones, you know, put the experienced with the inexperienced for this one? I mean, the Junior Rovers and Mounties, they just got here . . ."

"Yes, Wyatt," Viktoria said. "We'll follow the safety protocol as always. I'll be taking us only up to around twenty-five thousand feet today, and the CYPRES units are already in place . . ."

"This is the first time up for a lot of these kids, so I'm just wondering if we should jump the first time . . ." Wyatt, now unable to hide his exasperation, knew he was drawing attention, maybe even from the SecDef.

"Wyatt." Viktoria pulled her sunglasses down. "Would you like to lead this exercise?"

Wyatt shook his head. "It's just that . . . Cody can't do this. He's afraid of heights."

"Wyatt, what's your problem?" Cody's freckled cheeks reddened. "I can do this, same as anybody else!"

"Very good, then," Viktoria said, turning toward the C-130, its engines already whirring. "Wyatt, since you are so concerned, why don't you be the one to brief everyone before they jump?"

"Roger that," Wyatt said, and the campers filed in behind Viktoria and the heavy door slammed closed.

The C-130 taxied down the short runway, getting to the end of the pavement. They made a 180-degree turn in the opposite direction, and several jet blast deflectors popped up from the flat surface of the tarmac. Viktoria maxed out the turbo prop jet engines for an appreciable period, going to max power before releasing the brakes of the plane to begin takeoff.

Wyatt looked over at the young campers as the plane began to shake. Some clenched their eyes shut, others were wide eyed with terror. He counted in his head: *ten, nine, eight, seven . . .*

One. The plane jerked, throwing the campers backward in their seats.

"This is normal," Wyatt tried to say above the noise. He knew CJ had simultaneously engaged four JATO (jet-assisted takeoff) rockets attached to the sides of the C-130, hence the deafening roar. Though it wasn't uncommon in short runway takeoffs, JATOs were the closest thing to being on a NASA rocket that actually landed on its wheels at the end of the ride. Wyatt looked at his brother. "Here goes your first rodeo," he said as the plane climbed higher and higher into the wide, blue sky.

CHAPTER 25

The ascent to twenty-five thousand feet would take several minutes. Dur-ing the climb, as per protocol, the campers breathed pure oxygen and listened while Viktoria prepped them for the jump. She had warned them that the plane would be bumpy due to summer turbulence, but for Jalen, the bumps were less eventful than the JATO rocket "rush" on takeoff.

"Okay," Viktoria yelled out the instructions. "Essentially two campers will be locked together back to front. The Group-A camper will be riding behind—and then on top—of a camper in training. Cody, how 'bout you pair with me?"

Cody's face reddened again, but he nodded, and Wyatt breathed a visible sigh of relief.

Wyatt had been so worried about his little brother, but it was Jalen who really had a fear of heights. He stared at the other Rovers, searching for inspiration in their eyes, as they began strapping into all the harnesses necessary to do a tandem HALO jump. Once they were geared up in their jumpsuits, they began strapping onto one another.

"This procedure is crucial," Wyatt said, taking the lead as

Viktoria had asked him to. "Any mistakes, obviously, can be fatal."

"All good, partner," Samy said to Jalen, double-checking the clasps.

Jalen could not see Samy's face at this point, as the older camper was clipped to his back like a turtle's carapace.

"It's so cool, dude," Samy said, "Trust me, you're gonna love it!"

"Approaching twenty-five thousand feet!" Wyatt shouted. "Final prep!"

Jalen felt as if his own heart was humming with the plane's engine.

"Just breathe," Wyatt said to Jalen before his mouth disappeared behind the oxygen mask. "Breathe."

Jalen situated the mask on his face and took a deep breath, hoping the oxygen would travel to every cell in his being and stop his body from shaking. Final gear check began, each camper confirming the other was suited up correctly.

"Tuck that in!" Mary Alice barked at the goth-looking Rover named Sara. "You can't have anything hanging off your suit."

The jump light in the cargo hold was still glowing red, but Wyatt motioned the group to move down the ramp toward the wide opening in the rear of the aircraft. In order for them to land on the island, they'd have to jump from the aircraft nearly simultaneously. Jalen watched as the light from the rear ramp opening began to infiltrate the interior of the cargo hold. The wind, and the negative-fifty-degree temperature, came rushing in.

"Oh my god," Jalen screamed into his mask. Even with a jumpsuit on, it was like diving into ice water.

Wyatt looked at the group and gave an encouraging thumbs-up to all, and Jalen raised a gloved thumb in return. The rear deck was now completely open, and the jumpers waddled toward the void like crabs, strapped to one another.

The red light above the opening flicked green.

"Go time!" Viktoria yelled as she and Cody stepped off into the wild blue yonder.

"We good?" Jalen asked as they moved toward the whirring vacuum of air. "Samy?"

Jalen got no reply. He looked at Wyatt's face as he dropped off the edge, and instantly, he knew something was very wrong.

"Samy, Samy, can you hear us?" Viktoria stood over the teenager, holding the oxygen mask in place.

Samy smiled and gave a thumbs-up as some volunteers carried him away on a stretcher.

Once the kid had been whisked off to the medical ward for observation, Eldon knew the afternoon exercises were only going to make matters worse. He'd tried to explain to the SecDef that Samy's exciting HALO jump was actually an example of Valor at its finest: "We teach good skills, so that even if the exercise goes south, these kids are able to think on their feet."

"Yes, and this camper who suffered hypoxia, did anyone care to inquire what his recreational habits are at home? Did anyone bother to ask what he does the rest of the year, nine months of vaping and the hookah lounge? No wonder his lungs couldn't take it."

"You make a good point," Eldon said. "I respectfully note that. But Wyatt was right there. And had he not been there to assist Jalen with the chute, the CYPRES unit would have ensured it would have deployed . . . We do have protocol in place, Madam SecDef. Now, where should we go next?"

Ken held out his notepad, upon which he'd scribbled the schedule he saw in the lounge.

"Lifting the hood?" Elaine said, her eyebrows making a near perfect V. "It says it's to be conducted in the *kill house*."

"Yes." Eldon winced. "Right this way."

For the SecDef's viewing pleasure, this time it was Wyatt in the hot seat, hood over his head in the close-quarters arms training facility in the Caldera.

"So today is all about instincts," Cass began. She circled stealthily around Wyatt, up on her toes like something from the genus *Panthera*. "Your gut." She placed her nubby arm on her stomach. "The object of the exercise is to present the camper with a surprise scenario—a threat, a harmless passerby—and the trainee must react appropriately, having little time to think. Decision-making, reaction time, and close-quarters combat will all be tested. Since it is your third take with this exercise, we will be using firearms."

"Ah, Cass." Eldon raised his hand. "No arms today."

"Well, then, what's the point of the exercise?"

Eldon gave her a stand-down glare.

"Fine. So Wyatt will be demonstrating his martial arts skills and hand-to-hand combat. Are we ready?"

"Ready," Wyatt gave a muffled response and Cass pulled the hood from his head.

The other four Group-A members came charging at Wyatt, in padded suits, wielding padded weapons. Wyatt, recognizing the threat, immediately assumed an athletic stance. Mary Alice came first, swinging the stick, and Wyatt moved to the right, dodging the blow and kneeing her in the chest. Wyatt uppercut her lip, and MA dropped, blood splurting, but Wyatt pivoted, ready to take the next charging camper when the SecDef popped to her feet.

"Stop," the SecDef screamed. "Stop the drill!"

"Halt!" Eldon held his hands up. "Team Z, stand down." He turned to the SecDef. "Is there an issue?"

"Is there an *issue*?" Elaine echoed in disbelief. "Sir, follow me." The fabric of her pantsuit whisked as she charged out of earshot of the rest of the group.

"My god, this is insane. Completely insane. This program is going to be suspended until we can have a more thorough review."

"Madam Secretary," Eldon said. "With all due respect, we cannot just shut this down. Camp Valor serves a vital role in U.S. security. Countless lives have been saved by this program, including my own."

"They're kids. And last year, two of them died. Not to mention the senior staff member who also perished."

"That's correct," Eldon said solemnly. "This is a high-risk unit that sees a tremendous amount of action. It's why we are successful."

"At what cost?" She turned away. "Ken, Tui, come over here!"

Ken came running over like a lapdog, the henchman lumbering behind him.

"Mr. Director, I'm putting Camp Valor on indefinite suspension, and I'm leaving my chief of staff to make sure my wishes are enforced. You should know that until otherwise informed, there will be absolutely zero military training at this camp. No fighting, no arms, no bomb-making, no defensive, offensive, or tactical training of any kind. There will be no campers allowed into the Caldera. They'll be confined to the camp itself and its environs. My hope is this secret training nonsense will be forever stifled, but until further review, there won't be any activity resembling what I've seen today."

"May I have a word in private?" Eldon asked.

Elaine shot Ken and Tui a glance, and the two stepped away. "Make it quick."

"Ma'am." Eldon lowered his voice. "This is a *massive* mistake. The last five SecDefs who have visited our grounds—all of them would have engaged Valor to help hunt Encyte. Suspending the program right now is like taking the bullets out of your best gun, plugging the barrel, and putting a red plastic cap on the end of it."

"Mr. Director, if I hear of these campers doing anything more dangerous than hiking trails and lanyard making, so help me I will ship them all back to jail where they belong . . . I might even send you with them."

"Roger that," Eldon said, teeth gritted. He turned to Avi. "Shut down all training. Immediately."

CHAPTER 26

That evening, Eldon tried to put on a good face and for the second time that summer as he called the campers, candidates, and staff together for a postdinner meeting. But this time as he spoke, instead of Avi or Cass standing next to him, there was a tall, mustached man hovering over his shoulder with a snarky grin.

"It was a good job today, guys," Eldon said. "I want to thank each of you for your contribution. I've been informed that, in spite of our great work, or perhaps because of it—our formal review is going to continue. In the meantime, we're going to cease all military training and focus on survival and outdoor exercises. The same rules apply—you may quit at any time—the training and testing, however, will be purely physical and mental in nature."

Instant groans spread through those in attendance.

"Okay," Eldon said. "Before we're dismissed, Ken here will be sticking around for the duration of the summer. I think he has a few things to say." Eldon stepped aside, motioning the mustached man forward.

"Okay . . ." Ken consulted his yellow legal pad. "Some new rules are going to be implemented. No knives, no guns, no intense physical contact—wrestling, boxing—no swearing . . ." The list droned on, but no one was listening.

"Maybe I'll blow the horn," Samy said, taking his Buck knife and throwing it into the wall on the other side of the cabin.

"You wouldn't," Wyatt said from across the room. He sat on the bottom bunk, facing the window. In his clutched palm, the picture of Dolly. "We'll get there," he said, looking at her face. "We just have to be patient."

"Samy may have a point for once," Pierce chimed in. "It's already almost midsummer. You know how these Washington things go—it could take weeks to get reinstated, and then what? How many promises does the U.S. government make that they renege on? If we're going to be neutered this summer, might as well try to get out of it . . . I'll go crazy if I have to sit here."

"It's just temporary," Rory said, as ever trying to be the voice of reason. "Eldon is going to be on it, trying to fix this. Let's just see what happens." She looked out the cabin window as Ken Carl and the SecDef went whizzing by in the Gator, the large Samoan sitting on the back eating jerky. "Where they going now?"

"Avi's lair. They're going to take his toys, I'm sure," Wyatt said, knowing what everyone was thinking.

"Oh my god," Rory said. "Avi is going to lose his shit."

"Okay, enough. It's lights out," Samy said. "See you in the morning." Rory got up and left, headed for the girls cabins. Samy flipped the light switch.

Early the next morning Wyatt slipped from his bunk and walked down to the water. During the day, with the shifts in wind and weather, it was about the only time he could anticipate calm. Sometimes he would take a canoe out, his paddle cutting the mist that hung like breath above the surface. Other days he'd swim laps in the frigid water. But this morning, he couldn't bring himself to do anything but stare across the placid gray lake and watch the sun heave itself into the sky.

"Good morning," Avi said behind him.

"Avi." Wyatt nodded. "Morning. Up early."

"I couldn't sleep. Maybe it was the lack of radiation."

"How's that?"

"They confiscated everything with a wireless signal. Even the drones . . . that was a joke, Wyatt."

"Jeez. And I thought I wasn't funny." Wyatt sighed. "Avi, there's something—"

"Here." Avi forced a small, tightly coiled scroll in Wyatt's palm. "This came for you after the last Encyte attack. I wasn't sure if I should give it to you, but with the SecDef and that vile little man, and the islander the size of an elephant poking around, I thought it best you have it now."

"What do you mean?"

"It's a message." Avi turned to go. "I didn't read what it said, but it's from you-know-who. I know you saw him. He told me . . . I'm in the circle now."

Wyatt unwrapped the note. It was the same paper, dissolving almost as soon as it had been unscrolled.

> Las Vegas. Two weeks. You'll be playing her in the EVO gaming championship. The time to act is now. 3,000 people have died since we last met. Hope you don't feel that blood on your hands.—J.D.

"Gaming?" Wyatt said out loud. "Darsie wants me at a gaming conference?" Wyatt knew immediately what he had to do. "Avi, can you send a message back?"

"Yes."

"Tell Darsie I'll need to bring someone with me. If that's okay, I'm in."

"I don't even want to know what you're thinking," Avi said.

"No, you don't."

CHAPTER 27

It was close to 1 a.m., and the sun in the Far North had only been down for two hours. After a long day at Valor, all campers lay sleeping. Even those out on trips had rolled out their damp sleeping bags somewhere in the deep woods hugging Lake Tecmaga and fallen asleep. All campers but two.

Wyatt had been told by John Darsie: *Yes, you can take someone with you*. So he tied a knot and bit off the brown thread where he had carefully stitched a photo into the inside of his backpack. He slung the pack over his shoulder, slipped out of the rickety cabin, and hustled across the campus toward the Rovers cabin in the early-morning darkness.

Jalen was waiting on the porch, his backpack on as he nervously shifted from foot to foot.

"You ready to do this?" Wyatt asked softly.

"I guess." Jalen nodded. "Let's do what we have to."

"Okay, just give me a minute," Wyatt said as he slipped in the door. There they were: the half dozen boys breathing heavily. They'd already begun the transformation into strong young men, but now asleep, they looked like the children they were—slack jawed, dreaming, vulnerable. Wyatt tiptoed to Cody's bunk and knelt down, stirring him.

"What?" Cody's eyes popped open.

"Hey, it's me. Come outside."

"What are you doing?" Cody asked groggily.

"I want to talk to you."

"About what?" Cody said.

"Just come outside."

Bodies began to stir. Wyatt glanced around the cabin. Rayo had a pillow scrunched over his head.

"I wanted to say I'm sorry," Wyatt whispered.

"Sorry for what?" Cody asked, trying to be tough.

"I know I've been hard on you, but it's only because I need to be fair. I couldn't show you special treatment."

"But you *have* been showing me special treatment by pushing me down, singling me out. You've made it ten times harder for me. It's like you don't even want me here."

"I *do* want you here. You need to be tough. You need to be able to stand on your own, okay? You can't be coddled by Dad . . . or me."

"So that's why you're treating me like shit . . . to make me feel weaker than you?"

"Be quiet." Wyatt looked around, the campers again stirring.

"See?" Cody sat all the way up. "You're doing it right now. Get out!"

"Yeah, dude," a muffled voice called from the other side of the room. "We're trying to sleep." Clearly, it was Rayo's voice, but he tried to hide, so as to not bring on Wyatt's wrath.

A cacophony of voices joined Rayo's, yelling for him to get out.

"All right. Enough," Wyatt said, rising to his feet. "Have a good summer." He walked to the door and strode out and down the porch stairs, Jalen falling in step behind him.

They said nothing in the darkness. Across the field, the older campers had been in bed for hours. In the guest quarters, Ken Carl, mustache combed, was tucked under the covers. Even Mum softly slept, a copy of *Medicinal Herbs* on her chest.

Eldon, however, was awake. Slumped in an armchair in the lodge, in front of the last orange embers, his bloodshot eyes focused on a letter he was writing to the SecDef, a plea to keep Valor alive. Outside the windows, he could hear the night breathe: the insects humming, the water gently slapping on shore, the bullfrogs croaking in the shallows around the cove. He thought for just a minute he might close his eyes and sleep, but then a sound cut the air so violently he jumped up to his feet.

The horn. Three long blares from the porch bled through the air, sending panic to his heart.

Someone had just dropped out.

Slipping into his coat, he pushed through the double doors and rounded the porch, but saw only Ken Carl, emerging in his bathrobe, a confused look on his face. Eldon turned and there was Jalen, shifting nervously. His face stonewalled, but his dark eyes were turbid and on the verge of tears.

"I'm sorry, Dad." Wyatt stepped out from behind Jalen, the pale moonlight falling over him like a sash. Horn in hand, backpack slung over his shoulder.

Eldon dropped to his knees. "Wyatt . . . What . . . Why . . . What are you doing, son?" he stammered.

"We want out."

"But why?"

The question hung in the air, as the other campers slowly climbed the porch stairs and gathered around them.

"Wyatt, what are you doing, man?" Samy stood in his boxer shorts, rubbing his eyes. "You just told me not to do this!"

"And you can't. Guys"—Wyatt panned the crowd of campers, stopping on the members of Group-A, Team Z—"whatever you do, you have to stay. Do not follow me. The camp needs you more than it needs me."

"Wyatt, you can't leave. Please, this can't be happening," Rory bawled. "I would have never made it this far without you. Please stay."

"I wish I could."

"And what about you?" Rayo piped in, staring straight at Jalen. "I know we gave you a hard time and all, but damn. Have some respect. You can't quit your team, bro."

But somehow they all knew words didn't matter at this point. It was over. Wyatt and Jalen had sounded the horn, and the consequences would be swift and permanent. "Why" didn't matter; the two could never come back.

"But you won't remember this," Eldon said. "Valor—all of it—will be lost." He stepped forward and lowered his voice. "Even if the camp one day is no more, how could you let the experience disappear?"

Wyatt couldn't bear to look at him, but stared at his feet, wanting desperately to reveal his plan.

"That's enough!" Ken forced his way between them. "No more talking. These two have made their decision. According to the manual, they should be led to the medical facility, where they will be treated, and then returned home."

"I'll take them . . ." Eldon said.

Avi stepped forward. "Let me."

"No." Ken pulled Wyatt's arm.

"But I'm the senior staff on duty," Avi said.

"Understood," Ken said, "but given the circumstances, this should be done by an impartial party, lest there be any question about the finality of their choice. Don't you agree?"

Eldon felt the stares, and he knew what he had to do. Valor must be supreme, more important that any person, even his son. He knew that any bending of the rules, particularly at this point, would be to ensure the complete siege of an already compromised city.

"Take them to the medical ward," Eldon said.

Ken snatched up Wyatt's and Jalen's backpacks. "Arms behind your back," he barked.

"What are you doing?" Eldon asked.

"Until these two are processed out, they're a danger to themselves and to us, particularly your son," Ken added. "I saw how he bloodied up that girl in the Caldera."

"That's absurd." Eldon flushed.

"It's all right, Dad," Wyatt said calmly. "We'll do what he says." Wyatt looked at Jalen and the two put their arms behind their backs, crossing them at the wrists while Ken secured them with plastic zip ties.

"Let's get this over with," Jalen said as they started toward the medical ward.

Just as the three were out of sight, Mum appeared in the moonlight, in her nightgown.

"Where is he?" she panted, her voice a mix of confusion and panic. "I heard you say his name."

Eldon shook his head. "He's gone, Mum. And he took Jalen with him."

"Why are you just standing here?" She grabbed Eldon's thick shoulder, almost giving it a shove. "Go after them."

"They blew the horn, Mum! Come on. You know what has to happen."

Long seconds passed. "Back to bed, everyone," Eldon finally said.

The campers dissipated, slowly drifting to their cabins, but Mum stayed there, in her nightgown, in the breezy air.

"Oh, Wyatt," she whispered, staring at the rippling black lake. "What have you done?"

CHAPTER 28

"What are we going to do about this?" Cass followed Eldon into the director's quarters, literally fuming. "You can't just let him go back. Tell me your plan."

"My *plan* is to stay here at Valor. Get the SecDef off my ass and get this program reinstated."

"That's it?" Cass asked, "What about Wyatt's mother? What's she going to make of her son coming home unexpected from camp with another camper?"

"We have a cover story. They got concussions, decided to come home. Jalen's parents will come get him when they're back from a tennis tournament. Besides," Eldon added, "Wyatt's mom is not there."

"Where is she?"

"A retreat in Florida."

"Retreat?"

"Yoga, meditation. Just trying to get her life together."

"Valor for moms," Cass joked.

"Yeah and trust me it's better she's not there. Better for me, anyway. I can handle Narcy." Eldon looked out a window, shaking his head. "My wife . . . I can't figure it out."

"You sure you don't want to leave for a few weeks?" Cass asked.

"You know how this works. We can't break the rules, for my son. Or for me."

Cass sat down. "I know we have to follow a code. But Dolly's gone, and the only other person who gave a shit about that is getting his memory wiped as we speak."

"Don't know why the hell he would just up and leave. And take Jalen with him." Eldon rubbed his eyes and scratched the stubble growing on his neck. "Maybe he wanted to go home . . . maybe I didn't know him like I thought."

"No, he wanted the mission. That's all he wanted."

"Well, we don't get to ask him now." Eldon stepped toward the door, put his hand on the knob, and then stopped. "The thing Wyatt doesn't understand is that he'll forget everything. He'll go from superhero back to average kid. All of his talent, all of his training—gone."

The discharge of Wyatt J. Brewer—the only Top Camper in Valor history to blow the horn, aside from the illustrious John Darsie—was surprisingly quick and perfunctory.

"Now, I know it's here somewhere . . ." Ken's voice echoed and the three wandered down a dark corridor of the Cave Complex looking for the processing-out medical ward.

"Over here." Wyatt rolled his eyes and opened a hatch to a bunker ten feet underground.

"Right," Ken Carl huffed. "I would've found it."

"Not likely. We had to move it when a camper last year—Hudson Decker—escaped before his memory could be wiped."

"That sounds like a confidentiality breach," Ken said, stepping down into the creepy hatch.

"Would be if he wasn't dead," Wyatt said blandly.

Wyatt and Jalen entered a small room, similar to a doctor's office.

"Boys, please." Dr. Choy wasted no time in greeting them, pointing to the couple of medical beds lined with white paper. "Please"—she motioned to Ken Carl—"cut the ties."

Ken got out a pocket knife and cut the zip ties and then assisted Dr. Choy in clamping each teenager to a bed.

"Okay." Dr. Choy smiled. "You don't seem agitated, but we offer campers a sedative, if they so choose." She offered Wyatt a small white pill.

"I'm good." Wyatt turned his head and fixed his eyes on the panels in the acoustic ceiling.

Dr. Choy turned to Jalen.

"If he's good, I'm good." Jalen pressed his head against the crinkly white paper. "Let's do this."

"Suit yourself," she said and slid the white pills across a metal tray. She then uncapped a bottle and shook out two bright blue pills into her cupped palm.

She dropped the first blue pill into Wyatt's mouth while Ken looked on. She moved over to Jalen and repeated the procedure. "Now the injections." The doctor picked up a hypodermic needle loaded with dark purple fluid. She flicked the needle and felt in Wyatt's arm for a vein. "Wyatt will require more, as it's harder to erase more years," she explained to Ken Carl.

The serum burned through his arm, but Wyatt didn't flinch; instead he closed his eyes, embracing the instant effects.

"Man, I hate needles," Jalen said, extending his arm to Dr. Choy.

"Nice veins." She felt the boy's muscles in his forearm, and lifted a second needle. And in moments, Jalen, too, was instantly fluttering to sleep.

Dr. Choy readied an ECT machine, a device from the 1970s used for electroshock therapy that looked like a clunky stereo tuner.

"Wyatt," Jalen said. "Make sure Dar . . . make sure he can find me . . . on the train . . . I need to find insights . . .

and Vegas . . . I've never been to Las Vegas," he mumbled incoherently.

"What's he saying?" Ken Carl asked frantically. "Something's off." He leaned over Wyatt. "Stop it for a minute, doctor. I need to ask him something."

"I'm sorry." Dr. Choy dropped the needle into the orange sharps bin. "It's already taken effect . . ."

"You can't reverse it?"

"No."

Ken turned to Wyatt. "You're up to something." He leaned down and looked into the boy's liquefying blue eyes. "Tell me . . . can you hear me?" He grabbed Wyatt's limp shoulders and shook them.

"Sir, hands off the patient," Dr. Choy said. "It's too late."

Just before Wyatt slipped into a deep sleep, his lips curled into an up-yours smile.

"Dammit!" Ken stormed outside, pulling his cell from his pocket.

The SecDef answered on the second ring. "This is Elaine."

"We have a problem."

"I'm listening."

"Wyatt Brewer—the son of the camp director here—well, he just quit the camp."

"And this matters to me because . . ." the SecDef said, staring at her long nails.

"This kid is the best they've got. He's not going to tap out unless he has an agenda. And it looks to me like he's taken this new kid with him. They were saying something about a train and Las Vegas."

"What kid?"

"Jalen Rose."

Silence followed. "You mean the kid who was partly responsible for the attack in Austin? The kid who was Encyte's pawn? He's dropping out with the director's son?"

"Yeah, I didn't put it together until now, but yes, and they're gone."

Elaine sighed and muttered a curse. "I leave you there, and you let this happen. Incredible. Just incredible. So, what do you wanna do about it?" the SecDef said, lowering her voice to a whisper.

"Put Tui on him. Let him follow them for a while."

Elaine sighed again.

"These boys are up to something," Ken pressed. "And figuring out what that is might solve all your problems at once."

"Okay, you got the green light. But, Ken—"

"Yes, ma'am?"

"I'm sure I don't need to tell you, but our conversation never happened."

"What conversation?" Ken ended the call with an exaggerated click.

PART TWO

CHAPTER 29

Of all John Darsie's many eccentricities, perhaps the most outstanding was that he required only an hour or two—four at most—of sleep. His life was in constant motion—trains, cars, and planes (when he had to). Like a shark, he was ever coursing along, always alert, always hungry.

His morning began at 3:30 a.m. sharp. It was his practice to wake up and meditate for thirty minutes. This routine he never broke, not for any reason. Perhaps the most dramatic example of his dedication to his practice was when an employee tried (and failed) to reach him during meditation.

"Mr. Darsie, sir, I need a decision . . . or we're going to lose a billion dollars," the nervous assistant called through the door of the hotel suite to his cross-legged boss. Darsie knew what the assistant wanted. He could have taken a two-minute break to give him the information needed, but that would have violated one of his core beliefs—never break your own rules, at any cost.

Following meditation, there was his two-hour workout. Depending on where he was, he would swim, run in water, lift weights, power lift, ending with thirty minutes of cardio (usually jujitsu) for which he had a traveling personal trainer. After a massage and a shower, there was thirty minutes of speed chess, which alternated between in-person and virtual competitions. When possible, the flesh-and-blood opponents were flown in from around the world. On some occasions, Darsie liked to play multiple people at once, and like his meditation, he considered the activity sacred. It was a means of strategic training, but for Darsie, who'd found the sport a sanctuary during a lonely adolescence, it was somewhere in the realm of a holy practice.

With his spiritual, physical, and mental exercises out of the way, exactly three hours later, Darsie's real day began. Although he'd given almost forty-five minutes to Wyatt, his staff knew that he allocated no more than fifteen minutes for any meeting, unless critically important, and so business associates were ushered in and out accordingly. His evening activities alternated between his two relentless passions: learning and productivity.

But on this particular day, at 7:15 a.m., Darsie was in Paris, in the Louvre. He was, in fact, the only person inside the museum, as it did not open for almost two hours, but through his various contacts, he'd been granted special admittance. So there he was, behind the thick velvet ropes, when his phone rang, shattering the silence.

Darsie's habit was to avoid physical and verbal interaction when possible, particularly when he did not know the outcome, so he silenced the phone and slipped it back into his pocket. He could not be certain, but he had a feeling in his gut: Wyatt had blown the horn.

Darsie wandered through the exhibits, thinking, when the phone buzzed again. This time, a text: *As usual, you've gotten what you want. Hope you know what you're doing with these 2 young lives. One of them happens to be like a brother to me. Be careful.—Avi*

Darsie again pocketed the phone and stared into the muddy eyes and smirking face of the *Mona Lisa*. He wandered from room to room, his polished shoes echoing down the great corridors, stopping only when he reached the Winged Victory. It had always been one of his favorites—the cold, headless marble with wings outstretched like a crucifix. He took out his phone and snapped a picture of it. Maybe it was the beauty of the statue, or maybe it was that he always thought four moves ahead, but in uncharacteristic Darsie fashion, he dialed up an old friend.

The number he called from was untraceable, but as he predicted, the call was answered on the first ring.

"Eldon," Darsie said cheerily. "It's been a while."

"Who is this?" Eldon's voice was angry and frantic.

"What? Don't recognize your former camp buddy?"

Eldon paused. "John?"

"Bingo. Look, I won't ask how you're doing. No need to waste time with pleasantries when I know things are not going well. Here's what you need to know: I'm on the way to meet your son."

"You son of a bitch—"

"Ah ah, Eldon," Darsie interrupted. "Thought you were above the name calling."

"What the hell do you want with him?"

"He's going to help with a little mission I'm running. A crucial one."

"I bet. How many billions are at stake this time?"

"Actually, this doesn't involve money. This call was an olive branch. I have your son, and I need this to go right. Can't have Valor meddling and messing this up, so I need you to promise you'll steer clear. I'll take care of Wyatt and his little buddy. I'll keep you in the loop, but . . ." Darsie's tone shifted. "I can't make that promise if you get in the way."

"Is that a threat?"

"Chill out." Darsie could almost feel the heat coming through the phone. "I'm telling you the truth. Stay back, and I'll owe you one . . . agreed?"

"If Wyatt gets hurt in any of this."

"He won't. So long as you steer clear. And listen, if strange things happen back in Charlottesville, cover for me?"

"Don't see how you've left me much choice."

Darsie ended the call and immediately dialed up his secretary as he strode toward the exit. "I'm leaving for the airport now. Change the route. I'm going to Charlottesville . . . Yes," he said after a pause. "Virginia by 8 p.m. And I'll need four men and a couple syringes loaded with phenobarbital."

CHAPTER 30

Once the pills were swallowed, Jalen found himself in a semicomatose state. Lights and colors surrounded him, but it was like his whole body floated in a warm bowl of Jell-O. He felt his limp torso shifting to a gurney and then vaguely remembered rolling out of the medical ward and passing the enormous whirring propellers of an airplane.

And then, black. A long weighty sleep, like someone was holding him down by the forehead. Until suddenly, there was a light. It sliced below the curtain, burning Jalen's eyes as he blinked awake. His head throbbed and a wave of nausea washed over him. He tried to sit up, but his body would not do what his mind asked. He was in a room, in a bed he didn't recognize.

Where the hell am I? He strained, but he still had no recollection of the place. Lacrosse posters dotted the wall. The birds chirped outside the window, their songs excruciating to his pounding head. He turned and saw a boy on the other bed, eyes closed and mouth wide open. He remembered him vaguely from the safe house in Clarkston. The kid who beat up the interrogator. *Is he dead?* And then Jalen saw the boy's chest gently going up and down.

Again, the nausea. His throat and stomach seized. He rolled from the bed and batted open the door, tripping, then crawling down a short hallway where a toilet was visible through a cracked door. He punched it open and lunged for the rim and retched.

"Wyatt? You okay?" The woman's voice coming from downstairs was unfamiliar. He could hardly open his eyes in the blinding light coming from the vanity. A few seconds passed and the voice called again, "Wyyyyatt!"

Jalen stumbled back to the room and lay down. He was closing his eyes, trying to let his body relax, when he heard the stairs below groaning beneath a great weight. *Who was it?* A figure appeared in the hallway, eclipsing the light. He could make out a fuzzy pink bathrobe, and then a shrill, frantic voice.

"Oh, thank god, you're awake." A large woman hustled over to him and lifted him by the shoulders, cradling his head. "Jalen?"

"Yes?" Jalen said. "Who are you?"

"Narcy. Wyatt's aunt Narcy." The woman dropped Jalen's head back down on the pillow.

"Who's Wyatt?" Jalen said, gripping the sides of his aching head.

"My nephew." Narcy huffed over to the boy on the adjacent bed and give him a not-so-gentle shake. "Wyatt, sweetie."

Wyatt moaned and his eyes fluttered.

"Lord," Narcy said. "Thank goodness. Thought y'all were never going to wake up."

Jalen could finally make out the woman's full face in the lamplight. "That man from camp told me everything," she said. "About the fall."

"A fall?" Jalen said.

"Yes," Narcy said. "You and Wyatt were rappelling down a rock wall when the rope came loose. Should be dead. Both of ya."

"Rock climbing," Jalen said, rubbing his smooth head, feeling for bumps, but he had no memory of any of it: a camp, a fall.

"And I told him," Narcy went on. "I said this is pretty darn strange. That both of you boys would have the same reaction to a fall. Passed out for seventeen hours from a lump on the head?"

Now Wyatt, too, was attempting to sit. "Where am I?" he said.

"Home," Narcy said.

"Millersville?"

"Nooo. We left there almost a year ago. We're in Charlottesville . . . Virginia," she continued. "They said they gave y'all somethin' to help you sleep while they flew you home. But that must have been some Mickey they slipped ya."

"What about Mom? Where's she?"

"Took a little trip," Narcy said nervously. "She's fine. Just went down to Florida for a bit. To clear her head. She's on her way back to see you now."

She pointed to the backpacks at the foot of each bed. "Got your things here," she said. "I wanted to go through them, but didn't want Jalen to think I'm nosy, but I could wash your camp clothes."

"Camp?"

"Camp Tamagame. Or whatever it was called. You don't remember that?"

"No," Wyatt said blankly.

"Your dad and brother are still there. Ever since your daddy got back from driving trucks in Iraq, that's been his job. Remember your daddy was a driver?"

"Vaguely. How did I hurt my head again?"

"Rock climbin'." Narcy sat on the end of Wyatt's bed and observed him. "It's weird, though, I don't see any bruising." She squinted, then turned to Jalen. "Don't really see any lumps on you, either, honey," she said, and then let her mind go where it always did. "You boys want something to eat?"

At that, Wyatt flung out of bed and fumbled down the hallway to the bathroom.

Jalen looked at the woman and the woman looked back. They said nothing, just listening to the sound of Wyatt's vomiting.

"Well," she said, tightening the long cord of her gigantic bathrobe. "I'll be downstairs watching my programs if you need me."

Jalen nodded. There was so much more he wanted to ask, but all he could do was lay his head back down and sleep.

CHAPTER 31

Jalen's eyes opened as Narcy's shrill voice broke in. She was downstairs, arguing with someone. "James did *not* tell me you were comin' . . . And no, Wyatt's *not* here and no, you *ain't* comin inside this house!"

"It's vitally important that you let me speak to Wyatt and the other boy," a man said. "This cannot wait."

"Told you, no one is here."

"But he knows me," the man said.

Jalen pushed himself up to standing. He looked out the window—a gleaming Mercedes on the curb and a shiny black SUV behind it. A thick man wearing a black suit scanned the street. He wore sunglasses and an earpiece, like he was straight out of central casting for the Secret Service.

"If you don't back away from this door," Narcy threatened, "I'm calling the police."

"Ma'am, put the phone down . . ."

"I'm warning you. You've got five seconds to get off my porch."

"Ma'am, I just need a second . . ."

"I'm calling—"

Jalen heard feet shuffling and breaking glass. "Help!" Narcy screamed. "Intruder!"

Jalen ran down the hall, just as a man bounded up the stairs. Another man in black behind him.

"Jalen," the man said, approaching slowly. "You don't know me, but my name is John Darsie, and I am a friend."

The man looked like anything but a burglar: pleated pants, a fancy cardigan over his shoulders. He could have been coming from a racquet club except for the needle clutched like a dagger in his right hand. "You had a fall that hurt your memory," he said softly. "You need to let me give you this."

"Like hell," Jalen said, staring at the syringe.

The man came closer, and Jalen stood his ground, his hands and feet—guided by route training—assuming fight stance, his mind unaware of where he learned the posture.

"Wyatt!" the man yelled as Wyatt appeared beside Jalen. "Wyatt, I'm here. Just like I told you. Please . . . just let me get something for you to look at." The man ran through the hallway door to the backpack on the floor. He opened the center compartment and ripped out something from the inside.

"Here," he said, pulling out a Polaroid.

Jalen watched as Wyatt stared at the photo of a girl.

"Run, Wyatt!" Narcy bellowed from below.

In a split second, Wyatt kicked the man with the syringe squarely in the chest, sending him flying down the stairs, crashing into another man, who waited at the bottom.

Jalen noticed a narrow bookshelf outside the bathroom door. He tipped it, dumping the contents, and dragged it over to the small window at the end of the hallway. Strength suddenly returning, he threw the bookshelf through the glass. Three steps and Jalen crawled through the broken glass and scrambled out.

"Go, go, go," Wyatt said behind him, and they both sprang out, shards of glass and roof shingles under their feet.

One of the men in black crawled out behind them and chased

the boys across the roof. Jalen saw a nearby tree and without thinking, he jumped, grasping for a branch. He swung down and rolled, then popped up into a fighting stance. Once again, without forethought, his hands and feet flew into action as if they belonged to someone else. The first man tried to tackle him, but with speed he didn't know he had, Jalen dodged the man and came underneath his chin with a right hook, then a knee to the groin. The second man grabbed Jalen from behind, pinning his arms at his sides and pulling Jalen backward. Jalen kicked the man in his kneecaps, and as the man teetered back, he used the momentum to body-slam him. He rolled off his chest and was once again on his feet.

"You're definitely feeling better," the man with the cardigan said as he jumped from the roof.

Jalen could see Wyatt out of the corner of his eye. He'd knocked another man in black to the ground. Wyatt held him, his foot on the man's throat.

Jalen raised his fist and motioned the cardigan man forward. "Go ahead, try me," he said as if someone else were speaking for him.

"Jalen, I'm telling the truth." The man set the syringe on the ground. "Wyatt, look at this." Again he held out the Polaroid.

Wyatt could hear sirens in the distance, the loud whine growing closer. "Cops will be here any minute," Wyatt said to the man. "I'd run if I were you."

"Her name is Dolly," the man went on, stepping closer to Wyatt. "You told me to show you this." Again the man thrust the photograph toward him.

Wyatt stared, hesitating just long enough for the first man in the suit to twist Wyatt's foot, drop him to the ground, and quickly slam the needle into his shoulder.

And then Jalen too felt a sting in his upper arm. "Ahh!" he screamed. He looked over and saw the man in the cardigan retracting the needle. The burning radiated through Jalen's upper body, coursing into his chest, and then everything went black.

CHAPTER 32

Cass leaned over the garden—arms, elbows, knees covered in rich, black, ancient soil. She hadn't tended a garden since she was a girl, but she had enough of a green thumb, and given Valor's long summer days and Mum's four decades of labor, it almost seemed there was no better place to get back into the dirt. The sun would rise at 4:30 a.m. and set sometime after 11 p.m. In the light of long summer days, everything seemed to explode from the volcanic soil—the cucumbers, the currants, the massive heads of lettuce—like the children Mum never had, flourishing under her constant care. Row after row, Valor's organic horn of plenty.

Most recently, Mum had been teaching Cass the secrets of crop rotation, and planting a variety of fruits that would grow in cycles. "Tomatoes would spring up first," Mum said. "Then beans, summer squash, and sweet peas." The garden was roughly the size of two swimming pools and fed campers for much of the summer, which worked out, as Valor was not exactly convenient for food trucks. Mum had also shown Cass the spot in the garden where she kept her medicinal herbs.

"And this is the one I used last summer when Wyatt got a

tooth knocked out in a fight." Mum blushed. She knew Cass was also upset about the abrupt loss of her friend. Her comrade in grief.

The truth was, everything had shifted. There were no missions. Eldon, though he was clearly trying to unite the group, had lost every bit of spring in his step.

Cass sighed. She needed something to go as planned. To bear fruit.

"Dear, Wyatt will be all right. Something tells me he has a plan. He's far stronger—and smarter—than we think. All these kids are."

"Hope you're right."

She knew what it was like to have her plans literally blown to pieces, but for once, she was tired. Too tired to put them back together again.

She leaned over the outdoor sink, letting the cool water run over what was left of her scarred skin, her damaged right hand, unsure in that moment if she had the strength to fight again.

Across campus, the Rovers were having their midday downtime in their cabins. Cody, since he wasn't much for journaling or taking naps, sneaked down to the shooting range. Thanks to Ken, the campus had long been combed of weapons, but he had managed to steal a Beretta M9, a sweet little number, and sometimes, when he was certain no one was around, he'd get a few shots in, just to practice.

And he was doing just that when his pocket buzzed. He reached in and pulled out an old iPhone, and on the notification screen, six voice mails. Cody was confused and a little alarmed. Normally there was no cell service at Valor, and definitely no Wi-Fi access for campers, but he kept the phone with him, another form of contraband, and he would play the few games he'd downloaded before he left, *Minecraft, Fortnite.*

He played the first message, and it took only a couple of

seconds for him to recognize a voice he knew better than any other.

"Cody, it's me. You gotta get back here. They took him, they took your brother! Oh my god, oh my god," Narcy sobbed.

Cody looked around the empty range, wondering where his dad would be at this point in the day as the first voice mail ran over into the next.

"Cody, it's your aunt. Where are you? Oh my god . . ."

There was shuffling on the other end of the line. "Cody, someone wants to talk to you. Hang on."

"Cody," a male voice said. "This is Mr. Yellow. Do not overreact," the man spoke calmly over the chorus of Narcy's curses and screams.

"Overreact? I'm a hostage!" she bellowed.

"I know Narcy left you a disturbing message, but the situation is not as dire as you might think. We have men following Wyatt and Jalen right now."

"They stormed into the house," Narcy squawked. "Wyatt kicked their asses, doin' some kind of judo . . . he judo-chopped one of them right in the stomach."

"Narcy, please," Mr. Yellow said faintly in the background. "Why don't you have a Coke?"

"Well, thanks for the offering, for pity's sake."

"Cody," Mr. Yellow again turned his attention to his message. "I know this might sound disturbing, but truly, everything is fine. Right now, Wyatt and Jalen are with an individual—I cannot reveal his name—suffice it to say, he's a man of great means, and though we do not know exactly the intent, we believe they're on a mission to find America's most-wanted terrorist."

Cody knew where he had to go. He slipped the phone into his pocket and climbed out of the range, taking the long way instead of going up the trail on a path where he might encounter campers returning from training. He followed the shore north and west. He entered the bunker complex, which, at its entrance, was large enough to drive through. He sneaked past the security detail and headed toward the director's office. But instead of going to his father, he went down into the bowels of the bunker and followed a series of ladders and narrow staircases to find the thick metal door and biometric scanner that led to Avi's hideaway.

"Avi," Cody said, rapping on the metal door. "It's Cody. Could we talk?"

"What's going on?" Avi's bland tone blared through the intercom.

"Just let me in." Cody looked around, worried at any minute his father might see him.

There was a long buzzing sound, and the door unlatched. Cody found Avi inside his lair, goggles down.

"Now, what is going on?" Avi grunted.

"Avi," Cody said, wide eyed from the lights and sounds behind him. Though he had been at camp for a few weeks now, he'd yet to see Valor from this kind of James Bond vantage.

"Something's going on with my brother," he said. "And I think you know what it is."

Avi did his best "Who, me?" face, but feigning innocence—or feigning anything, for that matter—was not his strongest skill set.

Cody extended the old iPhone. "Here," he said. "I have messages . . . from my aunt Narcy. And Mr. Yellow. I know Wyatt's involved in an important mission and he's been kidnapped."

Avi began tinkering with something in his hand. Behind him, behemoth racks filled with servers, spy gear, and drones, and his staff of secretive computer geeks scurrying about.

"Come inside," Avi said after a minute. He waved the boy past a wall of knobs and screens and blinking lights, his own private world of security equipment.

"Now, where did you get this?" Avi asked, snatching up the phone. "You know electronics of any kind are prohibited."

"My aunt Narcy. It's her personal phone, she kept her one for business. Anyway, I'm sorry. I know Dad said not to contact anyone, but Narcy insisted I keep it for emergencies. I was worried . . . I just wanted to be able to check in on my mom. If I had to. She was really messed up when we left—"

"Well, your brother is fine. What your aunt witnessed was likely a recovery of assets."

"Huh?"

"Your brother and Jalen are in the employ of a powerful billionaire—Mr. John Darsie."

"Hey, I know him. The Paycard guy."

"Yes, Paycard and all of that. He's very well known. Your brother left camp because he's made a secret pact with this man in hopes of finding Encyte, but if I had to guess, it's for revenge."

"I knew Wyatt didn't give up on us."

"Of course he wouldn't do that. Especially not when it comes to you."

"What's that supposed to mean?"

"A brother's love is very important," Avi said, his tone going cold. "And that is why I'm allowing this total disregard for protocol. I want to help your brother find the man who killed mine."

"Hallsy?"

Avi nodded. "And it seems now, with Valor turned into a glorified amusement park and your father under a microscope, this man—Mr. John Darsie—is the only way."

Just then, the heavy steel door to Avi's lair clicked closed. He looked at Cody, wide eyed. "Did anyone come with you?"

"No. Just me."

"Well, then, we've got a bigger problem on our hands." Avi sighed and went over to a metal cabinet and pulled out the tiniest drone Cody had ever seen.

"What are you doing?" Cody asked.

"I'm going to see who was just spying on us."

"Why were you following Cody, anyway?" Rory asked, resting her oar across the hull and letting the kayak drift.

As was common, Group-A was out on the lake in the afternoon. One place they could get cool, be alone and away from the watchful eye of the landlocked Ken.

"Well, I was down in the Caldera and I thought I heard a shot . . ." Samy said from the other kayak. Pierce was in the seat behind him. "And I knew no one was supposed to be down on the range, so I followed him."

"And why do you think Cody didn't just go to his dad?" Rory asked.

"I don't know! Maybe because he didn't want to tell his dad he had a gun and a cell phone! But the point is, I heard it from Avi's mouth—Wyatt and Jalen are going after Encyte. Don't you see? Wyatt's getting a plan in place. He's going to bring us back in. So we gotta get off our butts already!" Samy said to the rest of his group, his passionate voice a little too loud for the still lake.

"Quiet, dum-dum. Sound travels on the water," Mary Alice snapped. "Anyway, what about Wyatt's memory? He's been wiped, so how will he remember us?"

"Yeah, I don't know how that works, but he must have planned for that. Come on, guys. Wyatt had balls."

Rory and MA looked at each other and rolled their eyes, paddling just ahead of the boy's kayak.

"You know what I mean," Samy persisted. "Courage. He made his own path. I say we get back to our training."

"And then what?" Pierce asked from the seat behind him.

Samy smiled. "And then we freaking go after him . . . He's going to need our help. I just know it."

CHAPTER 33

Jalen rocked, slipping in and out of consciousness as he felt a gentle roll-ing motion. His arms were heavy, like he was wrapped in a blanket, making it even harder for him to wake, but when he finally forced his eyes open, he found himself in a train car. He popped his stiff neck and looked down, realizing that it was not a blanket at all, but a straitjacket. His heart was now thudding to life.

"Good morning."

Jalen jerked his head up to see the man in the cardigan sitting across from him. "What's going on?" Jalen bucked against the canvas cloth. The dim memory was now coming back in Jalen's mind—the fight, the bookcase, the window he shattered.

"I'm Mr. Darsie, and you weren't part of my original plan, but," Darsie said, motioning for Jalen to lean forward, "I think it was a good call. Still, Wyatt was supposed to have been sworn to secrecy." He began loosening the heavy buckles on Jalen's back.

"Thank you," Jalen said, wrestling from the jacket like a molting snake.

"The headaches may continue for the next few weeks." Darsie motioned to a dish rattling on a thin golden tray. "These will help." The dish contained two white pills, and beside it, a bottle of Fiji.

Jalen picked up one of the pills. It bore no markings. "Think I've had enough unknown substances for a while," he said, setting it back down. The veins in the side of his head throbbed. "What are they, anyway?" he asked, wincing.

"Mostly a standard pain reliever . . . with a special mix that my doctors find particularly soothing for migraines."

Jalen stared at the pill.

"Muscle through on your own if you'd like," Darsie said. "I must say I'd like to be trusted at this point, but perhaps that's wishful thinking . . ."

"Trusted? Didn't you stab me with a sedative?"

"Touché. But I'm glad to see your memory is coming back. I wasn't positive that formula worked." He smiled and turned to one of his manservants standing behind him. "Please find some aspirin. And take this away." Darsie motioned to the golden tray.

The man lifted the tray and Jalen caught his hand. "Just a sec," Jalen said, reaching in the bowl and scooping up the pills. He stared at Darsie, popped the pills in his mouth, and slugged the mineral water. "Thank you."

A few moments passed. "A little extra caffeine," Darsie finally said.

"What's that?"

"Perfectly pure caffeine . . . in the pills."

"Oh."

"That's it. Nothing else."

"Well, I feel better already." Jalen finished his water. "Where's Wyatt?"

"He'll be joining us shortly, but first, I wanted to have a little talk . . . about your friend, Hi Kyto."

"She's not really my friend. I mean, I know her but I haven't met her."

"And I think you and Wyatt have discussed that she could be linked . . . to Encyte."

"Yes."

"Well, Hi Kyto is employed by me. She and I have an intimate working relationship, and in order for that to continue, I need to know some things."

Jalen nodded.

"You see, often when we think about who's bad, we have so many emotions and prejudices that lead us in a direction that objectively may be wrong. Innocent people are constantly harassed, accused, and found guilty of crimes they didn't commit, based on these prejudices. I don't think I need to tell you that."

Jalen nodded again.

"For example," Darsie continued, "many of my colleagues in the software industry or in tech in the government are convinced that Encyte is a Russian mole from North Korea."

"Think it's possible?" Jalen interrupted.

"Sure it's possible. Anything's possible, but jumping to that conclusion, I think, is lazy . . . not to mention dangerous. Other ideas we've heard . . . a political activist—which makes way more sense to me—domestic terrorists, a rogue politician, the idea of a Unabomber has even been kicked around." Darsie smiled, eyes glowing. "Some people think Encyte could be me."

"Okay, so?"

"So you need to think about *why* Hi Kyto is a suspect."

"Well, her ability, her technical skill, her disposable income from professional gaming."

"Right!" Darsie snatched an iPad off the nearby desk and swiped it open. "Maybe you've already learned a few things from Valor, but there's more. A hunt for a serial killer starts with a victim. You need to profile them."

He handed Jalen the iPad. Jalen studied the screen: a table, a mosaic of faces filling the sixteen-by-nine-inch frame. They were laid out in blocks of three—the sneaker attack, the Austin attack, the victims of the California fire.

"These are the victims," Darsie said. "Hundreds of them."

Jalen zoomed in, scanning each—every color, every gender. His head pounded. He thought he might be sick. "I . . ." he stammered, suddenly wanting to jump out of the train.

"Come on, boy. Get control of your thoughts. Push them back. What's done is done. Now, look at them and tell me what you see."

Jalen swallowed. He scrolled and zoomed. A song came into his head. "This is America," he said to himself. A few more seconds passed. "More young than old people."

"Correct," Darsie said gleefully. "Median age is twenty-three . . . What else?"

"Well," Jalen said, "they're young, but I don't see why."

"What do you mean by that?"

"As I understand from what Wyatt told me, the first attack involved a shoe drop with a brand that marketed to urban youth, so in that attack, I understand why the victims may've been young." Jalen slid the blocks of photographs to the right along the timeline, pulling up a fresh batch of images that looked almost like they could be in a college yearbook.

"Go on . . ."

"And the car attack in Austin, it would make sense that so many young people were there, because it's a city where young, cool people go . . ."

"Hold on." Darsie Googled quickly. "Median age for residents in Austin is thirty-one point eight."

"That still doesn't make sense. The median age for the attacks is a lot younger than that, so—"

"He targeted them as they ran through the park?" Darsie asked.

"Well, not really. I was driving, so I was choosing the victims, but if I remember the point scale correctly . . ."

"What, what about the points?"

"The points got higher the younger the victim," Jalen said, his stomach and mind swirling.

"So he was guiding you, to some degree." Darsie walked across the gently rocking train car and sat down at his desk. With great focus, he began hammering on his keyboard. He stopped and sat upright, staring at his laptop. Jalen watched his mind turning like gears.

"A birthday party for a high school senior, who was killed in the attack, had been planned that afternoon . . . it was to be held in the food court. The girl's name was Jill Mahoney . . . and her dad was a state senator. There are pictures of them setting up on Facebook . . ." Darsie looked up, face flushed. "She was a gamer."

"Her name did sound familiar."

"Ever play with her?"

Jalen shook his head.

"So maybe Hi Kyto had a beef with this gamer? Maybe she was plotting to kill her."

"Maybe." Jalen wasn't convinced. "But I'm sure Hi Kyto would have been ranked above her. I mean, so far beneath her that it wouldn't matter . . ."

"An aspiring club pro versus Andre Agassi?"

"Or club pro versus my mom," Jalen said under his breath. "Just doesn't make any sense, and statistically, I'm not sure if it means anything."

"They still teach statistics?" Darsie grinned.

"I'm no great student, but I can do basic math." Jalen consulted the iPad. "Sixty-four million kids play video games. Hit a kid, and you stand a good chance of hitting a gamer."

Jalen swiped the iPad to another block of images. "But our young theory breaks down with the fire," Darsie said.

"It killed old people because they were surprised in their homes and probably couldn't escape in time . . . and can someone truly predict where a fire will go? I mean, if the wind is blowing, its path would be pretty crazy." Jalen paused, reaching the dead end of his thinking. "You mentioned the Unabomber type."

"Yes, but political activists—what we like to call homegrown terrorists—are tossed into every investigation. Not saying Encyte is not a terrorist, I just don't know if his motivations are political or radical."

"But the Unabomber, Ted Kaczynski, wasn't he associated with universities?"

"Yes, he was a mathematics professor, a prodigy in his field. He was disgruntled, but that's about all he had to do with students. I don't know . . . maybe he held a grudge against them."

"Maybe this one does."

"Maybe so," Darsie said. "But back to the original question—do we have enough evidence that points to Hi Kyto?"

"No. Not based on this alone." Jalen stared at the block of faces. Those from the fire. He looked up. His mouth opened. "I remember something."

"Yes," Darsie nudged, eyes wild.

"You said the fire was started by a pill-head, right?"

"That's right, he was on Zovis."

"Well, when Hi Kyto played with Pro_F_er, she called him something else."

"What was it?"

"Highboy."

"Highboy? That's it?"

"Yeah, that's all I know. I just thought, since this Zovis kid started the fire. Maybe it could mean something."

"It just might."

"So what now?"

"We get close. Very close. You need to be her friend. You need access to her life, her friends, and then the opportunity will present itself."

"But I haven't even met this chick."

"No, but you will."

"Huh?" Jalen looked out of what should have been a window, but instead the image of a Western landscape—arid and mountainous—raced past.

"I'm assuming that's why Wyatt brought you here," Darsie said. "We're en route to the Evolution Championship Series . . . We'll be in Las Vegas in fourteen hours."

"You mean EVO? The fighting game competition?" Jalen panicked. "Wyatt said I was going to be a part of the mission. To stop Encyte. He didn't say anything about having to play."

"Oh dear," Darsie said. "Well, now that you're in on our little secret, I don't think you have much choice . . ."

"Hope you aren't threatening a thirteen-year-old," a voice came from the other side of the train car.

Jalen turned to see Wyatt, slumped in a seat, also in a straitjacket.

"Wyatt," Darsie said pleasantly. "You're awake."

CHAPTER 34

In his years with the CIA, Tui had seen some strange things. Like the time he was spying on an Iranian cleric suspected of terrorism. The cleric left his Manhattan hotel dressed smartly, his gray *labbaadeh* buttoned to his neck, and took a car service downtown. Tui followed him, surprised to find the cleric disrobing in the back of the dark limo, but when the man got out in Greenwich Village, he was in jeans and a T-shirt. Tui tailed him through the narrow streets into what looked like a basement-level apartment, and there on a small stage was the cleric, practicing a heavily accented and rather poor routine to a crowd of aspiring comics. Stranger than fiction, Tui had thought to himself.

In Bosnia, Tui had seen war crimes of every shade, same in the Soviet Union. In his experience, this was just the way of political people—weird clung to them like their cologne and vodka, but nothing he'd seen in his service was quite as odd as what he witnessed outside of Wyatt Brewer's house.

Not even twenty-four hours after Wyatt and Jalen had been dropped off by the Washington fixer, a Mercedes pulled up outside the Virginia ranch house and the billionaire tech investor John Darsie stepped out. Tui knew that Darsie himself was rumored to have been a part of Valor, but now, dressed like a J. Crew model and with four personal guards to keep his hands clean, it was hard to imagine.

Darsie got into an argument with an obese lady brandishing a cell phone, pushing his way into her house and shattering the window in the center of the door as he shouldered his way in. Then a bookshelf came smashing through a second-story window, and the kids came out on the roof. Wyatt beat the hell outta one of them, like Peter Parker turned Spiderman, and that other kid was all right himself until Darsie pulled out something that looked like a photograph, and they both were distracted and dropped like flies. Even with binoculars, Tui couldn't see what was in the picture, but pushing his earpiece into his ear, he thought he heard a name—"Molly"—before the boys were knocked out and tossed into the back of a Suburban.

Tui knew he could have intervened, but instincts told him better. And so far, in two decades with the CIA, his instincts had never once been wrong. That was all he had to hang his hat on—his work. Hell, it was time for his ship to come in. He was getting too old for this shit. He wanted to go back to Memphis. Open himself up a little barbecue pit, spend Sundays along the riverfront, drinking beer. He'd spent twenty years being patient, and now, by god, it was time to get paid. So the spidery Tui decided to lie and wait, following the caravan right up until they boarded the damnedest-looking train he'd ever seen—all black, futuristic, much more so than something that was simply military. But before he could get a really good look at it, it was gone.

Tui slurped his Big Gulp, noting the direction of the train—due west—and though he couldn't follow it on the track, he could call in a favor. He dialed a number.

"Hey, Bobby. Need you to get me an aerial on a train coming out of Charlottesville . . . No, it's not Amtrak," Tui said as he drove west with the train, his thoughts clicking along with the track. He wanted to get in the mind of John Darsie. What on earth could he possibly want with the boys?

"Yeah, just need you to keep eyes on that train," Tui said. "I owe ya a beer, Bobby."

It was only a few moments before an idea came to him. He picked up his phone again.

"Yo," Ken said on the other end of the line, his mouth full of something. "Starting to wonder about you."

"Yeah, well, I've been busy . . . but I got something for you," Tui said.

"'Bout time."

"But I don't want you to tell anyone, not even the Old Broad, until we get a little further."

"You got it."

"At this stage, it's total theory, but I think it's this Darsie guy who's behind it."

"Billionaires don't typically kidnap kids." Ken burped.

"I know that. The kids are pawns. This Darsie guy is shifty as hell, and we're going to figure out why."

"Be my guest."

"I don't think you get it, Ken. You need to think bigger. If we bag this guy and prove he's Encyte, it'll be better than getting Osama bin Laden. I'm talking book deals, the works—and you better remember me when your time comes."

Ken finished chewing and swallowed, suddenly *very* intrigued. "You know I will, Tui. Just keep an eye on the kids for now. And be in touch."

CHAPTER 35

"You're kidding, right?" Jalen asked both of them.

"No," Darsie said bluntly. "This was supposed to be a solo gig for Wyatt, but apparently he didn't feel up for the challenge." Darsie went over to one of his chessboards and moved a piece. Instantly, a piece on the other side of the board moved by itself. "Am I right?"

"I realized it was not a one-man mission," Wyatt said. "I don't play video games, and Hi Kyto is a champion." Jalen and Darsie looked over at Wyatt as he jerked and twitched in his straitjacket like a worm on a hook. "Can you get one of your butlers to get me out of this?"

Darsie nodded and the request was granted.

"Where's my aunt?" Wyatt asked, rubbing his shoulders and neck, which were now free.

"Narcissa? She's a little agitated, but she'll be okay."

"Did you hurt her?" Wyatt asked.

"Hurt *her*? Come now. That woman can fend for herself. Actually, she put one of my men in the hospital. Snapped his rib like a twig." Darsie chuckled. "She's in a hotel in Charlottesville, probably enjoying a breakfast buffet. She'll go home once the memory-erasing agent has taken effect."

"You wiped her?"

"Just barely. Can't have her remember that little run-in with me. But there's no time to worry about your aunt."

"Look, Mr. Darsie, I'm going to tell you something. All that matters is clearing or closing the suspect—Hi Kyto. Isn't that why I'm here? Why you had me leave Valor?"

"I didn't *have* you do anything."

"Whatever," Wyatt said. "I just want to figure out whoever is behind Encyte, so you'll help me find Hallsy so I can . . ."

Darsie held up his pointer finger. "You're getting ahead of yourself."

"That was our deal!" Wyatt slammed his fist on the arm of the chair.

"Sit down, Wyatt. You will get yours when I get mine."

"I better." Wyatt glared.

"Now." Darsie turned to Jalen. "You'll be playing *Street Fighter*. The Arcade edition. Kids these days are reviving the old games. It's not Hi Kyto's favorite, but she's very good. And at EVO, champions can play against newcomers, so it's the perfect place to meet her."

"No, no, no," Jalen said.

"Wyatt, looks like you chose the wrong guy." Again a piece on the other side of Darsie's chessboard slowly slid across the squares inlaid with fine wood. "Robotic," Darsie offered, satisfying his guests' curiosity without looking up. "I'm playing a computer."

"Look, I wanted to help with your little Mission Impossible here," Wyatt said. "But we need the right tools in place." He turned to Jalen. "Come on, buddy. I know you think you're not ready, but it's one series. All you have to do is meet her, and you're in. You can never touch a controller again after that if you don't want."

"It's not just that," Jalen said. "Yeah, I'm scared . . . what if it's hacked and instead of killing Ryu, I kill an actual dude."

"That won't happen. There's no way—"

"But this is just not cool on so many levels. First of all, this girl is talented and really cute, and I can't just go up and talk to her . . ."

"What if I promise you, I'll be there. I won't be more than ten feet from you the whole time. If something is fishy about the game—which it won't be—I'll know it. And sure, she's pretty but, dude, look at you," Wyatt said. "You're ripped out of your mind and that's from doing nothing. I spent six weeks at Valor, swimming and sweating, and I couldn't achieve abs like that."

Jalen sat, thinking.

Darsie piped in. "Jalen, I should say I don't choose people to work with me because of any particular skill set. I've always found that the ability to come up with a new way forward—that no one will see coming—is supreme above all . . . I think you are worthy of doing something great, and I've been told I have pretty good instincts in scouting young talents."

"Didn't you hire a potential mass murderer? Isn't that why we're here?"

"Another smart retort." Darsie golf clapped. "Well, we could always let you boys out at the next stop."

Jalen looked over at the 4K screens, which were now depicting thunderstorms. A crisp bolt of lightning popped just as he spoke. "I'm in."

"Wonderful. So Wyatt, you'll need to be in disguise. Dress like a fan or something? These places are very strange to me. Like Grimms' fairy tales on mushrooms. Jalen, the handle I have acquired for you to play under in the championship is CV_kyd."

"Cute." Wyatt smiled.

"Thought you'd think so. It's for old times' sake."

CHAPTER 36

Vegas isn't what it used to be, Tui thought as he burped up his cheese-burger, his gold Ford Taurus lumbering down the Strip. Used to be a city run by the mob, but now, it's all nightclub promoters and celebrity chefs. The city used to have mobsters, brawls, and casinos that smelled of cheap perfume, body odor, and bad buffets. But today, it was cover charges, pool parties, and DJs. And kids. Particularly this weekend, it was flooded with video game–playing kids. *Like a bar mitzvah on steroids.*

Tui wheeled into the Mandalay Bay, and tossed his keys at the valet—who missed. The keys went sailing past.

"You know, you can leave them in the car." The valet bent over to pick them up.

"Frank Sinatra is crying in his grave," Tui said as he loosed a dollar from his billfold and handed it to the valet, who muttered, "Dick."

Entering the Mandalay Bay was like walking into a world of pure weirdos, fans dressed as ghoulish, fantastical, gruesome characters. Lots of Asians in jerseys with Red Bull logos across their backs. For the life of him, he couldn't quite figure this circus out—pro football announcers and pop concert fandom. Foam hats and rhinestone microphones. Fireworks and DJs on every corner. *There better be some free drinks.*

But a couple hours inside the casino, and Tui—though he didn't want to admit it—was starting to see what all the fuss was about. Maybe it was all the oxygen they were pumping, but the atmosphere was electric. It was life or death. The kind of competition that harkened back to man's first sparring. This was gladiator crap. The ever-present sense of suspense gripped everyone from schoolgirls to team owners who'd groomed the young athletes and wagered their cash on groups of misfits to compete in battle. Here, at a mega-gaming championship, different rules apply. Some of the biggest weenies Tui had ever seen in his life, thanks to a little hand dexterity, morphed into gods. Pot-bellied, pasty nerds wielded all-powerful digital avatars who towered above the crowd in shimmering LED.

Tui found a cozy spot to wait and keep a lookout for Jalen and Wyatt. Beside him, a zitty kid stood next to a gaming console, promoting a new release. Tui snorted in the guy's direction, thinking about how the kid looked like someone he'd wanted to beat up in high school. He let himself stare as he sipped his Coke.

"Sir," the kid said. "Like to try this? It's a single-fighter game."

Tui looked around. "You talking to me? Oh no. Please don't take my eye contact to mean I wanna buy something, kid."

"Come on. It's totally free. You know you want to."

Tui, were he in his typical mood, might have moseyed over and rammed the glasses down the kid's throat, but since he was feeling generous and he had time, he thought he'd give it a shot.

"Not bad," he said, popping on the glasses. He looked around the casino, seeing the virtual world in glowing 3D. "Lightweight."

"Yeah. High-resolution liquid crystal display and they only weigh three ounces."

Forty-five minutes later, the zitty kid was tapping him on

the shoulder. "Sir, please. Other people are waiting." He pointed over Tui's gigantic shoulder, where a line had formed.

"Yeah, one more try, okay." Tui looked up and saw a crowd gathering at the entrance. They pressed the barricades. In face paint and purple hair and wearing all manner of bizarre accessories, they hooted and chanted.

"Like a damn Gaga concert," Tui said. "Kid, what's goin' on over there?"

"Looks like the players are here."

CHAPTER 37

"Try not to look so . . . normal," Wyatt's voice came through Jalen's ear-piece as he walked underneath the arches of giant palm trees and into the casino.

"You try not to look so freaky," Jalen said, his mouth closed like a ventriloquist.

As promised, Wyatt was ten feet behind him, in a red military costume with silvery shoulder pads and a service cap. "We can thank Darsie for my outfit," Wyatt said grumpily. "I'm M. Bison, Norwegian dictator."

"Or a deranged flight attendant," Jalen joked.

"Now, we're kinda cutting it close time-wise, so you'll need to go straight to your event. Hi Kyto will be sitting beside you, shoulder to shoulder. All you need to do is look like someone who is mildly competent at this game and somehow get her to notice you. Nobody cares about anything else. She never talks to players and she really doesn't go overboard talking to fans, so just do the best you can."

"Kinda throwing a lot at me at one time," Jalen muttered, taking his items from the check-in counter and following the signs to bag check. He gave the man his backpack and took a ticket.

"Stay loose. Keep breathing. Just play."

"Loose," Jalen said, trying not to look at the purple casino carpet, the pattern nearly giving him a seizure.

"Go kick some virtual butt," Wyatt said sarcastically.

Jalen took his place at his computer and tried to appear like someone who was supposed to be there. He took out the joystick Darsie had packed for him. "Good grief," he muttered to Wyatt. "What the hell is this?"

"A controller. It'll work, right?" Wyatt said, watching Jalen get set up. "Sorry we didn't have a custom arcade stick laying around."

"It'll work, but I expected more from a billionaire. Your peripheral—your controller—is like another appendage. The stick I have at home is the best there is. This is just . . . amateur."

Just then Hi Kyto appeared beside him, standing behind her chair, loud music bleeding from her headphones. She looked over at Jalen like she was looking through him. Then she actually looked at him, right into his eyes.

Jalen suddenly felt a rush of fear thinking what if she recognized him from the video—even with the VR headset on, what if she knew it was him? Her eyes cut away.

"Oh god," Jalen muttered, somewhat breathless. "I thought she'd recognized me from Encyte's video."

"Impossible. Play it cool," Wyatt coached.

"I'm trying," Jalen whispered, trying to calm his breath and not stare. The girl was fashionable in a damaged way—dark glasses, ripped T-shirt, and thick leather jewelry. Tough and a little boyish, but cute.

"Now get ready to play," Wyatt's voice came in. "Once you switch headsets, I'll still be able to break in."

Jalen looked over and spotted Wyatt in the crowd and

nodded. "Better act like a true fan if you're gonna wear that outfit . . . you know, cheer or something."

"Woooo," Wyatt mocked.

Jalen stealthily removed the earbud and slipped on the large gaming headset. He glanced over as Hi Kyto took her seat. *Oh my god.* He could smell her lip gloss. It was strawberry or something. *That should be a violation.* She smelled so good. He tried not to stare, but up close, the girl was utterly beautiful. Perfect skin, red lips, long dark eyelashes—a body that belonged not in *Gadget,* but on the cover of *Vogue.* The baggy outfits and the surly attitude were pieces of armor to conceal a porcelain doll.

Just as Wyatt had warned him, Hi Kyto stretched her fingers and popped her neck, looking neither right nor left. "How am I supposed to engage with this?" Jalen muttered. He didn't consider himself an unfriendly person, but flirting definitely wasn't his strong suit.

"Just think about the game," Wyatt coached.

"Okay," Jalen said, closing his eyes. *Hi Kyto is playing on the left, so she'll pick first. She's comfortable with Guile, but at public events, she usually reps female, so maybe she'll go with Rose . . .*

Just then, the announcers began to fire up the lights and music. Jalen looked up at the screen where Hi Kyto was choosing her player. Scrolling, scrolling.

"Ahh, Akuma!" one of the announcers said as Hi Kyto stopped on the huge, devil-looking dude with purple pants and red hair that looked like a lion's mane. "Somewhat unexpected for Hi Kyto, but she likes to keep us on our toes," he said with the enthusiasm of a football announcer. "Get ready to see some demon flips!"

All around, the fans went wild, but Jalen kept his eyes on his own screen, moving the joystick until he settled on the one he wanted.

"Cammy!" the other announcer bellowed into his microphone. "CV_kyd also making a surprising choice."

Jalen glanced at Wyatt as his chosen character filled the screen—long braids, a leotard, muscle-y bare limbs. "Okay, dude," Wyatt said into Jalen's earpiece. "I'm all for girl power, but this match is shaping up to look like beauty versus the beast."

"What I like about Cammy—" the announcer said to the roaring crowd.

"Aside from the fact that she gets buffer every season?" the other announcer interrupted with a chuckle.

"Exactly, but aside from great movement speed, she's got good pressure with throws . . ."

"Just trust me," Jalen muttered to Wyatt, pushing past the chatter around him.

"I do, buddy," Wyatt said. "Good luck."

In the distinguished history of the EVO championship, few head-to-heads had been over so quickly. Jalen did his part, wielding Cammy with a flurry of scissor kicks and lightning bolts as Hi Kyto's lion-demon man throttled CV_kyd in front of the bloodthirsty audience. In the corner of his eye, Jalen could see Hi Kyto, one hand toggling the joystick and the other hovering, working the half dozen buttons with more precision than a concert pianist.

The first round was over in a matter of seconds, the screen flashing the letters *K.O.* as his character lay dead. For the second round, there was little improvement. Jalen got a couple of good hits in, but the truth of the matter was Hi Kyto was playing much better than she did in the YouTube videos Darsie had shown him on the train. It didn't matter what character Jalen chose, his fighting avatar, Cammy, was a sitting duck.

"Oh my god! Full-meter burn!" The first announcer laughed. "Hi Kyto is brutal!"

"I know, I know," the second announcer chimed in. "My goodness. How many times can one man's heart break?"

After the game, Hi Kyto stepped up on stage for the medal ceremony. She received the clear glass championship trophy and promptly hugged it to her chest.

"Hi Kyto, congrats on another successful tournament," a moderator said. "Anything you'd like to say?"

"Well, there were some good rounds." Hi Kyto raised up on her tiptoes to speak into the microphone. "Aside from CV_kyd, which was a total waste of time."

Ohhhhh, the crowd said in unison, swamping Jalen with a tidal wave of boos. From the side of the stage, he felt his face burning with their stares.

"All right, everyone," the announcer said as the music began blaring and the heavy TV cameras panned the stage. "Why don't we give Capcom a hand and our competitors a hand. Thank you all for a wonderful event, and we look forward to seeing you next year!" he said as the fireworks rocketed on stage and the heavy metal band took their place again.

Jalen, still reeling from his public burn, forgot for an instant his one objective and caught the girl's arm as she stepped off stage.

"What was that for?" he blurted. "You know what, you're full of it. Maybe you're a queen in this weird little world, but I know a place where girls half your size would eat you alive *in real life,* not on this silly virtual one." He motioned to the screen that took up the wall behind them, where Hi Kyto's face loomed.

She stared a moment, stunned behind her glasses. "If it's so silly," she said slowly, "then why are you here?"

"Because I thought it was fun, until I had the misfortune of playing with you." Jalen turned and stormed toward the exit, furious at the girl, at the game, at Wyatt for getting him into this mess.

"Woah, dude," Wyatt's voice popped in Jalen's headset. "Not cool. Can you slow down?"

Jalen turned around and saw Wyatt bumping through the crowd behind him, his red service cap askew, but Jalen kept walking toward the exit. "I tried. It didn't work. I need a minute."

"Jalen—" Wyatt said, but Jalen pulled the hidden earpiece from his ear and did not look back. He found the baggage check and threw the ticket at the man. "I'm sorry," he said, quickly realizing what he had done. He paid for his backpack and gave the guy an extra five bucks.

"It's okay," the guy said. "It's hard to lose."

"Yeah. No kidding."

Unsure what to do, Jalen charged out of the casino and into the bright sunshine. He tilted his face, already feeling free of the cavernous space, the pulse of the casino. He walked off the Strip, looking to get away from the action—thinking, fuming, until he found a rare park in Vegas. There was an abandoned basketball by a picnic table, and he went over and picked it up and began dribbling around the court. Beyond the tables and the hoop, he noticed a painted brick building. The brick wall was actually a colorful mural, a love offering from a couple of artistic EVO superfans. It was several minutes of free throws before Jalen realized that the backdrop of his shooting—the mural—contained the faces of several professional gamers, and there, right in the middle of them—the thick glasses, intelligent eyes looking out through the lens—was Hi Kyto herself.

He began throwing up the ball with more fervor than before. Over and over, he fired—the more he shot, the slower his breathing became; his frustration started to subside and an almost meditative calm dropped over him.

It was nearly dusk when he heard a girl's voice behind him. "Can I try?"

Startled, he dropped the ball and it bounced, then rolled to the grass at the side of the court.

He turned, surprised to find Hi Kyto herself, standing shyly in the shadow of her own giant image. Everything about her—even her voice—had softened. "I guess." Jalen shrugged.

She picked up the ball that had stopped at her feet.

Jalen watched as she walked to the white line, her eyes squinting first at the ball, then back at Jalen, then at the net. Her determined tongue resting in the corner of her mouth as she aimed and heaved the ball from her shoulders, and the ball went sailing into the chain-link fence.

It was all Jalen could do not to laugh. It was truly the worst shot he had ever seen. With the greatest amount of effort.

"Gotta try that again." She awkwardly scooped up the ball and again shot with so much force that she knocked her glasses off her face. The next time, instead of shooting from her shoulders, she shot from her chest. The ball went slightly higher, but bricked off the backboard and nearly hit her in the nose.

She picked up her glasses and turned to Jalen. "Well, how the heck do you do this?"

Jalen laughed. "Lemme show you." He picked up the ball and dribbled around her. "Okay, first thing you need is a shooting position."

Her right eyebrow arched and her nose crinkled. "Like this?" She shifted. Her feet side by side, shoulders slumped.

"Never mind, let's start with the basics. How 'bout this . . . Stand like you're going to throw a baseball."

She shot another incredulous look.

"Never played baseball, either?"

Hi Kyto shook her head. "One time I was asked to throw a pitch at a Giants game," she offered.

"How'd it go?"

"I declined."

"So you're not a sports person."

"Not the ones in the *real world,*" she said in a mocking tone.

"Yeah, sorry about that. Guess I was a little harsh."

"I asked for it." She looked up at the mural. The sunlight was almost completely gone behind the wall. "Gaming is a very male-dominated world, you know."

"I saw some girls today."

"Sure, but all of us have had to fight hard for it. Those dorks you see, they're more macho than most frat boys. If you don't have an attitude, they'll run you right over."

"What about the guys who just wanna be nice to you?"

Again Hi Kyto crinkled her nose incredulously.

"You know," Jalen said. "Someone just trying to make conversation."

"You mean flirting with me?"

Jalen could feel himself blushing. "Whatever. Don't worry about it." He shook his head. "Now, stance. Here we go. Bend your knees slightly, put your right foot forward and your left foot back." Jalen stepped toward her. "Are you right-handed?"

"Ambidextrous when I play video games and when I write—" she said.

"Okay." Jalen tucked the ball under his arm and stepped away from the goal. "Come over here. First I want to show you how to make contact with the ball."

Hi Kyto stood in front of the wall and Jalen stood behind her. "When you shoot, your right hand is going to do the work and your left hand is going to guide. You see, you were shooting from your core, but you want to have some give in your legs . . ." Jalen said, bending his knees like he was on a springboard.

"Are you, like, a sports star or something?"

"No." Jalen laughed. "But both of my parents were . . ." Jalen thought about how much he wanted to reveal. He and Wyatt had worked on a backstory for this cover that was close to his real life but without details that would reveal who he was . . . "Pretty athletic."

"Like college level?"

"Yeah. For a bit. They always wanted to make it to the pros. Still do."

"What sports?"

"Football and tennis."

"And you didn't play either of them?"

"Nah." Jalen passed the ball from hand to hand. "But I always liked basketball. Never told my dad, though. If he knew I had any interest, he'd have me in camps night and day. He'd hire a private coach and be stressing about my play all the time."

"I get it. I mean, the Chens, we are more mental athletes . . ."

Jalen raised his eyebrows.

"I just mean," she stammered, "both of my parents are genius professors . . . It's part of why I started playing games. To escape their expectations . . . the pressure . . . Okay, so show me."

Jalen smiled. She was nervous, suddenly vulnerable. "So put your right foot slightly forward." He stopped her. "Don't look at your hand. Look where you're going. Right at the net."

"Okay," Hi Kyto said, and again the concentration dropped over her face and she stuck her tongue in the corner of her mouth. She shot, and the ball arched perfectly through the net.

"*Yes!* Oh my gosh," Hi Kyto beamed. "I've never done that before. You just made me an athlete."

"You know." Jalen grinned. "You're kinda strange."

"What do you mean?"

"Well, you just won a hundred thousand dollars in the EVO championship and didn't seem half as excited as you did for one little shot."

"A hundred and fifty thousand dollars," she corrected. "Want me to buy you dinner?"

CHAPTER 38

Monty's Diner was a classic greasy spoon. The bluish wraparound lunch counter, a long, narrow railroad-car layout, the kind that used to be found in towns across America, but now the sort of place that's frequented by locals with sky-high cholesterol and Instagrammers who want cool pictures but are frustrated they can't order avocado toast.

"How'd you find this place?" Jalen asked as he followed Hi Kyto through the front door into the diner, where a puffy Ukrainian short-order cook manned a flat-top griddle. "Doesn't feel like we're in Vegas anymore." The Ukrainian watched them, slinging hash like a samurai with his long metal spatula.

"I like to operate off-grid," Hi Kyto said, sliding into the red pleather booth.

Jalen took the seat across from her, shoving his bag into the seat beside him. She huddled in her hoodie and tucked her legs up to her chest.

"So you come to Vegas much?" Jalen asked.

"Once a year at least," she said. "And my dad likes this place."

"Ready?" The Ukrainian's wife wiped the table and tucked the rag into her apron.

"Uh." Jalen scanned the menu. "I'll try the Reuben."

"Monty Burger—rare," Hi Kyto said.

"Fries?" the Ukrainian asked.

"Absolutely," said Hi Kyto.

"Me too," Jalen said.

The waitress gave a nod and a couple of grunts and left the kids alone.

"So," Hi Kyto said. "I don't even know your name, CV_kyd?" She smiled.

"Right." Jalen said. "Call me Jay."

"And now that I know your name, where are you headed?" She nodded at Jalen's dingy camp pack. "I've known people with bags like that."

"Oh yeah?" Jalen stealthily reached down into the side pocket and felt for the earpiece. He turned it on, hoping Wyatt could hear the conversation.

"Yeah. And they live out of their car."

"Well, I prefer to travel by rail." He sipped his tea. "California."

"Where in California?"

"San Francisco."

Her almond eyes narrowed.

"My plan was to follow the gaming circuit. The next event is in San Fran."

"Call it the Bay Area," she said. "Not San Fran. But the tournament is not for two weeks. Why aren't you going home first?"

"No one's really home right now," said Jalen. "And my half brother is in California. I'll be staying with him."

"Where are your parents?"

"Training. Hoping to get a shot." Jalen looked out into the darkened street beside the diner trying to recall his made-up backstory. His parents were supposedly trying to make it in their respective sports but in the European leagues. "My story isn't that interesting." He found himself not wanting to lie to her. Not that he was sure of her innocence, but it just felt . . . bad. "My parents are training in Europe. I was in boarding school. Got kicked out and sent home."

"For?"

"Bad grades. I'm just not that smart."

"Not sure I believe that."

Jalen shrugged as he looked longingly at the grill, the short-order cook seemingly taking her sweet time with his sandwich. "I couldn't spend the summer sitting around the house with my aunt in her bathrobe," he said, conjuring up the image of Wyatt's aunt Narcy with a wince. "So I decided to do this."

"Follow the professional video game circuit?" Hi Kyto teased. "You just picked it up? Most of us have been playing since before we could read."

"It's not rocket science." Jalen smiled. "And I guess you could say I've always had good reflexes, always known how to react in a simulated environment."

She squinted again. "That sounds like a line."

"Well, also, I suck. Sorta. I mean, you saw me."

"Order up." The Ukrainian woman slid Jalen's plate across the table—variations of hot beef piled on bread with crisp fries.

"Thank you." Jalen nodded at the woman. "Of course I want to win," he said to Hi Kyto, "but I actually don't like video games like I used to."

"Really?"

"Yeah, I mean, like you, I started playing to escape. I couldn't change my reality, but I could in the digital world. In the games, I had power, I had friends. But lately I've been trying other pursuits, you know, with real people—" Jalen stopped himself, realizing he was saying too much. "I just mean the thing that makes me different from other players is that this isn't my dream. I'm doing it for the adventure, for a chance to see an entirely new world . . . meet people like you."

Hi Kyto smiled but then covered it up.

"What?"

"I just think it's kinda cute. That you wanna win."

Jalen shrugged. "Sure, I have a ways to go."

"A ways to go?" Hi Kyto teased. "Haven't seen poor Cammy that beat up since *Street Fighter Turbo*."

"Yeah." Jalen laughed, for the first time making fun of himself. "She took it pretty hard today."

"So what are you going to do between now and then?"

"Well, I gotta get to California first. Then I don't know. Maybe get a job, try to earn a little money before the next one . . ."

Hi Kyto didn't say anything but stared at Jalen for a long pause, as if contemplating putting another card on the table. And then she did. "I live near San Francisco," she said.

"Cool."

"Something tells me you already knew that."

"I've seen your Wikipedia page." Jalen wiped his mouth. "If that's what you mean. But I didn't really think anything of it."

Jalen suddenly felt a rush of heat. The uncomfortable disparity of being a mere mortal around a modern celebrity, and a beautiful one at that.

"Tell you what," Hi Kyto said, cutting a corner of her burger and dipping it in ketchup. "Why don't you call me when you get there? Palo Alto, where I live, is not that far out."

"What are you doing this summer?"

"Interning at a lab on campus. Maybe we can hang out . . . and practice or something. I might even be able to help you find a job."

"Deal."

After the diner, Jalen walked Hi Kyto back to the casino, where the Chens were waiting for their daughter by their rental car in front of the hotel.

"So your parents just let you go anywhere?"

Hi Kyto held up her phone. "They have a tracking app . . . on my cell."

"Ah."

"Well, I gotta run," she said, acting suddenly awkward as they approached. "Give me a call when you get to San Francisco." She slipped a piece of paper in his hand. "Safe travels."

Jalen watched her duck into the sedan, the smile on his face quickly fading as he caught the father's stoic stare. Her mother, likewise, glared. Wyatt knew they were both upstanding figures in their community, but at the moment, the pair—particularly the mother—looked as stoic as one of the nuns back at Jalen's school.

Jalen turned and headed toward the bus station, but he wasn't more than a few blocks away when a black Mercedes pulled up to the curb.

The tinted window rolled down and there was Wyatt's face. "I've been texting you." He had taken off the driver's cap, but he was still wearing the ridiculous red costume of the beloved *Street Fighter* character.

"I've been busy." Jalen opened the door and slid into the seat next to him.

"That was masterful. You went a little off script, but you're in."

"Yeah," Jalen said. "Guess so." Jalen reached inside his backpack and unclipped the recording device. He'd agreed to be bugged, but now, after meeting Hi Kyto, it felt a little sleazy. And maybe unnecessary.

"Don't forget what's at stake here," Wyatt said. "That girl could be Encyte."

"I know."

"She can be charming, but you have to remember." Wyatt looked into Jalen's eyes. "I've known girls like her. They seem innocent enough, but she's smarter than both of us put together.

She could be four steps ahead of us right now, so you gotta stay sharp."

"Not sure I know what you mean."

"I bet you do."

The email that came to Eldon's encrypted account was not signed, but as his eyes scrolled the brief message, he knew who'd sent it.

Eldon, as promised, a little gift. For your eyes only.

Eldon stood up and locked the door to the director's office as the video loaded. He clicked the link, and there was Jalen in what looked like a packed arena. He sat in a cubicle on a stage, wearing a large headset and a sports jersey, frantically playing a video game. A girl sat next to him. Her face was still as a stone, and her eyes, behind her thick glasses, were locked on the screen as her small fingers moved with precision and speed. The crowd cheered, the camera followed them, panning the faces of nerdy teens, stopping on one: Wyatt, in a strange red costume, wearing some kind of flat cap. Wyatt held his hand to his right ear, like he was talking into an earpiece.

The screen went to black.

CHAPTER 39

Leigh Ann Davidson had always been considered a little unhinged. There had been the stint in high school when she'd been the fiery head of the Young Republicans. Then, in college at Swarthmore, her thinking jackknifed to the Left, but with no less fire. She joined the Anti-Defamation League, which led to Leigh Ann learning about anti-fascist groups who were not afraid to tangle with the alt-right.

After graduating top of her class and working as a librarian in Portland, she participated in five antifa protests, and in her third, she actually wore a hockey mask and ended up punching a Tea Party demonstrator in the jaw. It was her first taste of violence in the name of public justice, and as she swabbed her bloody knuckles over the sink that night, she had to admit: it felt damn good.

But it only got worse for those in her wake. Friends who knew her, who were not antifa, found it difficult to be around her. Any discussion that smacked of politics whatsoever would send her into a tirade. Of course those nearest to her knew how unstable she was becoming. And eventually, mania hung on her like a stench so that even her frenemies, dentists, and the cousins she saw only at Christmas joked about her being on the edge. But it wasn't until a few years later that the core of Leigh Ann's mental, emotional, and psychological makeup was blasted into bloody, shrapnel-dinged, gunpowder-singed pieces when a seventeen-year-old walked up to a school in California with an AR-15 outfitted with a bump stock and blew her half sister, and her life along with it, to bits. The mentally ill assailant, still much too young to purchase a beer, was able to buy a small stockpile of weapons and armor-fitted rounds at a series of gun shows, several of which struck Leigh Ann's eleven-year-old half sister, killing her upon impact. Twenty-seven students, three teachers—all women—would follow before the disturbed student himself would be felled by a sniper's bullet.

For Leigh Ann, her grief for her sister, Ava, moved in phases. The girl, who was Leigh Ann's father's second child—was almost like a living doll. And in her late thirties, Leigh Ann knew it was the closest she'd ever come to raising a child of her own. So it was in the stage of Decimation that she read an article in which the head of the National Firearm Association mentioned the student's right to purchase the arms that had killed Ava. And it was in the stage of Sadness that Leigh Ann began to fantasize about avenging her death. And finally in the stage of Anger, these fantasies took shape, forming themselves into the anonymous post she made on the darknet in the middle of the night: "Plan 13: What I'd Like to Do to the Children of the National Firearms Association Leadership."

In this manifesto, Leigh Ann detailed finding, hunting, and killing NFA children in front of their parents with guns bought legally, at the same gun show where the assassin bought the AR-15 that killed Ava. She posted the article on a revenge forum she found on the darknet, taking every precaution to cover her tracks, knowing from her experience with antifa how these things were traced and tracked.

A few days later, while writing another missive, this time

encouraging a protest in Washington, D.C., in her half sister's honor, her in-box pinged with a message: *RE: Plan 13—How I can help.*

She looked at the sender—a name she did not recognize, Grieving_Dad12.

Leigh Ann's first response was fear. Had her anonymity been penetrated? But after a few moments, realizing her identity was likely still secret, she typed a simple response: *How?*

CHAPTER 40

Just as the black train sped across the California border, Darsie found Jalen in the adjoining car practicing *Street Fighter.*

"May I come in?" he asked, gently tapping the threshold.

"Sure," Jalen said. "Wanna play?"

The two had taken breaks on the long train ride from Vegas, playing *Street Fighter* but also dabbling in *Call of Duty* and even *Fortnite.* Wyatt had made it clear that after his encounter with the Glowworm, he didn't want a thing to do with gaming for the rest of his life, but Darsie was a skilled, compassionate gamer. He'd even taught Jalen about a little game of his own—chess.

"No," Darsie said, flipping his wrist to look at his beaming gold watch. "Don't have time at the moment." He sat down on the berth across from Jalen.

"Well, what's up?" Jalen said, eyes still on the screen as he toggled the joystick.

"It seems that word has gotten out that you and Wyatt are heading to San Francisco."

Across the train car, Wyatt bristled, and Jalen immediately hit pause.

"I didn't say anything. I didn't tell anyone," Jalen said.

"I know. I wasn't suggesting that, but it appears someone else knows where we're headed. And, well . . . I don't think you're going to like this."

"I'm not going back to Valor," Wyatt piped in.

"Oh, there's no going back to Valor—ever—for either of you. That ship has sailed." His words dropped like a stone on Jalen's soul. In a flash, he saw the green canopy of trees, the misty lake, the warmth of the campfire.

"So what's going on?" Wyatt said. "Out with it."

"You're going to have an extra chaperone in San Francisco."

"Who?"

"Your aunt—I believe her name is Narcy."

"Narcy? What do you mean?" Wyatt panicked.

"She'll be part of your cover. It's a little more believable that you two would be in San Francisco with a mother figure watching over you."

"Oh my god, I don't like this." Jalen shook his head and looked at Wyatt, who was utterly dumbfounded.

"I'm kidding," Darsie said after a moment. "Can't you guys take a joke?"

"Didn't really know you were the joking type, Darsie." Wyatt dropped back down in literal relief.

"From time to time." Darsie clicked his teeth. "But I will say, if that ole hominid aunt of yours doesn't stop making phone calls to your brother, she might have to become part of the plan."

"God help us," Jalen whispered.

"But luckily—and thanks to the good SecDef Elaine Becker—right now being at Valor is about like being exiled on the Isle of Patmos."

Jalen raised his eyebrows.

"You know, the island—"

"I know. In the Aegean Sea." Jalen rolled his eyes and returned to his game. "I took a history class."

"Well, hope you also took geography," Darsie said. "I'm dropping you two off outside San Diego."

"And where will you be?" Wyatt asked.

"Hawthorne, California. There's a rocket factory I'm thinking about purchasing, if you must know. You two can't arrive in the state with me, so you'll take a plane to San Francisco."

"That seems . . . complicated," Jalen said.

"It makes about as much sense as riding a Jet Ski to catch a train in the middle of the woods." Wyatt smirked.

"Misdirection. Never underestimate it," Darsie quipped. "Now, Jalen, you were on your own at the tournament, but here's where Wyatt will come in."

Jalen nodded.

"If Hi Kyto is ever to see Wyatt, the story is that he is your half brother." Darsie pointed at Wyatt, who was slouched in his T-shirt and camp shorts, looking something like a grungy Patagonia ad. "Your father was a traveling athlete. He had a little dalliance with a British woman a couple of years before you were born, and here we are—your older half brother, Wyatt."

"You don't think I'm too white?" Wyatt raised his eyebrows.

"It's believable. From the image I found on Google, Ronnie Rose is fairly light skinned. And now that it's summer, you're somewhat tan . . ."

Wyatt huffed in exasperation.

"You're the one who chose to bring Jalen into this. Not me. But come to think of it, it might work out better than planned." Darsie circled Jalen, his eyes narrowing. "Jalen and Hi Kyto will have the organic bond of gaming."

Jalen shifted as Darsie took another lap around him, assessing.

"My guess is Hi Kyto will think he's handsome enough. And . . . he seems to have the kind of softness she'll find endearing."

"Softness?" Jalen bowed up.

"Yeah. Kinda reminds me of those little Asian kitty cat stickers she puts on her backpack." He laughed. "Anyway, Wyatt, keep your distance. You're here to support Jalen and keep him safe."

"Think I know how to run my own mission, thanks," Wyatt said.

"There'll be a blue Ford truck waiting for you outside of the apartment where you'll be staying. And you'll need this." He handed Wyatt an envelope, and Wyatt pulled out several hundred dollars of petty cash and a shiny plastic card.

"A driver's license?" Wyatt said. "I've been driving for years."

"Yes, but now you're official. Cops in the city are ruthless. Get pulled over and even I can't get you out of it."

It was sometime just after dusk when Darsie, ever preoccupied with secrecy, dropped the boys off outside Yuma, Arizona, where a car was waiting to take them to a ritzy hotel in downtown San Diego.

A few hours later and still in camp duds, Wyatt and Jalen wandered into the lavish lobby of a four-star hotel in the Gaslamp Quarter, a fire roaring in the ornate stone fireplace.

"'Bout time." Jalen smiled at Wyatt as they walked across the marble floor toward the elevator. "This is the kind of treatment I've been expecting from Mr. Paycard himself."

"Yeah, well, we need to try not to stand out so much." Wyatt checked the exits and doors in full mission mode. "Take a different elevator than me and go straight to the room."

"So much for the hotel party," Jalen grunted. "At least we can relax."

But even after a long, hot shower and a room-service meal of the best chicken tenders Jalen had eaten in his life, he could not relax, and he definitely couldn't sleep. He tossed and turned on the giant bed, trying every pillow, but eventually surrendered and slipped from the hotel room in the predawn hours without waking Wyatt up.

He took Fifth Avenue across the trolley tracks, past the convention center to the Embarcadero, a waterfront attraction area where giant megayachts sat docked at the pier. Wyatt strolled down the sidewalk, smelling salt water mixed with chlorine and ammonia and a hint of what he thought was feces. As the driver said on the drive from Yuma, "They need to literally wash the streets of San Diego . . . so many bums, pooing and pissing all over the place. It's not clean. The whole state of California isn't clean, if you ask me."

Still, it was comforting to Jalen. He'd been to San Diego once before—his mother had taken him along when she was still playing tennis professionally—and it was one of the few good memories he had in a sea of unhappy ones. Jalen walked along, thinking about Hi Kyto and when he would contact her and what he would say, and what if she really was a murderer. The person who'd made him a murderer and ruined his life. And if there was even this chance, then why did his stomach drop in waves at the very mention of her name?

Jalen returned to the hotel and opened the suite door a crack, the light from the hallway spilling onto Wyatt, who was still breathing heavily in the darkness. Jalen, exhausted, crawled back into bed and finally slept till morning.

CHAPTER 41

"Don't look now, but I just saw a man . . . from Valor." Jalen stared over the rim of his orange juice at Wyatt. His heart jumped in his chest, but he tried to remain calm.

"What do you mean?" Wyatt said. The two boys sat at the Starbucks outside their gate waiting to board. "Stop staring. Do you mean one of the staff?"

"No, that lady—the secretary woman with the bug eyes—this guy was with her. The big dude. Looks like some kind of islander."

"Dammit." Wyatt again sipped his coffee casually. "Lean your head down."

Jalen's Gucci sunglasses rested on top of his head, and he leaned down, letting Wyatt look in the yellowish reflection on his face to confirm his suspicion.

"Right behind you and to the left . . ." Jalen said. "He's wearing a Grizzlies hat and headphones. Looks like he's gotten himself two éclairs."

"I see him. It's Tui. How the hell did he track us here?"

Jalen closed his eyes, a wave of realization washing over him. "So this morning, before you woke up—"

"Aside from Narcy's," Wyatt continued thinking aloud. "We've been on Darsie's train, essentially untrackable from the outside."

"Listen," Jalen said. "This morning. I couldn't sleep, so I took a walk."

"A walk? Where?"

"Well, just around . . . the wharf area."

"You gotta be kidding me."

"I guess he coulda followed me."

Wyatt sighed. "There's a reason why I'm looking over my shoulder all the time. And it's not my neurotic nature. Push your glasses back up. And pull something out of your backpack to look at."

"There's nothing but clothes. And the Valor manual."

"Well, pull that out and start at chapter one, where it says don't go prancing around the city, potentially exposing yourself to rogue agents while we're on a mission."

"I'm sorry, okay? . . . So what do we do?" Jalen fumbled in his pack. "Think he knows where we're going?"

"I don't know." Wyatt checked his watch. "Let's just wait until the absolute last second to board. If he's not on our flight already, he'll know we're headed to San Francisco, but he'll have to figure out how to meet us there . . . or have someone else pick us up at the airport."

"Pick us up?"

"Yeah, pick us up—have somebody in the airport to continue following us."

Thirty minutes later, Jalen boarded the plane, as he was told: seconds before the cabin doors were closed, just ahead of Wyatt. The two ran up to their gate, apologizing to the weary flight attendant, who looked at them like dumb kids who almost missed their flight home.

"Think he split?" Jalen asked as the boys crammed their

backpacks in the overhead and shuffled to their seats next to the lavatory. Darsie had booked them on a discount local carrier, the kind that wouldn't give you a pretzel even if you were about to go into a diabetic coma.

"I didn't see him. But there could be plants on that plane," Wyatt muttered. "So don't talk mission."

Jalen nodded. "That dude's so huge, he'd have to buy two seats on this plane."

"If I had to put money on it, I'd guess the SecDef is just following up. She's got red mustache guy at Valor to enforce her rules. And Maui Jim here to follow us around, but it's better to err on the side of caution."

Once they deboarded, Wyatt looked like something from a Bond film, cutting through the crowds, looking over his shoulder, slipping down to ground transportation.

"Don't think he's on us," he said to Jalen as he pulled up the Uber app. "Even so, keep alert."

Moments later, the Uber, a slick silver Tesla Model S, quietly crept up to the curb. The doors popped open.

"Holy moly," Jalen said of the vehicle.

The young, hooded driver, in the few moments it took for Wyatt and Jalen to pile in, had loaded the address to the apartment and pulled away from the airport.

"Are all the Ubers in San Francisco like this?" Jalen asked.

"Don't know, man. This isn't my main gig. I'm in between start-ups."

"Work on anything I've heard of?" Jalen asked, then looked at Wyatt, who narrowed his eyes at him for being chatty.

"Facebook, Instagram," the driver said, "but now I'm trying to do my own thing."

"Cool," Jalen said, feeling excited and invigorated. He could smell the ocean, and in the quiet cabin of the electric car, they could hear the gulls circling overhead.

"So this is California." Jalen smiled.

"Nah," the driver said. "This is Silicon Valley. California's another state."

"Yeah." Wyatt nodded, his scowl warning Jalen to rein in the excitement. "Don't let the salt air go to your head."

The safe house that Wyatt and Jalen shared was a former Airbnb. Darsie had found the single-bedroom apartment on the website, and in order to keep total secrecy, he bought it outright. "Guess you could say"—Darsie smirked—"I booked it for life."

The apartment itself was nothing to write home about, save for the location close-ish to downtown San Francisco. It was shabby chic, with a little more emphasis on shabby. But it came with a couple of Darsie's personal men.

"The room has already been swept," Darsie's head of security said to the boys as they entered. "It's clean. And we'll have someone out here day and night."

That seemed to satisfy Wyatt somewhat, though Jalen watched him proceed to do his own assessment: lifting up lamps, going through kitchen cabinets, taking the top off anything electric, and looking in air vents.

"Think I need a nap," Jalen said, flopping on the couch. "You can take the bedroom." Even though it was afternoon, the predawn trip to the airport had made them quite tired.

"Okay. But no more walks," Wyatt said dryly, going over to check the lock on the door. Out the window, a gleaming black Mercedes was parallel parking out front. "Actually, don't think we're getting that nap."

And sure enough, approximately one minute later, Darsie came barreling through the front door. He pulled out a barstool from underneath the kitchen island and sat down, his head in his hands, veins throbbing in his temples.

"Morning," Wyatt said, pouring him a cup of coffee. "To what do we owe the pleasure?"

"There's been a development. It doesn't look good."

Jalen watched Darsie's perfectly manicured hands shaking as he lifted the mug. "At Red Trident, we monitor all the internet traffic on the network. Every site that is visited, it's all tracked. Hi Kyto, of course, knows this, so we'd never expect her to make this kind of mistake."

"What did she do?" Jalen leaned in.

"Let me ask you, have you ever heard of a Raspberry Pi?"

Both boys shook their heads.

"Well, it's a device you can use to create a VPN—virtual private network. I noticed that Hi Kyto purchased one with a private credit card midyear."

"How did you know that?"

"I just know, okay? The point is a Raspberry Pi—or a device like it—can be used to make secure tunnels and then connections. They're practically unhackable. Two weeks before the fires, security cameras in the restaurant across the street from Red Trident captured this footage of Hi Kyto's laptop." Darsie flipped on his iPad and slid it over to Wyatt. There was Hi Kyto, having an iced tea and French fries and a salad. Her computer was open. Wyatt zoomed in.

"The security camera at the restaurant takes images only every five seconds, so it's possible she visited different sites, but what we've done is analyze URLs and imagery to build the following progression. Go ahead and swipe left."

Wyatt swiped through the photographs. "First she visited the website of the drugmaker Zovoricin. She looked at the chemical makeup of the drug," Darsie said. "Next she visited sites about the chemical process of addiction."

Jalen looked on in horror: public records, medical data, scientific reports, addiction specialists—in an hour and a half, she'd visited approximately forty-five information sources, everything from how a person becomes addicted, to the chemical process, to the spiritual deterioration, and finally, the change in the brain anatomy of chronic users.

"Since she has a photographic memory, this is only a snippet of what she could have learned over the days, weeks, months," Darsie continued. "The last image is most damning."

Wyatt flipped, and there was Hi Kyto on the Tor browser, searching for recovery groups in California.

"Days later, Encyte, armed with knowledge of the crippling effects of addiction, lured Daniel Acoda to strike the match that caused the biggest wildfire in California's history. And," Darsie said, pausing, "Encyte contacted Daniel through a chat group in Tor."

Jalen waited a few minutes to respond. "This topic is pretty common . . . there are a lot of people who have these addictions. Maybe she was looking for—"

"For what? She works for *me*. She's a student. Sure, maybe taken in isolation, this means nothing, but this is a *very* strong coincidence, and I don't believe in coincidences."

Jalen blinked, not sure if it was disappointment or fear he was feeling. What if he couldn't do this? Darsie, though he'd suspected the worst, clearly didn't want to believe it, either.

"I'm sorry," Wyatt said.

"Don't be sorry," Darsie snapped. "Just get to the bottom of this. Jalen, stay on her. Get me something definitive. I just want to move on."

CHAPTER 42

It doesn't have to mean anything. **On the sofa, Jalen stared at the ceiling,** thinking of what he would say to Hi Kyto, his motivations oscillating from anxiety to rage in light of what Darsie had shown him. Sure, it didn't look good, but it wasn't enough to convince him yet, so he turned the words over in his mind until he thought he'd crafted the perfect text:

Hey, just got here. What r you doing?

"That was lame, wasn't it?" Jalen looked at Wyatt. "Maybe I should say something funny."

"Just chill." Wyatt came over from the kitchen, took the phone, and set it down. "She'll write back."

Seconds later, the cell vibrated across the coffee table. *Bzzzzzz.*

"Told you," Wyatt said as Jalen opened the text.

Was wondering what took you so long. LOL. Wanna see my internship space?

Jalen felt a smile creep across his face. Hi Kyto *actually* wanted to hang out with him. She was looking forward to it. Then he felt a flash of guilt. He wasn't just hanging out with her, he was spying on her. He texted back.

Yes! Just getting settled.

Gotcha. Meet me here in the morning. Her response included a pin drop in the heart of the downtown tech scene near the new AT&T stadium.

"We're in." Jalen looked up at Wyatt and flopped back down on the couch. "You're gonna be with me, right?"

"Yeah, bud. The whole way."

"But I thought you were in school," Jalen asked as they walked into the tech campus.

"I *am* in school." Hi Kyto flashed her badge to a security guard, who herded them through the metal detectors with a distracted wave. "Yeah, I'm a student, but it's my summer internship. Well, I work year-round," she said, leading them into the large, almost futuristic lobby. "My boss—you know, the guy who funds my fellowship at Stanford—this is his building."

Jalen followed her, looking back over his shoulder through the glass doors leading outside to a courtyard with a Japanese-inspired rock garden where the overwhelmingly young employees from the various businesses in the Red Trident building took breaks, pacing among serene stones, frantically typing on their phones, blasting music through their headphones, and grimacing in the rare San Francisco summer sun. Wyatt blended into the crowd, wearing a hoodie, sunglasses, and backpack slung over his shoulder.

"Hey, dude," Wyatt said in the earbud. "Security's pretty tight. Not going to be able to follow you in. I'll be at the café across the street. The one where Hi Kyto was in the video Darsie showed us . . . Scratch your head if you copy," Wyatt said.

Jalen smiled at Hi Kyto, trying to act normal as he rubbed the back of his head, giving the signal. "So this is the stomping grounds of the infamous Hi Kyto," he said to her.

"That's my handle, but at work, they call me Julie."

"But everyone knows, right?"

"That I'm a gamer? Sure."

"That you're one of the most famous gamers playing today."

She nodded.

"Bet it's hard. At school, being recognized everywhere you go."

"Sometimes. But truthfully, I'm not all that special. I mean, sure, I'm smart."

"Yeah—uh, 'brilliant' I believe is the word," Jalen said and saw her blush.

"Whatever." Hi Kyto rolled her eyes. "For much of my life parents and teachers have put me up on a pedestal, but at Stanford I'm far from the smartest kid on campus, often not the smartest in the room. And I like that. Let me take you upstairs."

She led him to a big elevator and they whizzed up to the seventh floor. "Like everyone else in the Bay Area," Hi Kyto continued her tour, "my boss had a company that he sold for a lot of money, which he then invested in a bunch of other companies that are now worth a *ton* of money. Anyway, I work for one of those companies."

The elevator dinged and they stepped out. Below them, the Red Trident operations center, where dozens of people milled around on the floor. To his surprise, the people fell into different age categories. Some of them, like Hi Kyto, looked like they were in their late teens, but Jalen knew in actuality they must have been in their early twenties, maintaining a sort of nerdy, late-pubescent aurora about them. Then there was the grown nerd meets prepster who moved about confidently. The final third of people in the building were old—late thirties, forties, fifties. Soft-looking adults with round bellies stuffed into too-tight jeans and hoodies. Jalen had this feeling that everyone, even the old geezers, were putting on a show, doing this imitation of entrepreneur. He was surprised to see that even among the best and brightest, a group mentality seemed to predominate.

"Hands down the best perk about working here is the food,"

Hi Kyto said, grabbing a bottle of sparkling water from a long ice chest. "Everything's catered. Hungry?" she asked.

"Yeah," Jalen said. "Starving, actually."

Jalen grabbed an omelette and sausage, and Hi Kyto opted for a pastry and a coffee. Jalen got a fresh orange juice, overwhelmed by the sheer number of choices in Red Trident's café, which was more like a three-star restaurant. On the same floor where you could order anything you wanted for breakfast, lunch, or dinner 24/7, you could also get a haircut; play pool, Ping-Pong, or cornhole; or step into one of the several gaming centers.

"Yeah, so I work a lot," Hi Kyto said.

"Where?" Wyatt looked around at the sea of high-end cubicles.

"In a lab. I'll take you by, but I can't let you in."

"Big secrets goin' on in there, huh?" Jalen smiled, trying to flirt, but also knowing he needed as much information about that lab as possible.

"Yeah. But even as much as I work, there are people here who literally never leave. See that guy." She nodded to a man in a silver jumpsuit. "They call him the desk troll."

"Why troll?"

"Because he sleeps under his desk."

"Seriously?"

"No one knows why he does it because we have sleeping quarters, if you ever want to crash here."

"Cool," Jalen said.

"Dude, see if she wants to go somewhere," Wyatt broke into Jalen's earbud. "You've seen her world, now get her out of it."

Jalen cleared his throat. "Uh . . ."

"You want Hi Kyto out of her environment, her normal routine," Wyatt coached. "Let her experience something real and then she might confide in you."

"Wanna get out of here?" Jalen said to Hi Kyto.

"What do you mean?"

"Leave. Go find something to do. Doesn't all the Wi-Fi around here start to feel like it's burning your brain? Let's take a hike or something."

"A hike?" she said. "Like walk in the woods?"

"Yeah, like over the Golden Gate Bridge. I hear there's a park."

"That could be fun, but I want you to meet someone first," she said. "Remember I was saying that I'm not that brilliant?"

"Yeah, I do. And you're not a good liar."

Hi Kyto laughed. "Whatever. Well, I want you to meet someone who's truly brilliant. He's actually a student at Stanford—but a graduate student—not undergrad like me," Hi Kyto said, leading them to the elevators.

They went down to the fourth floor and through another security checkpoint into a less secure area. "So wait, what's that all about?"

"Remember I told you my boss owns the building?"

Jalen nodded.

"Well, I work for his security company, Red Trident. He has several other businesses housed here, but some of them have less stringent security requirements. It's kinda the deal with this one."

"Okay," Jalen said, following her down a long hall. They walked past a room that instantly took Jalen back to a more comfortable place. The air was damper, smellier. The clean, almost sterile decor of the Red Trident facility fell away and was replaced with tattered posters that smacked of public school as they entered a start-up called Ocean Guardian.

Although the medium varied, plastered on the walls and everywhere around them was one specific theme—the ocean—in watercolors and vintage postcards, even indoor graffiti. The employees, who looked decidedly more like surfers than the tech goons on the seventh floor, all smiled at Hi Kyto as she walked inside.

"In my opinion," Hi Kyto whispered, "this is the coolest start-up in the building." The guys and girls in the space all stood at drafting tables, working on designs. At the back of the room, up on a platform, was the head table, which was occupied by a tall, handsome man who looked somewhere between nineteen and twenty-four. His long, dark hair framed the sides of his face as he studied a drawing.

"That's the brilliant guy you wanted me to meet?" Jalen asked, not bothering to mask the annoyance in his tone.

But Hi Kyto hadn't heard the question, striding over to the good-looking guy on the elevated desk. "Morgan, this is Jalen. He's a gamer friend of mine." She smiled at Jalen. "Morg's going to save the world."

"Morgan Whittendale." The guy reached his hand out to shake Jalen's. "And I don't know about the whole world, but we're gonna start with the oceans."

"Morg," Hi Kyto said. "You've got to tell Jalen about Ocean Guardian."

"Love to." He flashed his polished white teeth. "First, I've just got to finish this sketch and send it to manufacturing in Singapore. Just give me five minutes . . . Grab a tea and I'll join you guys by the beanbags."

Within Ocean Guardian, Wyatt had noticed a sitting area where a cluster of people looked like they were squatting on the ground. Upon closer look, he realized it was a beanbag-themed lobby.

"In fact, I'll take a pu'er myself," Morg said. "If you don't mind letting it steep for me."

Hi Kyto poured two teas, one for herself and one for Morg. She extended the pot to Wyatt, who politely shook his head.

"Shoot," Morgan said, scrolling on his Apple Watch. "Gotta deal with something. Be right back." He jogged off to the other side of the room.

Jalen, having already worked up an appetite from his stroll

around Darsie-ville, was also starving. He scarfed down a gluten-free cookie and pounded a Red Bull, and they both fell back into the beanbag chairs, waiting a good forty-five minutes until Morg returned.

"Sooooo sorry, guys . . ." Morg said as he strode over and sat down. "We're trying to launch Phase Two of our project. I'm just completely behind." He'd fastened his hair back into a pony-tail, allowing part of his bangs to fall, hugging his perfectly symmetrical face.

He lifted the tea to his lips and frowned. He signaled his assistant. "This is cold. Can I have a new one? Well," Morg said, turning to Jalen. "So this all got started when I was fifteen. At the time, I was studying neuroscience and wanting to follow my hero, Robert Sapolsky, into the field of primatology. Well, I was surfing one day and I saw a dead sea turtle. An adult leatherback—a gorgeous, highly endangered creature. It had ingested a plastic bag, likely mistaking it for a jellyfish. For no reason but someone's laziness, it died a painful death . . . left to float and rot on the surf. It was awful, and I decided then that I had to do something to make a change in this world, and I would start with the oceans."

Jalen looked over at Hi Kyto, seeing in her face what was clearly admiration.

"I'm sure you're aware of the miles and miles of the plastic in our oceans today." His spiel began like the introduction of a nature documentary. "Well, the first stage is to clean that up. So we're launching the world's largest recycling project."

"Tell him about the fleet," Hi Kyto said.

"Yeah, so we have a fleet of boats armed with nets. And on the back of our boats are mini solar-powered recycling facilities . . . So basically, we compact trash with solar-powered compactors, making it into a string of blocks that we can pull behind our oceanographic vessels. We call it the Tail of Life."

Morgan paused to accept a fresh cup of tea from an enthusiastic young assistant. "So when the Tail of Life gets beyond ten miles long—instead of burning fossil fuels to tow it back—we set in motion a sea anchor and we combine all the Tails together in what we call an Ocean Harvest. With multiple tails connected front to back, we make what's effectively a giant raft of plastic. We then use water brakes and inflatable sail technology to let the prevailing westerly winds blow this giant flotilla, once assembled, back to a major city in the United States—Portland, Seattle."

"So, Morg," Jalen said, putting an almost sarcastic emphasis on the nickname. "What if it doesn't go?"

"Well, if need be," Morgan's friendly surfer tone teetered on irritation, "we can pull it back into the harbor. But I'm not inclined to do that, because I'd like to see it work with zero carbon footprint." He thought a minute. "Actually, it's not really zero because of the plastics we're taking out of the ocean . . . there's a massive negative carbon footprint."

"Okay," Wyatt broke into Jalen's earpiece again. "Enough of Mr. Blue Planet. Lose this guy and get her out of there."

Thankfully, Jalen noticed that the enthusiasm in Hi Kyto's eyes had glazed over a bit, so after another fifteen minutes of lectures from the young environmentalist with his fresh pu'er and his beanbag bully pulpit, Jalen stood. "This has been cool, but I'm gonna . . ."

"Wait," Hi Kyto said. "You know what Jalen was just saying?"

"Tell me." Morg leaned in, everything about him exaggerated.

"Do we ever do anything different? Do we ever break the mold and get out of our usual day?"

Morgan looked around him. "Our usual days are pretty remarkable." He nodded at the skyline view from the wall of glass.

Hi Kyto shrugged. "Work is still work. And the remarkable becomes . . . unremarkable after a while. What do we do that isn't studying, that's different or fun?"

"I've got an idea." Morgan grinned. "Something very different . . . give you a hint: it involves one of the most amazing fish in our ocean and buckets of blood. Who's up for an afternoon on the water?"

CHAPTER 43

Morgan kept his boat, a Bahama 41, at Pier 39. It actually belonged to the start-up, and thanks to the deep pockets of their benefactor, John Darsie, Ocean Guardian had what amounted to a fleet of boats, from giant workboats to fast, fishing-style center-console go-boats. Morgan preferred the latter variety. When he got to the marina, he picked up sandwiches from a restaurant, some drinks, and snacks. "All aboard!" he said cheerily to the group.

"Wait. I don't think you should go alone," Wyatt's voice came in through Jalen's radio. "See if you can bring me. Make something up."

Jalen stood on the dock, hesitating. "Hey, Morg . . . so my brother's in town. He loves boats. Maybe he should come with us?"

Morg laughed. "Well, unless he's hiding behind those crab traps over there, he's not gonna make it in time." He began untying the boat from the dock. "But it's cool if you don't want to come. The water's not for everyone." He gave Jalen a look and tossed a line into the stern.

"Come on!" Hi Kyto called from the bow, sunglasses on, waiting. "We'll meet your brother later. Promise."

"Jalen, don't do it." Wyatt snapped in the radio. "I don't

want you with her alone. Remember this girl has probably murdered scores of people. Don't risk it."

Jalen looked down at Hi Kyto, now slathering herself with sunscreen. He had to decide quickly. In a rapid motion, he removed his earpiece, put it in his pocket, pulled out his phone, and turned it off. "Let's go."

"Great," Morgan said, pulling two buckets of pigs' blood from his onboard refrigerator. "I have a friend who has an organic farm . . . the pigs who gave their blood for this were killed as humanely as possible."

"A merciful slaughter?" Hi Kyto asked.

"Well, yes. It's brought into a pen . . . the farmer, who the pig has come to know and trust, puts his arm over his forward shoulder." At this, Morg reached out and put his own hand on Hi Kyto's shoulder. "Then he draws a 9mm from his waistband, putting it behind the pig's ear, so the pig can't see it, and then . . ." Morg lifted his hand pointed like a gun, and raised it up behind Hi Kyto's ear. "Bam!"

She jumped. "You jerk!" She slapped his shoulder.

"So the pig doesn't know anything. They string the pig up and slit its throat so the blood fills buckets. Totally humane . . . Anyway . . ."

Morgan secured the buckets and started the engine of his boat, the *Kid Captain,* and continued his chatter as they eased out of the slip. "She's nine hundred thousand dollars new."

"Sounds like Darsie," Hi Kyto piped in. "Gotta have the best boat on the water."

Morg eased away from the dock. "This little number," he said, pointing to a joystick, "is a Helm Master, a control system that allows for simultaneous operation of both the engines and bow and stern thrusters. Basically, it's like training wheels. Makes it possible for inexperienced drivers to maneuver in tight quarters. You could probably even do it, Jay."

Jalen held up a hand. "No, thanks."

"Yes, sir, she's a pretty sweet little thing," Morg continued. "Got a center console, a fishing tower. We've got another seven boats in Stockton and twelve in Seattle, but those are mostly arctic fishing vessels, converted. I like the small boats, though. They're faster. More fun."

"Small?" Jalen looked around the yacht; from its bow to sleek stern, it stretched forty-one feet. He wondered if he'd ever been around someone so smug, even in his parents' supper club of ex–professional athletes.

"Don't see any fishing rods on board," Jalen said, looking around.

"No, man. We're not going to catch anything."

"Then why the four gallons of chum?"

Morg didn't answer. Instead he smiled and bumped it into gear, churning up a wake as they passed the yellow NO WAKE signs.

Morg at the helm, the *Kid Captain* cruised out into the San Francisco harbor; Jalen looked back at the marina and saw Wyatt back among the floating docks and yachts watching them slip away, powerless to help if something went wrong out on the high seas.

Morg throttled down, the triple Yamaha 425s effortlessly bringing the stepped hull to plane. Skipping along the blue-gray water, they cut a white, knifelike line under the Golden Gate Bridge. Jalen felt a chill as the morning fog whirred across his back and neck. Hi Kyto pulled up her hoodie and tucked her hands into her sleeves.

"Don't worry," Morg yelled over the thrumming motor. "It'll warm up once we get out into the water."

"Where are we going?" Jalen called out.

"Farallones," Morg called back.

Jalen nodded, though the name meant nothing to him.

The boat steamed out into the Gulf of the Farallones, leaving San Francisco behind, disappearing behind a fogbank. Feeling like he was slipping off the edge of the life he knew, and recalling some of his Valor training, Jalen kept track of the *Kid Captain*'s heading, nearly due west, driving for about an hour, talking little until the targeted series of islands rose out of the water like skeletal remains, a hunk of lower jawbone dotted with jagged, crumbing teeth.

"It's a natural preserve." Morg cut the motor and let the boat drift toward the islands. "This is my place. The one piece of this godforsaken planet where I can come and reset. We can't actually step foot on the islands, but to me—that's why it's perfect. Untainted. By the way, if we see any park rangers, I know most of them. They're cool with me."

"Kinda creepy," Hi Kyto said as they drifted into the cool shadows. Above them, gnarly protrusions of rock covered in seal and seagull shit.

"Yeah, American Indians who lived in the Bay Area used to call them the Islands of the Dead."

"That's not eerie at all." Hi Kyto smiled at Jalen.

"There's only one house on the island and scientists live in it," Morg said, checking the wind and tide. "It's pretty cool. I stayed there once. For a birthday party."

"Of course you did," Jalen muttered, pulling off his sweatshirt. It had gotten warmer, so hot in fact that he wanted to take off his shirt, but left it on.

"Now for the main event." Morg reached in the minifridge and retrieved the buckets. "The Farallon Islands—in fact, all of this area—is a habitat for great white sharks. They come out here to feed on the seals. Here, Julie," Morgan said, surrendering the leather captain's chair, "put the boat in gear and loop around the islands. Jalen and I will leak the chum. A great white can smell this blood from forty miles away, maybe more. Hopefully we'll see some surface." He pried the top off the first bucket.

Jalen drew back, wincing at one of the foulest smells he'd encountered in all his life.

"Yeah, that's what they like. Yum, yum, it's lunchtime." Morg leaned over, pouring the liquid into the cerulean waters.

Jalen did the same with his bucket, suppressing his nausea as a bit splashed on his cheek. "Organic, huh?" He snorted, the smell completely enveloping them.

"Every bit of it." Morg laughed.

They laid down about a thousand yards of chum, the blood and oil leaving a slick trail on the surface as they idled back through it.

Jalen thought of Mackenzie and how much he would have rather been on Lake Tecmaga in the *Sea Goat* than with Morg in these creepy islands, drifting through blood.

"What now?" Hi Kyto asked, her voice slightly echoed.

"We wait. Maybe eat something ourselves." Morgan retrieved his sandwich from the same refrigerator and offered her half.

"Kinda lost my appetite," she said.

"Too bad. It's just a little blood." Morg took a bite of his combo. "So Jay, you look really familiar. Are you a professional gamer as well?"

"Nah, man," Jalen said. "Just play for fun."

"That's funny, 'cause I *really* feel like I've seen you before."

"I don't think so," Jalen said, feeling a little annoyed.

Just then, a small splash on the port side. "Ah, looky, looky," Morg said. "Think we're getting lucky."

Hi Kyto laughed, almost delighted, as she crossed the bow. They all leaned over and saw a ripple along the water, followed by a gray fin breaching the surface.

"Woah, that a great white?" she asked. Jalen noticed her eyes, glistening with excitement, like they did in Red Trident.

"Nah, mako." Morg slumped down and returned to his sandwich. "They wouldn't even be here if there was a great white in the neighborhood."

And indeed, in the next half an hour, the shark activity

slowed down. Morg finished his sandwich and talked about what he called "the cause and effect."

"The shark reacts to the chemical," Morg said. "Like a dog and a dog whistle. It doesn't know why, but it simply comes. It's programmed to investigate. Chemicals. They are what link us to the beasts. Pheromones are in the blood. They trigger the shark's instincts to come sniffing around. What do you think makes a male human react more favorably to a girl? Or lets a girl instinctively know when a male is scared or aggressive?"

"He's ripping off Sapolsky, the biologist." Hi Kyto smiled, chiming in. "We're all slaves to chemicals, but it doesn't all add up."

"What do you mean?"

"Why would they react to pigs' blood? I mean, evolutionarily speaking, how many pigs are falling in the water?"

"Well, if I could get seal blood, I would. It would be more effective. Wanna go club some seals?" Morgan laughed. "I'm kidding." He reached down into a compartment under the helm and retrieved three masks with snorkels. "Who's hot?"

Hi Kyto again flashed a nervous smile. "Nooo."

"You really wanna get in?" Jalen said to Morgan, wiping the sweat from his forehead.

"What about the blood?" Hi Kyto looked down at the buckets.

"Ah, it's dissipated."

"And the sharks?" she asked.

"That's exactly why I want to get in." He winked at Jalen. "Don't you want to look back on your life, when you're fifty or sixty years old, and say, 'I swam with sharks'?"

"Think I'd like to at least make it to fifty or sixty," Hi Kyto said. "This seems like a good way to ensure an early death."

"Come on. We'll stay by the boat. If we see any activity, we'll just get out. Look, the ladder's right here." He flipped a fold-up metal ladder off the back. "Ladies first." Morg smiled at Hi Kyto.

Hi Kyto groaned. "Good thing I wore a sports bra." She rolled her eyes and snatched up a mask. She peeled off her top. "You coming, Jay?"

Jalen nodded. Her lean shoulders, the smooth dip at the small of her back. He turned his head, trying not to stare.

"You scared?" she teased.

"Scared of cold water?" He looked at her for a second, and then dove in, the temperature taking his breath the instant he hit the surface.

"Go, Jay!" she cheered. "Is it cold?"

"That would be an understatement."

"Hey, you may want this," Morg said, holding up a pneumatic speargun.

"Don't think that's going to do much to a great white," Jalen called back.

"Great whites aren't the only thing to worry about in the waters," Morg said. "But how 'bout this?" Again he ducked down into the boat and popped back up, this time holding out a sawed-off shotgun. "It's from the boat's tender. If ever traveling off the coast of Mexico or Africa, it's possible to run into—it's funny to say, but—marauders . . . you know, pirates."

"You always have weapons aboard?" Hi Kyto asked, taking the weapon from his hands.

"Absolutely . . . There are more in the hold. Be careful. It's loaded with slugs. Could punch a hole in a boat, or a human." Morg took the gun and put it back where he found it.

Still treading water, Jalen secured the mask to his face and dipped his head under. Immediately, Jalen saw something moving through the kelp directly underneath him. He felt a flash of panic, but then realized it looked more like a puppy with flippers.

"Look, seals!" He could hear Morgan yelling above the surface. Underneath them, down in the cold, blue water, dozens of seals.

Jalen turned back to the boat and saw a splash. A whirl of white bubbles. Two thin, pale legs gracefully breaststroked toward him. He purged his snorkel of water, took a deep breath, and dove down again. He could feel the cold constricting his muscles, shaking his whole body. During the wrong time of year, there was a real threat of hypothermia, but since it was summer, he knew the water, even if uncomfortable, was probably warm enough to stay in for a half hour.

Jalen surfaced and pushed his mask up on his head.

"Oh my god, oh my god," Hi Kyto said, treading water several feet from him. "It's cold. So damn cold."

Jalen dove down again, panning around until again he saw something, this time it was pale—the color of moonlight—and lumbering in a circle. He could still see the makos circling in the distance. But this was no mako. It was giant—thirteen feet, if he had to guess, longer than a Mini car.

The black eye caught sight of Jalen, and the creature's course shifted.

Jalen kicked slowly, trying not to make any sudden movements as he scanned the water. *Where is she?* Without taking his eyes off the shark, he swam steadily toward the surface. He'd almost made it when there was another splash, spooking the shark, and it dove back down. More bubbles swirled as Morg kicked toward him. Jalen surfaced and saw Hi Kyto lackadaisically backstroking toward the *Kid Captain*.

"I'm freezing." She climbed the ladder and shook the water from herself like a cat.

Jalen dipped his head back down and moved quickly, looking around for the shark again. He felt something on his shoulder—a hand—and he spun around to find Morg, also below the surface, his hands upturned in a what-do-you-see gesture.

Jalen shook his head. Nothing. The beast was gone.

CHAPTER 44

On the noisy voyage back, Jalen said nothing of what he'd witnessed, and again the trio fell quiet, entranced by the boat as it skipped along the surface.

"Can't believe it," Morg said. "Took the whole morning off and got skunked. What did we do wrong . . ." He trailed off, then answered his own question. "We didn't do anything wrong, that's nature. Sometimes it just doesn't work. Plus, man has villainized this creature and almost hunted it into extinction. I'll bring you guys back . . . it's better in the fall."

"I had a nice day anyway," Hi Kyto called out cheerfully, the wind drying her long black hair that she'd clasped at her neck.

As soon as they were within ten miles of shore, Morgan fastened his Apple Watch to his wrist and began furiously tapping on it again. "So sorry, Julie . . ."

Jalen, for the life of him, could not get used to him calling her that. She was Hi Kyto. She created Hi Kyto. Julie didn't fit. It was the name a parent gave a child so she could fit in in the United States. Julie was not a choice. Hi Kyto was who she wanted to be.

"I was hoping to spend the whole day with you guys, but I

got a film crew coming in from the Netherlands to talk. So I gotta take them out, give them a presentation . . ." Morgan finished his tapping.

"That's okay." Hi Kyto looked at Jalen and smiled coyly. "We can figure out something to do for the rest of the day."

"Hopefully, I can make it up to you tomorrow. Maybe we can hang out after work?"

"Well, Jay and I had planned to practice."

Morgan shot Jalen a funny look. "Oh right, the tournament. You guys are playing. You don't strike me as the gamer type, Jay. You seem too . . . built." Morg laughed.

"Genetics," Jalen offered, feeling his pulse slightly rise. He had put on some muscle weight in his short time at Valor. A few weeks of sunshine and hill runs, and his body had become what it was meant to be. "You a gamer, Morg?"

"Used to be," Morg said, steering toward the shore that was now visible.

"Whatever," Hi Kyto chimed in. "He was playing up until just a few weeks ago."

"Don't have time for that now. Gotta play games that matter in real life, ya know. You guys are lucky . . . still young."

"Aren't you like, eighteen?" Jalen asked. "How old are you?"

"Nineteen and a half. Just enjoy this time," Morg said, ignoring Jalen's question, "before responsibilities start to weigh you down."

"Hi Kyto—I mean Julie—has got a pretty important job," Jalen said. "Homeland security's not responsibility enough for you?"

"My god. Yes, Red Trident, for sure. Julie's phenomenal. But, it's just . . . different." He sighed. "So, where do you guys want me to drop you off?"

"How 'bout the Presidio Yacht Club?" Hi Kyto said, then turned to Jalen. "Wanna show you something."

"Okay," Morg said, a lilt of surprise in his tone. "You got it."

* * *

"I know it's nice now, but the weather might change and you're a long way away." Morg eased into the marina at the Presidio Yacht Club, which was on the opposite side of the Golden Gate Bridge from downtown San Francisco. "You sure, guys? I mean, at rush hour, it'll be a nightmare getting home."

"We're sure," said Jalen, who couldn't wait to be rid of the *Kid Captain*.

After Morg had said goodbye and pulled away, Hi Kyto led Jalen down to the clubhouse. "What are we doing here?" Jalen asked, looking down at his T-shirt, unsure if it was tainted with pigs' blood. "I'm not sure if I'm dressed for the yacht club."

"Yacht club is a misnomer. It's a little restaurant. And I needed to get off that boat."

"Wanna get a table?" Jalen asked as servers bustled by.

"Sure," Hi Kyto said, almost shyly. This felt strange, like a date. And he'd never really been on a proper date. I mean, there was prom and all at St. Mary's, but a date for no reason. He'd never had the courage for that.

They took a seat, the cold air-conditioning worsening their chills in their wet clothes.

"So, Morg," Jalen said, tracing the sweat beads on his water glass. "He's a real good friend of yours, huh?"

"Yeah, he is . . . and he can be a nice enough guy. Sometimes I admire him and think he's so amazing, but when he gets on his high horse it can get a little . . . annoying."

"You said it, I didn't."

Hi Kyto laughed. "I know what you're thinking."

"What's that?"

"You're thinking why would I hang out with a guy like that?"

Jalen took a sip of his water.

"I'm right, aren't I? The truth is, I'm also kind of an asshole myself. And beyond that—"

The maître d' came to the table and dropped a basket of bread. "Are you good with that menu?" the man asked Hi Kyto. "We also have a kid's—"

She jerked the tall menu off the table and scowled.

"Sorry," the maître d' said. "I'll just go . . ."

"Yeah, go do that." Hi Kyto shook her head as he scurried away. "It's like the two things I'm sick of—one: when people think I'm ten, because I'm Asian."

"How old *are* you?"

"Fifteen . . . almost. Next Saturday."

"Big plans?"

"Yeah, think I'll use my EVO money to throw a party." Hi Kyto looked out across the water, eyes twinkling. "Maybe I'll rent a party boat . . . Would you come?"

"Depends if you're going chumming for sharks . . ." Jalen smiled. "What's the second thing you hate?"

"When people think I'm a guy, because I'm an Asian girl."

Jalen cleared his throat. "Don't think anyone's mistaking you for a dude."

"Trust me. I put on a baseball cap and you'd guess I was in a Korean boy band." She laughed. "But the thing with me and Morg . . . we have a special relationship. He actually used to be a helluva gamer and he's smart. I think I like smart people."

For the first time in a long while, Jalen started to feel suddenly, inexplicably out of his depth. This notion of smart people. Of course he knew he wasn't dumb. In fact, he'd always scored well when he even slightly applied himself. But he wasn't a child prodigy. He didn't have a photographic memory, and he couldn't build a freakin' Venice-like floating recycling system to save the ocean. But he was a tough kid. He'd learned how to survive by himself. He learned at Valor that above all, he was resilient. But being around Hi Kyto—who was, by all measures, a genius, and who was feeling insecure herself around a genius—made him feel almost like a Neanderthal.

"I've lost you, haven't I?" she said, twisting her long hair into a knot.

"What?"

"That look on your face. You just went off somewhere."

"Guess I'm wondering," Jalen said. "I'm not like your other friends, I'm not brilliant or saving the planet. So I'm just wondering what happens when you figure that out. Will you still want to hang out with me?"

The words had come out of Jalen's mouth surprisingly without thought. Here he was, trying to find out if she was a murderer, a terrorist, and he felt insecure, shy, asking why she liked him.

"I like you," she said. "Because you're kind and safe. I mean, there are all these macho guys in San Francisco, all these 'bros' trying to outsmart each other. All these Type As. And you're normal . . . sweet."

Jalen didn't know whether to laugh or be truly offended. Here she was, calling a bunch of computer nerds Alphas, while *he* was her sensitive buddy. *Soft,* Darsie had said.

"Yeah," he said, biting his tongue for the hundredth time that day. "Guess I'm just not like them."

"And that's okay." She reached out and put her hand on his. "You know what I also see in you?"

"What's that?" Jalen said, trying not to be distracted by the warmth of her hand.

The maître d' again approached the table, and she slid her arms to her lap.

"Ready to order?"

"Yeah," Julie said dryly. "Kid's chicken fingers."

"And for you, sir?"

Jalen nodded at his glass. "Good with water."

"It's okay," Hi Kyto said to Jalen. "I'll pay."

"Don't worry about that. I'm not hungry."

"But you didn't eat on the boat."

Jalen looked out over the water. The boats coming and going. He should be hungry. "I'll have what she's having."

"Another kid's chicken fingers," the maître d' repeated the order, not bothering to hide his irritation.

"With fries and a cherry Coke. Jay, you?"

"The same."

"Guess you won't be needing these after all." The maître d' snapped up the adult menus.

"Actually, make those Shirley Temples," she called out. "What was I saying?" she asked Jalen.

"Well," Jalen said. "You were psychoanalyzing me. I'm not really sure what was coming next."

"Oh, sensitive," she said, smiling. "But for real, what I was saying is that as sensitive as you are, there's also something dark." She looked into Jalen's eyes. "Something happened to you."

Jalen suddenly found himself pushing back from the table. "What if we get those chicken fingers to go? I feel like moving."

"Okayyy. Where to?"

"I saw a bike rental stand. Why don't we get a little exercise?" Jalen signaled for the check.

Hi Kyto went to the bathroom and again Jalen pulled out his phone, which was still turned off. He thought for a moment. He knew he should check in with Wyatt. But he slipped it back into his pocket, still off.

With doggie bags dangling from the handlebars and sweatshirts wrapped around their waists, Jalen and Hi Kyto jumped on mountain bikes and rode up into the Marin Headlands. It was a steep series of cliffs and hills that looked west, out into the Pacific. The trails were great for mountain bike riding, especially for Hi Kyto, who was clearly new to the sport, and the rides, while challenging, were not too much of a strain. Not that Jalen was all that experienced, but unlike Hi Kyto, he'd at least grown up riding a bike around his neighborhood. They rode, talked a little, ate their lunch on a park bench, found a trash can, and were riding some more, up and down the hills and along the cliffs, when, as often happens in Northern California in the summer, the fog came rolling in like an offshore cloud and completely enveloped them. The air, which had been bright and clear, now swirled with moisture, beading on their skin. Like they were in a steam shower in a cold steam room. The sky grew dark, and they could hear thunder in the distance.

"I can't see." Hi Kyto stopped pedaling. "I'm not sure about this."

Jalen heard something for the first time in her soft voice: fear.

"It's okay," he said calmly. "Let's just get out of the way, in case someone else comes riding through."

He helped her take her bike off the path, and they sat on some rocks.

"I'm cold," she said. "Could you scoot closer?"

She pulled her hoodie up, and Jalen slipped his arm around her, feeling her breath on his cheek. She took his other arm and wrapped it across her, pulling herself into a hug, using his body as a barrier.

What am I doing? Jalen's whole chest felt flushed and heavy, as though he were under the influence of a drug. *This girl might be a mass murderer.* Probably she killed scores of people, Wyatt had told him. He sat there in intense silence and intense closeness. He thought about the theory of relativity and how a few minutes in a park next to a girl could feel like an eternity. He was stuck in a time warp, somehow endless, yet instant.

But then, as Morg predicted, the weather suddenly changed. The sky opened up and a light shone down. The fog lifted, and he almost felt angry when again they were under a clear, blue sky.

"Guess we can go now," she said, turning to him, her nose almost brushing his lips.

"Yeah," was all he could manage before she slipped from his arms.

"Think this is the way to get out," she called out, rolling her bike toward the path. She mounted and took off down the mountain, with Jalen following all the way to the bottom, where they came out, somewhere near Sausalito.

"Ready to go back?" she asked. "It's not that I haven't had fun. I just need to get home. Can't believe I've been gone the entire day." She looked down at her phone, distracted.

Jalen was still trying to process his own thoughts. He didn't want to go back. Not at all. "Yeah, me too," he said.

They rode back to the yacht club, returned the bikes, and took a water taxi to downtown San Francisco. On the ride over, Hi Kyto seemed to be lost in her phone, texting someone rapidly in Chinese, her smooth brow growing increasingly furrowed.

Jalen also pulled out his phone. He turned it on, but did not put in his earpiece. He was gonna get an earful from Wyatt, but that could wait.

"What's wrong?" Jalen asked her once they got in line to deboard the ferry.

"My parents . . . they're just so nosy, always wanting to know where I am . . ."

"Yeah," Jalen said, switching his own phone to silent. "I get it."

"I mean, they're following my location, asking what I'm doing away from my internship, spending the day with you."

"They know who I am?"

"They remember you from Vegas," she said. "But let's just say they don't refer to you as Jay."

"What do they call me?"

She smirked. "*Wàiguó rén*. It's Chinese. It's like the Japanese word—*gaijin*."

"Which means . . . handsome?"

"Foreigner." She flashed a quick smile and went back to her phone. "Someone must have told them I was with you."

"Morgan?"

She shrugged. "Maybe."

"So your parents don't like the idea of me, huh?" Wondering if it was because he was African American or just American. "I understand the cultural difference, but I'm not a bad guy."

"It's not a matter of good or bad," she said. "There's a Douglas Coupland book. Do you know him?"

"No idea."

"I'm such a nerd." Hi Kyto laughed. "He wrote a book called *All Families Are Psychotic*. And it's true. They are."

Jalen's own family flashed through his head: his mother, Ronnie, the years of au pairs who'd practically raised him. Yes, he could relate. "But your family seems pretty . . . I mean, your parents are professors and diplomats. They're respectable."

She laughed. "Respect has nothing to do with it. I've got secrets, too." Her eyes piercing him, and in them, a flicker of anger. "Everyone does, and if I've learned anything at Red Trident, anything from John Darsie, it's that everything's a conspiracy. And I don't want to live in a world like that."

"He sees people as pawns in his master chess game." Jalen changed his voice to mimic how he'd heard Darsie say it: "And the pieces don't need to know what the master is thinking."

"Oh my gosh." Hi Kyto laughed. "That's *exactly* what he says . . . how did you know that?"

"Uhhh, I've seen him on TV and in the news," Jalen lied, realizing his slip. "Who hasn't?"

"Well, anyway, my parents . . . they don't like the idea of anyone who isn't Chinese, female, and has already aced their PSAT."

"Bet they like Morgan."

"Funny, they actually do."

Jalen grunted. "Well, you better get home."

She started to walk away and then turned. "You know what," she said. "I want you to steal me again tomorrow."

Jalen smiled. "What do you mean, 'steal you'?"

"Get me out of there tomorrow. Please. Out of Red Trident. Mountain biking, water, I've never done any of that before. Let's not practice tomorrow . . . no video games . . . I just can't be inside."

"Where do you want to go?"

"What about Muir Woods? I've haven't been since my parents took me as a kid."

"Okay. Sounds good."

"You're awesome." She leaned forward and gave him a hug, then a slow kiss on the cheek. "I need to put in at least an hour. Meet me at Red Trident offices at 10 a.m. We can leave from there."

"All right," Jalen fumbled. "I'll see ya."

She waved and bounded to the curb as an Uber pulled up and stopped. "See ya, Jay," she said as she jumped in and drove away.

CHAPTER 45

As soon as Hi Kyto was gone, Jalen pulled out the phone that was already vibrating in his pocket. "Hey, dude," Jalen said, wincing for what he knew was coming.

"What the hell is wrong with you?" Wyatt yelled on the other end.

"Yeah, the yacht club was a little stuffy, so after the boat, we biked, and—"

"I told you to take me with you," Wyatt fumed. "And not only did you hop into a boat and head out to open water with a potential serial killer, you kept your phone off—for hours—so I couldn't even track you."

"I'm sorry."

"You're not ready to go off by yourself, dude."

"It was a split-second decision. And Morgan was there. She wasn't going to do anything with that blowhard around. By the way, that dude is a little crazy. He started asking about how long I'd been playing video games, and I nearly freaked. You think Darsie—"

"Yes. It's covered. He gave you a fake game history."

Jalen looked out over the city, the inky night blinking with headlights and buildings. He felt invigorated—less boy, more man. "I'm sorry, okay? Come pick me up?"

Just then, Wyatt pulled up in the truck Darsie had left them. He leaned out the driver's window. "On this mission," he said calmly, "you do what I say."

"Got it," Jalen said, reaching for the door handle, but Wyatt slowly eased the truck away.

"Seriously, dude?" Jalen threw his hands up.

"Seriously. Follow orders. You can think about that on your jog back." Wyatt checked his watch. "Our apartment is four miles away. I'll see you in thirty-five minutes. Don't be late."

"Jerk," Jalen muttered as the blue truck sped away.

CHAPTER 46

Leigh Ann and Grieving_Dad12 began exchanging messages using Wickr, an encrypted messaging service. Their bond was instant. Her friend, who she met on the darknet, shared two of her greatest passions: their country and gun control. And also like Leigh Ann, Grieving_Dad12 had lost someone—his only daughter, who'd been born with a muscular disorder that had left her paralyzed from the waist down and been killed in a school shooting years before. On that sunny day, he dropped her off at school like always, and in a few short hours, Grieving_Dad12 lost his very reason for breathing.

Although they kept conversations mostly to broad ideologies, Leigh Ann—or 4Ava as she was called on the darknet—had learned a bit about her new best friend. He was a software developer, independently wealthy. Leigh Ann was not only moved by his dedication to his daughter's memory but also by his productivity. He wasn't just going to talk about the relentless gun violence in schools and other safe zones; he was going to do something. The vision they'd collectively arrived at was that they needed to change the thinking of the gun lobby. Talk, talk, talk, what they needed was some action, something to open their eyes.

They need to really feel this, Grieving_Dad12 said. *This is war and there will be casualties. And it's got to start at the top.* And after months of philosophizing, they came to one conclusion and it was certain: the bastards had to pay.

@4Ava don't you think that if a child of NFA leadership was to be the victim in a school shooting, perhaps then the forces behind the gun lobby might feel what so many others have felt? the senselessness of loss?

Her answer, an unequivocal, unspeakable *YES*. Who couldn't? Who wouldn't change their mind when one of their own was a victim?

Leigh Ann made it her day's work to familiarize herself with the organization and its leaders. She learned that the NFA president himself had twins—a daughter and a son who were fifteen years old. Details of his private life, due to security threats, were hard to discover, but with the help of Grieving_Dad12's software skills, they learned that although the twins attended an elite private boarding school in New Hampshire, the twins, Frank Jr. and Coleen Henryson, were signed up for the Fairfax Band Camp, a summer program focused on music hosted at a public school in Northern Virginia—Fairfax Middle School. And as fate would have it, Fairfax Middle School was just across town from where Leigh Ann lived and seethed.

Though she'd been marginally mentally ill her whole life, Leigh Ann didn't realize just how ill she had become. She knew she was depressed. She rarely left the house, relishing hours at her desktop, chatting with Grieving_Dad12. That could not be healthy. Crying all day long could not be healthy. Her fits of anger were not healthy. She knew all of that, but the more time passed, the less she cared about her own health. What parts of her mind were sound were shrouded in an angry fog, and she could think of nothing but executing the plan.

It's pure karmic justice, she wrote to him one night. *We will do this. Whatever the cost.*

Let's do it together, Grieving_Dad12 said. *If you support me through this, I can execute. We can gain access to the school by posing as parents . . . the girl plays cello, the son plays percussion. I can get my hands on the band camp schedule.*

A sudden thought occurred to Leigh Ann, gripping her with fear. *But you can't die,* she typed furiously. *You have other children. You need to be with them. I'm going alone.*

@4Ava I can't let you go alone.

It has to be this way, she typed back. *With you helping me, Ava's life will finally have meant something. Mine would have meaning. Our pain will be felt by those who caused it. This is my destiny. Let me fulfill it.*

If this is what you want, I'll support you. You are an angel.

Leigh Ann powered off her computer and climbed into her unmade bed for the first time in days. She fell sound asleep.

After studying the calendar, a date was chosen. That day, there would only be twelve campers in total, so collateral damage would be minimized. Security would be at its lightest, and chances of success highest.

Leigh Ann had received the guns in a series of packages and instructions for how to assemble them. She'd gone to the thrift store and purchased an old wheelchair, which would serve as a central part of her cover, hopefully aiding her entrance into a school run by friendly Southern folk. And though he didn't say it, she knew the wheelchair was also a tribute to Grieving_Dad12's daughter, the one with the muscular disease who was slain on that somber Florida day.

Leading up to the date, she took the gun to the range in the early mornings and practiced shooting until after lunch. She was not necessarily athletic, but since she knew she might have to run, kneel, and fire, she began a modest workout routine—running laps around her suburban neighborhood outside D.C. and doing a few push-ups and crunches beside her bed while she watched the nightly news. She almost felt happy—she was going to change the world.

It was 10 p.m. one night and Leigh Ann paced from living room to kitchen, disassembling and reassembling the M4. CNN was playing in her dingy kitchen, as it did all day and night, the sound of human voices commenting on current events, the only thing to keep the house from utter loneliness.

Leigh Ann looked out the kitchen window. The wind blew through the green trees. A hint of summer storm in the air. She thought about opening it to freshen the kitchen, but she suddenly felt sluggish. Maybe she was hungry. She set down the M4, grabbed a cold slice of pizza from the fridge, and put it in the toaster oven on broil.

They had been hyping the evening's interview all day. The host, Indra McCall, was discussing Encyte and the upsurge in attacks across the United States with a special guest, Secretary of Defense Elaine Becker.

Leigh Ann almost shut the TV off. She was so sick of hearing about Encyte, but she was curious to hear what the secretary of defense would say.

"He's making a point . . ." the SecDef said. "He picks big issues and uses them as mirrors to hold in the face of society—violent gaming, technology, drug addiction—then he takes it a step further. He builds a trap that we walk into. We spring the trap, inciting a chain of events that results in the horrific act. He makes us the change agent of his will. Or that's his intent. He's trying to make us feel like we're the change agent. The truth is, he's manipulating everything. We're just pushing a button, pulling the trigger of his gun."

Leigh Ann listened, leaning in closer to the small TV set.

"You mention change and change agent," the host said. "Is that his goal? To change the world?"

"I believe he *thinks* so. Of course, all terrorists have an ideology."

"How do you know that's his intent?" Indra asked.

"He tells us so. His messages tell us his thinking, about gaming, for example—the reality that exists within the virtual world. Or his reference to dominion in the Book of Genesis. It's very pedagogical."

"Pedagogical, interesting," Indra said. "Can you define that . . . umm . . . for the audience?"

"It means teaching, you dummy," Leigh Ann said to the TV.

"Intending to teach," the SecDef said, "his notes feel scholastic in nature. Like a teacher, he wants us to consider the lesson and find the answer. Also like a teacher, he wants us to do the act—to pull the trigger. He sits back and observes us acting. Like a test, a game. But in the end, like all terrorists, he thinks he has a point and will create change."

"Can you explain this trigger mechanism a little further for our guests?"

"Sure. He's trying to incite violence, but he makes us the trigger. A kid playing a video game unknowingly kills fifty-three people when he thinks they're not real. Encyte did not run over those people, the player did. A number of people launch drones near airports. And those drones are steered into planes. Encyte didn't launch a single drone. A drug-addicted son of a Big Pharma CEO lights a fire to get high, not knowing he's lit the spark that will burn a huge portion of California. Again, Encyte did not light the match. And here's another example: we strongly believe Encyte is behind the SoHo Sneaker Riot of last year."

"How did you make that connection?"

"In the case of the SoHo Sneaker Riot, teens were led to an event where there was a shortage of shoes and a surplus of angry customers. But the basement was artificially suffused with hormones and pheromones that made the crowd more prone to violence and agitation. He didn't leave a note, but the riot fits his MO."

The host nodded. "I know the Department of Defense and

the FBI are trying to solve this. But what can we, as average citizens, do?"

"We should all be vigilant. Be aware. Encyte often uses the web—the dark web—to engage his triggers, so we should be mindful of strangers online who want us to do something . . . out of the ordinary."

Leigh Ann stood frozen in her kitchen. Blinking at the TV. Could it be? Her mind was struggling to process when an alarm blared through the house. Smoke poured from the forgotten pizza in the toaster. She pulled out the pan, and forgetting a rag, threw it in the sink, running the hissing pizza—and her burning fingers—under the water.

She opened a window. A cool, wet breeze fanned the smoke until the alarm stopped. She leaned out and drew in the fresh air. With every breath, her mind cleared a little bit. And then she glanced over at the kitchen counter where the M4 lay on its side, a magazine loaded into the breech, trigger gleaming.

CHAPTER 47

Three thousand miles away, the same CNN interview played in the small apartment in San Francisco.

Jalen sat on the couch, ice packs draped across his legs and an aspirin bottle and a glass of water beside him. Wyatt watched from the small kitchen as he dumped two pounds of steaming spaghetti into a strainer. He divided it into salad bowls and dropped a half stick of butter into each, sliding one bowl in front of Jalen. "It's not Mum's cooking, but eat up. After your triathlon today, you need the calories."

Jalen normally might have wisecracked, but he stared at the TV, rapt as the interview wound down. "Pedagogical," he repeated. "Meaning teaching. Hi Kyto's not a teacher. She's a student . . . it just doesn't fit."

"Both of her parents are teachers." Wyatt swirled his spaghetti and shoved a forkful in his mouth. "They're professors. The gaming angle, the teaching angle, the tech angle. For me, it's all adding up."

Jalen leaned forward to pick up the bowl but stopped. "They keep referring to Encyte as male. *He does this, he does that*. It's like they know it's a guy," he said hopefully.

"They don't know. They just assume. And I'm damn sure the SecDef and ninety-nine point nine-nine percent of the population isn't thinking there's a fourteen-year-old girl behind this."

"She's nearly fifteen. Her birthday's coming up next week. She's gonna have a boat party and I'm invited."

"Dude, let's hope you won't be here in a week. You gotta keep your head, okay?"

"You said *get close*. Darsie said get close. I'm doing my job!" Jalen threw his napkin on the counter. "You focus on yours."

"Yeah, I am," Wyatt shot back. "It's called babysitting you."

CHAPTER 48

The summer sun had not yet risen over D.C. and Secretary of Defense Elaine Becker had just finished an early-morning interview with a European news outlet. She was wanting nothing more than a black coffee and a few moments with her heels off when her trusty assistant, Jennifer Sloan, came rushing up.

"Madam Secretary," Jennifer said timidly. "Sorry to bother."

"What is it, Jen? I need a minute."

"Understood, but I think you should hear this," Jennifer said. "There is a woman in custody right now. She wants to speak with you."

The SecDef sighed.

"She showed up at the White House early this morning. She's been vetted and is currently being detained," Jennifer said. "She didn't go to the FBI because she wanted to talk with you directly, but"—Jennifer lowered her voice—"it looks like she's been corresponding with Encyte."

"Where is she?" the SecDef said, barreling toward the door. "And somebody get me some freaking coffee!"

* * *

Always a good judge of character, Elaine recognized immediately that the woman in front of her had a psychological issue. One could argue that the arm restraints were a dead giveaway, but even so, there was something about the woman's eyes, the way they bounced like pinballs to different points on Elaine's face.

"What's your name, miss?" Elaine asked in the kindest tone she could muster.

"Leigh Ann," the wild-eyed woman responded softly.

The SecDef could smell her—body odor mingled with coffee and cigarettes. She clearly hadn't showered in many days.

Jennifer slid a couple of coffees on the table, and Elaine motioned for the guard standing behind Leigh Ann to remove the restraints. "I'm sorry for the precautions," Elaine said.

Leigh Ann's hands shook as she accepted the steaming cup.

"I've been debriefed on your communications," the SecDef said. "But why don't you tell me yourself why you are here."

"I saw you on CNN," Leigh Ann began, "last night. You were talking about Encyte and the potential threat, and I knew you were the one I had to come to . . . my half sister is dead," her voice quivered. "Killed in the California school shooting a year ago."

"I'm sorry to hear that," the SecDef's voice softened a little. "Tell me more about what you have planned."

"I don't know for sure if it's him, but someone approached me on the Tor browser. His name is GrievingDad_12—" Leigh Ann stopped. "I know what I'm telling you is awful, but I didn't do it." She looked frantically around the interview room. "I'm not going to do it. That's why I came here today. I'm not going to be arrested, am I?" She pushed back from the table.

"Please." Elaine's mind raced. She shouldn't have let them take off the restraints. This woman was a wanna-be serial killer for goodness's sake. She thought about her own daughter and what she would tell her later.

"Please sit," the SecDef said as two guards came over. "Laura Ann . . ."

"Leigh," she said, slumping back in her seat, rubbing her wrists.

"*Leigh* Ann," Elaine corrected herself. "You came in here talking about a shooting. That's something very serious."

"I know. And I need your help to stop it. He wanted me to shoot all the kids at a band camp . . . we were targeting children of the executive of the NFA, Frank Henryson. We've been planning this for weeks, very detailed. I have a wheelchair to help get me through school security, so the guns won't be detected. I can show you screenshots of the messages we exchanged, if you'd like."

The SecDef sat in silence, thinking. "You said you planned to attack a band camp?"

"Yes. There's an end-of-the-summer performance at Fairfax Middle School. We planned to . . . attack them at the rehearsal. We wanted the shooting to be at a school."

The SecDef turned to her assistant. "I want you to set up a virtual meeting with Ken and the director of Camp Valor . . . now."

CHAPTER 49

It was 7:30 a.m. on the East Coast. A war room had been set up in the DoD's NOC—Network Operations Center—where a series of desks manned by network operators were lined up across from a large dynamic screen. The SecDef sat in the long center table beside Mr. Yellow. Glowing on a big screen across from them was Ken Carl, sitting in Valor's NOC in the Caldera.

"Madam Secretary," Ken said. "You're looking well."

"Don't patronize me, Ken. Where are they?"

"I'm in the director's office. They should be—"

The door behind Ken opened and Eldon filed in followed by Avi Amit, grumpy before his morning coffee.

"Madam Secretary," Eldon said into the camera as he took a seat.

"Eldon . . ." Elaine smiled her widest smile. "Please. Call me Elaine."

Eldon cleared his throat. "Elaine." He nodded at the camera.

"Listen, gentlemen, I'll get down to the point. Something critical has been brought to my attention, and we don't have much time . . . I need a favor."

"From us"—Eldon's brow furrowed—"or from Valor?"

"Both, actually. There's someone here who I think you'll be interested to meet." The SecDef stepped to the side, revealing the stringy-haired woman. She still looked as though she hadn't slept in days, but her eyes were clearly more alert.

"It's all right, Leigh Ann," Elaine said. "They are friends. Now please, tell them everything."

Unbeknownst to Leigh Ann, within an hour of her confession, a bomb squad had slipped into her row house, and meticulously waded through the laundry and piles of papers and all manner of trash, searching for ordinance and weaponry. They took their time: lifting prints and looking for booby traps. Since they couldn't rule out explosives on the property, they went ahead and brought the dogs, one of which was howling at her freezer.

"Easy, Yeller," the technician said. The dog's nose seemingly pointed at the water dispenser.

The technician got on the radio, summoning his partner with a quick click.

"What's up, Kev?" his partner responded from outside.

"Yeller's going crazy about this refrigerator. Practically biting the door handle."

"What are you thinking? Booby trap?" his partner asked.

"That or a serious diet plan." Kev laughed. "Keep you out of the ice cream. But for real, doesn't make sense. You'd booby-trap the front door, not the freezer. Gotta be something in there."

"Like what?"

"Ordinance. I'm trying to remember what compounds would be favorable to cold."

"Lots of 'em, if I had to guess."

"We don't have time to debate this. What do you wanna do?"

Kevin reached out, put his hand on the freezer handle, and the dog leapt forward, jumping up toward the ice maker, practically biting in the air.

"What the hell's he doing?" Kevin stuck his head in the freezer and studied above the ice bin. "What's this?"

An aide strode into the DoD's NOC in the middle of the video conference and handed the SecDef a note. The SecDef read it and looked up. "We've searched her apartment."

"And?" Avi said.

"And it looks like someone has tampered with her water filter," Elaine said. "Boosting it with testosterone and norepinephrine."

"Where is she now?" Avi asked.

"Under surveillance." Elaine turned to a tech in the room. "Can we show Leigh Ann?"

A window appeared on the big screen, and there was Leigh Ann, sitting in a chair. "She's guzzling coffee and looking like a confused puppy. Mr. Yellow, I'm right to assume this matches Encyte's MO?"

"It *is* his MO." Mr. Yellow, still slumped in the corner, straightened up in his seat. "He's used the same neurotransmitter cocktail in previous attacks."

"So why are you talking to us?" Eldon said. "What can Valor do here?"

"I have been thinking of a way to entrap Encyte." The SecDef looked dead into the camera. "We need to let Leigh Ann and Grieving_Dad12 proceed with the attack."

"I'm sorry?" Ken coughed. "Have the crazy woman shoot twelve band campers?"

"Obviously, no one will get shot. We'll make sure Leigh Ann uses blanks and insert child operators from Valor to stage the shooting. We'll get the real band campers out, and the Valor campers in." The SecDef walked over to a display, a replica of Fairfax Middle School. "In every attack, there's been a commonality. Encyte has used video and digital interfaces to document the crime and the perpetrator so he can show the world what he has done. In the case of the school, there is a security camera system, with cameras in all hallways, classrooms, and in the auditorium where the rehearsal will take place." The SecDef pointed to a room in the administrative wing of the school. "The school recently upgraded its security system to use IP-based cameras. They are monitored on site and remotely. We believe Encyte intends to hack into the camera network to observe and record the shooting. We must let him do this. He must think the attack is occurring, so we can trace him online."

"So what does that mean?" Ken Carl sat like a parrot, perched on Avi's shoulder.

"She means," Avi said, "that within the school, you have a network and firewalls. Within the network, there exists a closed-circuit television feed that's hackable."

"So how would Encyte record this attack?" Ken asked. "With a camera? In the network?"

"Obviously." Avi nodded. "Unless he's going to show up with a smartphone and watch somebody blow away a bunch of kids, he's going to hack in, get past a firewall, and duplicate the closed-circuit camera feed. If we can observe him doing this, we can trace the data back to wherever Encyte is watching. Naturally, he'll bounce the data around the globe so it can't be traced, so it won't be easy, but it's possible to locate his IP address if he hacks in during the shooting."

"And how do you do that?" Ken asked.

"I can't do it." Avi looked at Eldon, who shook his head. "Perhaps the DoD has a cybersurveillance team?"

"Of course we do," the SecDef said, "but I don't want to engage them. You can imagine what the press would do if it got out the DoD faked a school shooting involving the children of the NFA. A political bloodbath."

"I hate to say it," Avi said, "but missions like these are exactly the reason you don't want to shut down Valor."

"Yeah, we get that," Ken sneered. "But what the hell are we talking about here, for Christ's sake?" He jumped up from his seat. "How can we do this?"

"I know someone who can help," Eldon said. "Elaine, we can handle what happens on the ground, but we need a third party to help us with the technical stuff."

"Who?" Elaine asked.

"Red Trident . . ." Eldon said. "John Darsie owes me a favor."

CHAPTER 50

"We want Red Trident's fraud detection bots crawling all over the school's network," Avi said.

It was 5:30 a.m. in California, and John Darsie, drenched with sweat, leaned on the handlebars of his Peloton bicycle.

"Yes, I can do it," he said. The screen mounted to the handlebars no longer played a Peloton trainer in a New York City studio, but the face of Avi Amit. "My team will need at least fifteen minutes to trace the IP address. Avi is right, there's no doubt Encyte will send this thing all over the earth and beyond." Darsie dabbed his brow. "We'll be able to find the point of origination, but like I said, we need time."

"So she'll have to be inside for fifteen minutes?" Avi asked.

"Yes," Darsie said. "It's like finding the first stitch in a sweater. You would need to pull each thread, slowly tracking back to its point of origin, being careful not to break it. That's what we're trying to do here, with one wrinkle. To truly understand who Encyte is, we need to have somebody physically in his environment."

"We don't know where Encyte is," Elaine said. "He told Leigh Ann his daughter was killed in that school shooting in

Florida, but he could literally be anywhere—one of the seven and a half billion people on earth."

"Well, at Red Trident, we have some key suspects," Darsie said.

"*You* have suspects?" Ken Carl yelled through the Peloton screen. "You're an IT contractor. You're not supposed to have suspects. What are you doing spying on the American people?"

"With all due respect, Kenny boy," Darsie said. "There's a killer in this world, and I'm one of the only people capable of finding him."

"I'm not sure we're not looking at one of the suspects," Ken muttered and pointed at Darsie's face on his screen.

"I don't have time for fools," Darsie said. "So who's going to be on the ground? If it's Ken, I'm not making promises."

"Screw you!" Ken shouted.

"Ease down, everyone. I've temporarily reinstated Camp Valor," the SecDef said. "Eldon has assembled a team of campers, and they'll be en route to D.C. within the hour."

"When's the rehearsal?" Darsie said, again starting to pedal the stationary bike, grinding out his thoughts.

"Tomorrow," Elaine said, "4 p.m."

"To me, our biggest concern is if you can get this woman mentally prepared to go through with it. One thing that may help—change the timing."

"What?" Elaine said.

"Aren't we worried Encyte will spook if she changes the plan?" Avi asked.

"No, he's right," Eldon chimed in. "We have no idea what Encyte might do. If Encyte has planned this attack, don't you think he has a fallback if Leigh Ann doesn't go through with it? He could be there. He could have another shooter. He could have five other shooters. A guy like this is not going to all this trouble without a contingency, so we should switch it up."

"So he might have to shuffle to put a Plan B in place?" SecDef said.

"Exactly," Darsie said. "It's an aggressive chess move, and we must get him on his heels. A show of force. Otherwise, he controls everything. Let's have the school change the schedule, so it doesn't look like Leigh Ann is calling the shots. Have them move the rehearsal to today at 4 p.m."

"Today?" Ken balked. "How can we assemble a mission of this scale in one day? I mean, it's . . ." Ken looked down at his wrist, realizing he'd rustled out of bed without his watch.

"It's eight thirty on the East Coast. We have seven and a half hours. That's two hours more than you put in in a work day, Ken." Darsie saw the SecDef had to stop herself from snickering. "I'm ready. Always ready. Eldon, can the team from Valor be in place and ready by 4 p.m.?"

"Yes," Eldon said without a moment's thought.

"Okay," said Darsie, "I suggest we get the school to publish the change online before 9 a.m. Leigh Ann needs to contact GrievingDad_12, and then we set the trap."

"I might not like to admit it, but Darsie's right," Eldon said. "Elaine, what's your decision?"

The Sec Def sighed and sat back, propping her head in her hands.

"If I may—" Ken Carl leaned in behind her.

"Hush," the SecDef snapped. She took a few deep breaths. "Let's do it," she said, and the screens went to black.

In the shadow of the Washington Monument, Ken sat down on a bench and called up Tui, who didn't answer until the third ring.

"What are you doing?" Ken snapped. "Shit's getting serious over here."

"What do you mean *what am I doing*?" Tui said. "I've been following these kids all over San Francisco. They went bike riding for five hours yesterday—do you have any idea how hard that was to track? Hang on—" Tui paused and then ordered, "Yeah, five soft tacos and five bean burritos . . . and a large Mountain Dew."

"Taco Bell?" Ken scoffed. "It's breakfast! Listen up. It's going down, and I mean now."

"I'm listening."

"You were right—the Ole Broad is all in with this guy Darsie. He's hiding something, and she's too close to see it. There's another attack coming today. Find John Darsie and don't leave his side."

"You understand what you're asking, right? The guy has his own security detail and a Tesla outfitted like the damn Batmobile."

"I don't think you're hearing me. Today!" Ken screamed, spooking some geese into flight. He lowered his voice. "Everything we've waited for . . . is happening . . . today. Now, do you want this or not?"

"Yes."

"Lose the kids. Find Darsie. Whatever you have to do, just do it."

"Okay, I'll figure it out."

CHAPTER 51

"Do you want me to drive you to the cabins?" Avi asked.

"No," Eldon said as he strode out of the secure communications room in the Caldera. "I wanna walk."

Eldon left the Cave Complex alone, walking quickly in the cover of the thick, wet evergreens. He followed the path that led up and out of the depression that was once the heart of a volcano, his mind erupting in thought. He'd gotten his wish. Once again, the American people had a need—a desperate and mortal need—and Valor had been called to meet it.

If he had to be honest, there was a part of him that felt relief when the SecDef halted kinetic activities at Valor. The heart of his concern was Cody, the fragile younger son who Eldon knew was not ready. Brave and eager to prove himself, Cody was more than willing to invite danger, but it was this willingness that worried Eldon. Cody was the good son, the one who not only wanted but *needed* a pat on the back.

In his two sons, there were two kinds of boys: the one who wanted the pat on the back, and the one who wanted to survive. Wyatt was the consummate survivor. The kid who did what he had to do to get through a challenge. Wyatt was uncomfortable with pats on the back, and before his time at Valor, he had received a scant few.

There was a certain aggression about Wyatt. When he saw an opportunity, he attacked it with violence and purpose. Cody, on the other hand, tried to do the right thing, to perform at the highest level. The gun range was the perfect example: while Wyatt sought only to shred the bull's-eye, Cody saw it just as much for the art, choosing the right firearm and conditioning and oiling it.

And Eldon knew all too well that in a kinetic environment, violence and action—attacking a goal to get it done—was the difference between the survivors and the martyrs, the heroes and the fallen. And so he was thinking of all these things when he pushed through the doors to the lodge and went back to the kitchen to find Mum, sitting at a small table with Cass, having coffee.

"Morning," he said to them. "Cass, didn't expect to see you so early."

"Couldn't sleep," she said. "But want me to . . ." She stood and he motioned for her to sit.

"I'm glad, actually. I was coming to tell you both something."

"You look worried," Mum said. "Coffee?" She motioned to the fresh pot.

Eldon nodded and filled a mug, joining them at the card table.

"So what's up?" Cass asked.

Eldon thought about how he'd break the news. "The SecDef finally came around. We've gotten our first mission of the summer."

"What?" Cass said excitedly. "That's great." Cass looked to Mum, who had risen out of her seat.

"This is wonderful," Mum echoed, holding her hands up clenched. "Yes." She looked to Eldon. "Is it really happening? They're not canceling the program?"

"Orders come from the SecDef herself . . . The short version is that we're intercepting a school shooting that we assume is being planned by Encyte. But it's going to be . . . complicated."

"How so?" Cass asked.

"Because she doesn't just want the Group-As . . . she wants the Rovers, too."

"Oh dear," Mum said, nervously biting the inside of her cheek.

Eldon looked over at Cass. "Well, orders are orders," she said hesitantly.

"Yes," said Eldon. "But do you think they're ready?"

"The Rovers?" Cass said. "Or one of them in particular?"

"I don't know." Eldon lowered his eyes. "Is he?"

"Eldon," Cass said. "My sister is dead because of what she did at the camp."

"I know. Don't you think I know—"

"Let me finish. My sister is dead, but she was ready and willing. She knew exactly what she was getting into. She knew the danger."

"Dolly was special, we all know that."

"So is every kid at this camp," Mum chimed in.

"If you want," Cass said. "You could hold him back, put him on a detail here, but if you ask me . . . he's ready. Whether you like it or not."

"That's all I needed to hear, because there's one more thing."

"What?" Cass said.

"You'll be the one leading them on this mission."

Eldon stomped up the steps to the Rovers cabin, the beetles bumping against the lone porch light. He looked around; his breath hung in the cold morning air, but sweat dotted his forehead and under his arms. He put his hand on the cabin door and knocked.

"Come in!" one of them called.

He entered and they all stood to greet him, the eyes around

the room so young, so innocent. "Rovers." Eldon cleared his throat. "I'm going to make this brief. A C-130 is inbound to the Caldera to pick you up for your first mission. Get your gear ready. We'll debrief you on the plane. You guys have twenty minutes."

A moment of silence. Excited, bewildered eyes blinking back at him.

"Well, let's get moving," Cody said, looking around and then quickly packing his rucksack.

Exactly fifteen minutes later, Eldon found Cass standing on the tarmac, her hair slicked back, boots laced tight as she did for combat. "Is everyone ready?" he asked.

"Ready as they're gonna be with two hours of prep."

"And Viktoria?"

"Already in the cockpit."

"How 'bout you . . . you good?"

"Scared shitless."

They watched the Group-As—Mary Alice in the lead—walking in formation, cutting through the misty grass toward the C-130. "Think the Old Man would've done what we're doing?" Cass asked.

Just behind them, the Rovers tripped along like puppies. A fresh-faced Cody first among them.

"God, I hope so," Eldon said, slapping her on the back. "Let's go."

CHAPTER 52

"Get up." The voice was not Wyatt's.

Jalen lurched up on the couch and his eyes popped open. There, in the studio apartment, was John Darsie.

"I am up." Jalen yawned, settling back. "Now."

"Your body's up. Get your mind up . . . Where's Wyatt?"

"Don't know." Jalen rubbed his face, looking around the small space. "Captain America works out in the morning. Probably went for a jog."

The door opened and Wyatt came in, dripping with sweat. "Morning, Darsie." Wyatt went over to the kitchen and wiped his face with a towel. "Saw your car and I turned around . . . To what do we owe the pleasure?"

"I couldn't risk calling." Darsie locked the door and went over to the kitchen counter. "We have highly credible evidence"—Darsie lowered his voice—"that there's to be an attack . . . today. Let me rephrase—Encyte is going to attack. I should say, he's going to use a pawn to conduct the attack. But we're ahead of it. We have a team in place to mimic the motion of the shooting, while our cybersurveillance team will trace Encyte as he tries to record it."

"Where?" Wyatt said.

"Fairfax, Virginia. There's going to be a school shooting. A middle school. Encyte, like in other attacks, has someone else pulling the trigger. A lady came forward, tipped the DoD."

"But Hi Kyto's here," Jalen said. "She can't be in Virginia and California. Can't be her, right?"

"No. Doesn't matter. All she has to do is log into her computer and she can coordinate a strike. You need to be with her all day."

"I will be. We're going hiking. In Muir Woods."

"That's perfect," Darsie said. "No computer access. I don't even think there's cell service in the park."

"So if she's with me and she's not online and this thing occurs, then it's not her, right?"

"Yes. Let's hope that's the case," Darsie said. "For me . . . and now it seems you, too, have something invested in her."

"She's a friend," Jalen said defensively. "Of course I hope she's not a killer."

"She's your mark," Darsie said tersely, then turned on Wyatt. "Your little disciple needs some help in the spy game. Emotions should not be involved."

"You don't even want to hear about lover boy's field trip yesterday," Wyatt said. "He cut off all comms so they could go boating and biking."

Jalen's face flashed hot. "I just need to operate on my own—" he started to explain why he shut off comms, then stopped himself. "You're right. Gotta get my head in the game."

"Darsie, how do you know about the attack?" Wyatt asked.

"SecDef Becker has contacted Red Trident."

"And who's going to be at the middle school? Is Valor involved?"

"Red Trident is handling the technical stuff, and a third party will get the kids out and provide stand-ins in their place," Darsie said.

"Third party? You mean Valor?"

"Valor?" Darsie said, feigning ignorance. "Don't know what you're talking about."

"Don't give me that crap, Darsie. If there's a military team providing stand-in for a bunch of kids, it's gotta be them. Tell me!"

"Wyatt, calm down. Yes, it's Valor, but as you're no longer a part of it, I can't talk to you about its missions."

"I'm a part of Red Trident. I am on your team."

"You are a subcontractor. And our agreement was that you stay here, with Jalen and Hi Kyto."

"Yeah, dude," Jalen chimed in. "You can't just leave. What'd you say last night? I'm not ready."

"Screw the agreement," Wyatt said. "My dad will be there, *Cody* will probably be there. I need to go."

"It's not me who doesn't want you there. It's Valor. Their rules." Darsie shrugged. "I'm like you, a contractor."

Wyatt's eyes shifted to the knife block on the kitchen counter and thought about how easy it would be to draw one out and put a blade to Darsie's neck and ask again.

"Let me rephrase," Wyatt said. "I'm going to do what you do all the time—break rules. I *am* going. You can help me or try to stop me. Either way, I can figure out how to get to Virginia."

Darsie thought for a second, then nodded. "A Red Trident spy plane headed to Fairfax is leaving from SFO in twenty minutes. If you can get on the plane, you can go."

Wyatt ran for the door. "I'm taking your car!"

CHAPTER 53

As Wyatt took off in the Red Trident spy plane, the C-130 carrying the team from Valor was taxiing down the runway at a secure hangar at Fort Meade.

The door to the Valor plane opened, and there began one of the swiftest mission preps in U.S. military history. Hair and makeup teams descended; the Valor kids were assigned their instruments and shown how to mock playing them. And while the ground team was getting ready, everyone kept an eye on the main event, like she herself was a grenade with a loose pin.

"Leigh Ann," said Mary Alice, approaching the woman who stood just outside the group, nervously biting her cuticles. "I'm the team leader for Group-A. They told me you have been training on your own, but there are some things I need to go over with you before the mission today, okay?"

"Yes, the mission," Leigh Ann repeated, watching Mary Alice load the M4.

"This weapon looks exactly like the weapon you received in the mail, but it's been replaced with the kind they use in Hollywood."

"Okay," Leigh Ann said nervously.

"It's been modified, so it can fire in automatic position, but you have to be careful—these are prone to jamming." She held out the assault rifle. "Now, you're going to hold the rifle to your shoulder like this . . . and you want to aim your sights right at the head or the chest."

"Oh my god," Leigh Ann whispered, taking the M4 and shouldering it as she was told.

"Steady. Look where you want to shoot."

"Are you sure those are blanks?"

"Yes," Mary Alice said calmly. "They're blanks."

"What if I can't do this?"

"You have to. Stop thinking of yourself as a victim . . . you're a soldier. And in doing this, you're not going to hurt us, you are going to save us . . . Now, aim and squeeze the trigger."

Leigh Ann looked through the crosshairs at the dummy—a head with the little Henryson girl's picture attached to the face—and pulled the trigger.

In the NOC war room, all eyes were on Leigh Ann Davidson, the emotionally damaged woman now at the center of the operation to ensnare the world's most wanted terrorist, as she sat down at a table and logged into Wickr. Her interface played on the big screens, and everything was silent except for the sound of tapping as she hunted-and-pecked keys.

Today is the day, she typed, including with the message a link to the school's website that detailed the change of locations for the band rehearsal. *Rehearsal moved up due to weather. It's in the auditorium.*

She waited. Less than thirty seconds later, she got a response.

GrievingDad_12: *This is distressing news. This changes a lot.*

4Ava: *Should we abort mission?*

GrievingDad_12: *No. We must adapt. Plan remains the same.*

Change your schedule. I will be with you, watching. And able to help if you fail.

Elaine looked over at Mr. Yellow and saw a flash of alarm in his bland eyes.

"What does that mean? I thought I was going in alone," Leigh Ann said as another message dinged.

GrievingDad_12: *I am doing this for all of the lost children.*

"We need to be on high alert." Elaine rose to her feet.

"What does he mean, 'able to help if you fail'?" Leigh Ann was still frozen in her seat.

"I think he's trying to mind-game you, to make you feel like if you fail there's a backup plan. Take the pressure off you. But I can't know for sure." The SecDef paced. "We're going to stage a shooting without a single run-through. This is insane."

"They're professionals," Mr. Yellow said calmly.

"If this goes sideways, I'm gonna kill you." Elaine jammed her finger in his chest.

"If this goes sideways, I'd welcome it," said Mr. Yellow.

CHAPTER 54

Jalen sat alone in the safe house and hit send on a text to Hi Kyto: *Morning. Still feel like playin hooky?*

The reply was quick: *Yeah! Definitely.*

OK, be by in half an hour.

Do I need to bring anything special?

Good shoes. We may go off the trail a bit.

Jalen stood and walked around in circles as he waited for a response. Minutes later, the phone buzzed again.

Hey, I need to stop at Red Trident. Let's push our trip until noon.

No problem, Jalen texted back. He thought about what this meant, if anything. The rehearsal was planned for 4 p.m. Eastern. If she can't meet until noon Pacific, that's 3 p.m. on the East Coast. She'd be away from her computer at noon and hiking during the attack. She'd be cleared. But it would be close. If she pushed the trip back any further, it would be possible she could launch the system to record the attack and go hiking.

But there was another fear that gripped Jalen, an idea about Encyte that had not yet been shared, which he felt had been overlooked and which he, in fact, was afraid to even mention, lest it come true. *What if Encyte was more than one person?* It made sense. Why couldn't Encyte be more than one person? What if Hi Kyto worked as part of a team?

Jalen paced around the room, circling and hypothesizing, wishing to god that Wyatt was still with him.

The Valor campers, in military formation, filed out of the hangar toward the bright yellow school bus that was already running on the tarmac. Bringing up the rear was Cass, dressed in a pantsuit and a red wig, hair pulled back in a bun like she'd seen in pictures of the Fairfax band instructor. There were twelve in total, their ages ranging from eleven to sixteen. After a seven-hour flight with the world's best makeup artists, their own parents wouldn't have recognized them, though from a distance, the proud parents of twelve band campers would.

"Let's move quickly, guys," Viktoria said as the bus doors hissed open and the Valorians climbed inside. Though it was against decades of Valor protocol to send Junior Rovers into the field—particularly ones who had not completed a first summer of training—with only seven hours to execute, Eldon had no choice. So the members of Group-A—Mary Alice, Rory, Samy, Pierce—were joined by the Junior Rovers, the freckle-faced Cody leading the team.

Viktoria hopped in the driver's seat, and the bus pulled out, heading for Fairfax Middle School. Along its way, it passed another school bus, one loaded with the real band campers en route to a secure facility where Mr. Yellow and a team of local police would be waiting. The real Fairfax band members—grumpy and confused—were informed that this was a safety drill. All of them were completely unaware that kids their same age had just voluntarily taken their place in a potential slaughter.

Mr. Yellow stood in the cool vacant warehouse, under the fluorescent lights, answering their many questions:

Yes, you have to participate in the drill.

Yes, you will get your instruments back at the end of the day.

No, you cannot call your parents.

"Where are the Henrysons?" Mr. Yellow asked, looking over the dozen kids for the twins.

A well-dressed, good-looking brother and sister raised their hands. "Right here," the boy said politely.

Mr. Yellow stepped away from the group and whispered into the radio. "We got them. They're safe."

"Roger that," Eldon said from the school parking lot where he and Avi were stationed in a tactical van outfitted with communications linked directly to the school's IoT infrastructure, the Tor browser, and Red Trident.

Once the Valor kids were in position, Eldon again briefed the local SWAT and FBI teams on what would be taking place in less than fifteen minutes. "There will be one female shooter with a weapon loaded with blanks . . . Be alert. We don't know what's coming. There could be other forms of attack: drones, planes, hidden bombs . . . just about anything could come through those doors."

CHAPTER 55

The doors of the Darsie Pavilion swung open, and Hi Kyto stepped out wearing her trademark hoodie, a signature T-shirt, tight blue jeans, torn at the knees, and a backpack slung over her shoulder.

"Hi," she said cheerily. "Been waiting long?"

Immediately, Jalen noticed something different about her face. She had her same natural beauty, but her dark eyes had been lined and her lips slightly glossed.

"Just got here." He smiled. "What's up?"

"You ready to do this?" she asked excitedly.

"You bet." Jalen pulled up his Uber app and requested a ride to Muir Woods. "You look really . . ." Jalen paused, feeling his stomach swirl again. "Pretty."

Hi Kyto smiled, about to say something as a motorcycle hummed toward them. "Oh, look," she said. "Morg!"

Morg eased his Tecate motorcycle to the curb alongside them and flipped up the black visor on his helmet. "Hey, guys." His eyes gleamed. "Jay, what brings you over this way?"

"What's up?" Jalen gritted his teeth and reached to slap Morg's hand, but Morg kept his grip on the handlebars.

"We're going hiking," Hi Kyto said cheerily.

"Aw man, I'm slammed today. Otherwise, I'd come with."

"Next time," Jalen said, not mentioning that Morg was not invited. Jalen flagged down the Uber driver who'd just pulled up.

"You know, Jay," Morg said. "Ever since the boat ride, I couldn't shake it. I knew you looked familiar, and then I did a little research into CV_kyd's game history. Decent record. Interesting what else I found out."

Jalen wiped his forehead, which was suddenly soaked with sweat. "What's that?"

"You're just not who I thought you were."

"What's that supposed to mean?" Hi Kyto laughed and looked over at Jalen.

"Nothing." Morgan stared at Jalen. "Nothing at all, really." His Apple Watch buzzed, breaking the trance. "Gotta take this," he said, putting his mouth to his wrist.

Jalen ducked into the back of the waiting Uber. "Let's go."

Hi Kyto slipped into the back seat beside him. "See you, Morg!" she said as she closed the door.

Makeup aside, there was another glow about Hi Kyto as she leaned against the window in the back seat of the sedan, the blue sky and red cables of the bridge as her backdrop. She was a postcard: sunlight streaming in on her smiling face.

"I was up all night," Hi Kyto said, almost manic with enthusiasm. "Thinking about our ride yesterday, and then I started Googling mountain biking videos."

As their driver headed north out of the city, Jalen tried to relax. If he could just get her to Muir Woods, she would be safe, assuming she was not part of a network. The farther they got from campus, the more he felt like he was waking up from a dream. From a nightmare that Hi Kyto was a monster killer. This would be over soon. In a matter of hours, they would have the truth, and Wyatt and Darsie would see that they'd been wrong. All the lying could stop.

"Think I'm gonna buy a bike," Hi Kyto continued, still in her own world. "I want a Kona. I was looking at them last night. It's just crazy that, like, I literally don't think I've ever jogged around the corner. I mean, in gym class, I might've pretended to jog, but yesterday was the first time that I've actually sweated from exercise. I'm so sore, but I don't even care."

Jalen glanced at the clock on the dashboard: *12:25.* Almost go-time on the East Coast. He took a breath. Nothing to worry about.

"Sure you're okay?" Hi Kyto asked. "You seem . . . like you wandered off somewhere . . . in your own Muir Woods in your head."

"Yeah, I was just . . . I'm sorry." He looked into her eyes. "I'm here now."

"You gotta relax." She rolled down her window. "It feels so good. Breaking routine. Breathing real air. Being free."

"Yeah, it does." He reached over and without thinking, took her hand, lacing his sweaty fingers between hers. The sea glittering and eternal beneath them.

CHAPTER 56

At 3:45 p.m., Leigh Ann's sedan pulled into Fairfax Middle School and parked in a handicap spot. Limping, she got out and walked around to the trunk and with great effort, she pulled out the ratty oversized wheelchair, unfolded it, and rolled her way to the entrance ramp.

"Hello, ma'am, who are you here to see?" The guard at the door wore a starchy brown uniform and a wide smile.

"Principal Skinner," Leigh Ann said, rifling through the purse that sat on her lap. "My daughter may come here in the fall."

"You know there's an open house at the end of the school year."

"I just recently relocated, so I had scheduled a meeting now." Leigh Ann smiled.

"Okay, write your name down on the badge, and we'll have you go through the security detector."

Leigh Ann scribbled the name *Carolyn* on the name tag and stuck it to her chest, right above her pounding heart.

"Here, darling, let me help ya." The security guard held out his hand, and as predicted, made it all too easy. He pulled her to her feet, and holding her breath, she hobbled through the metal detector without a beep.

Leigh Ann looked nervous, but she hoped the guard would chalk it up to being without her chair.

"Just a sec." The guard gave her a wink and wheeled the chair around the scanner and helped her sit back down.

"Whew," Leigh Ann said, adjusting her purse back in her lap. "Thank you so much. You're too kind."

The guard nodded and left Leigh Ann to wheel herself down the hallway toward the sounds of a classical symphony that drifted underneath the double doors of the gymnasium.

She stopped in the bathroom, and shedding her limp, wheeled into the handicap stall, disassembled the chair, and reassembled the M4 assault rifle she'd hidden inside it. In the seat of the wheelchair were eight extra magazines loaded with sixty rounds of blanks each. Seeing the ammunition, which looked so real, her heart spasmed and her face began to sweat. She sat down on the toilet seat, prayed that a mistake had not been made, and real bullets were not in the gun. She logged into Wickr, and sent a message: *I'm in.*

CHAPTER 57

The Uber was nearing the north exit of the Golden Gate Bridge when Hi Kyto's phone buzzed. Her warm hand slipped away and she pulled her phone from her hoodie pocket.

"Oh shit," she said, looking at the message.

"What?" Jalen sat up. "What is it?"

"I totally screwed up . . . I've got a deadline. Back at the lab. I've got to get back right now."

"Now?"

"Yes, I'm so sorry." She tapped the Uber driver on the shoulder. "Sir, can we please turn around? I'll pay the extra fare."

Jalen's heart thrummed in his ears.

"Miss, I'll try," Uber driver said. "But look." He pointed to the wall of red taillights ahead of them. "It's a parking lot."

"You're right. You know what, I'm just going to get out right now. I can walk to the other side and catch an Uber headed south."

"Hang on." Jalen tried to grab her hand.

"I'm so sorry I ruined the day, Jay." She opened the door. "But I'll call."

"Julie, what the hell?" Jalen was so panicked he used her real name. "Please. Just wait."

He grabbed her hoodie, but she jerked away.

"I told you. I have a deadline. One of my labmates just texted me. If I don't get back, we can't ship our product, we can't ship updates."

"What do you mean . . . ship software?"

"Jay, you gotta let me go. Look, we can do the hike another day. Maybe even today, but I just need three hours—I'm sorry."

Jalen watched as Hi Kyto jumped out, bobbed through the cars, and began running south on the bridge. *Dammit!* He banged his fist on the seat. He reached into his backpack and pulled out his phone and called Darsie. "She's running," Jalen screamed as he jumped out of the sedan.

"What do you mean *running*?" Darsie yelled.

"Down the bridge. On the 101. Headed south."

"Where the hell is she going?"

"The lab," Jalen said, his legs pumping, cars honking, and he dipped and ducked through traffic.

"The lab?" Darsie said in his ear. "That doesn't make sense. If she operates from the lab, we'll be able to track her. Don't lose her!"

"I'm trying," Jalen said, watching as she slipped into a gray sedan with the U sticker in the window.

Jalen's thighs burned, weaving between cars and pedestrians. He grabbed a bike outside a coffee shop and pedaled hard, trailing the sedan, a hipster behind him screaming, "Hey! Someone just stole my bike!"

He followed for at least eight or nine miles, but in one of the hilliest cities in America, on a two-foot peddler, it was a lost cause.

He watched the sedan hook a hard right and head north, in the opposite direction of the university, and speed-dialed Darsie.

"Tell me you still have eyes on her," Darsie said.

"Lost her," Jalen panted. "But I know the direction. She was lying about going back to the lab. The Uber is headed to the Mission."

Jalen looked at his watch—12:45. Fifteen minutes. Leigh Ann must be arriving at the school.

"Think I can catch her," Jalen said. "Traffic ahead."

Thanks to some construction, Jalen caught up with the car and watched from a block and a half away as Hi Kyto got out and began walking briskly north, into the heart of Chinatown. He ditched the bike and ran, following her for a few blocks, the smells of food wafting out of the stalls, the streets bustling and busy. Hi Kyto, her hoodie now pulled up, was a dark figure, dipping and ducking just a hill ahead of him. He knew that running down the streets of Chinatown was attracting too much attention, so he slowed down to a fast walk and followed as she cut through a dumpling stall and down an alley. He peered around the corner, fifty yards into the alley, just as Hi Kyto entered the rear ground floor of a tenement-style building, a steel door slamming behind her.

Jalen dialed Darsie. "She's gone into a building in Chinatown," Jalen yelled. "Darsie, do you hear me?"

"What kind of place is it?"

"Don't know." Jalen looked at the steel door, which was spray-painted white with Chinese characters. "But I've lost sight. What do we do?"

"Could she leave out the front?"

"It's possible, but she won't, right? She doesn't have time—she needs to log in." Jalen kicked the steel door hard.

For a few seconds, they just listened to each other's breathing. Jalen scrambled up a dumpster, thinking if he jumped, he could reach the cement ledge of the second-story window above him. He leapt, but it was still a couple of feet within reach, and he dropped hard to the street.

"My god," Darsie said. "Encyte has hacked into the network."

"What's happening?" Jalen dusted himself off, still looking for another way in. "What do you see?"

"He's cloning the school systems, the camera feeds, every piece of data coming in and out of the school . . . downloading them onto the on-premise . . ." Darsie muttered. "Through a VPN tunnel to another IP address. Yes." Darsie paused. "Encyte is watching."

Jalen banged on the steel door.

"Just wait. I'm coming right now. I can see your address. You're just a few blocks away. My team will trace the hack and follow the IP trail. I'm coming for you."

"I'm going to try the front door."

Jalen ran down the filthy alley. He pulled the handle. "Locked! Dead-bolted from the inside! There's no way I can get through."

"Okay, hang tight. Be there in three minutes."

CHAPTER 58

Never in his life had Wyatt seen anything like the Red Trident company jet, aka the Red Trident Spy Plane. As one might expect, it was outfitted with all the technology in San Francisco, but modified with Darsie's own personal touches: polished leather, gold fixtures, and wall-to-wall screens showing various footage. Inside the cabin, forty thousand feet above the earth, the brightest computer minds in the world were frantically hammering on keyboards, in a very complex virtual game of cat and mouse.

Wyatt sat behind the pilot, his gaze shifting from the clock on his iPhone to the blinking control panels, then back to his phone. Outside, all around them, nothing but white. The jet bounced and jerked, the Red Trident team buckled tight into their seats so as not to be thrown from their makeshift desks by the turbulence.

Darsie's plane—his secondary form of transportation—had been converted to a mobile NOC. Over the beeps and dings of computers, Wyatt listened to the layered voices: Darsie at Red Trident, Avi in the surveillance van, the comms where his Valor team was waiting for the fake shooting, and even the auditorium where the recorded symphony played.

"All right, you guys," Wyatt heard his father's voice over the radio. "She's in. Be ready."

"She's in?" Wyatt said in horror; he tried to scrambled to the front of the plane, but the turbulence knocked him down.

The pilot kept his eyes on the small window of glass in front of him. "I'm sorry," he called back to Wyatt. "The summer air is so turbulent over the Midwest! It's going to be tight. Not sure if we are gonna be able to get your boots on the ground by 4 p.m."

Leigh Ann waited in the stall, looking at her watch, convincing herself she would not run away before the signal. Two signals, in fact. The first from GrievingDad_12 to say that the operation was a go, and the second from the SecDef's security team, letting her know that they detected Encyte in the network.

GrievingDad_12 came through first, the Wickr message buzzing on her Apple Watch: *Good to go.*

A second message immediately followed the first: *We found the hack. He's in. Take your time. Follow the plan. God bless.*

Leigh Ann took a deep breath and told herself for the hundredth time that this was her penance. With the mind-altering drugs now completely out of her system, she was now painfully aware of her own culpability. Some deeds are so horrific that the very meditation of them makes one guilty.

She left the stall with the huge rifle at her side, feeling what so many killers before her must have felt: a surge of adrenaline, almost disorienting, as she put one foot in front of the other, determined to elaborately act out the evil she'd originally planned.

Unnoticed, her heels clicked down the quiet hall from the bathroom to the auditorium, and she pushed open the doors. The children were on stage on the far side, in midrehearsal of Bach's March in D Major. The stand-in kids could not play instruments, of course, but they went through the motions as a recording played. Leigh Ann closed her eyes and listened. Only for a moment. The notes so perfect, swirling to heaven like the souls that would be if she failed.

She made it to center court and raised the bump stock to her shoulder. She put her eye to the cold scope, seeing first the stand-in band instructor. A beautiful woman with pinned-up red hair, whipping the conductor's baton back and forth as though she'd done so all her life.

From there, Leigh Ann shifted her scope until she found the one she was told to hit first: the stand-in for the Henryson girl. A small girl. Dark hair, probably only half the size of her cello.

Leigh Ann breathed, then opened fire. The girl dropped instantly, the squib—a small firework inside a packet of fake blood—exploded and covered the little girl with the sticky red liquid. Around her, other kids began screaming, the music stopped as they flailed around on stage. As she was told, Leigh Ann methodically shifted her scope, moving to the next kid—a dark-skinned boy who stood at a drum set. The squib hit him in the chest, and he dropped alongside the girl. The pattern continued: the gun jumping in Leigh Ann's hands, the kids banging against the locked double doors below the green exit sign. Leigh Ann had completely lost herself, pulling the trigger over and over, seeing the bodies go down.

A minute and forty-five seconds later, she executed the last part of the plan, and with great relief, she reversed the gun to point the barrel at her own chest. "I'm so sorry for all of this," she whispered as she pulled the trigger. Instantly, two bags filled with fake blood and triggered by squibs detonated under the clothes at her chest and behind her back as if a bullet had passed through her body. She slumped to the ground.

CHAPTER 59

Darsie bypassed the elevator and went straight for the stairs, four of his top security men falling in step behind them. A private police car was waiting outside, flashing red and blue lights, and the traffic was already cleared. They were going over eighty miles per hour, through the narrow San Francisco streets, grabbing air and bottoming out. When they reached Chinatown, the men were out of the car, running.

Darsie tossed Jalen a bulletproof vest and a Glock. Jalen slung on the vest, flipped off the gun's safety, and waited for the battering ram.

One, two, three—the metal door swung off the hinges, and the team ran, in SWAT formation, down a dingy hallway. They could hear voices speaking Chinese. Jalen's mind raced. *Oh my god. This is big, bigger than a lone wolf. What if it's the Chinese mafia?*

The team entered a room where thirteen Chinese people sat, cross-legged and shoeless, in a circle, blinking at him. In the back of the room, coffee was burning in a cheap pot and a few men smoked. Hi Kyto sat next to a woman, holding her hand.

Jalen recognized the woman instantly, from the night outside the casino in Vegas.

"Mrs. Chen?" Jalen sighed.

Seeing the men with the guns filling the room, the women began crying, and the men yelled, "Get down, get down!"

There was a folding table, covered with coffee mugs. Several big blue books, and a large art easel with a poster board, half in Chinese, half in English: NARCOTICS ANONYMOUS.

Narcotics Anonymous? She's a . . . drug addict?

Jalen let the Glock drop to his side as the SWAT team held guns in the faces of Mrs. Chen and Hi Kyto. "Put your hands up and lie down on the ground!"

"Mr. Darsie!" Hi Kyto's face flushed. "What are you doing here?"

"Face down with hands behind your head!" a SWAT guy shouted at Hi Kyto.

She did as she was told, belly down beside her crying mother, as her hands were zip-tied hard.

"What's happening?" Hi Kyto said and managed to lift her head, and her eyes met Jalen's, tears filling the corners of them. "Who are you?"

The SWAT team searched the entire building and found no weapons of any kind. "Yeah, seems they're using this building for a church . . ." the SWAT leader said to Darsie. "Other than some evidence of gambling in the basement, I hate to tell ya, we got nothing."

Darsie let out a long breath. "Okay, let them go."

Zip ties were cut. Confused recovering addicts rose to their feet, muttering, angry, relieved.

Jalen offered Hi Kyto his hand but she batted it away, and pushed herself up.

"Why'd you jump out of the car?" he asked.

"My mother," Hi Kyto said, eyes still burning with fury. "She was addicted to Zovis. She's been clean for a month now, but since I've been hanging out with you, she's started to worry . . . that I would give up my studies, that I was taking the wrong path."

Jalen glanced at Mrs. Chen sitting in a chair, a woman consoling her.

"She texted me this afternoon that she found an old bottle she'd hidden, so I told her to meet me here, at the nearest meeting I could find on my phone."

"But why couldn't you just tell me?" Jalen asked softly.

"The secret wasn't mine to tell. My mother is a well-respected woman—at Stanford, but also in the Chinese government. She was ashamed . . . and if this got out, she could lose her fellowship, or get deported."

"I didn't know."

"Yeah, well, you could've trusted me . . . but what about you? Here you are, leading a SWAT team against my whole family and our church! Who the hell are you, anyway?"

Jalen opened his mouth to speak, but Hi Kyto held up her hand. "You know what? Don't. I don't care. But whatever this little game is, I bet it has something to do with him." Her eyes cut away to Darsie.

"You don't have the exact address?" Darsie shouted into his phone, listened, then hung up. "We know he logged in somewhere in the Bay Area using a mobile connection," he told Jalen. "But we don't have an address. Damn it."

"What's going on?" Hi Kyto asked.

"Encyte is close," Darsie said. "And if it's not you . . ."

"Not me?" Hi Kyto rose up and shoved Darsie in his metal-plated chest. "A terrorist! Oh my god, this is good. You guys thought I was *Encyte*!"

Darsie took the phone off speaker and put it to his ear. "What do you mean you lost the signal? Keep looking!" He ended the call and looked at Hi Kyto. "Julie, please. I know you're angry, but I can explain."

"I think I've heard enough."

"Please." Darsie caught her arm. "Give me one hour. Meet me in my office."

She looked at Jalen, then back at Darsie. "I'll meet you at the Ocean Guardian office. I want Morgan as a trusted third party to witness whatever you are going to say . . ." She stared at Darsie, her eyes narrow behind her glasses. "I'm never going to be alone with you again." She then looked at Jalen. "Or you."

CHAPTER 60

As planned, news of the shooting was intentionally leaked, and with only immediate law enforcement agencies and FBI aware that it was fake, the campus was put on full lockdown. Reporters flocked to the scene, cameras rolling just outside the police barricades. But inside the school, there was only silence. Smoke hung in the air. Deathly quiet. And yet not dead at all.

"Leigh Ann," a voice said in the earpiece. "This is the team leader from Valor, Cass. Don't move. Try to speak without moving your mouth. Are you okay?"

"Yes," Leigh Ann said, keeping her lips closed like she was told. She turned her head to the side and saw the blurry carpet on the auditorium floor, layered with broken glass. And the stage where children posed dead in front of the heavy velvet curtain. "Where are you?"

"Lying in front of you," Cass said. "By the podium. Thirty feet ahead."

Leigh Ann glanced up and saw the redheaded band instructor covered in blood—fake blood.

"Mary Alice . . . Samy . . ." Cass began rattling off the names of her team, and each of them responded with an "okay."

Leigh Ann fought tears as she heard their names. She leaned up slightly, trying to see the faces of the bloodied kids.

"Stay down," Cass said. "We'll be outta here in no time. Good work, guys. Let's just hope they got this guy."

Frank Henryson had just finished up his eighteenth hole at Congressional in Bethesda. He'd shot an eighty-five—not terrible—especially with his lower back soreness. Toweling off his face, he strode over to the bar where his wife was perched with a chardonnay in front of the TV. Frank squinted, reading the white letters scrolling across the bottom of the screen. *Another School Shooting.*

"Shit," Frank sighed. He signaled the bartender, who began filling the cocktail shaker with ice. It was going to be a long day. A long couple of days. Months even. He would be doing press, defending the NFA against all the nuts who blamed the Second Amendment every time a deranged person got hold of a gun. In Frank's opinion, it was a matter of more and better arms training and arming folks in schools that would solve the problem.

"Hey, turn the TV up," someone said to the bartender. Frank wanted to turn around and punch the guy. Couldn't he get one moment of quiet before the storm? Before the press conferences.

"The usual." The bartender slid the martini glass in front of him.

Frank sat down by his wife and lifted the cold gin to his lips, intentionally avoiding the TV screen. "Honey," he said, noticing his wife's pale, blank stare. "Barb?"

Her eyes were glued to the TV, jaw hanging like an epileptic fit. He followed her gaze to the screen where a jerky cameraman showed children crying, fleeing a campus. A campus he knew well, as it was in his neighborhood, Fairfax Middle School. On one hand he was devastated to think of the parents of the children at the school, some of whom he was sure to know. And on the other hand he was relieved—his kids went to a private boarding school. But what confused him is the school was out for the summer, wasn't it? Why were kids at the school? Thank god his kids were at band camp. And then in a rush of terror and panic he remembered—the rehearsal was moved to today. Suddenly Frank could not pull his eyes and ears away from the TV.

"We don't know anything for certain," said CNN's Mario Bombisuito, "but at this time, it's believed that the twin son and daughter of Frank Henryson, president of the NFA, were targeted in this attack during a summer camp activity. A band rehearsal." He paused. "Up to a dozen children are reported dead, the Henryson twins thought to be among the victims."

A wineglass slipped to the floor, shattering as Barbara Henryson wailed.

The SecDef's office in the Pentagon was still in utter chaos. While Leigh feigned dead on the video feed, teams frantically tried to track the IP address of the hacker, essentially chasing a white rabbit through a Byzantine network of point-to-point communication, data-packet traveling, satellites, buildings, IP address to IP address, somehow managing to find the thread no matter where it went.

The news played on low in the background and the SecDef sat at her desk, taking a minute to decide what to do. Already, the folks on the left touted that this was to be expected, and folks on the right, while grieving, still doubled down on Second Amendment rights.

The shooting was over, and now it was time to call the parents of the students at Fairfax and tell them their world was not. That their children were actually sitting in a warehouse, perfectly safe, pawns in the game to draw out a terrorist, but no longer innocent in the ways of the world.

The SecDef opened the manila file with the list of numbers, and decided she would call the Henrysons last. Let them feel this, she thought. She lifted the phone from her desk, but then glanced over at the photo of Ming Lu in the gold frame on her desk, in her school uniform plaid, hands crossed in her lap. What if it had been Ming?

She'd hardly had time to contemplate when Mr. Yellow came running over. "There's a second shooter!"

CHAPTER 61

"Looks like he's logged out," Avi said on the crackling radio. "Okay, boys, it's a go."

Eldon had been waiting for the call. He nodded at the SWAT team, and they moved silently and in formation, guns drawn, clearing rooms per protocol, making sure there was no other madman or -woman—or Encyte himself—hidden in the building.

They worked their way across the east wing and down the long hall. "All clear," Eldon said in the comms. "We're going into the auditorium."

Eldon kicked the door in, gunpowder and smoke spilling into the hallway.

"Dear god." Eldon looked around the silent auditorium. Though he'd seen many gruesome things, both as a hostage and in service to his country, there were few sights more horrible than his young team—bloodied and sprawled out dead on the floor.

He stepped around the fallen kids. *Rory, Samy, Mary Alice . . .* accounting for each in his head. *Pierce, Rayo . . .* Eleven.

"Guys, we're one man down," Eldon said into the radio, his heart hammering, and then he saw at the far end of the stage:

Cody, face up, T-shirt drenched in fake blood. His blue eyes were opened wide, like in death.

"Hi, Dad," Cody muttered into the comms, still playing dead, but angling his head slightly toward his father. He gave a quick smile.

Eldon cleared his throat. "All accounted for," he said into his radio. "We're all clear on the—"

The sound of gunfire echoed through the silent auditorium. Eldon spun around. "Everybody down!" he screamed. "We got a shooter!"

A bump from turbulence threw Wyatt to the cabin floor. Wyatt had just listened as Darsie, back in San Francisco, told the Red Trident team that the Chinatown raid was a bust and the suspect, Hi Kyto, was cleared. Now, there was another shooter on the ground in Virginia. The entire mission was falling apart.

"Shooter!" Wyatt heard his father's voice blare through the jet's radio. "Everybody down!" Wyatt ran over to the tech, his face hovering just above the plane's radio.

Bam-bam-bam . . . bam-bam! More shots rang out. Wyatt looked at the wide-eyed tech as they listened to the sound of feet shuffling, then silence.

"Eldon!" Avi's voice crackled through the radio. "Sounds like it's coming from the west wing! Near the audio visual center."

"Roger that," Wyatt's dad said. "We've got noises coming one hundred feet ahead of us to the left. No shooter in the hallway."

Wyatt waited. More silence. And then, his father again: "Avi, it's Encyte. Did you get that? He just came over the intercom. He's in the building. He's got one kid hostage with him."

"We just did a body count," Cass's voice broke in over the comms. "Everyone is accounted for."

"We've got a little girl screaming," Eldon said. "We're following."

Wyatt leaned over the screens, one showing grainy footage of the auditorium where his comrades lay in fake dead poses. Another screen showing the school's hallway, where his father and a couple members of SWAT crept carefully toward the school's audio visual center.

"Oh my god, Dad, please be careful," a muffled voice broke in.

Wyatt's heart dropped. "Cody!" he screamed. "That's my brother!" he said to the tech.

The sound of more shots ricocheted down the hall: *bam-bam-bam.*

"Dad, something's not right," Cody said after a couple of seconds. "The sound is off—"

He was interrupted by a scream. The high-pitched, guttural scream of a young girl.

"Dead. They're all dead . . ." a maniacal voice came over the intercom again. "Don't try to find me unless you want to join them."

"Avi, are you tracking?" Eldon asked.

"There is nothing to trace!" Avi yelled over the radio. "He's not in the network. Someone physically is in the building."

"We gotta move. We've tracked the shooter. He's at the AV center. There's smoke in the room. It's sealed, but I can see behind the glass. We're going to open fire."

More shots over the intercom, and then more silence.

"It's not live fire," Cody said in the comms, the sudden realization obvious in his tone.

Wyatt watched on the small screen as Cody stood up and began running across the auditorium toward the door. "Dad, stop! It's not right! It's not real!"

"Get me into the comms," Wyatt said to the tech.

The tech hesitated.

"Do it!"

The guy began frantically pushing buttons and then handed Wyatt a headset. "You're in."

"Dad, listen to Cody," Wyatt yelled into the radio. "He knows what he's talking about. Please, stand down."

"Wyatt? How are you on this—"

"Doesn't matter. Dad, you gotta listen." Wyatt held the earpiece tight against his face. "It's a trap! Listen to Cody!"

"Please, Dad," Cody chimed in. "The sound is a recording. I promise."

"We got eyes on him right here," Eldon said. "I see the smoke from his gunfire behind this glass."

The SWAT team leader's voice came in, "If you're not going, I am."

Silence. Wyatt listened in horror to the sounds of gurgling, choking, gasping.

"Nerve agent! It's a trap!" Eldon yelled. "Everybody out!"

On the screen, a man's body shook. He put his hands to his neck. The foam from his mouth visible even in the low-def footage.

"We're landing!" the pilot called from the front.

Wyatt braced as the Red Trident jet tore through the low-hanging clouds and bumped down for the landing at Fort Meade.

CHAPTER 62

It was only moments after the shooting that the SecDef arrived. Her hair freshly pinned back and her lips glossed and ready for the storm of press. In her shadow, Ken and a flurry of entourage as well as five black Suburbans.

"Elaine," Eldon said as he walked across the parking lot to greet her, unclipping his helmet. His face was tired, but it twinkled with victory. "We did it."

"Yes, we did." The SecDef extended her hand. "My thanks to you on behalf of the American people." She looked over at the campers all huddled, drinking water, stripping off the gear they had under their school clothes. "And to your team."

"This is what we're here for. We're happy to help. I see you brought the cavalry." He nodded in the direction of the vehicles. "For us, I presume . . . an escort back to Valor."

The specious smile faded from the SecDef's lips. "Actually, it's an escort home. You and your team will caravan to a secure hangar, where everyone will be routed back to their respective cities, to their lives."

"Excuse me?" Eldon stepped closer, so close he could see the blurred liner gathering in the corner of her eyes. "You lied to us, to me. It was a trick."

"Eldon, come now—"

"You brought me here to run this mission, so that you could get us out of our fortress. Why trust us at all?"

"I played the odds and I won. We won here today. That counts, and you should embrace that." She tapped him on the shoulder, then shrugged. "But the risk is too high to do it again. We're cashing in, Eldon. Quitting while we're still ahead."

Ken stepped over from behind the SecDef and opened the door to her vehicle. "Elaine, you've got CNN waiting. We need to get moving," he said.

The SecDef nodded and turned back to Eldon. "Have these kids cleaned up and at the airport within the hour."

Eldon glared. "These kids just saved your ass."

Wyatt stepped out of the car, taking in the scene: the police beating back press, who waved cameras and microphones, trying to get a glimpse of the kids. The SWAT team leader, still convulsing, was being treated with a nerve agent antidote on a gurney. And the Valor team huddled to the side, high from their first mission as Wyatt walked up.

"Holy crap, Cody," Mary Alice said, wiping the fake blood from her face. "How did you know?"

"All those hours in the gun range"—Samy patted Cody's head—"finally paid off. You did well today, little Brewer."

"He's right," Wyatt said, walking over to where the campers were gathered. "If Dad had started shooting, it would have been a catastrophe." Wyatt held up his hand and Cody smiled, slapping it in the air. "Avi said there was a canister of sarin in the ceiling, rigged to the sprinkler system. Would've killed everyone, and any responders who came in after."

"Dude." Samy came over and folded Wyatt into a hug. "So glad you are back. How did you find us?"

"I had help. I took something to reverse the effects."

Samy squinted. The rest of the team leaned in. "Who helped you?"

"A former one of us," Wyatt said.

"What are you doing talking to my team?" a voice said just beyond the ring of kids.

Wyatt and the rest of the group turned to see Eldon, his face smudged black from gunpowder. Cass stood behind him, a pained look on her face as she began un-Velcroing the bulletproof vest.

"Son, I'm going to have to ask you to leave," Eldon said. "This area is restricted. No civilians."

"Dad, come on." Wyatt glanced around the circle—his family, his team, no eyes would meet his. "You gotta understand. What I did—it was the only way. And we're close. So close. The mission is not over."

"It is for us," Eldon said, his words dropping like an iron curtain.

"But Darsie said they'll have the IP. Jalen has cleared a suspect, we know the area—"

"We have orders from the SecDef," Eldon said. "Valor is no more."

"Samy . . . Rory?" Wyatt looked to his groupmates, who just stared at their hands. He turned to Cass. "Come help me."

She pulled off her wig and looked at Eldon, who shook his head.

"Oh my god, Dad, what am I supposed to do?" Wyatt said.

"I don't know." Eldon said. "Maybe Darsie can help."

CHAPTER 63

Jalen took the long way home. He walked slowly, turning the day over.

It wasn't Hi Kyto. I'm the liar. Thoughts zipped through his head over and over again, electrifying him. *She's not a murderer. She's just a girl. A perfect girl.* He wanted to throw up. He thought about her face, tearful as she climbed into the car with her mother. "I don't ever want to see you again," she said.

He weaved his way through Chinatown. Along the streets, vendors were taking down shop. The winds blew and with the sun now sinking, he felt cold.

He cut across the street, wandering, not wanting to go back to the apartment. Wyatt and the Valor kids were safe, but it would be hours before Wyatt was back. Jalen bumped through the crowd, passing an electronics store with TVs in the window all playing the news footage of the fake shooting.

Encyte was there. So close. Jalen stopped at a meat market. A whole suckling pig hung upside down, bloodless, staring at him. And then, the connection to Encyte hit him.

That's it. He wrestled his phone from his pocket and dialed up Wyatt.

"Hey, dude, I can't talk," Wyatt answered, the exhaustion immediately evident in his tone. "I'm getting on a plane—"

"I just have one question—what do you think about Morg?" Jalen asked.

"Morg? I don't know. Why?"

The shopkeeper standing behind the pig stared at Jalen. "When I was on the boat," Jalen said, "Morg was talking about pig pheromones. Do you think . . . ?"

In the background, the loud hum of a jet's engine. "I don't know," Wyatt yelled above the noise. "I don't see it. I mean, he works for Darsie."

"And so does Hi Kyto!"

"Look, Jalen, don't do anything. Stay there. I'll be back in five hours," Wyatt said and hung up.

Jalen looked at his watch. Hi Kyto would be meeting Darsie in thirty minutes. He pulled up the search bar on his phone and typed the name "Morgan Whittendale."

The first hit, an article from the *San Francisco Chronicle*. Jalen scanned the words: *For such a young man, Whittendale speaks with a professorial tone.*

Jalen's eyes scanned the words: *"They used to call me 'the professor' when I was in high school," Whittendale said. "I didn't really like that. Being a hacker used to be taboo, but now technical skill is a badge of honor. And hacking is something that can be taught."*

Professor? Jalen stopped in his tracks, the busy people of Chinatown bumping past him toward home. He pulled up his Uber app as fast as he could and ordered a ride to Red Trident.

Hi Kyto was perched in the Ocean Guardian beanbag chairs, her shoes off, her face hovering above a steaming cup of tea. She held her phone to her ear, tears of anger in the corners of her eyes as she explained the day to her best friend.

"I just can't believe it," she said into her phone. "I mean, of all of us, Darsie was closest to me, and he actually thought I was Encyte."

"I know," Morg said gravely. "It's just insane, Julie. Such a violation. And I saw there was another attack today."

"Yeah, there was. But it was staged. The whole thing."

"Staged? What do you mean?"

"That woman—the shooter—went to the feds. The kids weren't the real ones."

Silence. "You there?" Hi Kyto said.

"Staging a school shooting," Morg said slowly. "What the fuck is Darsie doing? This is giving me the creeps. Look, just let me handle some emails and I'll just be in my office. You can see me through the glass."

"Okay, I just really couldn't be alone with him right now. I'm, like, really freaking out."

"Of course," Morg said. "I've got some essential oils. Just take a breath. Let me handle a couple of things and I'll be right back."

CHAPTER 64

Tui had known eventually everything would come to a head. And when it did, there would be chaos and he'd be able to swoop in like a hawk and pluck the unsuspecting fish from the river. Sure, it was difficult to keep up with Jalen, but again, his instincts had paid off. He'd watched the failed raid on the Chinese Kumbaya circle, enjoying the contrite look on that bastard Darsie's face when the crowds started swarming around the church.

But still, Tui knew this could be the billionaire's elaborate scheme. Make a to-do about suspecting someone else to keep the attention away from yourself. Sounds just like something a punk like Darsie would do. Funny, he's the world's greatest hacker and yet he somehow lost the trace. How convenient.

Even so, Tui couldn't believe his eyes as he watched Darsie's Tesla leave the data center, weave back through Chinatown, and then pull back into Red Trident where Hi Kyto was waiting. That sleazy MFer was headed right back to the nest. To meet with the prime suspect.

Tui got out his phone and texted Ken: *Polish the fuckin medal of honor for me.*

This is all about to pay off, my friend. Ken texted back. *Big time.*

From the back seat of the Uber, Jalen's hands shook as he texted Hi Kyto: *I know you hate me. And I promise I'll never lie to you again.*

Seconds passed. Then a text popped up: *What do you want?*

The handle Pro_F_er, Jalen typed furiously, *have u ever seen it?*

Maybe. I've played like 1000 handles.

Morg's handle? Was it his?

Don't think so. He had a bunch. His main one was like Ocean Boy. Or Sea Boy. Please stop.

Sea-boy? Jalen's heart pounded in his throat. *Not high boy?*

No.

Jalen looked out the window at the late-afternoon traffic. Hi Kyto texted again: *But hai is sea in Chinese.*

"Oh my god." Jalen tapped his driver's shoulder. "Please, man, can you please go faster?" He called Hi Kyto.

"Jay, I can't do this right now," Hi Kyto said.

"Julie, listen to me. You're not safe. Please, where are you?"

"I'm in Morg's office right now. Look, if you have questions, you can talk to him yourself. He's walking in."

Jalen listened in horror as she passed off the phone.

"Hey, Jay," Morgan said.

Tui flipped his FBI badge at the salad-eating security guard at the pavilion entrance and ran to the elevator, jamming his thick, tan hand between the doors before they could close.

"What floor?" Darsie asked as he pressed the fourth.

"Same, thank you." Tui smiled.

The fourth floor pinged and Darsie stepped out, almost charging down the dingy hallway. Tui fell in step behind him, feeling for his gun as he entered the business office of Ocean Guardian. Everything was grungy. Like stepping from the sleek future back into the year 1989.

Tui watched Darsie duck inside the office where the Asian gaming chick and a young college-aged kid with stupid-looking long hair were waiting. It was dark. The overhead fluorescent lights were off as the staff and volunteers were leaving for the end of the day. Tui's eyes shifted to the glass, peering through the sea of stickers.

Now was the time. Tui entered the waiting area, where the three were sitting in beanbag chairs. He leveled his gun. "Think I need to have a little talk with you guys."

Morgan jerked Hi Kyto by the wrist and started stepping backward toward his office. "Yeah, I don't think so." Morgan slammed the door, peering at Tui and Darsie through the glass.

"Morg, what are you doing?" Hi Kyto writhed in his grip. "Let me go!"

Tui leveled his gun at the door.

"*No!*" Darsie called out. "It's bulletproof!"

"Then I'll kick it in." Tui slammed his giant foot into the door.

Tui began slamming his whole body into the glass door. A few more kicks and slams and suddenly, the door gave way. He was in.

He made it only a couple of feet before—*BOOOM!*

A horrible explosion rocked the room, blowing glass and knocking Darsie to the floor. Black smoke and flames permeated the air. Darsie looked out into the chaos: water raining down from the ceiling and Tui, legless on the floor, eyes open, body severed in half.

Darsie stared blankly, then shifted his body, seeing a giant chunk of glass piercing his torso, blood seeping around it. He peered into Morg's office—filled with smoke and broken glass, the windows completely blown out. He watched as Morg secured a neon yellow rappelling rope to a cabinet and slipped over the edge, struggling to support a limp Hi Kyto tucked under his arm.

He dropped from sight, and moments later, Darsie heard a motorcycle engine rev.

CHAPTER 65

As soon as Jalen stepped out of the car at the Darsie Pavilion, he could hear the chaos following the explosion. He looked up, above the wall of fire engines and first responders, and saw where the fourth-floor office windows had been blown out.

A pack of EMTs were wheeling a man out on a gurney.

"Darsie!" Jalen yelled and ran toward him, the EMTs barely giving him any notice and not slowing.

Darsie's pale face turned to Jalen. He'd lost a lot of blood, but he tried to speak as Jalen ran alongside the gurney: ". . . has Julie," Darsie said to Jalen, his hand flopping off the gurney. He dropped a key fob as the EMTs whisked him away.

Jalen snatched the fob, clicked the key. The lights to a BMW i8—the sleek all-electric coupe—flashed. Jalen ran to the car, instinctively taking the passenger side. He checked his steps and corrected, heading for the driver's seat. He had no doubt where Morg was taking Hi Kyto.

Jalen raced the i8 into the marina parking lot and jammed on the brakes. The car skidded and slammed into a Mercedes G-Class, setting off a crescendo of car alarms and chaos. Jalen abandoned the vehicle, leaving the door open and key on the driver's seat as he ran down the dock. He scanned the Ocean Guardian fleet, one of the slips open, like a missing tooth. The *Kid Captain* was out to sea. The Bahama 41 with the three Yamaha 425s. The fastest in the fleet. There was no other boat that could possibly catch it.

Thinking, he looked around then stopped, noticing the glint of the pneumatic fishing spear tucked in the stern of one of the dive boats. There was no choice; he jumped into the boat and grabbed the spear.

"Hey, what are you doing!" a man called after him.

Jalen tucked the spear into his waistband and ran down the dock, dropping down onto a shiny new Yamaha WaveRunner FX Cruiser SVHO. It was maroon and super light. He took the key, which was still in the ignition, and cranked it up.

"Hey, kid!" Another man screamed as Jalen, with no life vest, went from zero to sixty out of the marina and toward the open ocean.

He had no radio, no GPS, only his memory and a hunch. He headed straight out toward the Golden Gate Bridge and the Farallones beyond them.

Recalling the trip and its heading on the *Kid Captain,* Jalen kept the throttle down, punching through the swells like he was on a bathtub-sized bullet. Just like the previous day, the fog rolled in, and the northern Pacific churned and bucked. The sunset he rode into was a red wash of haze. By the time Jalen approached the desolate islands, he could barely make out the jagged formations against the black sea. His gas tank was nearly empty, and it was dark and soupy with fog. He killed the motor and let the WaveRunner drift, listening.

A voice cut through the greasy night air. "Technology, brother. There's nowhere to hide anymore, and that's a shame."

Jalen spun around, seeing nothing.

"I just wanted to help, you know," Morg's voice echoed as the *Kid Captain* came into view like a ghost ship. Morg stood in the helm, a preacher's grin on his face. "But then it hit me—I can clean up the oceans all day, but what about all the shit going on on land?"

The *Kid Captain* began circling Jalen, wrapping the WaveRunner in a whirlpool of waves and wake. Jalen held the handlebars, goosing the jets, steadying the watercraft, riding it out.

"What side of history do you want to be on?" His voice bounced off the rocks. "I was changing the world and then you had to show up, Jalen. Or should I say, *Javelin*?" Morg paused, reaching down and lifting up Hi Kyto by her long black hair. She cried softly through the gag in her mouth.

"Put her down!" Jalen yelled. Walls of water coming over the nose of the WaveRunner.

"There are many killers among us," Morg continued. "Kids like you and Julie, who think their actions in a virtual world have no consequences. But I say a little pinch to wake us up is a good thing. I mean, think about it, Encyte only killed a few thousand people—a hundred-millionth of the planet. A tiny prick. We're all so . . . insignificant in terms of life . . . but a nice wake-up call for the planet. Until you showed up. You really ruined things. And that pissed me off."

Morg reached down under the helm and once again retrieved the sawed-off shotgun. He leveled it at Jalen and fired. A slug tore into the rear quarter of the WaveRunner, punching a five-inch hole a foot behind Jalen's leg. Morg racked the gun. Jalen dove off the side of the WaveRunner as another slug hit it. Gas and oil poured from the hole. Wyatt took a breath and dove down. He looked up at the surface and felt the concussion of the water as the WaveRunner exploded on the surface. A flashing, burning light pulsed through the water around him.

Jalen turned in the water and swam toward the *Kid Captain*.

He felt a tug at the back of his pants. He panicked, then remembered the speargun. He reached back and retrieved it from his waistband.

He pointed the gun at the *Kid Captain,* holding on to the handle as he kicked toward the surface, lungs now burning for breath. In the faint light from the flaming WaveRunner some ten yards off, he saw Morgan leaning out, peering into the sea around the wreck, now with a submachine gun in hand. He scanned the water, looking for Jalen to surface.

Jalen aimed for Morg's torso and squeezed the tight trigger. A firm burst of air jerked the gun back in his hand as the spear whistled from the barrel like an arrow without feathers, wobbling through the air. Morg, hearing the shot, turned just as the spear came angling up toward the helm. It caught him in the neck, just below the jaw, and came out his cheek, a pin rammed through the face of a doll. He was hooked, fishlike. He turned the gun on Jalen, bullets tearing through the water. Jalen yanked hard on the handle of the gun, jerking Morg forward as he fired down at his feet. Jalen pulled again. Blood poured from Morg's face as he stumbled to the side of the boat. Morg dropped the gun and held on to the boat. Jalen yanked hard once more, pulling Morg overboard, face first, his fresh blood pouring into the sea.

Jalen treaded water, still holding the speargun. He felt the bump of something underneath him. Sandpaper skin. Another bump. Jalen looked down and saw what looked like a car in the water. At first, he thought it was the remains of his WaveRunner. But it swam. The shark now moving toward the young scientist who bled and thrashed in the water a few feet from him. He felt the handle of his speargun gently tugged from his hands. Then—a terrible pull, a giant jerk—as the speargun was ripped from his hands, tearing the skin on his palm.

Jalen swam hard for the boat that was drifting away. He took several strokes and then—a scream. A gurgling scream. He turned to see half of Morgan's body above the water as the great white thrashed him back and forth like a seal's plaything.

Jalen swam harder, lungs screaming, until he reached the *Kid Captain*. He was unsure how he was going to get up on deck. He took off his belt and, looping it over one of the rear motors, he pulled himself up on the motor mount and flopped into the stern.

He looked down to see his own legs bleeding. He scrambled to his feet and glanced around for Hi Kyto. He went to the bow, belowdecks, and pushed the door to the small aft cabin, and there she was, curled like a bird on a nest of life jackets. All around her, blood.

He lifted her up and held her. "He's gone," Jalen whispered, loosening the gag on her mouth as she sobbed. "It's over. He's gone."

CHAPTER 66

Though the body of Morgan Whittendale was never found, there was sufficient evidence to prove categorically that he was, in fact, Encyte. His young life and utter brilliance misdirected and wasted. The absence of a corpse caused a problem for Jalen, and though he and Hi Kyto both testified to what they had heard him confess that night, both teens were still grilled by various authorities: FBI, San Francisco PD, and even zealous park rangers who were the stewards of the Farallones.

Even Mr. Yellow joined in the questioning. "You have to understand," he said to Jalen. "It was a foggy night, and with the gunfire and the waves, coulda been easy for him to slip away."

"I saw him being ripped in half by a great white," Jalen said. And to him, it was the most appropriate death for what the press was calling a "deranged ecoterrorist. An entitled millennial who used his talents to terrorize the world and teach it a lesson." This sparked a political debate, followed by finger-pointing from the Left and Right. To Jalen, labeling Morg anything other than a monster and making his life fodder for politicians to sling mud at one another was a sin in itself and a terrible shame.

Before Jalen left to go back to Detroit, Hi Kyto agreed to meet him on the bike trail. No phones, no tech, no tricks—that was the rule.

"Don't even know why I'm here." Hi Kyto stood arms crossed, looking out at the summer moonrise above the bridge. "I can't trust you. I can't trust anything about you."

"How's Darsie?" Jalen asked, hoping that she'd gone to the hospital to visit him. That maybe from his recovery bed, the great Mr. Darsie had put in a nice word.

"John?" She snorted. "His currency—his heartbeat—resides in his secrets . . . he sees no problem with deception, conspiracy."

"So what did he say?" Jalen persisted.

Hi Kyto rolled her eyes. "He said you were in a secret military spy group . . . and you were one of the bravest kids he'd ever met."

"I can't tell you how sorry I am . . . for deceiving you. And I know it doesn't mean much, but . . ." Jalen stepped behind some bushes and pulled out a new mountain bike. "Here."

"What? It's awesome—" Hi Kyto stopped, catching her own excitement. "But you didn't have to . . ."

"It's a Kona, like you wanted. The seat might be a little high, but you can lower it."

"It's great, but I can't accept this . . ."

Jalen took a deep breath and nodded, looking out at the bay and the city beyond it.

"You thought I was a terrorist," she said softly. "The world's worst. Which is sorta flattering, but . . . it's just . . . done. Whatever we had is gone."

"I understand, and I promise I will leave you alone. But before I do, do me one favor?"

She laughed. "You're something else, you know that? I don't owe you shit." She pulled the sleeves of her hoodie down over her hands. "What?"

"You know how you said all families are psycho?"

"Yeah?"

"Well, I was thinking. The thing I'm most afraid of is letting someone meet mine, to see who I really am. I know you say you'll never trust me, but I want to show you . . . ya know . . . that you can."

"I have no idea what you're getting at," Hi Kyto said. "Are you saying you want me to meet your psychotic family?"

Jalen shrugged and nodded.

"Where?"

Jalen waited shyly beside a large Latino family, probably awaiting the return of a cousin or grandmother, holding balloons and signs that read, BIENVENIDOS. He checked his watch. It was 7:30 in the morning in the McNamara Terminal at the Detroit Metro Airport. The red-eye from San Francisco should have landed minutes ago. He had no sign and he didn't need one. As arrivals started shuffling past TSA security and into the baggage area, he saw her: Beats headphones on, eyes puffy from a nap on the plane. Backpack slung over her shoulder.

Hey, she mouthed, smiling as he approached. Should he hug her? Fist bump? Jalen hadn't decided before she slipped off her headphones, reached out, and grabbed him.

"Hey, you," she said, pulling him in for a quick hug. Her cheek brushed his under the hoodie. He could smell her face lotion.

"Welcome to Detroit," he said, pulling back and smiling. "I thought Darsie wanted to give you the jet."

"He did. He wanted me to work along the way . . . probably wanted to keep an eye on me." Hi Kyto rolled her eyes. "But I didn't take it. I want to disconnect. I want this to be a break. In fact," she said, pulling out her cell phone, "I'm going to turn this off."

"Okay." Jalen pulled his phone out of his pocket and turned it off.

"And . . ." She took a small paperclip out of her pocket and proceeded to eject the SIM card.

Jalen did the same; both kids smiled, ensuring there would be no connection. "Me too. You know, I'm surprised you still work for the guy."

"Yeah," Hi Kyto said, "but the truth is he does cool work. And I get paid a lot."

"Sign me up." Jalen laughed. "This way. It's bright outside." He took off his Guccis and handed them to her, then stopped. "You sure you're up for this? My parents can be a bit much. They're trying things out again, so that's like weird too."

"Up for it?" Hi Kyto smiled. "I'm just an observer. You're in the hot seat."

"Okay, well, you've been warned." Jalen texted his dad: *We're out.*

His dad responded with a black thumbs-up emoji, and moments later, a white Range Rover pulled to the curb, and his mom and dad both stepped out of the car.

"What up, what up?" his dad said as he came around the car and shook Hi Kyto's hand. "Heard so much about you. My name is Ronnie Rose, but you can call me Mr. Rose."

"What?" Jalen said.

"Ah, I'm just kidding. Call me Ronnie. And this is Tyra, my beautiful and hopefully soon-to-be wife again."

"Don't get ahead of yourself." Tyra turned to Hi Kyto. "Thank you so much for coming to Detroit. We're happy to have you. Now, let's get back home. We've got a lot to do."

Jalen slipped in the back behind Hi Kyto and Jalen caught his dad giving him a wink in the rearview mirror. The drive back to Jalen's house in the Palmer Woods neighborhood of Detroit included a short tour of the newly resurgent downtown area of Detroit, Jalen's father pointing out the casino, Comerica Park, then slowing by Ford Field. "Here's where the Lions play," Ronnie said. "What I used to call my office, back in the day." He pointed out the Shinola Hotel, the Nike store. "You wouldn't believe it, but fifteen years ago there was nothing here but woodshops and bars."

"He's not lying," Tyra said.

"I used to have to drive around with a—you know what, we're not gonna go there."

Jalen's mom rolled her eyes. "Ronnie, you never had a gun in your car in your life."

"You don't know everything about me," Ronnie said, joking.

Back at Jalen's house, the Rose Labor Day reunion was already in full swing. In front of the house—a large, renovated home formerly owned by one of Detroit's pioneering auto executives—was a big tent filled with Jalen's family who'd already arrived. The cousins were playing in the yard and Ronnie's brother had already fired up the grill and was bragging about his special rub.

Ronnie wasted no time making his rounds, introducing Hi Kyto as Jalen's girlfriend, and each time, Jalen followed it with a wince. "No, no, no," he said. "We're just friends."

"Friends? Oh, from where?" his aunt asked.

"A gaming tournament."

"Gaming? What do you mean?"

And at this point, Ronnie stepped back in and said that Hi Kyto was a genius, professional gamer. Not only was she taking college courses, she was already working as a professional. "Some spy kind of shit."

"I do a little programming for a security technology firm." Hi Kyto smiled politely.

After these somewhat embarrassing introductions were made and guests started digging into the food coming off the grill, Jalen and Hi Kyto found themselves having a pretty good time. Jalen's cousins had fired up the Xbox in the living room. The game for the day: *Call of Duty: Black Ops*. The cousins grew raucous, as the bullets streamed down, firing incessantly.

"You want in?" Jalen looked at Hi Kyto. "Clean these fools up?"

She smiled and shook her head. "No. We're disconnecting, remember? Besides, I don't think humiliating your family is the best way to get them to like me."

In the backyard, sprawling along the lush sweep of green grass, a game of pickup football had started. Mostly Ronnie, his brothers, two cousins, and a neighbor who'd already sprained his back. They'd divided themselves into two teams: Ronnie and Tyra's brother (who'd actually played running back at Clemson) against everyone else.

Both families were full of great athletes, so the competition every year was fierce. It was apparent that Ronnie, who'd spent eight years in the NFL, had a clear advantage and probably should not have been playing in a pickup game. But still, Ronnie was in heaven: to stretch his legs and run and pull down balls from someone who, Ronnie admitted humbly, could actually throw a football.

So Ronnie was loving the shit-talking and joke-cracking, especially at the expense of the neighbor who had instantly pulled his back. He was having such a good time, in fact, that he hadn't noticed Jalen stepping quietly onto the other team.

"Can I play?" Jalen asked.

"Sure, Jay," his cousin said. "Jump on defense."

Hi Kyto raised her eyebrows from the sidelines, hearing him called Jay.

"See." Jalen shrugged. "I wasn't lying about everything."

Jalen lined up, not across from his father but on the opposite side. As instructed, he took the guy with the bad back. Jalen's family was all too aware that Jalen had no interest in live sports, only electronic ones. No one had noticed that over the summer,

Jalen—the scrawny video-game king—had put on a solid ten pounds of muscle, grown almost a half inch, and also simultaneously became harder, sharper, and more present.

The snap went back to the former Clemson running back, and Ronnie broke off the line, threw a juke, danced past his defender and was halfway to the makeshift end zone, marked by a paper dinner plate. The ball hummed through the late-summer air. Ronnie watched it, his eyes clocking the brown torpedo as it cut a line through the blue sky. He came up, hands in position to receive yet another touchdown pass, when another set of hands entered his view. Thin and wiry, they rose up between him and the ball. The look on Ronnie's face showed where his mind went, the look of *Oh shit. Someone's about to pick me off*. And indeed, the ball was snatched out of the air.

"Intercepted!" someone yelled across the backyard.

Ronnie was confused to see his son switch the ball from right to left and throw a spin move, sending the Clemson QB sprawling. And then, to Ronnie's utter disbelief, Jalen actually put ground between the two of them and ran back for a pick-six. Jalen crunched over the paper dinner plate smeared with barbecue sauce and dropped the ball.

A cacophony of cheers and whistles tore through the yard.

Jalen's uncle stood up from the grill, tongs in hand. "Ronnie," he yelled. "Your boy just schooled you!"

Jalen stood awkwardly in the imaginary end zone, wondering what would happen next. His dad in the yard, bewildered, the family laughing, Hi Kyto on the sideline, smiling proudly.

Ronnie put his hands on his hips and shook his head, a hint of humiliation on his face. "Damn, boy, you got me." He slapped his son's hand. "Where the heck have them skills been hiding? You're awesome."

The gazpacho soup sat untouched in the iced terrine. The salads, covered in late-summer fruit slices, slowly wilted on the edge of bone-white place mats. And the Chilean sea bass, cooked head on, lay on its plate wide-eyed in the center of the heavily waxed dining room table, watching as Barbara and Frank Henryson argued with each other from opposite ends of the long wooden table. Their twin son and daughter sat in the middle, each as wide-eyed as the dead fish, watching the fight unfold. Hanging on the wall behind the table was a Revolutionary War–era musket and a plaque with the NFA coat of arms and the Second Amendment written out in golden script.

The veins bulged on Barbara's neck, her hands shook, and tears ran from her eyes. "Frank, I have never argued with you on this issue before and would never say a word against you in the press or to our friends. But"—she breathed deeply, trying to calm herself—"after our kids were nearly in a mass shooting you have to tell me—by the love of God—that our laws need to change. Now that it hit home you *have to tell me* you agree that we have to take these goddamned machine guns out of the hands of mentally deranged and dangerous people! Tell me you see it. Or I am going to lose my mind."

Frank dabbed his lips. The only item on the table being consumed with any regularity was the red wine enjoyed by both parents that evening. "Babs," Frank shook his head softly. He did this when she was being silly. "I am very sorry and ashamed to hear you speak like this. I sure as heck agree that we got a mental health issue in this country. We got an overeating epidemic, too. Should we ban spoons cuz fat folks can't stop eating ice cream?" Frank laughed. "Yeah, I think we should change the laws. Right now you know there's lawmakers in the state of California that are trying to make it illegal to buy a thirty-round magazine for an assault rifle. If you got a nutcase with four magazines and you're trying to stop him with a magazine with five rounds, how the hell do you think that's gonna work out?"

Barbara laughed and then screamed across the table. "Don't you see? More guns and more bullets will not solve this problem!"

"No, I don't see! What the hell do you think will stop the mass shootings? More Band-Aids? That's goddamn crazy talk! And I'm not gonna sit in my house and listen to crazy talk!" Frank stood up and slapped his napkin down into his seat.

"You are insane," Barbara yelled back as she stood. "And this, don't you forget, is not your house. It's our house!"

"Dad . . . Mom . . ." A quiet voice rose up from the center of table. Frank Jr. addressed his parents timidly. "Please, let's settle down. I . . . we . . . don't know what the solution is, if it's what you're saying, Dad, or if it's what Mom is talking about. I don't know. It's probably not either. But it's clear there is a problem." Frank Jr. looked across the table at his sister, Coleen. "And we need to fix it. The good news is, we can figure it out together. It might take some time and lots of talking, but there is a solution."

"Mom . . . Dad," Coleen said, "please sit back down."

The elder Henrysons looked at each other from across the table and slowly each slid back into their seats.

CHAPTER 67

Though he was forced to alter his schedule somewhat, from his suite at UCSF Med Center, John Darsie still found a way to conduct business. In the early morning, Wyatt slipped in and found the billionaire propped in his hospital bed with a fresh glass of tomato juice, sliced San Francisco sourdough, and a copy of the *Times*.

"Not a bad setup," Wyatt said, pulling up a chair.

"Suppose it helps to rent out the entire floor." Darsie folded the newspaper in his lap.

"How do you feel?"

"Never better." Darsie motioned to his heavily bandaged torso and smiled. His face, though cut and bruised, was clean shaven and smelled of a light cologne. "Didn't turn out as we predicted, did it?"

Wyatt looked out past white orchids lining the windows that let in the bright morning sun. "No."

Darsie sighed. "Red Trident is still swarming with feds. They confiscated all of Morgan's files, all of his work."

"I figured."

"Just too bad they didn't get there first." Darsie grinned mischievously.

"Wait, you didn't take any of it . . . did you?"

"Of course I did. And let me tell you, that boy was more of a genius than I ever gave him credit for. What he was doing with facial-recognition software . . . it's unprecedented."

"Jeez, Darsie."

"Yes, well, what's done is done. And I don't suppose I need to ask why you're here. I made you a promise, and you want me to make good on it."

"Yes," Wyatt said eagerly.

"I'm not one to moralize . . . but are you really sure you want to take this step?"

"What step?" Wyatt asked, confused.

"I'm not going to mince words, Wyatt. But to me it looks like you are hell-bent on finding Hallsy and killing him. Is a revenge killing really what you want to do with your life?"

"Hallsy's a rogue agent. He's dangerous and he needs to be brought to justice. What do you think I should do . . . become like you . . . a privateer? No, thanks."

"Very well. But from an objective perspective, the odds are you'll not gain what you seek."

"Guess we'll find out."

"There are two types of men in this world, Wyatt—ones who live for themselves. They see the best path and they take it. They do a lot of good, yes, but only if it is a by-product of serving themselves."

Wyatt rolled his eyes. "And the other?"

"Like your father. The kind who must live for a cause. A group. Whose relentless altruism grows like kudzu in the summertime." Darsie smiled. "The more you chop it, the more it persists. I'm sure I don't need to tell you which kind I am . . . but perhaps my one redemptive quality is that I am able to admit it."

Wyatt shrugged. "Or you could change it."

"At my age, not likely. But you still have some time." He took a notepad from the table and scribbled something down. "Here you go."

"No dissolving paper this time?" Wyatt said sarcastically as he took the note.

"Fresh out. So those are the coordinates, but I'm not sure how much it will help."

Wyatt's eyes lit up. "You found him?"

"Hallsy is currently hiding out in one of Rio's most dangerous favelas. The U.S. military cannot operate without clearance, and Hallsy has paid hundreds of local mafia handsomely for his protection. In short, they are the hive, and he is their queen. So yes, I found him, but I'm not sure what you're going to do about it."

"I have an idea," Wyatt said. "Just need one more favor from you."

"Which is?"

"I need to borrow some technology."

EPILOGUE

The motorcycle chewed dirt as it wound up the mountainous path that wove through the neighborhood, the favela built from stolen cabling and housing a giant makeshift city above a city. Squalid and overrun with poverty, the favela, lit pink with the setting sun, was altogether a different planet. With its own rules, its own terra firma.

The motorcycle that the young boy rode looked like any of the other ones used by the millions of Brazilians who couldn't get around by car. Two bikes rode up into the town that operated outside of the law, stopping when they came to a rusty gate. A young Brazilian came forward to see the teenagers step off the motorcycles and remove their helmets. One was a gringo, and with him, a local. The foreigner handled the money and the Brazilian did the talking.

There was a thumb drive and a shoebox full of cash—American dollars. The Brazilian told the sentry, "Take this to the Gringo." He pointed at Wyatt. "The boy just wants to speak with him."

The sentry studied Wyatt. "Você conhece ele?" he asked in Portuguese.

Wyatt looked at his Brazilian guide, who translated. "He wants to know if you know the Gringo."

Wyatt nodded.

The sentry looked into the shoebox of cash, weighing the decision. He shrugged, took a few bills out for himself, then ran it up through the rabbit warren of tunnels and shanties where Wyatt imagined a large gringo paced in a small room high above Rio.

"Someone is here for you," the sentry said, extending the box of cash.

"What?"

"Someone's here and wants to talk to you."

"In Rio?"

"Yes, a boy has brought you cash."

"Let me see that," Hallsy said. He took the box and very carefully removed the top.

"I didn't take any money," the sentry said, but Hallsy ignored him, dumping out the cash and fishing through the shoebox looking for something until he found the thumb drive.

"What the . . ." He inspected it closely, realizing that it was not a thumb drive at all. It flashed. Hallsy turned it over. It was a beacon—with facial recognition software. That's when he heard the faint hum of drones.

"Identity has been verified . . . Attack," Rory told the gamers through her headset.

"Roger that," Samy said.

"I'm on him," said Pierce.

Some six thousand miles away, logged into the technology called Infinite Warhead, Jalen and the members of Group-A, Team Z—outside of Valor sanction—were in their respective bedrooms back home, flying drones outfitted with infrared cameras and warheads. Like bats swooping over Rio, they whirred under the nearly full moon and the newly risen stars. They soared over the favela.

Standing outside the gates of Hallsy's compound, Wyatt saw the missile streaking out of the sky, exploding behind the walls like the sky erupted, shooting fireworks down at the ground.

The missiles were small, but deadly. His guide sped away on his bike back down the mountain, and Wyatt pulled the seat off his motorcycle, containing a handgun and an Israeli carbine called an IWI Tavor. He tucked the gun in his waistband and holding the Tavor, Wyatt kicked the gate open and passed into the compound. In his hand, Wyatt had a tracker, showing where the beacon was. Seeing the attack had come from the sky, the panicked mafiosos shot up at the clouds, and in the pure pandemonium, Wyatt was able to weave his way through. He wound up the stairs, taking down two guards in the process, and kicked in a door that led to a room overlooking the city. He saw the shoebox and the beacon, men's clothing scattered on the floor. On the ground, a couple of bloody footprints leading out.

"Hallsy, come out and face me," Wyatt said.

"I never meant to hurt anyone." Hallsy's once-familiar voice was weak. "It was the money. It was always about the money."

"I don't want any excuses. Step out."

Hallsy broke left and Wyatt saw the hulking gorilla limping toward a railing of the small balcony, blood dripping from his foot. Wyatt sighted his back. Two bullets: one in the brain stem and one in the lungs. Sergeant Eric Hallsy was no more. Wyatt felt an intense wave of pure cruel joy wash over him. That was for Dolly. He spat on the body. He then felt the desire to kill Hallsy a thousand times more. But he could not. The joy dissipated and the hollowness Wyatt had been feeling since Dolly's death washed back over Wyatt. Time to go home.

Wyatt pushed open the door to the condo his mother had rented. It was only a mile from the house Wyatt's father lived in, and she had only rented it for a year, but it was a space for her to start something new, a way to reset and see if—on her terms—her real husband and the reality he offered were right for her. Wyatt agreed it was the right move. And both chose to move in with her and Narcy. Cody chose to stay with his father.

Before he even opened the door, he knew Narcy was home. From the front steps, he could smell the fried chicken, Aunt Narcy's love offering, her welcome-home meal whenever Wyatt or Cody came back from a camping trip or a sports game.

"Hi, honey," Wyatt's mom greeted him at the door. "How was the camping weekend?"

"Great," Wyatt said, slipping off his backpack.

"Want me to take that?" His mom reached for the pack.

"It's okay, Mom." Wyatt held it back. "Pretty heavy."

And it was heavy, the rucksack laden with drones and weapons and thousands of dollars in various South American currencies.

"So did you and Uncle Avi hike the whole trail?" Katherine asked as she swooped about the condo picking up.

"Yep." Wyatt nodded and put the bag in the small room he slept in on the first floor.

"Well, then you must be starving," Narcy bellowed from the kitchen. "Get in here and eat some chicken!"

Wyatt rounded the corner, and was stunned to see his father, sitting in his mother's kitchen opposite the SecDef at the folding table his mother had bought at a garage sale and had been using until she could afford a proper dinner table. The SecDef smiled. She was wearing red lipstick and a crisp navy suit. "Hi, Wyatt."

Wyatt said nothing. He simply walked back out of the kitchen and found his mother in the landing. "What's Dad doing here? I thought this was your space."

His mother stepped close and practically whispered, "Your father called me and asked if he and the secretary of defense could talk to you, alone . . . That's not something you say no to. And he asked? That's a start."

"Okay." Wyatt walked back into the kitchen but did not sit

down or smile at the SecDef. He nodded to her politely and said, "Madame Secretary, with all due respect, I'm not sure why my father would bring you here. You canceled the Valor program." Wyatt looked at his father. "I don't know why you'd let her in."

The SecDef's smile dropped. Narcy made a face. "Think I'm goin' back into the kitchen."

"Why would you say that, Wyatt?" Eldon asked.

"She killed Valor. The world is less safe because of that decision." Wyatt glared at the SecDef.

"Well, it *was* less safe," Elaine said. "And your father was not the one who asked me to come see you or him. I'm here now at the order of the president . . . Camp Valor is being reinstated." She let that hang in the air. "And he, the president, wants you to rejoin. I need to know now."

"How is that possible?" Wyatt asked. "I'm out. I quit Valor. I can't go back."

"That, too, is changing per the order of POTUS. If you're interested . . . But I need to know now."

"I'm certainly interested," Wyatt said, cutting his eyes at his father and taking a seat at the table. "What's the rush?"

"We have a situation," the SecDef said. "Are you aware the president has a teenage son?"

"Of course," Wyatt said. "They keep him out of the media, but of course I know about him."

"Well, he's in trouble. The president is aware of your skill set. And he's convinced only you and Valor can help." The SecDef leveled her eyes at Wyatt. "So what's it going to be?"

ACKNOWLEDGMENTS

The authors want to thank Marc Resnick, Hannah O'Grady, the Valor team at St. Martin's, Elizabeth Bohlke, and Ian Kleinert, for the tireless work, patience, and unwavering commitment to bringing the Valor books to life.